Ghosts
of the Assassins

Ian Todd

Ghosts

of the

Assassins

E. A. SEEMANN PUBLISHING, INC.
MIAMI, FLORIDA

To Tom. . .

Contents

Most characters in this book are based on actual persons. In some cases the names have been changed for obvious reasons. But any similarity between living or dead people and characters in *Ghosts of the Assassins* is intentional.

IAN TODD

Ghosts
of the Assassins

E Force Alerted

Colonel Richard Ormond Douglas (Rod) Paulisen, United States Army Air Force, retired, received the cryptic call from Washington at his Palo Alto, California, home on Thursday night. He checked his watch. It was 7:40 P.M. Next morning, soon after dawn, his wife Jean drove him in the family station wagon to San Francisco airport.

The Paulisens had been married for over 25 years. Ever since Rod had retired from the USAAF and the diplomatic service, he had operated a small, fairly successful publishing company from a three-room office in downtown San Francisco. Jean suspected that her husband was still connected with government work. But she knew nothing about it. She loved and trusted him. This was the second time in three months that he had been called out of town.

Rod Paulisen was fifty-six. He was five-feet-nine, of medium build. His eyes were light blue and his complexion fair and fresh. His gray hair was slightly curled at the top and carefully trimmed. He was always well groomed. He preferred to wear light gray or light brown suits and white shirts. He also preferred striped ties, and those with small figures. He frequently had a pipe in his mouth, which he rarely smoked.

Rod Paulisen was the top Middle East expert of the Central Intelligence Agency. His security clearance rating was one of the highest in the United States. He spoke and wrote Persian and Arabic fluently. He had studied Arabic history and literature at Harvard and Cambridge. He had also served as U.S. Air Attache in Cairo, Damascus, Teheran, and Baghdad. Though not on the CIA payroll, he was on call. During World War II Paulisen had served with the famous Office of Strategic Services (OSS) in Cairo. He was trained as a parachutist, sabotage expert, and karate killer. He was the only American to serve in the mysterious, British-led "E" Force. This was a wartime outfit so secret and ruthless that its leader, a British Secret Service regional chief by the name of Thomas Buchanan, had not even divulged its existence to his own boss in London. After the war, when Paulisen happened to read some of Ian Fleming's James Bond thrillers, he often smiled when he saw references to "M," the head of the British Secret Service. Few readers would ever realize how accurate Ian Fleming was. "M" stood for Lieutenant-General Sir Stewart Graham Menzies, who *was* head of a British intelligence service for many years during and after the war.

The 9:00 A.M. United Airlines Flight 52 from San Francisco to Washington was called at 8:40. Paulisen again told Jean that he would phone her from Washington. Then he submitted himself to the routine antihijacking screening, and minutes later was on his way to Washington.

The long flight gave Paulisen time to review the call from his CIA contact, Sam Gerber, who had asked him to take the nine o'clock flight. Gerber's brief communication was given over the phone in code. He had identified himself as Solon Ginalis—a prearranged signal. All that Gerber had first said was: "Is that you Rod? This is Solon Ginalis." Paulisen had replied: "Well, what do you know! Where have you been all these weeks, Sol?" Then Gerber had given him the message. "I got news for you. Look, why don't you drive over here first thing tomorrow, and we'll work out some kind of united approach to that contract deal. That's the only way. Believe me."

Paulisen had replied: "O.K. I'll be there." Gerber had said "fine" and then hung up.

The words: "Well, what do you know! Where have you been all these weeks, Sol?" were Paulisen's part of the identification process. "I got news for you," meant *you're wanted urgently*. "United approach," though not a code expression, was an easily understood request to fly United Airlines. The first UA flight from San Francisco to Washington was at 9:00 A.M. Gerber's parting remark: "That's the only way. Believe me," was also a code expression. It meant *this is an order, do exactly as you're told*.

This was only the second time that Paulisen had been contacted by the CIA since he had resigned from public service. The arrangements he had made with the CIA were only verbal and vague. In the State Department he had cooperated with the CIA a number of times. When he left, they simply asked whether he would make himself available for special assignments.

Paulisen had agreed. And he had practically forgotten all about it until three years later. His first assignment had seemed very strange to him at the time. Also pointless. Pat Connolly, deputy chief of covert operations, had asked him to suggest any wartime colleagues who might be suitable for a top-secret international assignment. Paulisen mentioned E Force. There were four other members besides himself. He hadn't kept in touch with them after the war. But they were all experts in their fields and absolutely reliable.

The OSS had been succeeded after the war by the CIA. General Donovan (the wartime head of the OSS) had died, and so of course could not be contacted in 1974. After a two-day search of Donovan's files and other CIA documents, Connolly told Paulisen that there was absolutely no mention of E Force. A request for information had gone to London. The reply, just received, was also negative.

Nobody in the British Secret Service (now called M.I.6) had ever heard of E Force. In the files of Special Operations Executive, the British wartime counterpart of the OSS, there was no mention of E Force either. Nor did M.I.5, a British security outfit, know anything about it.

Paulisen was puzzled. He explained that "E" stood for *elimination*. He said its leader was Thomas Buchanan, British Vice Consul in Athens before World War II, and head of the Balkan section of the British Secret Service during the war.

Connolly told Paulisen he wasn't particularly concerned with the lack of official evidence. He knew of several wartime outfits which did not exist officially. He asked Paulisen to track down the other four members of E Force and find out if they were willing to combine once again in a special operation.

Buchanan, known among his staff as Uncle Tom, was officially Thomas E. Buchanan, O.B.E. (the Order of the British Empire is a decoration for civilians), the Vice-Consul of His Britannic Majesty in Athens. This position barely concealed his real job, which was head of the Balkan Section of the British Secret Service. When General von List's German armies overran Greece in 1941, Uncle Tom merely transferred his headquarters to Cairo. Extra facilities and funds were then provided to him, and he expanded his organization into the most powerful, most ruthless, and efficient Allied intelligence group operating against the Germans and Italians in the Balkans. From Cairo an assortment of spies, saboteurs, and killers would be dispatched to Athens, Tirana, Sofia, Belgrade, and Bucharest. They wrought havoc on German, Italian, and other enemy plans in the Balkans.

Buchanan's five-man E Force was only one small unit of the large organization he controlled. Each man was directly responsible to him. These five secret agents didn't even know each other. They only found out that they were members of Uncle Tom's elimination squad after the war, when Buchanan brought them together for a reunion and farewell party in a London hotel.

No other British or American intelligence outfit knew about the E Force, either. The five E Force members were paid from the large funds available to Uncle Tom for general intelligence activities. In his accounts to London, which were in any case cryptic and very general, no mention was made of sums paid to E Force members. This was Uncle Tom's own private spy outfit.

Four of the E Force members were serving as Allied officers. They had been detached from their units for service in various "bona fide" intelligence groups—such as the OSS and the SOE, the British Field Security, the II Bureau of the Greek General Staff, etc. They were then detached, under a top security cloak, to such innocent-sounding outfits as the British Embassy in Cairo, the Y.M.C.A. administration in Jerusalem, and the Alexandria Port Authority. And from there they operated under the direct orders of Uncle Tom. The fifth E Force member was a Greek civilian, operating under a variety of names, also of course directly responsible to Uncle Tom.

The job of the E Force was to eliminate enemy agents inside and outside occupied south-east Europe. The world "elimination" was used in its widest possible meaning. It was not restricted to the murder of "dangerous persons"—the expression used by Uncle Tom when handing out murder contracts. They might be asked to eliminate a particular building, the plans of a new German secret weapon, a file in the vaults of the Serbian secret police, or the apartment where a captured British agent had been interrogated and the tape recordings of his confessions were kept.

When the war ended, three of the five members of E Force were quietly returned to their units, where they obtained their discharge from the military services. One of them was Rod Paulisen. Another was Jim Atherton, a Canadian. The third was Londoner Colin Young. The other two—Aris (for Aristides) Dimitrakopoulos, a Greek civilian, and John Menzies, a Scotsman (but no relation to Lieutenant-General Menzies) for a while remained close to Buchanan in Athens. They were no longer on the Secret Service payroll, but they were available for little jobs. They operated in the tradition of the disbanded E Force, but their work did not include murder. Their job was to root out collaborators who had caused serious harm to the Allies, or who had been involved in the disappearance of British undercover agents during the war.

Menzies was only twenty-two at the end of the war. He was Uncle Tom's closest friend. For Menzies, Uncle Tom's word was law—to be blindly obeyed. In peace as in war.

The DC-8 of United Airlines Flight 50 from San Francisco landed at Washington at 4:55 P.M. It was a cold, rainy March afternoon, and Paulisen was glad he had brought his raincoat with him. He collected his suitcase, stepped out of the airport terminal, and briskly walked over to the taxi stand. He spotted Gerber straight-away, despite the disguise. Gerber wore a taxi driver's cap, and the moment he saw Paulisen he picked up the suitcase and opened the door of a Yellow Cab. Soon they were rolling toward downtown Washington, dodging traffic on the freeway at 60 miles an hour.

"What's up?" asked Paulisen.

"Kissinger wants you. That's about all I know."

Paulisen stretched his legs and adjusted himself in the seat next to Gerber. "How long's this gonna take?" he asked.

"I don't know, Rod. You were supposed to see Henry here today. But he took off for Florida about two hours ago. You'll be seeing him in Miami tomorrow."

"That's just dandy," said Paulisen. "Anybody remember I'm supposed to be running a business?"

Gerber grinned. "It'll be taken care of."

"Thanks!" There was a trace of sarcasm in his voice.

They lapsed into a long silence. Gerber finally broke it.

"How's Jean, by the way?"

"Fine. Only a bit curious."

"Anything I can handle for you while you're away from Frisco?"

Paulisen pondered over the question for a while. "Maybe. I better make a couple of phone calls. Perhaps from your office."

The Yellow Cab stopped at a red light, and Gerber took a pack of Luckies from a pocket and lit one. "That's where we're going." The cab moved with the traffic, and Gerber continued. "What have you told Jean?"

"Nothing. But as I said, she's curious."

"That's O.K. We got a sweet cover for you all fixed up."

"Great! Tell me more." The sarcasm was still in his voice.

"Just a phone number in Montreal. A publishers' convention you can't afford to miss. I'll give you the full story when we get to my office."

Paulisen sat up and pushed his head back. It was his turn to grin. "Just like old times—eh, old buddy?"

"Yeah. Only more. A helluva lot more."

Gerber drove to the Chief of Naval Operation's house on Observatory Circle and double-parked next to a late-model Ford van. A man got out of the van. He was about the same height and build as Gerber and identically dressed. Gerber opened the rear door of the cab for him and at the same time asked Paulisen to get out and walk the two blocks up Massachusetts Avenue to where Gerber's undercover office was located.

Paulisen climbed out of the cab, with only his briefcase in his hand. Gerber and the other man drove off just as a prowl car approached.

Minutes later, Paulisen got out of the elevator on the seventh floor and strolled over to a door marked S. G. GERBER & ASSOCIATES, International Public Relations Consultants.

The door was opened even before he had pressed the bell. Gerber was already there waiting for him, and Paulisen's suitcase was standing next to Gerber's slim, pretty black secretary, Marilyn Armstrong. A brief, white fur-type cap held her hair together, and a heavy gold-chain necklace hung from her slim neck. Beneath it, a plunging neckline joined her tight-fitting white velvet dress. A wide brass-chain belt was wrapped around her waistline, and it seemed to lift her mindress just a little bit higher up. Her feet, hugged in white suede low-heel casual shoes, were perched on the wrought-iron desk support which was a few inches above the floor. From the angle where Paulisen was standing, he could follow the lines of those sheer nylons above the knees, almost all the way to the top. This is some broad, Paulisen thought. Maybe the CIA is undercover—but Marilyn ain't.

S. G. GERBER & ASSOCIATES operated out of a three-room, tastefully appointed suite. The front room was occupied by Marilyn and her L-shaped desk, three pigskin leather armchairs, and a large table, highly polished. On its black marble top lay issues of *National Geographic, Time,* and *Newsweek*. The doors of the other two rooms were closed. But from previous experience Paulisen knew that one was occupied by two young, athletic looking, perfectly groomed men—both former reporters of the *Washington Post*. The third room was Gerber's office. Paulisen wondered where the microphones and the hidden cameras were planted but quickly dismissed these wasteful thoughts when Marilyn followed them into Gerber's office and handed an envelope to Gerber. "It's for Colonel Paulisen," she said. She stepped out of the room and closed the door behind her.

Gerber opened the envelope and took out a message. He consulted a small book which he kept locked in a drawer and deciphered the message. Then he wrote it out in plain English on a different piece of paper and showed it to Paulisen. It said: REACTIVATE E FORCE.

When Gerber was satisfied that Paulisen had seen the message, he put the piece of paper, together with the original coded message and the envelope, into a paper-shredding machine, the size of a tennis ball, affixed to the corner of his desk. Then he lit a cigarette and blew a puff of smoke in the direction of the ceiling. "I guess that's all I got for you," he said. He got up and walked to the door." I'll be talking to Marilyn. If you need me, just press that button over there." He pointed at one of the multicolored buttons on the left side of the desk. "Use that phone," he added, pointing to one of the three on his desk. "It's an outside line. By the way, you'll be staying at my apartment tonight. Airforce II is booked to take you down to Homestead tomorrow morning. At six."

When Gerber left the room Paulisen filled his pipe and lit it. It was his first smoke of the day, and it tasted good. He was impressed with Gerber's security plans. This must be something really big, he figured. He was certain Gerber knew nothing about E Force. Or about the job he had been picked to do—whatever it might be.

He puffed at his pipe for a while. His mind was just a jumble of swift, flashing ideas. Memories, possibilities, riddles. One thing was fairly clear. Whatever his mission, it wouldn't be controlled by the CIA. The CIA was just providing the background, the organization, the facilities. His job might come under the NSC and perhaps directly under Kissinger himself.

He tasted the bitter, tongue-burning nicotine dregs and heard the sizzle in his pipe which told him the tobacco was burnt out. It was the same old Players Medium Navy Cut stuff he had first tasted in Cairo during World War II. He liked this soft, dampish, English-made tobacco. And he had missed it when he was on a job behind enemy lines. It would have been a dead giveaway if he had been caught carrying it. Even the smell of this tobacco would have been enough to betray him. Paulisen replaced the tin tobacco container in his pocket, emptied and cleaned his pipe, then stuck it back in his mouth. He reached for the phone and lifted the receiver.

Paulisen's meeting next morning with Secretary of State Kissinger was brief. Kissinger was alone when Paulisen was ushered into a small office in the CIA's downtown Miami setup, just off Flagler Street. Paulisen explained to the Secretary of State that he had contacted the E Force members with one exception—Menzies. Menzies was somewhere in Mexico's state of Colima, or Michoacan—but nobody knew exactly where. CIA headquarters in Mexico City had spent 16 hectic hours trying to locate him. They had even called in the Mexican *Federales* police, under the pretext that Menzies was a suspect in the murder of two Mexican farm workers in Indio, Southern California, and that the FBI was looking for him. To ensure that the request sounded genuine, the CIA had got the Federales looking for Menzies at the request of the FBI office in Mexico City. The CIA had also contacted the British Secret Service office in Mexico City.

Paulisen told Kissinger that the other three members of E Force were already on their way to London. He said he was ready to operate without Menzies for the time being. But he must be found—hopefully alive but dead would also be satisfactory—because he knew enough about E Force and its members to compromise the success of whatever assignment Kissinger had in mind for them. Menzies running loose all over Mexico and Central America was an unacceptable security risk. He must either work with the reactivated E Force or he must be eliminated. There was no other way, Paulisen said.

Having explained his activities and his thoughts that far, Paulisen paused to hear Kissinger's instructions. Suddenly a disturbing thought flashed through Paulisen's mind. Watergate. The Plumbers. Indictment. Jail. Could he get himself into something like that? In any event, Kissinger hadn't been involved in Watergate.

Kissinger interrupted his thoughts. "The President and I, with the unanimous agreement of the members of NSC, have entrusted you with an assignment of the utmost national and international importance," he said. He looked very grave. His words were spoken quietly, clearly, slowly, evenly. His German accent, guttural at times, seemed to add extra severity to his husky voice.

"You will report directly to me, and through me to the NSC and the President. The CIA has been asked to provide you with every assistance and facility you require. But the purpose of your mission and the progress you make may be discussed only with me. Your contact with me will be through the United States Ambassador in London. But such contact will only be in case of absolute emergency. He has no knowledge of the details of your mission.

"The British, Canadian, and Greek governments have consented to the employment of their nationals in the former E Force, under your direction. They will have dual responsibility: to you and to their respective prime ministers. The governments of West Germany and Israel, through their respective defense ministers, are also aware of your mission and have offered their cooperation. Your contacts there are personally with the two defense ministers. President Giscard d'Estaing of France is also aware of your mission. But you have no contact with France except through me. The French are conducting their own investigation independently. But we are satisfied that they will pass on to me any information which is relevant to your own investigation. And we would expect you to do the same with any information which might affect the French. All other NATO heads of state have been informed."

Kissinger paused. From his breast pocket he drew three sheets of letter-size typewritten paper. He handed them over to Paulisen. "These are your instructions. Please memorize them. I will be back in half an hour." Kissinger then got up and walked out of the room.

When the Secretary of State had left, Paulisen looked at the single-space small type, which he instantly recognized as coming from a late-model, cartridge-ribbon, electric portable typewriter.

As he first glanced quickly at the succession of neatly spaced paragraphs, his eyes began to glare. "Fantastic," he murmured. Three bird-cages of plutonium were missing from Brussels. The French security, SDECE (Service de Documentation Extérieure et du Contre-Espionage), had traced them to unknown Arabs. Their whereabouts were unknown. When he reached the end of the last paragraph of the third page, he felt like swearing. So he did, in fluent Arabic, using the slang of Alexandria's dock-side slums. After this brief, whispered outburst, the thought flashed through Paulisen's mind that the room was bugged. For just a brief instant a playful grin wandered over his face. He thought of the surprise the President's staff would get when they translated his Arab swear words.

Then he reverted to his earlier grim mood and read the three pages three times over. He mentally repeated his orders, checked himself for errors, digested the information sentence by sentence, and rechecked with the typewritten pages. Then he unclipped his Cross ballpoint and copied a portion of page two on a blank sheet. He read it once more, using a memorizing system he had learned while serving with E Force. At last he was satisfied. He had committed the three pages to memory with minutes to spare. Kissinger walked in.

"Any questions, Colonel Paulisen?"

"No, sir." He handed the pages back to Kissinger. The interview was over.

Rod Paulisen caught the 7:30 P.M. BOAC Flight 660 to London from Miami International Airport the same evening. He set his watch five hours forward, as the pert English stewardess suggested. After watching the feature film on the jumbo jet's double screen, he went to the first class bathroom and spent half an hour checking and improving his disguise. He was now Mr. Leonard Hans Rickbauer, assistant general manager of the First National City Bank of New York's branch in San Francisco. And he had all the necessary papers to prove it.

To be sure, a real Leonard Hans Rickbauer held that position. The real Rickbauer was spending a month's holiday on Grand Cayman Island in the Caribbean, while the phoney Rickbauer was on his way to London to organize the biggest anti-terrorist drive the North Atlantic Treaty Organization had ever launched.

BOAC's Flight 660 landed at London's Heathrow Airport on time, at 8:45 A.M. Twenty minutes later Rod Paulisen was met at the immigration check point by Colin Young.

Young was fifty-five. He was five-feet-eight, stocky, not fat. He wore a dark blue striped suit, a regimental tie (11th Hussars), and a goatee. His left, gloved hand held a black rolled umbrella and his right glove. On his head was perched a black homburg. His ox-blood calf skin buckle shoes were shined to mirror-brightness.

After a moment's hesitation, Young recognized Paulisen, despite the disguise. Paulisen now wore a fancy hair piece with long black sideburns and plenty of hair to cover most of the neck, a false nose and false ears. Paulisen had put on this outfit in a men's room in Miami Airport, minutes before he had checked in at the BOAC counter. He knew very well that international airports are usually alive with cops, intelligence agents, and spies. He didn't want anybody to recognize him.

As Young and Paulisen walked down the corridor to the customs and luggage collection point, Young casually remarked: "Not bad at all, old chap, considering you didn't have much time." He looked Paulisen up and down. Young's face was blank.

Paulisen smiled. "Your disguise is better. Establishment black."

Young grinned.

Paulisen was whisked through customs. Young carried his suitcase for him, and minutes later the pair were speeding toward London in Young's 1974 Jaguar.

"Aris and Jim are here already," said Young. "Any news from Menzies?"

"Not a darned thing. Just vanished into thin air. I understand your people in Mexico City are also trying to find him."

"Yes," said Young. "He's moved to a seaside bungalow in Manzanillo.
We've checked it. His luggage and typewriter are still there. Also about a
hundredweight of manuscripts, reference books, carbon paper, and so
on."

Young paused for a while. He seemed to be considering his words. "I
don't think there's anything to worry about. Dear old John has probably
found some beautiful deserted beach; some sexy señorita, and he's
fishing, swimming, sun bathing . . ."

"And probably screwing himself to hell," Paulisen interrupted.

"Naturally," said Young. "But not to hell necessarily—possibly to
heaven."

"Or to death," Paulisen said.

"My dear fellow, please don't be so morbid so early in the morning,"
said Young. "I'm sure we have enough problems without having to worry
about John's sex habits. After all, John doesn't know we're looking for
him."

"True enough," said Paulisen. "The CIA has the Federales looking for
him. They've told the Mexican cops Menzies is wanted for questioning
about a double murder in California. I guess CIA thought this suggestion
would stir quick cooperation. Hopefully a real manhunt."

"I doubt that was wise, at least at this stage," said Young, picking his
words carefully. His voice was icy. "It will make John furious. Besides,
there might be an accident —"

"I know," said Paulisen. "But if there's any accident, it's likely to be at
the expense of the Mexican cops." He cleared his throat. "Look, what else
could I do? "We just can't afford to have John Menzies running around
loose in Mexico while the rest of us are working on something big. And I
tell you, this *is* big. Menzies is the only other man who knows the E Force
set-up. He's either got to be into it, with the rest of us, or be eliminated.
There aren't two ways about it. And I'm telling you, we haven't much time."

"Carruthers, our man in Mexico, got through to me last night," said
Young. "He wants another 24 hours to track down Menzies. The Old
Man has approved it. This brings us to late this evening. Let's call it midnight. If there's no positive contact by then, we'll go out to get him—dead
or alive."

Paulisen allowed a long pause before replying. "O.K.," he said. "That's
fine with me."

Fifty minutes after leaving Heathrow, the Jaguar slowed down and
then stopped in the Strand in the middle of a traffic jam. Paulisen had

stripped off his disguise and stuffed all the paraphernalia into his brief case. The hectic activity of the past two days and the near-sleepless night on the plane were making him a bit irritable. "Why don't you limeys knock down some of those old buildings and make room for a proper highway," he said. "What the hell are you trying to do, turn your country into a complete museum?"

Young turned and looked at him. "Don't complain about London traffic," he said. "How long is it since you've been in New York on a Friday afternoon? At least over here, my dear fellow, we have done something about air pollution."

Fifteen minutes of inching through traffic brought them to the Strand Palace Hotel. Paulisen got out, and a porter took his luggage. Young went to park the car; minutes later he was back. Aris and Atherton were waiting for them in the hotel cafeteria, sipping tea.

The four men took the elevator to the fifth floor and walked down the hall. Atherton took the keys from his pocket and unlocked the door of suite 513. Three young, neatly dressed men were already seated in the room. At a nod from Young they left, quietly closing the door behind them. Paulisen let his eyes roam around the heavy, comfortable, antique furniture. Five large armchairs were arranged in a circle in the middle of the room, around a mahogany table.

On a desk at the far end of the room, near a large window, were several phones. On another table were a coffee percolator, a number of Wedgewood china cups and saucers, a large teapot with an electric water boiler, a bottle of White Horse whiskey, a bucket of ice, a jug of water, an old-fashioned soda siphon, a jug of milk, some glasses, two large platefuls of sandwiches, and some silver cutlery. There were two doors in addition to the entrance door. One led to a very large bathroom which included a huge bathtub but no shower. The other led to a comparatively small bedroom with two narrow single beds, a wardrobe, a few chairs, and a desk with more phones on it. Paulisen looked at the heavy chandelier hanging from the ceiling in the middle of the room and at the massive frames enclosing Rembrandt reproductions on the walls.

Young guessed his thoughts. "All the furniture and other props have been brought in from outside," he said. "The hotel stuff has been put into storage. The rooms on either side are occupied by our people. And so are the three rooms across the corridor. There are two tape recorders. They are controlled from a single switch. It's over here." He pointed at a white button on the occasional table. "When the recorders are switched on, a red light shows on the switch."

"Last thing we want is to put our thoughts on tape," said Paulisen.

"We'll operate the same way Uncle Tom did. No documents, nothing. Just by word of mouth. But this is only as far as E Force members are concerned. I can see your point. Instructions to people outside our group, reports from people outside our group, things like that need to be recorded."

"You're right," said Atherton—a very tall, thin, angular man with wide shoulders and tough, weather-beaten, leathery complexion. Atherton wore a heavy Harris tweed sports jacket and dark gray flannel trousers. He was clean-shaven. His fair hair was cut short—almost crew length. He didn't smoke and didn't drink. His voice was raspy.

Aris, about six-feet-two-inches tall, almost as tall as Atherton, was slim, lanky, and moved with an almost cat-like grace. One of his upper front teeth had a gold filling. His thinning hair and his complexion were fair, his eyes dark blue. He wore a light brown suit and brown suede shoes. His pointed shoes and the style of his wide-collar, single-button jacket revealed a taste for southern European fashion.

They sat around the occasional table, waiting for an opening. It was Paulisen's move.

Paulisen filled and lit his pipe and took a few puffs. He resisted a strong desire to reminisce and told them so. "Here's the story," he said.

"One of the two survivors of last Saturday's air crash on the Island of Rhodes carried a Libyan passport. It identified him as Abdul Aziz Sidaoui, 31, a mechanical engineer, born in Derna.

"He was still unconscious when he was flown to Athens and admitted to the general hospital. He had a number of head injuries, none of them serious, and some minor burns on the legs. He was suffering from mild concussion. One of the doctors who attended him was George Polymenopoulos, formerly professor of medicine at Alexandria General Hospital.

"Sidaoui regained consciousness on Sunday morning and he was put under sedation. He kept mumbling in Arabic, a language which Polymenopoulos understands perfectly well.

"As a result of certain things which Sidaoui said while under sedation, Polymenopoulos called in the Greek Idiki Asfalia, the Special Security Police.

"An Arabic-speaking nurse, an agent of Special Security, was placed in attendance. By Sunday afternoon Sidaoui appeared to have completely recovered. The nurse, Aliki Dimitriou, reported to her superiors further statements by Sidaoui. As a result an exhaustive search was made of his clothing and some belongings recovered from the crash.

"A roll of microfilm was found hidden in a secret compartment in the hollow heel of Sidaoui's right shoe. The microfilm contained Arabic writing. It was in code. Decoding experts and linguists of the Greek General Staff deciphered a remarkable report."

Here Colonel Paulisen reached into his jacket pocket, pulled out a single sheet of paper, and smoothed it flat.

The report, literally translated into English, read: "By the will of Allah, as transmitted through his only true representative on earth, the illustrious Sheik-el-Jebel, you must now complete final preparations for Operation Mushroom in London, New York, and Paris. Our two Mexican brothers have the triggers almost ready. The sacks will be delivered to you within two or three weeks. Finish your plans and preparations and await the final word of Allah, to be transmitted to you by the Sheik-el-Jebel, may his prosperous life never end. May the infidel dog hear the roar of the lion, and experience the anger of Allah, and repent. So be it." Paulisen crumpled the paper, placed it in the ashtray, and set a match to it. The five of them sat in silence, watching the flames consume the document. Paulisen crushed the ashes with the heel of his pipe, then mixed them carefully with the ashes of his Players tobacco.

"The Greek police removed Sidaoui to the headquarters of Idiki Asfalia, and there he was subjected to interrogation. He was not beaten nor tortured in any way. The interrogation was carried out in conjunction with hypnosis, sedation, and lie detectors.

"From Sidaoui's disclosures it became clear that he was a senior official of a hitherto unknown Arab terrorist organization calling itself The Society Of Seven. He was carrying a one-way ticket from Beirut to Athens, Rome, Paris, and London. He also disclosed that he would be traveling to New York, Miami, and Mexico City.

"Operation Mushroom is the code name for a conspiracy to place three 100-kiloton nuclear devices—at Piccadilly Underground Station in London, in the lobby of the Terminus St. Lazare Hotel in Paris, and in a locker at Grand Central Station in New York."

Paulisen cleared his throat, refilled and relit his pipe. "As we all know, a 100-kiloton atomic bomb is several times bigger than the bomb which destroyed Hiroshima. Our experts in Washington believe that such a bomb, exploded at Grand Central Station, would instantly destroy all life and all buildings from thirty-second Street to Central Park, and from the East River to the Hudson. There would be severe damage to buildings from the Metropolitan Museum to Washington Square, and a population loss of perhaps 25 to 50 percent in this area. Depending on the time of day, we estimate that up to 200,000 people would die instantly; perhaps a million others would be injured or suffer radiation effects. Destruction and loss of life in Paris and London would be similar.

"A 100-K bomb can be carried in a small suitcase by a very strong man. We don't know how such a bomb would be detonated. We shall have to assume some sort of remote-control triggering device. But these electronic devices are probably the most securely kept instruments in the world. Very few nuclear engineers know how to build one."

Paulisen paused to empty his pipe.

Young shifted in his chair. "Fantastic," he said.

"Did Sidaoui divulge any names in London, Paris, New York?" Atherton asked.

Aris shook his head.

Paulisen smiled and puffed at his empty pipe. He answered Atherton. "No, he didn't know his contacts. Apparently he was to have been followed on arrival at the airports and met by the local members of the organization as soon as they felt it was safe. The Greek authorities believe Sidaoui told them all he knew.

"Of course, Sidaoui is not his real name. It is Gamal Hormuz ibn Sidki. He is a Palestinian trained in Moscow and Damascus."

"Did he give us any information about the Society of Seven?" asked Atherton.

"I really don't know," Paulisen replied. "Aris probably has the latest news on Sidki. My information is second-hand, by way of Aris."

Aris stretched his legs, his eyes half-closed, allowing only the narrowest slit necessary to maintain vision. He yawned. "The news I have is not good," he said, at last. There was only the faintest trace of foreign accent in his voice. "Sidki died. He committed suicide. Just six hours ago."

"That's unfortunate," said Young. "How on earth did this happen?"

"Very strangely," said Aris. "While he was being questioned, we searched his trunk, and we found a small ball of hashish buried in a tobacco pouch in his pocket. There were two or three ounces of tobacco in the pouch, and the hashish was covered by it. In the remnants of a tin trunk which belonged to Sidki, in the burnt-out wreckage of the plane, we found the pure silver bowl of what was a pipe. Most of the wooden stem of the pipe had been destroyed by the fire.

"Last night Sidki was exhausted by the continuous questioning. Because he was cooperating so well, we allowed him to drift out of sedation. He had refused food, had eaten very little all this time. We told him we would let him smoke some of his own hashish. We thought this would help him relax. We heated the pipe bowl over a gas flame, put some hashish in it, and let him take a few puffs. He seemed to go into a trance. Soon he fell asleep.

"We decided to let him sleep for a while. We carried him down into a padded cell. There was no possible way he could commit suicide. Nothing sharp. Nothing hard. No shoe laces, no pajama cords, no belt. His wrists were handcuffed. The cell was checked every three minutes. And yet he did it. In a way which is—what shall I say?—inhuman, almost impossible. With his teeth he bit open the veins of his right hand and covered his handcuffed wrists under the blanket. He bled to death."

"Damn," said Atherton softly.

"Too bad," said Paulisen. "We'll have to go along with what we've got. Before we go any further, let me fill you in on the Sheik-el-Jebel."

"And who is he?" Atherton asked.

"Let me tell you," said Paulisen. He unlocked his briefcase and took out four sets of typewritten pages. He passed them around. "One of these is for Menzies," he observed. He put the extra set back in the briefcase. "While you're reading I'll fix you some drinks. What would you like?"

"I'll have tea," said Atherton.

"Whiskey for me please," said Young. "With a splash of water and no ice."

Aris got up to go to the bathroom. "I'll have the same, but with ice and soda," he said.

Atherton, Young, and Aris composed themselves to read the story of the Assassins.

> The origins of the Assassins (the word comes from the Arabic *hashishin,* users of hashish) is traced back to the eleventh century. In 1078, the Ismailite faith of the Moslem religion was facing a leadership crisis. A small group split from the main body of the Ismailites.
>
> Leader of this group—the Shi-a sect—was Hassan-i-Sabbah. He was accused of heresy and banned from Cairo, Baghdad, and many other cities. Hassan rode to the remote Erbruz mountain range of northern Persia in search of religious asylum. He rightly guessed that the tidings of his heresy would not have reached the faraway outposts of the Persian empire.
>
> Together with three hundred armed followers, Hassan reached the walls of the Persian fortress city of Alamut—gateway to the Erbruz mountain region south of the Caspian Sea.
>
> The garrison commander, mistaking them for religious pilgrims, allowed them to enter the city. During a ceremonial dinner to welcome the visitors, Hassan and his followers attacked and slaughtered the Persian garrison. They took over Alamut, which controlled one of the three passes into the Erbruz highlands.
>
> The Erbruz highlands were inhabited by nearly six hundred thousand people, most of them peaceful nomads recently converted to the Moslem religion. Hassan terrorized and converted the highlanders to his own particular version of the Ismailite faith. He formed them into a fanatic army which at one time numbered nearly one hundred thousand warriors.

Hassan used ten thousand workers to undermine mountains and cause huge landslides which closed the other two passes into the Erbruz highlands. He diverted rivers, honeycombed mountains with tunnels, and built a string of impregnable forts.

The Erbruz highlands are a fertile, beautiful area, 3,000 to 7,000 feet high. Ice-capped mountain peaks divided the lush, narrow valleys. Torrential rivers poured down abysmal gorges. Magnificent alpine grassland provided pasture for tens of thousands of cattle, camels, sheep, horses, and goats. Luxurious orchards nourished millions of orange, lemon, apple, peach, apricot, mulberry, and olive trees. Thousands of acres of grapevines and strawberries grew on the southern mountain slopes with vast vegetable gardens. This was Hassan's ten thousand-square-mile domain.

Because this stunning mountain scenery so contrasted with the dry, featureless plain of Central Persia, Hassan claimed his territory was paradise. His followers believed him. He adopted the title of Sheik-el-Jebel, which means leader of the mountain. Because the title "sheik" is common-place in the Islamic world, his friends and enemies preferred to call him Old Man Of The Mountain.

Only one pass now led into the Erbruz highlands. Blocking it was the fortress city of Alamut—its walls, parapets, and battlements extended and strengthened by Hassan. This pass consisted of a three-mile-long mountain trail torn in the side of the mountain. On one side of the path the mountain rose sharply to the 7,000 foot level. On the other there was a 1500-foot drop to the rolling waters of a fast-moving river. The Erbruz highlands stronghold was considered impregnable. "One man on foot can stop one thousand horsemen for a day," claimed the Old Man Of The Mountain.

From this mountain fortress Hassan now began to dispatch an assortment of killers and extortionists, all operating under the cloak of "the true Ismailite faith." His messengers of death ranged all over the Islamic world. They demanded supplies, gold, and jewels for the true faith.

The first targets of the assassins were the Caliph of Baghdad and the leaders and followers of the main branch of the Ismailite faith, scattered throughout the vast Moslem area from Morocco and southern Spain to present-day Pakistan. The Ismailite faith was recognized and respected by the Moslem religion, which is split up in a number of branches, much like modern Christianity. The Ismailites, a devout, generous, and benevolent group of Moslems, were hunted down and murdered from Marrakesh to Aleppo, from Cairo to Samarkand, Abadan, and the shores of the Hindus River. Some survived, and their spiritual leader today is the Aga Khan, as benevolent now as his ancestors were one thousand years ago. The terrorized Ismailites considered Hassan and his Shi-a sect murderous heretics.

When Hassan had sufficiently dealt with the Ismailites, he moved in other directions. Those Moslem potentates who paid up were allowed to live. Those who did not were murdered. The princes and religious leaders facing this extortion doubled and redoubled their bodyguards. But they had no way of telling who was a secret hashishin among their own bodyguard, their own harem, their own family. The killer might be a favorite son, a younger brother. He might be the *muezzin* who called the faithful to prayer three times a day. He might be the most trusted general, or the gardener, or the slave who cooked his master's sumptuous dinner. They had no way of telling who the killer might be because he never had an apparent motive. Of one thing the threatened person could be sure: if he disobeyed the Old Man Of The Mountain he risked death at the hand of a hashishin.

The secret society which the Old Man and his hereditary successors controlled had an unbreakable hold over its *fedayeen*—the faithful— the name they gave to their executioners. The assassins appeared to be under a hypnotic spell as well as being drugged with hashish. Some hashishin owed their lives to their victims, yet upon the command of the Old Man or of his three lieutenants (called Dai-al-Kirbal), they plunged their daggers into the hearts of their benefactors.

Recruiting of prospective killers was done in the following way: A young man, perhaps a shepherd in the Erbruz highlands, a teenage Bedouin youth in Arabia, or a Cairo university student, would be approached and invited to smoke specially-made hashish to enjoy the wonders of paradise. He would agree, and soon he would be in a trance, a hallucination which seemed delightful. The recruiters, all highly trained, had spent weeks, possibly months, studying the prospective recruit. They knew his weaknesses, his aspirations, the qualities of his character, his family background. They used the right psychological technique to gain his initial confidence, much as a master spy today, operating in a foreign country, might study and gain control of the personality of a man or woman employed in a sensitive defense or intelligence department.

Once the prospective recruit had taken the first heavy dose of specially-concocted hashish he could never escape from the tentacles of the hashishin. He was doomed because his brief career almost always led to his death. While still in a state of hallucination from this first "fix," the victim would be removed from his surroundings and taken to the Erbruz highlands. In the case of longer journeys, the recruit would be kept in a constant state of narcotic trance induced by regular doses of hashish. He never knew where he was going or how long he had been traveling.

The young shepherd, or the teenage Bedouin, or the university student would recover from the drug to find himself in a palace surrounded by beautiful young girls anxious to please him. The most delicious foods would be brought to him by an array of slaves. To the tunes of exquisite Persian music he would make love to the girls, swim in the cool waters of lovely mountain pools, eat the most exciting dishes that Persian culinary genius could offer. The "friends" who had recruited him were almost always beside him. "You are in paradise," they would tell him, and of course he would believe them. His Moslem faith had already taught him that there is a paradise; that the lucky people who carry out the commands of Allah secure for themselves a place in this paradise.

After a few days of this magic treatment he would be drugged again, and if convenient, he would be taken back to the spot where he had been originally picked up. If the recruit had come from a faraway place, he would be taken to a desolate hillside in the Erbruz highlands and left there alone, but under supervision, to recover from his latest fix. Then the Old Man's master agents would return. "You have been in paradise," they would tell him. "If you wish to live there forever you must join the sacred faith of the Old Man and do as he orders. If you carry out his commands, and if you die, you will live forever in paradise."

For the young recruit the choice was simple. He had already tasted the marvelous wonders of paradise. He had seen with his own eyes that paradise exists. So he begged his "friends" to let him serve the Old Man Of The Mountain, the true and only agent of Allah on earth.

After a period of training in the skills of murder, the new hashishi would be alotted a "thought" teacher. This teacher was a master psychologist whose job was to brainwash and reform the character of the new killer. "You will be a killer of the Lord," he told his student. "You have been chosen to serve Allah. Your first duty is to obey. Your second to carry out your orders. The third to preserve your mortal life and risk it only when you do the job for which you have been chosen."

Finally the new hashishi got his orders and was briefed to the last detail. He rehearsed everything he had to do again and again. The Old Man's intelligence system was superb by Middle Ages standards. But of course it could not always be up-to-date, because of the great distances involved. So the hashishi was also trained to use his own initiative, to adjust his plans to suit changing circumstances. There were branches of the hashishin secret society in almost every major Moslem city. Local hashishin were instructed to assist the killer in his job, to provide him with money and a suitable cover.

Not all the hashishin serving the Old Man Of The Mountain were trained to kill. In fact, the actual killers were a very small elite found suitable for this kind of assignment. Most of the hashishin served as spies, recruiters, and couriers who brought information to the Erbruz; local "office" administrators in various cities; collectors of extortion money; planners; or special envoys of the Old Man Of The Mountain.

In effect, the leader of the Assassins controlled a fantastic network of secret agents, killers, and terrorists. He commanded an organization which in terms of numbers, dedication, absolute freedom of action, ruthless efficiency, and influence outclasses the combined powers of the

Soviet KGB, the American CIA, the British Secret Service, and the Sicilian Mafia.

Drummed into the heads of the hashishin killers until it became part of each one's subconscious as well as his conscious thinking, was a strict code of behavior.

First of all, for the hashishi to die before committing the murder for which he was earmarked would instantly disqualify him from eternal bliss in paradise. So the hashishi must look after himself well, lead a healthy life, preserve himself for the act for which he was picked. To betray his mission meant that he would end up in hell instead of in paradise. And examples of hell were also shown to him at the time of his training.

Second, a hashishi must not take an alcoholic drink, or have any sex relations, until he carried out his job. The sex ban was not imposed without reason. It drove the young man to hunt down his target and complete his assignment at the earliest possible moment. The double element—he *must* kill before he dies and keep away from sex until he kills—acted as a powerful emotional and psychological force. This force sometimes drove the hashishi to the point of recklessness. But this attitude had its compensations. When blackmail and extortion victims heard of the reckless, fearless way the hashishin killers operated, they were terror-stricken.

Thus equipped, the young shepherd, or wandering Bedouin, or university student set forth from the Erbruz highlands to do the job required by the Old Man. He might have to travel to Damascus, Jerusalem, Cairo, Baghdad, Samarkand, Constantinople, Venice, or Paris. It might take weeks, months, or years before he carried out his mission. But the hashishi seldom failed.

In a matter of two or three generations Hassan and his hereditary successors began to wield immense political power within the Islamic world and also in many parts of Europe. Sometimes they were even able to dictate who would succeed the shah of Persia, who would be the next caliph of Baghdad, who would become governor of Alexandria, who would marry the beautiful daughter of the emperor of Kwarizm in Central Asia.

Some Byzantine emperors in Constantinople paid vast yearly sums to the Old Man to buy immunity from assassination and to win his support for various international political schemes.

The treasury of the Old Man at Alamut was crammed with gold, jewels, and precious works of art. Caravans laden with supplies of every kind wormed their way along the narrow mountain pass to bring gifts and ransom payments from every corner of the Islamic world.

The Assassins were noted scholars. The Old Man encouraged members of his sect to read, to study literature and history, to write books, and to admire poetry and the fine arts. Often he kidnapped Arab professors of mathematics and history and provided them with luxury apartments in Alamut. He kidnapped, threatened, or bribed famous astrologers, doctors of medicine, and other scientists, and made them work for him. Leading Arab and Persian writers were brought to Alamut and put to work revising old manuscripts, preparing various histories, or writing distorted versions of the story of the Shi-a sect. Of course, the Shi-ites were always described in such stories as the true representatives of the Ismailite faith.

The Old Man kept records of the murders committed by his hashishin. He instructed his writers to glamorize these monstrous killings, to justify them as the will of Allah. Each successive Old Man took pride in revising old manuscripts. He compared them with originals and had books written on numerous historical, literary, and scientific subjects. By the middle of the 13th century hundreds of books had been written and illustrated by gifted artists.

To ensure that original manuscripts and irreplaceable reports would not be accidentally destroyed by fire or become unreadable through deterioration of the scrolls, the Old Man ordered his writers to make many hand-written copies, and he placed them in the vaults of various forts.

It was part of the hashishin terrorist system to supervise the execution of each murder assignment. Undercover agents always followed the killers. They secretly reported on their behavior and the way they carried out their job. One of the jobs of these supervising hashishin was to provide full reports of the murders committed in the name of the Allah. The Old Man knew that few of his killers would escape death— probably torture and death. So he made sure that the gruesome story of the crime was not lost to him with the death of the hashishin killer.

Some Moslem leaders began to use the services of the Old Man to get rid of opponents. Suddenly the hashishin became the hired killers of the world. The payments went to the Old Man, but each killer believed he was carrying out the commands of Allah.

When the crusaders arrived in the Near East to capture Jerusalem, the Old Man at first declared neutrality. He was an enemy of the Caliph of Baghdad, whom the crusaders were fighting. But in the 1190s he rose to the cause of Arab nationalism and sent killers to murder some of the most illustrious knights of England, France, Germany, Italy, and Spain. Richard the Lionheart twice narrowly escaped hashishin daggers while fighting near Jerusalem and at Acre. But the man chosen in 1192 to become Richard's successor in the command of the armies of the crusaders, Duke Conrad of Montferrat, did not escape.

For devout Moslems to change sides publicly and join the ranks of Christian "infidels" at the time when the crusaders were trying to storm the holy Moslem shrines of Jerusalem was the absolute maximum disgrace in the eyes of the Moslem world. Yet, so single-minded and determined were the hashishin that they endured even this supreme insult in order to carry out their mission. They stabbed Conrad to death as he walked with his bodyguards in the streets of Tyre. One of the two assassins was immediately cut down by Conrad's companions. The other tried to commit suicide but was captured alive. He later confessed and was executed.

Saladin, the great and chivalrous Moslem leader fighting Richard the Lionheart, was a bitter enemy of the Old Man Of The Mountain. Nonetheless he was approached by hashishin agents with the offer to assinate the three most prominent crusaders, King Richard among them, for a low down payment and yearly installments of one thousand pieces of gold for ten years. Saladin refused and treated the hashishin offer with contempt. He told them: "I have not fought all these years in order to steal the victory. I want to win it with the pure sword of Islam."

Often the hashishin disguised themselves as Arabic language teachers and traders and traveled to Europe in order to carry out the commands of the Old Man. Venice, Constantinople, and Thessaloniki experienced repeated hashishin visits. Agents of the Old Man even traveled to France, Germany, and Spain.

The Old Man did have certain ethics. He never ordered the death of a Moslem at the request of an infidel. But he gladly accepted death contracts involving the murder of an infidel at the request of another.

From the 1070s to the 1250s more than a million people were murdered on the orders of the Old Man. Perhaps 95 per cent of the victims were Moslems.

Compared to the number of people slain in the savage wars which plagued the Middle East and Central Asia during that period, the number of the victims of the Assassins was small. But it was the sensational, cruel, and treacherous way in which the killings were carried out that gripped the imagination and spread fear and hatred.

The shahs of Persia, the caliphs of Baghdad, and the emperors of Kwarizm did not always take this terror campaign quietly. During the 11th, 12th, and 13th centuries a total of 31 campaigns were launched against the Erbruz stronghold. On one occasion, these three potentates, who were often at war with one another, even joined forces to stamp out the Assassins. They failed every time.

The beautiful Erbruz highlands became a cancerous sore in the heart of Islam—at that time the most civilized and technologically advanced part of the world after the twin empires of South and North China.

Key to the power of the Old Man Of The Mountain was hashish. Without it his whole complex system of terror could not have functioned. Hashish is nowadays obtained from the juice of the leaves and the stalk of the Indian hemp (marijuana) plant. In the days of the Old Man Of The Mountain a special method was used, though the net effect on the user of hashish was perhaps similar.

Marijuana plants, which were either cultivated or grew wild, were cut and placed in a warm, dark, damp room. After a few days, the foliage and later the stalk began to rot. When the dead plant became soft, moldy, sloshy, it was placed in a wooden strainer.

The wooden strainer where the hashish was prepared was made of the juicy green timber of a freshly-cut olive tree. The rotting marijuana plant was compressed by hand in the strainer until the juice of the plant began to drip into a large solid silver or silver-plated metal bowl. This bowl had previously been rubbed with fresh cow dung or horse manure in order to give the concoction a characteristic smell—in much the same way as a chef today may rub garlic in the inside of a salad bowl before adding the tomatoes and the lettuce.

The dark green, moldy, thick, somewhat smelly liquid was then allowed to simmer over a slow fire until it became a dark brown, clay-like substance. A few drops of olive oil were added, and the concoction was kneaded and shaped into a ball of several pounds in weight. Then a goat was killed and skinned, and a portion of the skin cut and made into a suitable bag. The bag was dipped in a container of olive oil and drained, and then the hashish was placed into it. After a few days the drug was ready for use. The olive oil ensured that the hashish stayed soft and malleable for a long time. The preparation of hashish in the Erbruz mountains was accompanied by strange rituals: the recital of the heretical principles of the Shi-a faith, psalms and other incantations. The goat skins containing this special hashish were hung from the ceilings of the vaults in the castles of the hashishin.

Hashish made in this way by the Assassins was not for sale. It was for the exclusive use of cult members. It was strictly rationed according to sets of rules, at certain times. For example, an army unit about to fight a battle would receive a hashish ration—much as soldiers in World War I sometimes were given a ration of brandy before they climbed out of the trenches for a dawn attack.

Hashishin on individual murder contract assignments would be given a large lump of hashish and instructed to use it in specified amounts only at certain times. Small amounts of hashish would also be distributed at the time of religious festivities and celebrations. Women were forbidden to use it in public.

Hashish was used in several ways. Perhaps the most popular method was to smoke it in long curved pipes. The stalk of the pipe was made of wood, the bowl and the connecting joint were made of metal. A silver bowl and connecting joint were thought to produce the best flavor. The bowl of the pipe would be placed over a fire until it had become nearly red hot. Then a tiny piece of hashish, perhaps the size of two match heads, would be torn from the large piece inside the goat skin and rolled into a ball. The hashish would be placed inside the pipe bowl and would immediately begin to sizzle. The user inhaled the smoky gas emitted by the sizzling hashish. When the pipe grew cold and the sizzling stopped, the user would again place the bowl of the pipe over the fire and smoke until the tiny ball of hashish was burnt out. It was necessary to clean the bowl before putting it away; otherwise the dried hashish would stick to the sides of the bowl and it would be very difficult to clean later.

The usual way hashish is smoked in the Middle East today is through the well-known hubble-bubble water pipe, which can be seen in most parts of Egypt, Syria, and other Arab countries. Hashish still has religious uses, and for all we know, it continues to play a role in ritual terrorism.

Atherton put his sheaf down and sat forward. "Do you think, Rod, there's a connection between the Assassins and today's terrorist organizations?"

"I'm sure of it," said Paulisen. "But of course they have made some adjustments, both to their organization and in the way they operate."

"Right now what we've got wouldn't convince any Canadian judge or jury," said Atherton.

"My dear James, you're thinking like a policeman," said Colin Young. "We don't have to convince anyone but ourselves."

"I didn't mean it that way," replied Atherton. "What I'm saying is that the connection between the ancient Assassins and the present Arab terrorist groups is not, as yet, so firm as I would like it. Before we swing, let's make sure the punch hits the jaw, not a punching bag.

"Let's see what we've got so far. The present Palestinian commandos call themselves fedayeen and so did the Assassins. That by itself doesn't mean a helluva lot.

"Second, we've got the name Sheik-el-Jebel—Old Man Of The Mountain—mentioned in the microfilm. This evidence is much stronger. But it's still not conclusive.

"Then we have the silver-bowl pipe for smoking hashish. Important evidence of an association between the hashishin and some Arab terrorists today. But still not enough. Until a hundred years ago, this was the fashion, the style in the Arab world. Hashish was often made exactly the same way the Assassins made it in the thirteenth century. Once the secret formula became known at the time the Assassins were wiped out, everybody started doing the same. My guess is that even today thousands of Arabs and Persians use the same method. As a form of traditionalism."

Atherton spread his hands on the table, looked straight at Paulisen. "Look, Rod," he said. "I'm not knocking it. I'm not trying to bust your theory. What I'm saying is the facts I've mentioned so far don't constitute conclusive evidence. That's all. Talking about traditionalism. The whole government, the whole country in Libya is reverting to traditionalism as official policy! Let's face it. This guy Kadafi, who runs Libya, he's said a thousand times that he's a traditionalist. He's trying to get Egypt and Tunisia to become traditionalist countries, too. He's a pan-Arabist. If they're reverting to Arab traditionalism, why not also use the traditional methods of smoking hashish? It's as simple as that."

Paulisen put his pipe down. "OK. I'll buy that. But what about the modus operandi?"

"Ah! Well, there you've really got something. The MO of some Arab terrorist groups today is very similar, I'd even say almost identical, to that of the hashishin.

"Now that's good standard, solid circumstantial evidence of a possible connection. But it's not proof.

"I'm particularly impressed by the way Sidki killed himself. It shows a kind of superhuman control of his conscious and sub-conscious mind-control perhaps by someone, some organization, the like of which we've never heard in the twentieth century.

"Suicidal missions we've seen plenty, including the Japanese kamikaze pilots. But tearing your veins with your teeth is something else. The will power! The fanatic dedication."

Young shifted impatiently in his chair but said nothing. Aris stretched his legs all the way under the table and sipped some whiskey.

Paulisen sucked his empty pipe and again unlocked his briefcase. He took out a sheet of paper. "I got some more evidence," he said. "I think we're all aware of the details of the massacres at Lydda, Athens, and Rome airports, and of the more recent Tel Aviv hotel massacre.

"Now let me read you from a statement made by Sergeant Moshe Shapiro, of the Lydda airport police, about the arrested Japanese killer: 'I noticed that his eyes were strange, glazed, feverish. He muttered words which I could not understand. There were drops of perspiration on his forehead, and his hands were wet, shaky. He showed many characteristics of a man under the influence of a drug, perhaps a heavy dose of hashish. . .'"

"Now a statement from Warrant Officer Emmanouil Karmoulis of the Greek Chorophylaki—Rural Police—who interviewed a suspect immediately after the Athens massacre. 'His eyes were funny, appeared blank, unseeing. He appeared to be in a trance. He kept muttering words in Arabic which I could not understand. His hands and face were sweating. From my personal experience of people with similar symptons I think he was a drug user. . . perhaps hashish.'

"And here's part of a statement by Lieutenant Giacomo Marinelli of the Rome mechanized police squad: 'He was trembling. His eyes were those of a madman. Inhuman, animalistic . . . he trembled and spoke strange words. He appeared to be drugged. Perhaps hashish.'

"And I'll give you one more example, though in this case I'm not suggesting any direct connection with the hashishin. How many of you are acquainted with the Charles Manson case in California—the convicted mass killer who ran a secret society of drug users and killers?"

"Say no more," said Atherton.

"I've read about it," said Aris.

Young nodded.

"Right," said Paulisen. "Compare what I've just read to you with the Assassin summary you've just seen—" He looked at Atherton. "I'd like to ask you one question, Jim. Consider the hypothetical situation in which all these indications of a connection point to one suspect, say a murder suspect. Consider that there have been a number of murders with the same MO. Would you be prepared, in the normal course of your duties as a Royal Canadian Mounted Police officer, to ask the city prosecutor in Vancouver or Toronto to issue an arrest warrant? Would you advise the city prosecutor's office to prosecute such a case in court on the basis of only such circumstantial evidence—use of same name (fedayeen); same patron (Sheik-el-Jebel); same MO; same drug; similar symptoms after the crime is committed?"

Atherton replied immediately, "You haven't put the question to me fully, properly, legally—so to speak; but I know what you mean. My answer is 'yes.'"

"That's all I wanted to know," said Paulisen. He turned to Young. "Colin, what do we know about the Arab commando organizations?"

"Not very much," Young said. "Before I give you a résumé, I'd like to make one thing clear. We in Britain don't consider all Arab commandos to be hashishin. In time of war—and many Palestinians feel themselves at war with Israel—assassination is nothing new. That is, assassination of enemy leaders, enemy agents, enemy soldiers. After all, that's what we in E Force did. And let's not forget that British commandos tried to assassinate Rommel, more than once. But of course, indiscriminate assassination, involving people who are completely unconnected, the senseless murder of civilians for purposes of pure sensation, is a different story. And in this category come the massacres at Lydda, Athens, and Rome. Also the slaughter of the Israeli athletes in Munich. And many, many other examples, like the more recent Tel Aviv hotel slaughter. So we have to draw the line."

"If we can find it," Aris said.

"Quite so, quite so," said Young. "If we *can* find the line. But we should try.

"Here's a summary of what we know. First of all we have *Al Fatah,* largest of the Palestinian commando groups. It has about 7,500 men under arms, by our latest intelligence reports, mostly in Lebanon, Syria, and Libya. Financed from Arab oil sources. Trained and supplied by Soviet and Chinese experts, with some American and French weapons. Leader of Al Fatah is Yasir Arafat, 46, a highly educated man. He is of medium height, fleshy, sports a moustache, prefers to wear Arab traditional clothes. A great womanizer. A moderate among Palestinian commando leaders. Al Fatah operates a radio station from a crossroads village near the Jordanian border. The station calls itself Falastin Al Thawra—the Voice of Palestine Revolution. We believe that most Arab oil countries provide money for Al Fatah. The radio station is frequently used to broadcast messages in code to Arab commandos operating inside Israel.

"Then we have As Saiqa, the second largest organization. It's based in Damascus. It's controlled by the Syrian government. Its leader is Colonel Zuhair Mohsen, a member of the ruling Ba'ath Party. As Saiqa is a paramilitary organization which includes one fully trained infantry brigade and one armored brigade. Also, of course, various underground groups operating inside and outside the Middle East. We estimate its total strength at around six thousand. Mohsen is a hard-liner. Though he often disagrees on policy with Arafat, it is doubtful whether As Saiqa is an enthusiastic advocate of indiscriminate international terror. Mohsen is frequently in touch with the Soviet KGB *apparat* in Damascus.

"The Palestine Liberation Organization (PLO) now incorporates Al Fatah. But it was previously independent. There was an administrative reshuffle of the Palestinian commandos in 1974, and the two groups have been linked closer together under Arafat. Arafat presides over an executive committee which includes three main branches. They are Al Fatah, with political, administrative and paramilitary responsibility; an indiscriminate terrorist branch, only theoretically under PLO; and an intelligence branch with a bureau in nearly every capital in the world. At the November 1974 Arab summit in Rabat, Morocco, Arafat was picked as the official representative of all Palestinian Arabs. He was the most moderate choice available to the Arab heads of state—a choice that would also be acceptable to the hard-line terrorist groups. The present PLO is very loosely held together. The real power does not lie with Arafat. It's in the hands of a secret society about which we know practically nothing. We believe Arafat is a figurehead—a figurehead that might lose its head if it doesn't toe the line.

"The Popular Front For The Liberation of Palestine (PFLP) is headed by Dr. George Habash, a Christian doctor of Palestinian Arab background. He operates out of Beirut and has an active organization in Israel, particularly in the Gaza Strip. The PFLP runs a weekly newspaper called *Al Hadaf*. The PFLP is communist-oriented, though we don't think that Habash himself is a communist. PFLP keeps in close touch with communist groups in Syria and Iraq. Responsible for numerous terror acts within Israel and many international plane hijackings. Mostly financed by Libya.

"The Black September Movement is the foremost and most notorious ITG (indiscriminate terrorist group). Has admitted responsibility for all three airport massacres, the slaughter of Israeli athletes in Munich, the murder of American and Belgian diplomats in Khartoum. BSM has liaison with Al Fatah through a Palestinian commando leader called Abu Daoud.

"Daoud was Arafat's deputy in Al Fatah. He was part of a conspiracy to murder King Hussein and his generals. He was arrested in Jordan and sentenced to death.

"But terrorist groups put the squeeze on Arab leaders. They got them to plead with Hussein, to threaten him. They claimed Daoud was the innocent victim of Hussein's vindictiveness.

"Hussein finally let Daoud go. But he first got a pledge from Al Fatah. There would be no more murder attempts against Hussein. He got the pledge in writing—a sworn agreement signed in front of three top religious leaders. They represented three different Moslem groups, including the Shi-a sect, and—"

"Now I get it," said Paulisen. "This explains why Hussein nowdays doesn't seem to worry very much about his personal safety. He travels to Miami and to London without his usual bodyguards—"

Atherton interrupted. "He's bought himself insurance."

"Only short-term insurance," said Young. "If that."

"What do you mean?" asked Aris.

"I mean," said Young, "that Hussein's insurance is only good as long as these religious leaders live and hold down their jobs. We've got excellent reason to believe that Hussein's insurance is likely to be cancelled, sooner than he thinks! Look what happened to King Faisal. He thought he'd bought insurance, too.

"Now, Daoud's connection with BSM suggests that Al Fatah, PLO, and BSM are linked. But we're inclined to doubt this theory. I'm not suggesting that Al Fatah and the PLO wouldn't provide facilities to BSM in an emergency. Far from it. All I'm saying is that the leadership of BSM and the leadership of PLO are not the same. The BSM is not responsible to the PLO and vice versa. BSM is a completely different organization. It operates hashishin style. Arafat must know who the BSM leaders are, and we think he's scared to death of them. And he's bloody right!

"What's happened here is that Daoud acted without Arafat's consent or knowledge in the assassination attempt against Hussein.

"We don't know who the leaders of BSM are. We can make a few guesses. We don't even know where their headquarters are.

"There's also been a development, only a few days ago, which convinces me now beyond all doubt of the connection between the hashishin and some types of present terrorism. Bits and pieces of this . . . development have even been reported by the *New York Times,* in a report from Beirut. Listen to this: a Shi-a sect leader, *from Persia,* has arrived in Damascus to take over the leadership of the 30,000 Shi-a believers in the Lebanon. He is the Imam Gamal el Shereeff, Sheikh Moktasar. Moktassar, according to medieval history, was the illegitimate son of Rukn-ad-Din, last Sheik-el-Jebel in the thirteenth century.

"Now the Imam Gamal el Shereeff has been reported to be the leader of a fanatical terrorist group operating out of the Lebanon independently from Arafat's PLO. Our intelligence men in Beirut are checking the possibility that the Imam is one of the top leaders of the Black September Movement and other such ITGs which recruit their fedayeen from among the Shi-a population of Lebanon.

"BSM is part of a vast network, part of a very rich, most influential, most powerful international terrorist organization.

"Both the Soviet and Chinese governments have privately, through diplomatic channels, denounced BSM's horror tactics. But this doesn't mean very much. There has never been a clear public denunciation of BSM either by the Arab leaders or by the Communist leaders. At least the Arabs admit they are scared of BSM."

"And what's the diplomatic angle?" asked Atherton.

"The Soviet Union has all the oil it needs," Young answered. "Western Europe hasn't. Without Arab oil Western Europe faces economic and industrial paralysis. It'll be knocked out of NATO. Become a ripe plum for Soviet take-over. Yet the Soviet Union at times appears to be encouraging the Arabs to squeeze Europe. So much for détente!"

"Yeah," said Atherton. "The Russians have already persuaded the Iraqis to kick out some Western oil companies. They've built a big naval and air base on an island just off Aden, blocking the southern exit from the Red Sea. They could switch off Arab oil to Japan and Australia just like that!" He snapped his fingers.

"Of course. Exactly what I mean," said Young. "Trying to get the Arabs to stop the oil flow to Europe is clearly an aggressive act. No mistake about it fortunately, the Kremlin has blundered. It has exposed its hand a little early.

"Now let's get back to what we were talking about. There is good reason to suspect that some Persian Gulf sheikdoms are supplying the bulk of BSM money, in conjunction with Libya. But much of this is the result of blatant extortion, not voluntary donations.

"Al Saada Fatah is BSM's prime weapon for extorting money from Arab leaders. It is also BSM's murder squad within the Moslem world.

They operate only inside the Middle East, Arab North Africa, and possibly Persia. They claim responsibility for the assassination of Jordanian Prime Minister Wafi Tal in Cairo. We believe they're also responsible for the murder of Faisal.

"The Palestinian Democratic Front is a propaganda outfit whose main job is to justify and explain Arab terrorist activity within the Arab world, in western Europe, and in the United States. They specialize in "planting" suitable newspaper articles in West German and French publications. Several key journalists in western Europe and America are believed to be on the payroll of PDF—either on a cash retainer or on a 'bonus' system.

To finance its operations, the PDF has joined the heroin pipeline from Turkey, Syria, and Lebanon to France and the United States. If we assume that Black September operates in classical hashishin style, then the hashish they use is probably channeled to them via PDM.

"These, gentlemen, were the main clandestine Arab organizations identified by us—until two months ago. At that time a British agent on a mission to Hamburg was found stabbed to death. He had gone there to track down a source of arms supply to the Irish Republican Army (IRA). On his body was pinned a piece of paper with the words 'Debt repaid by the Society of Seven!' We had no evidence at the time that the Society of Seven had any connection with the Arab commandos. The Sidki case, of course, now puts a different complexion on the whole matter. On the face of it, it tends to strengthen our suspicions that the IRA is somewhere along the line connected with Arab terrorism. We already know that Arab oil money goes to the IRA through Libya."

Young got up and looked at his watch. It was 3:45 P.M. "Sandwiches?" he asked. They all nodded. He walked over to the table and brought two plates. They munched stale bread in silence. Even the beer had gone flat. Then Paulisen said: "Well, that's about it. Now let's get down to the real business."

"Where do we start?" asked Atherton.

"Before we start I have one or two questions," said Young. He turned to Aris. "Why didn't you contact our office in Athens about the Sidki case at the same time you notified the CIA and the SDECE?"

Aris sipped some beer, lit a cigarette, looked at Young and then let his eyes drift away. He said nothing.

"I'm really quite curious. Why didn't you?" Young repeated.

Paulisen sensed the tension and quickly said: "Oh hell! We let you know within an hour we were told ourselves. What does it matter?"

Young turned to Paulisen. "It doesn't *really* matter all that much. Maybe. When we hear anything which affects a friendly nation we tell them straight out. We don't let them find out secondhand. That's all."

The slits in Aris' eyes became narrower. Again he said nothing. Atherton grinned." Maybe Aris wanted the CIA and the French to scoop the British Secret Service," he said.

"Cut it out," said Paulisen. "The guy hasn't had time to eat or sleep for nearly a week. He told us, and he knew we'd tell London. That's about it. Isn't it, Aris?" Paulisen was becoming curious himself. He knew the excuse he had manufactured wasn't valid.

Young looked at Aris. "I want to hear that from Aris himself," he said. "What's more, if nobody has any objections, I would like Aris' reply and the whole of this particular bit of conversation on record."

"I have no objections at all," said Aris. "Just tell me when you're ready."

"I have no objections," said Paulisen. "We might as well have this thing sorted out right from the beginning."

"That's fine with me," said Atherton.

Young pressed the recording button. "All right, it's over to you, Aris. Let me put the question again: Why didn't you notify the British Secret Service in Athens at the same time you alerted the CIA and the SDECE?"

"Colin, I didn't tell your Athens office because this matter is so big I don't feel I should trust them. I've had doubts about your Greek and Balkan operations since 1974."

Young's eyes flashed and then clouded. He smiled. "Whom do you suspect? Is it Dogberry, or is it Verges?"

"This is no joke," said Aris. "Let me spell it out for you. I have reasons to believe that at least one branch of British intelligence in Greece, during much of the period from 1946 to 1950, was compromised by Russia. I also know that at least one person involved with that particular branch of British intelligence is still in Greece. Not active any longer; he is too old for that now. But nonetheless he is still in—circulation. This former chief may or may not be involved; I would say the chances are about fifty-fifty. But his subordinate, his second-in-command, definitely *was* involved. I have no idea where he is at present. For these reasons, I decided it was wiser not to inform British intelligence in Athens. I knew that CIA would alert London direct. This was good enough for me."

Atherton's ears pricked up. He bent slightly forward, as if to listen better to what Aris was saying. Paulisen refilled his pipe and lit it. Young remained absolutely motionless.

After the silence, Young spoke again. His words were casual, the tone even. "I'm wondering why you didn't report your suspicions at the time directly to London—through me if you had no contact with anyone else."

"If I had done so, I might have been dead, and you too—judging by what became public knowledge a few years later."

"I think you are probably referring to Kim Philby," said Young. "Am I right?" He turned to Paulisen. "You recall the Philby case, Rod, I'm sure you do. The Russian spy who headed the Soviet Section of the British Secret Service for years and did incalculable damage, including the liquidation of numerous British secret agents all over the world. He finally fled to Moscow. He even wrote a book about his . . . treason. And other books were written about him from this side."

"Oh yes," said Paulisen. "I recall the case very well indeed. I was involved in trying to stop the American wife of McLean, one of Philby's associates, from disappearing into Russia from the Swiss resort where she was staying."

Young turned to Aris once again. "Could you be more specific? I still fail to see the connection."

"I'll be very specific," said Aris. "And John Menzies could be even more specific."

"Just a moment," said Paulisen. "Come to think of it, John did tell me that he didn't want to have anything to do with the Greek branch of the British Secret Service. I've been wondering ever since exactly what he meant."

"Well, yes," said Aris. "And I don't blame John at all. He was the one who suffered most as a result of the treachery." Aris looked straight at Young. "You asked me to be more specific. Well, listen to this" He paused, lit a cigaret, then continued.

"Way back in 1947 Menzies was in Salonika, Greece, on an assignment for Uncle Tom. By accident, he stumbled on a gun-running racket; British guns, ammunition, supplies were being smuggled from the British troops stationed in Salonika to the communist guerrilla forces led by Markos Vafiadis who was fighting the Greek government at the time.

"He reported this to a local British intelligence outfit—Balkan Counter Intelligence Service (BCIS), to a man called Captain Stacey, who was second-in-command.

"Stacey told Menzies he'd get together a posse and that he, Menzies, should wait for him at a certain Salonika restaurant to help in a dragnet through the various British units in Salonika and in the arrest of the gun runners.

"Menzies went there, and a few minutes later a team of Greek General Security police detectives all but murdered him. Menzies was saved because the sergeant in charge happened to be an old buddy of his who recognized him.

"Stacey was the only person who knew that Menzies would be at that restaurant at that time. The order to kill Menzies had been passed to the deputy chief of the Greek General Security police, a certain Captain Mouskoundis, by Stacey.

"Mouskoundis had no idea why Stacey wanted Menzies dead. But he was being blackmailed by Stacey, who had found out that Mouskoundis had killed British agents during the German occupation, and did exactly what Stacey told him.

"By the way, do you remember George Polk, the CBS correspondent found murdered near Salonika?"

Paulisen nodded. "Yes, I do remember him. But why don't you refresh my memory."

"Well, listen to this," said Aris. "On his way to London from Salonika in March 1948, Menzies spent a few days in Athens. He saw Uncle Tom there and arranged some contacts in London. One of these contacts was to be a certain Colonel Cripps, a cloak-and-dagger operator who had worked with Menzies during the war. Cripps, incidentally, was murdered on Philby's orders a few years later."

"One day in Athens," Aris continued, Menzies happened to meet an old friend. He was Karl Compton, vice-chancellor of the American Anatolia College before the war and head of UNRRA (United Nations Relief and Rehabilitation Administration) in Greece immediately after the war.

"Menzies and Compton sat down at Zonar's Café to chat. Another American, whom Compton knew, happened to pass by. He recognized Compton and came over. He was introduced to Menzies as George Polk. Compton left after a while, and Polk and Menzies were alone. Polk, then thirty-four, a native of Fort Worth, Texas, talked animatedly about the political situation in Greece. Menzies was bursting with anger and frustration about his recent experiences in Salonika, where an intelligence leak had almost killed him. Menzies, of course, did not know, and couldn't suspect the Philby connection at that time. All he knew was that Stacey—another double agent and Philby's man in Salonika—had tried to get Mouskoundis, deputy chief of the Greek General Security Police, to murder him.

"Menzies told Polk part of his story. He was careful not to implicate BCIS (Balkan Counter Intelligence Service) or Stacey directly—for he had given his word to Uncle Tom to keep quite about this. But he did tell Polk that he had reason to believe that British guns and ammunition were reaching the guerrilla leader, General Markos Vafiadis, from Salonika. He told Polk to contact Johnny Sotos, an American in Salonika. He also told Polk that if he went to the Pavlou Mela prison in Salonika and was able to reach a certain jailed German collaborator called Vavaveas, he would obtain information that Captain Mouskoundis and Captain Tsonos of the Greek General Security Police had been the closest and most trusted collaborators of the Gestapo and the Abwehr during the German occupation. Vavaveas would know what he would talk about, because he had been an interpreter for the Abwehr in Salonika during the German occupation. And that was, of course, one reason why he had been jailed after the war.

"Menzies had met Vavaveas in prison. They had shared a cell at Pavlou Mela, a British agent and a German agent jailed together. Menzies left Athens for London shortly after his talk with Polk.

"George Polk was found murdered—blindfolded and shot through the back of the head—on May 9, 1948. The investigation was carried out by Mouskoundis. Mouskoundis' General Security Police were involved in all aspects of the investigation right from the beginning.

"There was an uproar in the United States, especially among the news media, particulary of course at CBS.

"Even Major General William J. Donovan, head of the OSS during World War II, went over to Greece to help investigate the murder. He came up against a brick wall.

"The Greek government at the time naturally supported Moukoundis. The offical story was that Polk had been murdered by communists in order to throw the blame on the Greek authorities, discredit Greece, and stop U.S. military aid to Greece.

"Simply a cover story, of course. To be sure, George Polk was sympathetic to anti-government opinion in Greece. Mouskoundis said that Polk had been on his way to visit General Markos Vafiadis, the communist guerrilla leader, when he was killed by the communists, by the very people who had agreed to invite him to visit the guerrillas.

"What an absurd suggestion! Markos and his men were trying their best to get some favorable publicity in the United States and knew that Polk would give them precisely that—most likely! They had no reason to kill him at all.

"Mouskoundis may have fooled Bill Donovan and perhaps the State Department. But he never fooled the American newspapers and the other media—not completely, anyhow.

"One of those who were never fooled was columnist Drew Pearson. He wrote again and again about the Polk murder, casting doubts on the offical story from Mouskoundis.

"Pearson had no more evidence than anybody else. But he had a hunch. And he happened to know Polk very well. For Pearson, the pieces in the jigsaw puzzle just didn't fit, and. . ."

"Just a moment Aris," Paulisen interrupted. "The theory that Mouskoundis murdered Polk isn't new. That was the party line of Moscow Radio—right through 1948! Soviet propaganda even suggested that British intelligence was mixed up in the Polk murder. Don't tell me you really believe this Soviet propaganda line!"

Aris' eyes lit up, and his face broke into a wide, sardonic grin. "Rod, that's the beauty of it—the exquisite, Machiavellian beauty of it.

"Moscow knew precisely what had happened. Stacey told them so, through his boss Philby, who was a Soviet agent. Moscow knew that Stacey had to eliminate Polk because Polk was onto the gun-running story."

"If that's so, why should Moscow want to expose its own spies, its own plans?" asked Atherton.

Aris laughed. "Because that was the best way they could protect them. Moscow already knew that suspicion was being cast on Mouskoundis, and that this might lead to Stacey and eventually Philby. So they thought that if they first accused Mouskoundis, the Greek Security Police, British intelligence in Salonia, the Americans, and the British would automatically discount the theory. They would consider it Soviet propaganda.

"And who was the person most capable of discounting this Soviet propaganda? Why, Philby of course. It was a masterful Soviet plan. And it succeeded."

"Where's Mouskoundis now?" asked Atherton.

"He's dead," said Aris. "He died under very mysterious circumstances in Salonika some years ago. If you ask me, he was murdered on Stacey's orders. Here's why. When Philby ran away to Russia, Moscow knew that the game was up. They tried to plug all the loopholes and protect their remaining agents inside British intelligence.

"Moscow knew that as long as Mouskoundis was alive, they could not be sure he wouldn't one day point the finger at Stacey, the man who was blackmailing him to do what he did. Mouskoundis was certainly not a communist. He had unwittingly become the tool of Stacey who was. Mouskoundis had become all-powerful in Greece. A partial amnesty had been declared against all Greeks who had collaborated with the Germans. Mouskoundis no longer feared Stacey or the British. He was likely to spill the beans and tell everything. So Moscow *had* to eliminate him.

"Come back to Polk. A Greek newsman, Stachtopoulos, was convicted as an accomplice in the murder. But Polk's death has never been properly explained.

"There's only one theory in which all the pieces of the Polk puzzle fit in nicely, securely. Here's the theory. Stacey, and possibly Hutchinson, operating under the instructions of Philby, had discovered that Mouskoundis was a collaborator, and that he had murdered British and Greek agents during the war.

"Stacey did not take action against Mouskoundis; he decided to blackmail him instead. Stacey did not tell Mouskoundis that he, Stacey, was running guns to the communist guerrillas. But he told Mouskoundis that he must murder George Polk, because Polk was on his way to the Greek guerrillas, allegedly to obtain incriminating evidence against Mouskoundis. In fact, George Polk had found out about the gunrunning and was on his way to interview General Markos, the guerrilla leader, and clinch the story. It would have been a world-wide scoop for CBS.

"So Mouskoundis did Stacey's dirty work for him. He arranged to have George Polk murdered. Stachtopoulos, the convicted accomplice, hinted in his original testimony that George Polk had been murdered by agents of the Salonika General Security Police under Mouskoundis. Later, probably under pressure, Stachtopoulos changed his testimony.

"Now, I ask you this. Bearing in mind the well-publicized often contradictory, facts about the George Polk murder, don't they all fit nicely into the framework just described?"

"Yes—they do," said Paulisen. "But all this is speculation. It wouldn't be conclusive in any court of law—as our Mountie over there," he pointed to Jim Atherton, "would hasten to confirm."

"Sure it's pure theory," said Aris. "I'm not suggesting it's anything else. But you get Stachtopoulos out of Greece, get him over to the United States and have him interviewed by the CIA, and you will come up with some very interesting information."

"Why hasn't John Menzies reported all this in the last twelve years—when he knew that Philby had been exposed and gone to Russia?" asked Young.

"For several reasons," replied Aris. "First of all, Hutchinson was still active in British intelligence in Greece. If Hutchinson *was* in league with Stacey, then obviously in self-defense he would arrange for Menzies to be liquidated. Second, Menzies didn't want to expose all this and embarrass Uncle Tom. The whole situation would have drawn suspicion on Uncle Tom, Menzies' friend and patron. And I bet Menzies has other reasons, too."

"All right," Young said. "Let's take a look at another theory. Suppose Menzies is lying—and mind you, I'm not saying he is. I know him too well for that. But let's suppose he's lying. Doesn't all this theory of yours collapse?"

Aris smiled. He stretched his legs. "Not so, Colin," he said. "Menzies isn't lying. You see, as our American friend Rod would say, a Libyan lurks in the lumber. That's Kellenis—Captain Kellenis of the Greek Aliens Police. Kellenis was present when Uncle Tom and Menzies discussed Menzies' assignment from Uncle Tom. That assignment was to stick close to John Sotos and discover how a British SOE agent, Captain X, was murdered in the Peloponnesus during the war. Kellenis is a witness to the fact that Menzies was consorting with Sotos for official reasons; he is a witness that Uncle Tom had instructed Menzies to investigate the case. Uncle Tom had taken this precaution, letting Kellenis know about Menzies' assignment, in order to safeguard and support Menzies. Kellenis and Uncle Tom knew that many Greek police had collaborated with the Germans. If Menzies discovered that one such collaborator was responsible for the murder of Captain X, obviously Menzies couldn't entrust the information to the Greek police at the time. Menzies was to contact Kellenis if he needed police officers to make arrests, etc. Kellenis would then pick reliable officers to make the arrests.

"Let me make one thing clear. Of course I don't know all the information surrounding these cases. Only Menzies does. No doubt in his memoirs he will give full details, adding more incriminating evidence against Stacey and possibly Hutchinson."

Suddenly Young lost his temper. He let his fist drop on the table. "Damn it, what I can't understand is why Menzies is putting all this in his memoirs. Why the hell doesn't he get in touch with us? Surely he's got plenty of contacts right here in London. When he arrived in London from Greece, the old firm helped him. I was asked to help him establish himself here. I did so. He got a certain government job only because the old firm gave him a high security clearance. He was accepted without question in the intelligence panel of the Army Officers Emergency Reserve. Is this some kind of vindictiveness on his part? Damn it, the very fact that his arrests and rigged confessions in Greece were disregarded in Britain should have been enough to convince him that the old firm knew, that it knows, that he had been framed, that he was completely innocent. Isn't that enough?"

Aris was quiet for a while. When he finally replied, he seemed to be picking his words very carefully. "Menzies does not, at all, blame the firm—British intelligence—as a whole. In fact, I know he thinks that man-for-man and dollar-for-dollar, the British Secret Service and British intelligence generally are the best in the world. But he is not at all sure that the dregs of the Philby cup have *all* been drained. He has evidence of this. If all the Philby gang had been cleaned out, why was he, Menzies, never questioned about the Stacey-Salonika business?"

"I'll tell you why," said Young. "Maybe because no one so far has had the courage and the common sense to tell us about this. That's why."

"Colin, I think you're oversimplifying matters," Aris said. "All this is speculative and circumstantial. People would have laughed at Menzies in London. And most likely Menzies wouldn't have gotten within a mile of the top man in the British Secret Service to report his suspicions. "M" was the only person he could really confide in—knowing that at least one tentacle of the Philby era is still alive and kicking."

"All right," Young said. "We can still trust Menzies. But let's look at it from another angle. Doesn't Menzies realize that putting all this in print, in a book, will harm the public image of British intelligence, the image cf his former associates?"

"Menzies has changed a bit since he left England," said Aris. "He believes in the American way of handling such things. He is also a journalist. He feels that the public is entitled to know. He believes Britain will be better served by the exposure of certain facts rather than by keeping them undercover.

"Menzies quite realizes that the Philby gang, if they continue to exist within British intelligence, may go gunning for him, all the way to Mexico, when this book is published. That's why copies of his memoirs have been placed with a second publisher for safekeeping if anything should happen to him—anything, even if he gets knocked down by a truck."

Atherton shifted in his chair. "I think we're becoming a bit melodramatic," he said. "I've known Menzies for some years—I met him again and again when he was visiting Canada. We got to know each other fairly well. If he is writing in his memoirs what you suggested he might be, then he must be certain what he is saying is true. He has a very strong imagination, I know, but he can also control it."

"Look," said Paulisen, "in view of all this, I think it might be wiser for us if we keep the Greek sections of British intelligence out of this—until things get properly clarified one way or another." He looked at his watch. It was 10:30 P.M.

"We've got a lot of work to do," he said. "So let's get down to business." He turned to Atherton. "Jim, would you please go over to the British Museum and take a look at the Gibbs collection. Some of the books refer to the ancient Assassins. I'm particularly interested in what happened to the cult of the Assassins. I want to know exactly how the Mongols went about destroying them. What methods did they use? They couldn't storm the passes that led to the Erbruz Mountain strongholds—nobody could. I want to find from historical sources exactly how the Mongols tackled the problem. Maybe we can get a few ideas from them. If the Black September Movement and other similar ITGs operate on exactly the same system as the Old Man Of The Mountain seven centuries ago, then maybe the solution to the present problem will be similar to the solution used by the Mongols seven centuries ago. We've got to look at all angles, that's for sure. Right now we haven't got much to go on. Three 100-kiloton atomic bombs are being fixed to explode in London, Paris, and New York.

"Meanwhile, if we don't hear from Menzies by midnight tonight, I'll get the CIA to put a black alert on him. Are we all agreed on that?"

"What's a black alert?" Atherton asked.

"Just a term we picked up from the KGB. Call it a murder contract," Paulisen replied. He grinned.

The other three nodded. Said Young: "I'm reluctant, but I'll have to go along." Atherton looked at his watch. "It's just gone 10:45 P.M. That gives our people in Mexico only another hour and a quarter to find Menzies. I do hope they succeed."

"What exactly does a black alert mean in this case?" asked Aris.

"A black alert means that Menzies will be shot on sight anywhere he is found from midnight onward. No chance to explain, nothing. The Federales, the CIA, the FBI, the Secret Service, the SDECE, the whole lot will be out to kill him on sight. Too bad, but there just ain't any other way."

"What if Menzies finds out we're looking for him and gets in touch with us here first?" asked Young.

"Too bad," said Paulisen. "We won't have time to call off every man looking for him—not in Mexico, anyhow. For the Federales and the other Mexican police, we'll post a one-million-peso cash reward for anyone who kills him. There'll be plenty of enthusiastic hunters, that's for sure."

A deathly silence spread over the room, broken only by the almost inaudible whiz of the nearby tape recorders. Suddenly Paulisen pressed the button switching them off. "Oh hell," he said. He turned to Young. "Make sure, Colin, you erase everything other than the Menzies-Polk stuff. Also that only your old man, personally, hears Aris' disclosures."

Young nodded. "Yes, I'll do that," he said. "I'll do it right now." He got up and walked over to a chest of drawers where the recorders had been placed. He played back the tape recordings and erased the unwanted part. Then he walked over to the phones, dialed, and spoke to someone briefly. He returned to his seat. "We're getting the Museum staff straight away," he said.

"Fine," said Paulisen. "Now while we're waiting for Big Ben to strike midnight, let's see what else we can do."

"Chief Inspector Donaldson of Scotland Yard's Special Branch is coming over here eleven-fifteen," said Young. "Every Palestinian Arab in London has been placed under surveillance."

"Fine," said Paulisen. Then he got up. "I better make some calls, too," he said.

CHAPTER TWO

Death Warrant in Mexico

John Menzies lowered his muscular six-foot, 200-pound frame onto the bar stool of the roof-top garden restaurant and let his eyes roam over the great city below. Guadalajara glittered in the clear night sky. Its myriad lights stretched in a radius of ten miles all around him and blended in the faraway horizon with the stars.

"The usual, señor Menzies?" asked Pepe, the chubby, mustachioed bartender, widening his grin.

"Sí, por favor," said Menzies. He allowed a fleeting glimmer of recognition.

The "usual" was in fact rather unusual. It was Menzies' own invention. He felt that it was an ideal drink in Mexico. It consisted of a tot of the finest tequila, twice that amount of fresh lime juice, a splash of Mexican *agua mineral,* a few drops of Pernod and some ice. It was a fairly long drink, served in a tall glass. Menzies thought it refreshing.

The roof garden restaurant of the Roma Hotel on Guadalajara's Avenida Juarez is a long, rectangular affair decorated with scores of Aztec and Mayan murals. At one end of this partly glass-encased space, two huge doors lead to a roof-top swimming pool. At the other end another pair of doors, always open, lead to a large hall. In this hall are the exits of two elevators, a passage direct to the swimming pool, the staff entrance-doors to the bar and the kitchen, and the doors to the men's and women's bathrooms.

The bar and restaurant consist of a double row of dining tables with a corridor between, a decorated platform for Enrico's Cuban Band, a dancing area, some cocktail tables and deep arm chairs, and the bar. At that time of the night the restaurant was nearly full. But the diners had finished their meals, the kitchen had just closed, and the waiters served only drinks. Only half the cocktail tables were occupied. But every stool at the bar was taken, mostly by American tourists. Menzies sat at the very end of the bar, near the window. From his position he could see the entire 100-foot length of the restaurant and most of the entrance hall.

Enrico's Cuban Band was a five-piece combo—a piano, electric guitar, and two sets of drums, played by trim, sleek, swarthy young men, all dressed in tuxedos—and a tall woman singer swinging a pair of hot maracas. Enrico, in his early thirties, sat at the piano. His eyes were half closed as he moved his fingers over the keys. From time to time he jerked his head forward and let a suggestion of a smile wander over his pale, thin face. Women, especially American women, thought he looked very sexy.

The girl, Geralda, was in her early twenties. She wore white shoes with modest heels and sheer stockings. Her skirt, also white, was embroidered with colorful Aztec designs. It was a longish skirt with numerous pleats. She was standing on a two-foot-high dais. When she swung her hips to the rhythm of the rhumba, some male patrons, if they were lucky, could catch a glimpse of three inches of thigh. This was some thigh, Menzies mused. It was lily-white and supple. Considering that Geralda was Mexican, she was unusually fair-skinned. Above Geralda's skirt was a narrow strip of bare flesh, revealing her exquisite, tiny navel. Above this circular band of flesh she wore a rose-colored blouse with long, loose, white-and-red striped sleeves ending tight at the wrists. Her blouse ended in a modest neckline, which allowed only a small fraction of her bosom to show. Her long white neck, free of any necklace, blossomed into the most beautiful Castilian face Menzies had ever seen. Her lips, neither wide nor fleshy, on occasion parted to expose perfect teeth. Her blue eyes, heavy with mascara and eye shadow, moved across the cocktail tables and the dancing couples. Her hair was naturally golden-red. It shone brilliantly in the yellow spotlight. And it flowed, with only a gardenia clip to hold it, at least six inches below her shoulders. When she shook her head, her hair sometime revealed delicate ears from which depended tiny, heart-shaped golden *cadeñas*.

Menzies sipped some more of his drink and lit a cigarette. Pepe was watching him. "Wow! Madre mía!" he said in his serviceable Spanish, for Pepe's benefit.

Pepe's grin widened. He touched his moustache. "Sí, señor," he said. The señorita's name is María di Carmen Geralda Porras-Castro." He continued in a torrential vernacular, the upshot of which was lust, the international language.

Menzies himself wore white leather Hushpuppies with brass buckles and flared white trousers, held by a wide, light-brown leather belt with a heavy brass buckle. A padless, close-fitting navy-blue jacket hung from his wide shoulders, and a blood-red Mexican silk kerchief portruded an inch from his left breast pocket. Under the jacket he wore a white cotton turtleneck sweater. His neck and face were tanned from recent exposure to Mexican sun and the Pacific Ocean. His thick, dark-brown hair showed plenty of gray around the temples and descended down his face in well-trimmed sideburns. In the subdued light of the restaurant bar his age was hard to guess. It could be anything from thirty five to fifty five. Also impossible to determine was the color of his eyes. They could be dark green, hazel, gray, or light brown. His feet and his hands were somewhat small for his frame. But a careful observer would notice something unusual about his hands. The sides of the palms, from the wrists to half-way down the little fingers, seemed to be bulging, wrinkled, and cracked. This was the result of hours of recent daily practice chopping wooden planks and metal bars. His clothing and appearance blended naturally with the Mexican styles and fashions. In the multi-racial environment of Mexico, his dark gray hair and face structure did not mark him outright as a gringo.

Menzies had arrived in Guadalajara four days earlier. He had no idea that E Force has been revived for a special assignment and that just about every Western intelligence agent in Mexico was looking for him. Neither did he know that at 4:00 P.M. Guadalajara time that same day (midnight London time), a deadline for his capture had expired. He didn't know that scores of bounty hunters all over Mexico were already on the prowl, scouring every hotel and restaurant, every possible hideout, anxious to earn a million pesos.

Before driving up to the 5,000-foot level of Guadalajara, Menzies had spent a month on one of his rare health jags in Manzanillo — that delightful seaside resort north of Acapulco. A Menzies health program was a special kind of reconditioning to which he gladly subjected himself.

Taking such health trips was a Menzies peculiarity. The month-long health and strength program was his own invention. Menzies liked doing things his own way and didn't care a damn whether anybody agreed with him or laughed at him. He took these health trips not because he needed an overhaul, but for pleasure—the pleasure of bringing himself to the peak of physical and mental fitness. Menzies liked operating at peak condition. He needed only three things to launch himself into this special training program: a good place to swim, a long sandy beach for running, and a semi-tropical background for relaxing.

His program consisted of three parts. The first was purely a physical training plan. The second was a special diet. The third involved practice in shooting, knife-throwing, boxing, karate, and Kung Fu. He combined all three parts so that by the end of a month he had reached his peak.

The physical-training plan was very simple, and he could think of no physical instructor who might disagree with him. He started by swimming a quarter of an hour the first day (and by swimming he meant just that, not merely romping around in the sea). He gradually increased this period to two full hours. After each daily swim (and sometimes before it), he would walk or run along the beach—at the beginning about a mile, at the end about ten miles.

Much of his diet wouldn't arouse much controversy either. He ate what he normally ate, with extra amounts of fresh fruit and juices. But there was one more plus. It was *bringole,* also known as eggplant. A celebrated Egyptian physician had once told him in Alexandria, many years ago, that bringole contained certain food values that reacted instantly on the muscular system. Menzies had tried it, in a special progressive formula prescribed by Dr. Fawzi, over a period of a week. The results were astonishing. He had tested his strength on various instruments before and after and had noticed an improvement of more than twenty percent! His bringole diet consisted of five ounces the first day; he gradually increased it by five ounces a day till he reached the fifty-ounce mark. He'd maintain this rate for about ten days and then gradually decrease the amount until by the thirty-first day he ate none.

To make bringole more palatable he had studied a number of recipes—including the Greek *kapama,* the Turkish *imam baeldi,* and the Bulgarian *mes patlijan.* He weighed his bringole raw. Cooking usually reduced it to one-third its original weight.

He had once mentioned his strength formula to some friends in London. They laughed at him. He told them not to take his word for it—just try it. They never did. From then onward, Menzies decided to keep the information to himself.

Menzies settled down to this kind of health program about once every three years. Though he always practiced karate, Kung Fu, and boxing, seldom since the end of World War II had he exercised the more deadly arts of straight shooting and knife-throwing, at which he was also expert. When

Paulisen had met him a few months earlier at Puerto Vallarta, however, and had mentioned the possibility of resurrecting E Force, Menzies decided to give himself the full course in Manzanillo.

Menzies had three knives left from his wartime set of ten. He had kept them over the years as souvenirs and enjoyed the rare occasions when he had time to test his skills. These knives had been specially made for him in Damascus by the celebrated Syrian sword and knife manufacturers Salah el Faisal & Co. They were unusual knives—if indeed they could be described as knives at all. They consisted of a seven-inch, specially forged Damascus-steel blade, reputedly made by the same secret formula as Saladin's swords. The blade was so fashioned that it looked more like a flattened dart than a knife. It was thick and heavy toward the needle sharp point, slimming gradually toward the handle. Though the sides of the blades were sharpened and could cut, the knives were not really made to cut—only to penetrate. The short handle, a very thin aluminum tube, weighed perhaps a tenth of the blade's weight. Such knives were for throwing, not for slashing. One could throw them any way one wanted; they would always race toward the target point-first. Unlike the ordinary kind of throwing knife, one did not have to calculate the distance of the target accurately and launch the knife from one's open palm in a sudden forward jerk. Menzies' knives could be thrown in a variety of ways—including the overhand way used by the pitcher in a baseball game. In his practiced hands they were deadly—provided the target was at least twelve feet away. During many hours of target practice, Menzies had found that for his strength and arm action the best distance was between twenty and thirty-five feet. At thirty feet he could hit a standard-size competition English dart board ten times out of ten throws.

Menzies' other weapon was a German-made Luger-Parabellum 7.65 millimeter, seven-bullet automatic pistol with a specially-made windage and elevation correction adjustment. The trigger mechanism had been checked and adjusted at a Munich gunsmith shop to correspond to his particular finger pressure. He carried only soft-nosed dum-dum cartridges, whose bullets split into several pieces the moment they hit the target. These bullets were not made to penetrate; they were made to kill. Menzies could hit a rolling dime at fifteen feet, and a packet of cigarettes at forty.

Menzies appearance and usual behavior were serene, suave, polished, worldly. Almost invariably polite, friendly, humorous, his manners exuded just a trace of old-fashioned gallantry. Nobody could ever imagine that behind this casual, streamlined facade lurked, in times of fighting, a savage, cruel, and sadistic temperament—and the deadliest killer that Uncle Tom could lay his hands on in World War II.

Menzies looked at his watch. It was past one o'clock. In another half hour the band would stop playing. And he had a date with Geralda. He had watched the demure, attractive singer with increasing interest for three nights running. She had noticed him, too. The previous evening, during an interval, she had walked up to him and asked him if he had a favorite tune. Yet, he did have one. He couldn't remember what it was called—perhaps the "Cuban Love Song," a very old tune from a very old film, starring Ronald Reagan—or was it Ronald Coleman?—which he had seen many years ago. He hummed the tune in her ear, sniffing her gardenia perfume. She knew it. Minutes later, when the band resumed, she sang it for him. It was the hottest, most romantic, most danceable Latin-American rhumba he had ever heard. During the next interval he thanked her and offered her a drink. She asked for coke. Menzies wondered whether she would be demure in bed. He asked her to have supper with him, to go dancing with him at one of Guadalajara's famous night spots. This was the first time he had invited a woman for anything for nearly six months—ever since he had split up with his wife. The trauma of separation and the divorce proceedings had sickened him. During all this time he had led a life of celibacy. Though physically he craved women, emotionally they repelled him. He had spent many nights alone in bed, unable to sleep, unable to subdue thoughts about sex. He'd get up and walk around the room, have a shower, try to read a book, and wait and wait until dawn—when he could rush into the sea and let the ocean soothe his muscles and cool his thoughts.

Menzies had been wounded. Such scars take time to heal. He knew that. His latest conditioning program in Manzanillo had calmed his emotions. Time turned raw wounds into scar tissue. So when he arrived in Guadalajara he knew, instinctively, that he was now ready—but only with the right woman.

When he asked Geralda to meet him after the show, she looked at him in silence for a long time. She seemed to hesitate for hours, though he knew it was only fleeting seconds. Then, evading the question, she said: "How long will you be in Guadalajara?"

"I don't really know," Menzies had replied, truthfully. "I have no special plans."

She looked up at him. Her blue, candid, eyes seemed to scrutinize his face. "You are a tourist," she said. "You're on holiday, to amuse yourself. It is better that you go dancing with someone else." She looked in the direction of two voluptuous young women, very attractive in their minidresses, who were sitting alone at one of the cocktail tables. They had spent most of the evening dancing, but they were unescorted.

Menzies' reply had leaped out of his lips before he had time to check himself. "It's only *you* that I want to meet . . . I need *your* company."

The words, spoken in broken Spanish, sounded earnest, urgent. But it was his tone, and the way he had spoken, that made Geralda look once again. His face was unsmiling, sincere. Her eyes met his glance. It was steady, demanding. His eyes conveyed his hunger. He needed her; oh yes, he needed her. She felt a shiver along her spine. She remained speechless. He touched her hand. She didn't move it away. Then he took her hand in his and felt it trembling. When he spoke again, his voice was even more husky. "I'll wait for you tomorrow night at one-thirty. At the all-night coffee shop across the street from the hotel."

She moved her eyes away, then turned them up and looked at his face again. His eyes seemed to magnetize her. The tremor in her hand vibrated through her nervous system, to her neck and shoulders, to her whole body.

"I'll be there," she said. Then she gently withdrew her hand and walked the few steps to the microphone. When she began singing again, she was visibly shaken. She avoided his eyes. Because she wouldn't look at him for the rest of the evening, Menzies thought he might have offended her. But when the band had finally stopped playing and she was about to go, she turned and smiled at him. It was a smile full of promise. Menzies was so shaken that he was unable to smile back. He lifted his hand in recognition and followed her with his eyes as she walked away. She kept fiddling with the back of her dress, adjusting the back of her hair, all the way to the elevator. When she was out of sight, Menzies relaxed. His breath came out in a gasp. He ordered another drink, noticing the twinkle in Pepe's eyes. He ignored it.

That was yesterday. In half an hour Geralda would meet him. As if to confirm it, she turned and looked at him, simling boldly. She said something to Enrico. Then the band struck up his favorite tune, "El Manicero," the one he had requested the previous night. Menzies let his eyes roam. From his position he could see every part of the restaurant. He took a sip of his drink. He felt good. He felt happy. For the first time in over a year. He felt so relaxed and carefree that at first he hardly noticed the two men who appeared at the main entrance of the restaurant. But then he saw Ramon, the cocktail waiter, practically stumbling over the chairs to reach them. So he looked at the visitors again.

There was something very unusual about the two late-comers. First of all they were formally dressed for the occasion, unlike most other male patrons. They wore suits, white shirts, and ties. They also carried fedora hats in their hands. One of them, about six feet tall, Menzies guessed, was slim, pale, intense-looking. Perhaps in his early forties. The other, much younger, was shorter, bulky, thick-necked. Ramon seemed to know them. He was fussing around them, pulling out chairs for them. For a while they remained standing. They looked around the restaurant.

Menzies noticed the slight bulge in the front left part of their jackets. "Cops," he thought. "Carrying guns, both right handed, obviously on duty." He smiled. Funny how you could tell a cop in any part of the world. Though obviously on duty, because they both seemed to be staring around the restaurant as if they were looking for someone, their assignment must have been an urgent one. They didn't bother to disguise their appearance. "They must know that they look like cops, that they stick out like sore thumbs in this environment," Menzies thought. Who knows, with a bit of luck, he might see some action tonight before getting into a more serious hassle with Geralda. When this particular thought flashed through Menzies' mind, he had no idea how right events would prove him to be.

Then, something more unusual happened. Ramon, who was talking to them, turned and looked in the direction of Menzies. Both men then gave him a quick, furtive glance. They turned and smiled at Ramon and sat down at a table which the waiter had quickly cleared. For Menzies, the sign was clear. They had asked Ramon about him, and Ramon had pointed him out.

"What the hell do they want?" Menzies asked himself. "Maybe they're not cops at all. Maybe they're immigration officers checking out the tourist permits of all foreign visitors. Darned unlikely. These two are C-O-P-S."

The more Menzies considered the situation the less he liked it. Why hadn't they come over the moment Ramon had pointed him out? The pair had planted themselves near the exit — the one which led to the hall with the elevators. Whatever the two cops wanted to say, or do, they didn't want it done in public. Very, very, strange, Menzies thought. Potentially an ugly situation. The word *ugly* somehow seemed to stick in his mind. Menzies knew of no reason why cops would want to bother him. This very fact, in his mind, made the situation even more ugly — because it was mysterious, unpredictable.

Suddenly his flesh crawled. A hunch gripped him. He sensed danger. Menzies never disregarded his hunches. His mind raced back to the war days. He had met and dodged death a hundred times. He could smell it. It had become part of his everyday life. Now he smelled it again. A strong presentiment of impending peril and death. Oh hell! Surely there couldn't be any danger to him from cops! He had nothing to fear from cops. What then? Maybe there was going to be some kind of a shoot-out, and he would find himself in the middle. That might account for the danger and death hunch which now urgently prodded him to do something—while there was still time! But, no. It couldn't be that. Those two cops were looking for him. They had asked Ramon, and Ramon had pointed out Menzies.

A whole variety of subdued, long-dormant instincts now seemed to rise to the surface. These instincts combined with his meticulous, logical mind to produce one answer. He had to test the situation. But how? This is how: he had to test the situation under conditions and locale which were favorable to him. He had to take the initiative.

Menzies slid off his seat. He left his cigarettes, lighter, and half-finished drink on the bar. Casually he walked toward the two men. He moved past them, not even glancing in their direction, and entered the hall. He was only a few steps away from the elevators when he turned abruptly, at a right angel, towards the men's bathroom, marked *caballeros* in fluorescent lighting. From the corner of his eyes he noticed that both men had stood up. But they settled back into their seats when they saw that he was going to the men's room, not the elevators.

This was the last clue Menzies needed. He reasoned as follows: The plainclothes cops, who were on an urgent job and were armed, neither intended to question him or to arrest him. They could have done so already. But they were ready to intercept him if he had gone to the elevators. What then was their purpose? Could it be to work him over, perhaps murder him? This idea didn't strike Menzies as improbable. Every country had crooked cops. No reason why there shouldn't be a few in Mexico. Why they might want to work him over or kill him didn't matter. He felt reasonably sure they would try. He wasn't going to let anyone work him over. Since they were both armed, he might have to kill them.

The *caballeros* of the roof-top restaurant was a rectangular room, 25 by 20 feet. One side of the longer wall consisted of urinals. Facing the entrance stood three wash basins with cheap mirrors above them. On the other long side of the room were five toilet booths.

Six-foot plywood doors hung a foot from the floor—so visitors could see the shoes of men sitting inside the toilet booths and choose alternative ones. Above the toilet bowls were jacket hooks which could be seen from the outside. The doors swung out. They had big brass handles, and they could be secured with a latch only from the inside.

There was nobody in the Caballeros when Menzies entered. He closed the door behind him. Then he entered the middle booth, took off his shoes and placed them so that the tips could be seen from the outside. He took off his jacket and hung it on the hook above the toilet bowl. He left the booth and entered the next one. He latched the door, raised himself over the seven-foot partition, bent down and locked the other one from the inside. Then he slid back into his booth, lowered the toilet seat cover and crouched on it. He decided to wait and see what would happen.

In the next five minutes a number of men entered the *caballeros,* used the urinals, washed their hands and left. Time seemed to drag on. He looked at his watch. It was 1:25 A.M. He had been in the *caballeros* for nearly ten minutes. His thoughts drifted to Geralda. She might be wondering what had happened to him. From the stage she could see that his lighter, his cigarettes, and his drink were still on the bar. But he dismissed Geralda from his mind when he heard the entrance door swing open, followed by two sets of footsteps. They did not move toward the urinals. They seemed to hesitate outside the next booth. Menzies held his breath.

Suddenly a succession of gunshots shattered the air. In the confined space it seemed like a dozen hand grenades had exploded. Menzies eased the latch out just as he saw the face of the taller cop rise above the next toilet booth door to take a look inside. In that same instant Menzies hurled himself at the unlatched door. It swung out, and the handle smashed into the back of the taller Mexican. Menzies had followed the door out, and this movement brought him next to the shorter, burly Mexican. He grabbed the gun-toting wrist with both hands, lifted it upward and hurled the Mexican against the urinals across the room. With his free left hand the burly Mexican swung a vicious hook at his ribs. Menzies winced as a shiver of pain ran through his body, but he lifted his knee sharply at the Mexican's groin. The Mexican groaned and sagged into the urinals, his face a tortured picture of pain; but he didn't let go of the gun. Menzies saw that the other cop, who had dropped the gun when the swinging door handle smashed into his back, lay sprawled on the floor. He was groping under the closed toilet booth door, trying to reach his gun.

Menzies knew that time was running out. He pulled the burly Mexican's hand to his mouth and sunk his teeth into it. The Mexican screamed and dropped the gun. It fell into a mess of urine and vomit a foot deep. Menzies dragged him a few feet away from the urinals, then leaped up and latched the entrance to the Caballeros. Almost in the same movement Menzies returned to the taller Mexican, who had meanwhile raised himself on his knees. Menzies kicked him in the face. Too late he realized that he wasn't wearing shoes. A sharp pain shot up his leg and for an instant paralyzed it. But the effect of the kick on the Mexican was nearly lethal. His head jerked back and banged up against the toilet booth door. He collapsed in a heap, a mixture of froth and blood dribbling from his shattered lips and teeth. Menzies went back to the other Mexican, who was pressing his bitten and bleeding right hand to his chest. With the other hand he had picked his gun from the filth. Before he could fire, Menzies grabbed his arm in a standard wristlock and shook the gun free in a succession of arm twists. The Mexican lifted his knee into Menzies' groin, even as Menzies launched an uppercut into his liver. The punch exploded with a sickening thud, half burying Menzies' fist into a mass of splintered ribs.

The knee blow to Menzies' groin had found its mark and he backed away clutching his crotch. He began to vomit. Painful spasms tore his body. For a few moments all three of them were helpless. The burly Mexican, whose stamina had amazed Menzies, was first to recover. He stood up erect, then limped toward his gun, now lying a few feet away on the floor. Menzies, doubled up and in agony, saw him. In desperation now he hurled a left-handed karate chop at the Mexican's throat. It lacked speed as well as force, because the Mexican managed just in time to lift his shoulder and lower his head. The killer blow was taken by his chest and chin. Menzies rallied, enough to grab him by the jacket, and swung him around. He pushed him away from the gun. The Mexican turned on Menzies, swinging a tremendous right hook which grazed Menzies' chin. A short, straight left thudded into Menzies' stomach muscles, but by this time Menzies had recovered from the groin blow. Menzies stepped back, as if hurt, ducking under another right swing. Then Menzies feinted another left-handed karate chop to the throat of the Mexican. The tough, bull-necked cop quickly lowered his chin to evade the death blow. But then Menzies hit him on the back of the neck with a right-handed rabbit chop. The man crumpled on the floor, groaning.

Menzies now stood away, straightened himself up, and gave himself a few seconds to take stock. His thoughts and instincts at the moment were guided by only one principle. They had tried to murder him, so he was going to kill them. Instinct, anger, and latent sadism now combined to condition his thinking.

Casually he walked back to the short, thick-set man who was already trying to get up. Menzies grabbed him by the hair, twisting his head face upward. Then he rammed the extended, rigid, fore and middle fingers of his right hand into the Mexican's eyes, gouging them out. He grabbed the Mexican's head with both hands and rammed it up against his knee. The fearsome ogre with the eyeless, bleeding, pulpy face then thudded onto the floor. Menzies carefully evaded the shudders and dying spasms of the man's limbs and moved to the other Mexican, who was still unconscious. He put the man's neck up against his knee, then jerked the head down suddenly a few times until he heard the crunch of the spinal cord. Menzies picked up the lifeless body, opened one of the toilet booths and threw it inside. He made sure that the man's shoes could be seen from the outside. Then he went back to the eyeless Mexican. He picked him up and carried him headdown to another toilet booth. He rammed the man's head into the toilet bowl, put his foot on the head to hold it in position, flushed the toilet, then let the body roll over. Another c-r-u-n-c-h of the spinal cord told Menzies his job in the Caballeros was finished.

Menzies heard knocks on the entrance door. He ignored them. He went back to the toilet booth which had been his original hideout, lifted himself over the partition, unlatched the other toilet door, went inside and put his shoes on, grabbed his jacket. He picked up the gun of the first cop. It was a Colt 45. He checked it, put his jacket over his right hand, kicked the other gun across the floor into the stinking urinals. He noticed how filthy his white trousers and sweater were. He did his best to cover some of the stains with his jacket. He moved to the entrance and unlatched the door, his finger on the trigger of the Colt, ready to fire from beneath the jacket.

It was Ramon. Before the waiter had time to speak Menzies yelled with feigned anger: "What the hell's going on? This bloody door is all screwed up. You guys better do something about it."

Ramon's face, anxious at the beginning, quickly twisted into an apologetic grin. "I am very sorry, Señor Menzies, very sorry. Tomorrow we fix it, seguro."

"And there are two gentlement using the lavatories," added Menzies, pointing at the toilet booths. "So keep this door open. Otherwise they might be locked in here all night."

"Sí señor, sí señor," said Ramon. His grin now was much broader, "Some people heard some noise. . .

"Sure they heard some noise," Menzies interrupted him. "I've been banging in here; trying to get out for the last hour."

Ramon took a heavy flower pot and placed it up against the open bathroom door so that it couldn't close again. "I'm very sorry; Señor Menzies; very sorry;" he repeated; and walked away.

Menzies strolled over to the elevators and pressed the button. While he waited, he looked at his watch. It was 1:33 A.M. The whole business had just taken eight minutes.

Menzies got off on the fifth floor and limped around the corner to room 513. His mind worked feverishly. Why did those cops want to kill him? Obviously they couldn't have acted within the law. Mexico prides itself, and rightly so, on its liberal, democratic policies, on its hospitality to visitors. A man, or a woman, is much safer walking the streets of Mexico City after midnight than doing the same in New York, Chicago, Paris, Rome, or London. Quickly Menzies reached the conclusion that the two cops—if they were cops—had acted on their own, for reasons unknown to him.

Menzies knocked on the door of room 513 and yelled through his jacket, "Señor Menzies, telegrama, telegrama!" He hoped his muffled Spanish would be good enough to deceive anyone inside. He had guessed right. He heard footsteps. His room *was* staked out. He heard someone unlock the door, and as it began to open Menzies fired two shots through his jacket. The impact of the big bullets hurled the man into a backward somersault. Menzies got inside and locked the door behind him. He went over to the dying man and kicked the gun out of his limp hand. For a moment he considered whether the two rapidly growing red stains on the man's upper right chest were fatal. He decided he better make sure. He wrapped a towel around the muzzle of the pistol to muffle the shot, placed it up against the man's temple and pressed the trigger. A mixture of hair, brains, and blood splattered the floor and the opposite wall.

He rifled the man's pockets. He pulled a wallet with a Federales Police badge and identity card, some other papers, 2600 pesos in neat one hundred peso bills. He stuck the money, the badge, and the identity card in his pocket and threw the other papers on the floor. He made a mental note of the cop's name. Fernando Jesus María Porras-Castro. Menzies grinned!

He wrenched his clothes off, spent a minute under a hot shower, put on clean clothes, stuck his sheathed throwing knives into his hip pocket and his Luger into his French-made leather shoulder-holster. He picked up his passport, credit cards, his wallet with three thousand dollars in travelers' checks, and five thousand pesos, and stepped out of his room, locking the door behind him. He decided to use the stairway rather than the elevator and leaped down the six flights of steps in giant bounds until he reached the door which led to the hotel's basement parking lot.

Menzies opened the door gingerly, and in the dim light he saw his 1974 Ford LTD station wagon parked where he had left it 50 feet away. As he stepped into the parking lot he noticed a shadow move on the far side, and instinctively he hurled himself on the floor and began to roll over, even as two shots blasted the silence of the basement. Menzies kept rolling over and over again, got behind a nearby Volkswagen and began to groan in a loud voice. "Help, help, police, police!" he yelled.

A moment later the shadow on the far side materialized into a short, swarthy man. He held a gun in his hand and was cautiously approaching the Volkswagen. Menzies let him get within thirty feet. Then his right hand reached in his hip pocket, and a knife flashed through the air. The seven-inch blade thumped into the man's throat to the hilt. A deathly gargling noise, the sound of a gun clattering on the cement floor, and the frantic movement of hands to the throat convinced Menzies that his knife had found its mark. The man staggered, swayed, then collapsed. Menzies got up approached him. He was now holding his Luger in his right fist.

Another shadow moved about fifty feet away and Menzies was about to fire when a voice yelled: "Please, Señor Menzies, please it's me, Gonzales."

At the sound of the voice Menzies swerved behind a nearby car but kept his new target covered. "All right, Gonzales," he yelled, recognizing the voice of the hotel parking lot attendant. "Now just start walking over here, and keep your hands above your head."

Having spoken and thus disclosed his position, Menzies instantly moved to the cover of another car. He saw Gonzalez coming forward. He waited until he was close enough, then leaped up and hit him in the back of the head with the butt of the Luger. Gonzalez went down without a word.

Menzies now stepped over to the dying cop. His legs moved in convulsive spasms; his hands clutched both the hilt and the tip of the knife, which protruded on either side of his neck. Blood poured out of the two wounds in diminishing spurts. Menzies tore the man's fingers from the hilt of the knife, then grabbed it himself. In one, powerful, sudden jerk he slit the throat altogether. Then he wiped the blade on the dead man's clothes and stuck it back in the sheath in his hip pocket.

At that moment Menzies heard the clip-clap of a woman's shoes on the ramp which led from the street to the basement parking lot. Quickly he hid behind a car, the Luger once more in his fist.

He first saw the white shoes and white skirt, then the torso of Geralda, whose head was now covered in a red mantilla. She seemed unconcerned and strolled along towards the Volkswagen behind which Menzies had originally hidden. Menzies saw her open her handbag and fiddle with the car keys. He leaped across the intervening twenty feet in three giant bounds and slapped the palm of his hand on her mouth. He used his knee and body to pin her up against the Volkswagen and showed her the Luger and the dead man on the floor thirty paces away. "Now start talking," he hissed. "And make it good—if you want to live."

Geralda began to struggle. Menzies put the gun in his pocket, grabbed her hand and turned it behind her back until he saw the twist of pain in her face. "Are you gonna answer my questions? Are you gonna do what I tell you?"

Geralda's frightened eyes moved down and up in the affirmative. Menzies released some of the pressure on her arm and body. "You're getting into your car, with me behind you, and you're gonna drive up Avenida Juarez real fast, you understand?"

She said "yes" with her eyes. Menzies heard the distant wail of sirens. "I'll be behind you," he said. "If you stop, for any reason, I'll shoot you. Understand?"

She said "yes" the same way. Menzies slowly took his hand off her mouth. She didn't scream. She got in the car, and Menzies squeezed himself behind her, the Luger once again in his fist. Then the Volkswagen roared up the ramp and tore along the deserted Avenida.

They passed the screaming sirens and the flashing lights of two police cars going in the opposite direction. Minutes later Menzies asked her to stop. He got out and told her to move over. Then he got in and pushed the Volkswagen at eighty-miles-an-hour toward Guadalajara's western suburbs. "O.K., baby, now start talking," he said.

She turned and looked at him. She was terrified at the way he drove. He had run nine red lights. She saw the slight twist in the corner of his mouth, the strange glow in his eyes. That frightened her even more. Geralda thought he looked insane, inhuman. But there wasn't a trace of fear in her voice when she spoke. "What do you want from me?" she asked. "Where are you going? Are you mad?"

Menzies lifted a hand off the wheel and slapped her across her face. Her head jerked back, bounced off the headrest, and fell against the dashboard. She said nothing. She didn't even scream. Menzies eased the pressure on the accelerator and looked at her. She was fully conscious. He noticed the small stream of blood trickling from the corner of her mouth.

"Talk!" he yelled. He stuck the same hand in his pocket and raised the Luger, just enough for her to see it. "Was that your husband, your brother, your father?"

"My father is dead and I have no husband," she said. Her voice was firm. It sounded sincere to Menzies. She didn't bother to wipe the blood from her face.

"Then it was your brother," said Menzies. "And he's dead now. And that's what's going to happen to you, too, if you don't talk."

"What do you want from me?" she snarled. "I have four brothers, and none of them are in Guadalajara. I know that."

Menzies stuck his hand in his pocket, pulled out the Federales police badge and identification card, gave them to her, switched on the inside lights of the car. "Who's that?" he said. "My grandfather?" He paused to give her time to see the photo and read the name on the identity card. "I've just killed that bastard. In my room. He and three others had staked out the whole fucking hotel. They tried to kill me. Only I got them first."

"His surname is the same as mine, but I don't know him," said Geralda. "Porras-Castro is not an unusual name in Mexico. I saw the two Federales at the restaurant. I saw you leave. When you didn't come back I picked up your lighter from the bar and waited for you at the coffee shop. I waited for more than half an hour. When you didn't come, I went to the hotel to get my car. . ."

"Shut up," Menzies said. "Show me the lighter."

She was about to open her handbag when Menzies grabbed her hand. Over the years he had seen many things come out of a woman's handbag. He took his foot off the accelerator, slowed down the car, then stopped it.

He pulled the handbag from her hands, opened it, searched inside, found no guns or knives, felt around for his lighter, and took it out. "Sorry," he said. He felt bad. His mind became a jumble of new thoughts, new plans.

She interrupted him. "Are you telling me that you killed a Federales?" she asked.

"Yeah. Not one. Four. They tried to shoot me first. I don't know why."

Geralda stirred in her seat. She took her handbag from his lap, got a handkerchief, moistened it with her lips, and began to clean the dried blood off her face. "If you killed four Federales you are no enemy of mine," she said. "The Federales murdered my father. My four brothers are *guerrilleros* up in the Sierra Madre Occidental."

Menzies had heard of the guerrilleros. They rode horses. They operated in the old-fashioned romantic tradition of Pancho Villa. Or at least they thought they did. They considered themselves Mexican Robin Hoods, fighting for some great political cause. What this cause was Menzies didn't know. What he did know was that the guerrilleros had terrorist branches operating in some Mexican cities, especially Guadalajara. They had abducted the United States consul there in 1973 and released him for a ransom. They had also kidnapped the British honorary vice consul in Guadalajara the same year but had later released him. Reputedly they were responsible for dozens of murders and holdups. The Mexican police considered them *bandidos*. They gave them no quarter whenever they happened to find them, which wasn't often. The activities of the Mexican guerrilleros and their affiliated city terrorists were similar to those of the *tupamaros,* and others who operated in Argentina, Uruguay, and Paraguay.

For the first time that night Menzies began to doubt his hunch. It could just be that Geralda had nothing to do with what had happened at the hotel. But he could not afford to take any chances. He knew he was about a mile from the intersection of Avenida de las Torres and Calle Lopez Mateos. A turn to the left at the intersection would eventually take him to the 200-mile stretch of mountain road which led to Manzanillo or Puerto Vallarta. If he stayed on Avenida de las Torres, he would soon get onto the northern highway which led to Mazatlán, and to the United States border one thousand miles away.

Geralda interrupted his thoughts. "I can help you, but you will have to trust me. I know how the police operate in Guadalajara."

"Cut it out, baby," said Menzies. "Why should you want to help me? I know you're scared but I'm not going to harm you — if I can avoid it."

"I'll help you because we have the same enemies. That's why. Also because you're a *periodista* — a newspaper man. We need somebody to tell the truth about the guerrilleros — to the whole world!"

Menzies grinned. "How do you know I'm a newsman?"

"Because when you asked me to go dancing with you tonight, I checked with the hotel. I have many friends in the hotel. In the registration form you filled at the hotel you gave your profession as a *periodista*. But I want to check something out first. And if what you say is true, I will help you."

"Is it true? You bet it's true," said Menzies. "I've got a big problem and I know it. But I'll figure things out for myself. My biggest problem is what to do with you, Geralda."

Geralda spoke calmly and slowly. "First of all, move the car from here. We're right in the middle of Avenida de las Torres. Pepe, I'm sure, knows that you were going to meet me tonight. He has probably told the police. They'll be watching for my car. Take any turn to the left and park in a dark, quiet side street. Hurry up, do it now."

There was quiet authority in her voice. And Menzies knew her words were backed by plenty of common sense. He drove off without a word, turned left at the next corner, went down the street about ten blocks, turned left again, stopped the car.

"Now you'll have to trust me," she said. "I have another radio in the car, a special radio. It's linked to the police radio. I want to listen for a few minutes. I've to check out what you've told me."

Menzies hesitated. Then he took out the Luger and pointed the muzzle at her chest. "All right, Geralda," he said in a slow, casual voice. "But remember, you'll just listen."

Geralda nodded. Then she took a coin from her handbag and unscrewed part of the dashboard. She pulled out a small tray on which stood an assembly of wires and batteries in matchbox-size containers. She gave an earphone to Menzies and took one herself. She switched on the radio and a jumble of static and fast, metallic-sounding Spanish words rang in Menzies' ears.

They listened for more than five minutes. Menzies couldn't understand a thing. But he did hear the words Roma Hotel repeated a few times. Also the words Volkswagen, followed by some numbers. Geralda prodded him with her knee. She switched the radio off, took the earphones and replaced the radio. "You see? Are you satisfied?" she asked.

"It isn't me that has to be satisfied," said Menzies. "It's you." He put the gun back in his pocket.

"This means that this car is no good now; it's marked."

"Yeah, I know, I know," said Menzies, a trace of irritation in his voice. "The car is hot, and so am I. But maybe not you; at least, not yet."

He took out a pack of Fiesta cigarettes, offered her one which she refused, lit one himself. "You can tell them you were kidnapped. And you wouldn't be far wrong."

She took her time answering. "Yes; I will think of something when the time comes," she said quietly. Her voice changed, she added: "Now, Señor Menzies, *vamos, vamos!*"

Geralda got out of the car, and Menzies followed her. They both sensed the captor-hostage relationship had ended. Menzies could find no flaw in her story, her reasoning. The mention of her link with the Mexican guerrilleros, had put a new complexion, a brighter complexion, on his immediate problem. And Menzies knew that right now he didn't have much of an alternative.

They walked several blocks before a car from behind lit up the deserted street. Suddenly she took his arm and put it over her shoulders. "Come close," she whispered. "Let's pretend we're lovers."

Menzies felt the curves of her hips glued onto his. He smiled and said, "That's fine with me, though maybe you're the good old Mongolian ruse, the queen gambit."

"I do not understand," she said. The car raced past them. Switching to Spanish, she added: *"¿Qué dice?"*

"Forget it. Nothing."

She made him turn right at the next corner and he asked: "Where are we going?"

"I must telephone," she said. "There is a public telephone along this street. Please hurry up."

He lengthened his stride to match hers. Two blocks further along the lights of another car came around the corner ahead of them.

"Police," she said, and before she finished speaking she lifted herself on her toes and glued her lips onto his.

He felt the vibrating softness of her breasts up against him, wrapped his arms around her waist and buttocks and put plenty of zest into this imitation love scene. The prowling patrol car crawled down the street but didn't stop, and Geralda responded to his embrace with traditional Mexican passion.

The police car slowly turned right at the next corner and was out of sight, and Menzies suddenly grabbed her shoulders and pushed her away from him. He knew that had he not done so, the next second he'd have probably torn her clothes off and raped her right there up against some wall, or on the garbage-littered damp pavement.

She stood there panting, her eyes flashing, her breasts heaving. "Come, let's walk," she said. A minute later they reached the phone booth.

"Who are you going to phone?" Menzies asked.

"My. . . friends," she said. "They can help us."

Menzies knew that for him, this was the ultimate moment of trust. He looked at her in silence.

"Señor Menzies, we do not have much time to lose," she said. "I cannot take you to my apartment, because the Federales will be watching it. In another hour it will be dawn. They will find the car, then they will find the police radio. And then they will start looking for me, too. You understand?"

"O.K.," said Menzies. "Go ahead and phone." But instantly he changed his mind. "Listen, why don't you get out of this while there's still time. I'll be all right. I'll just take a cab and get to the British Embassy. I'll tell them exactly what happened. The police can't touch me there."

"Señor Menzies, you are being very foolish," she said. "Every taxi driver in Guadalajara is a police informer; and he has a radio in his car. And the first place the police will stake out is the British Embassy. They already know you are *inglés* from the hotel registration. Besides, we need you as much as you need us. And we can help you get out of Mexico." She didn't wait for him to reply. She got into the phone booth and began dialing. She spoke for a minute or two, then got out. She took him by the hand. "Everything will be all right. Now we walk back along this street. A car will come for us."

Less than half an hour later a Ford Pinto stationwagon pulled up beside them, and a plump middle-aged woman beckoned them inside. Geralda introduced her as Doña Tina and the car sped away toward the street where they had left the Volkswagen. They passed it three times before finally drawing alongside. Geralda leaped out and a moment later returned with the radio. Then they drove through a maze of side streets until they reached a two-story house standing in its own private garden, in the Zaporan suburb of Guadalajara. It was 6 A.M., and the great city was already beginning to stir. They got out. Doña Tina gave a bunch of keys to Geralda, spoke to her in rapid Spanish, then drove away. Menzies and Geralda walked about 100 feet along a cobblestone path, climbed a dozen steps to a wide patio, and entered a large hall. Geralda locked the door behind them. "First thing we want to find out is why the Federales tried to kill you," she said. "There's a telephone here, but I want you to promise me not to use it."

Geralda showed him around the house. It consisted of a kitchen, living room, and bathroom on the ground floor, and three additional bedrooms and a bathroom on the upper floor. The furniture was old but serviceable.

"I'll have to go now," said Geralda. "It is best for me to face the Federales' questioning straightaway. We have people working for us inside police headquarters in Mexico City. We'll know all there is to know about last night within a few hours. Doña Tina is already working on this. Some members of our organization will come to visit you this afternoon. Doña Tina will bring them over. Please speak to them truthfully, Juan. For your own sake. I'll come and see you after the show at the Roma tonight. About two o'clock. If I'm sure I'm not being followed." She went over to him and kissed him, but had slipped away from his arms and was on her way to the exit almost immediately.

Menzies watched her from the window as she walked down the street. Then he went over to the kitchen and made himself some coffee. He noticed the phone on the bedside table in the ground-floor bedroom. He hesitated for an instant, then decided to leave it alone for the time being. He needed time to think.

CHAPTER THREE

Nine Yak Tails

At 2 A.M. Greenwich time, two hours after the deadline for John Menzies had expired in Mexico, Sir John Hillary Brigstocke, special executive in the British Prime Minister's office in London, dialed an unlisted telephone number in Berkshire.

The phone rang only twice before it was answered. "Mr. Spiegelstein? This is Brigstocke, the prime minister's office," Sir John said. "I have a very urgent request from the Prime Minister. We want a word-for-word transcript, in Arabic, of all *Falastin* al *Thawra* broadcasts in the past week. We need it by 8:00 A.M."

There was a long pause, on either end of the telephone line. Then Sir John continued, "Priority one, classification one. A helicopter will be over at Caversham Park to pick up the transcript. We should like it suitably catalogued, with a one-page introduction from you."

"We'll do our best," the voice at the other end said.

"Thanks," said Sir John, and rang off.

Spiegelstein took the message, nodded curtly at the invisible Sir John, and set to work.

By the time Sir John had dressed, hopped into his Austin, and driven the back roads from Henley-on-Thames to Caversham, Spiegelstein had reached 17 Arabic translators—the other two were on holidays overseas. And by 3:00 A.M., when the lights of Caversham blazed into pre-dawn darkness, all 17 Arab news analysts were busy transcribing the thirty-three news bulletins and commentaries of Falastin al Thawra from the past week.

Precisely at 8:00 A.M. a helicopter landed on the lawn at Caversham Park. The pilot picked up a bulky package from a waiting ash-blonde Swedish secretary. Twenty minutes later he delivered it to two men standing on the rooftop landing pad of a building less than half a mile from Piccadilly Circus.

The third, fourth, and fifth floor of the building, whose exact whereabouts is one of the most closely guarded secrets of the British government, are occupied by the Foreign Office cryptography section. Awaiting the package were thirteen American decoding experts. They had been fetched overnight via supersonic Concorde. Traveling at an average speed of 1300 miles an hour, the plane had crossed the Atlantic twice in less than six hours.

By 9:00 A.M. forty-two British and American decoding experts, most of whom were also Arab linguists, were busy checking the twenty thousand-word copy which had come out as news and comment in the short-wave transmissions of Falastin al Thawra the previous week.

An hour after the helicopter landed on the roof-top landing pad of the cryptographic section building, Colin Young and Jim Atherton returned to the suite in the Strand Palace. They found Col. Rod Paulisen alone, chewing an empty pipe and sipping coffee. All three had spent a sleepless night. Paulisen, who had had very little sleep for three days, was feeling the strain. He had taken a Benzedrine tablet to prevent him from falling asleep. The drug would keep him going until 4:00 P.M. After that he had to get at least four hours sleep if he were to maintain a clear mind. Meanwhile, he forced his mind to concentrate on three million American, British, and French lives.

Young and Atherton sat down. Young pulled an envelope from his breast pocket. "It took a little longer than expected, but I think we've got the information from the British Museum," he said. I've got it all typed out, and I'm going to give you a copy. Or should we rather wait until Aris comes back? By the way, where is he?"

"He's flown back to Greece," said Paulisen. "There's been a message from a man called Kokkinellis, a Greek undercover agent in Damascus, and it probably has some bearing on this case."

"Hope there's some new clue there because right now . . ."

"Hold it," said Paulisen. He got up, poured coffee for the three of them, and brought it back. He sipped his coffee quickly, as if nibbling the cup. Young took a deep gulp, winced, and shoved it away. Atherton simply toyed with the handle.

Paulisen paused to fill his pipe and light it. He noticed impatience in Atherton's face but decided to ignore it.

"O.K., now let's see what you've got from the British Museum," he said.

Young took a number of closely typed pages out of the envelopes and handed them to Paulisen. "It's all there," he said.

Paulisen gave them back to him. "Colin, if you don't mind, read it aloud," he said. My eyes are feeling the strain. Besides, I find your voice, and your accent, rather soothing at the moment." He sat back against one of the overstuffed leather chairs and closed his eyes.

Young was about to begin reading when Paulisen raised his hand. "Just a moment," he said. "I forgot to tell you. Ten minutes before you got here I got a message from the CIA in Mexico and . . ."

"They got Menzies," Atherton said.

"Like hell they did," said Paulisen. "Menzies has knocked off, has savaged four Mexican bounty-hunter cops, and he's now holed up with a lush Mexican broad somewhere in Guadalajara. But they're really after him now. Every exit from Guadalajara has been blocked off. And they found his getaway car. It belonged to the girl."

"Good for Menzies," said Atherton. He looked elated. "I'm glad they didn't get him with his pants down."

"We all feel that way," said Paulisen. "But what do you suggest? If the other side gets him, he could be forced to talk. We're operating together, with government backing and facilities. Menzies is on his own. Can we take the chance that he might be arrested, tortured, forced to talk? His former E Force association would be disclosed, and our names would come up. To Mexican cops, this wouldn't mean a thing. But cops are known, sometimes, to sell information.

"Suppose they sell this information to the KGB in Mexico City. They have the world-wide facilities to check us out. We already know that the KGB in Syria has a connection with the As Saiqa.

"Now that would blow our cover. We'd be useless. We might as well be four more cops trying to stop the most ruthless and powerful international terrorist gang of the twentieth century. We wouldn't have a chance.

"You see what I'm getting at? We've just got to get Menzies. If he were in London and walked into this office, I'd welcome him with open arms. Believe you me, there's nobody I'd rather have with me. But where he is right now, roaming around with enough information in his head to bust the whole revived E Force, he's just too dangerous for us."

Young interrupted him. "Just a moment, Rod. If the Mexican police are officially looking for him, he might be caught alive, right?"

"Sure," said Paulisen.

"The situation has changed," said Young. "We expected the bounty hunters to kill him on sight. The last thing we want is for Menzies to get arrested for a serious crime and be interrogated. So think the situation is now reversed. We have to find Menzies *before* the Federales get him. And then we've either got to eliminate him or smuggle him out of Mexico and bring him over here."

"Listen, fellows," said Atherton. "Let's consider this thing properly. If we can get Menzies in a safe place, and somebody he could trust tells him he must report immediately to us in London, there wouldn't be any need to eliminate him. Right?"

"Sure, sure," said Paulisen. "But we've been through all this before. How the hell do you propose we get him into a safe place? And what's a safe place for Menzies? The Bastille?"

"All right," said Atherton. "We know Menzies is holed up somewhere in Guadalajara with a Mexican chick and every cop in Mexico is looking for him. Now where would he go? Where would he consider it safe? Remember, he considers himself completely innocent. We have to presume that the four cops he killed were bounty hunters, and that Menzies killed them in self-defense."

"O.K. Where does that get us?" asked Paulisen.

"If you were in Mexico, or in any other foreign country for that matter, and you were wanted for a murder, and you knew you were innocent, where would you go?" Atherton paused, but he didn't wait long enough for Paulisen to answer. "I'll tell you where you'd go, or at least where you should go. You'd go to the American Embassy, tell them everything, seek protection, legal advice. Right? The American Embassy would have to try to protect you, if they were convinced you were innocent, framed, and unjustly persecuted. On this basis I'm suggesting that what Menzies is doing right now is trying to reach the British Embassy in Mexico City."

"From Guadalajara to Mexico City it's four hundred miles, and he can't even get out of Guadalajara," said Paulisen.

"Also, the first place the Mexican police will stake out is the British Embassy in Mexico City," said Young. "They must have found out that Menzies is British."

"Precisely," said Atherton." So if he can't get there himself, he'll try to reach the embassy by phone, or by messenger. I think Menzies, being Menzies, will take the precaution not to use the phone. There's a huge dragnet and manhunt on in Mexico. He'll be cautious enough to assume that telephone lines to the embassy are tapped.

"So my guess is that Menzies, pretty soon, will get someone he can absolutely trust to go to the embassy, give the ambassador a message explaining his situation, and seek help."

"Who would do that for him?" asked Paulisen.

"That's unimportant at present," said Atherton. "We must assume that it will be someone that he believes he can trust. And let's hope he does have a trustworthy messenger—for our sake as well as his. Because we certainly don't want the Mexican police to take Menzies alive."

"O.K.," said Paulisen. "Where do we go from there?"

"We'll have to lay a trap for him," said Atherton. He turned to Young. "Colin, I suggest you contact your man in Mexico City. Tell him to get in touch with the British Ambassador. Ask him to tell the Ambassador that when a message reaches him from Menzies, he must immediately alert the British Secret Service office in Mexico City."

Young lit a cigarette and took his time before answering. "We have a good man in Mexico City, Archibald Carruthers. He's a dentist. Been there for ten years."

Paulisen grinned. "What? A dentist? Some cover. I give you full marks."

"Well," said Young, "we're sick and tired of foreign correspondents, foreign news stringers, import-export company managers, and travel agents."

"Now let's get back to Menzies," Atherton said. "As soon as Carruthers has been tipped off by the Ambassador, he should make the trip to Guadalajara, contact Menzies, tell him to get the hell out of Mexico and come over to London.

"If Menzies agrees, Rod calls off the CIA and the FBI and gets them to cooperate with Carruthers to smuggle Menzies out. If Menzies doesn't agree, if he hesitates or is doubtful, Carruthers eliminates him on the spot. That's what I'm suggesting. We have enough to do without diverting time and effort for Menzies.

"This seems reasonable," said Young. "I know the Firm will agree with it."

"I'll go along with it, too," said Paulisen. "But all this right now is just hypothetical. There are too many 'ifs' involved. In the meantime, I say we stick to the original plan. I'm not calling off anybody until Carruthers has Menzies alive and willing to cooperate."

"Of course, of course," said Young.

At that moment a light flashed on one of the phones. Young got up, went over to the desk with the phones, spoke briefly, and returned. "A messenger is coming up in a few minutes with a report from Aris," he said. "It's priority one. We have two decoding secretaries in the suite across the corridor. Should know what it's all about shortly."

Atherton looked at his watch. It was 11:30 A.M. "By the way, has anybody thought about breakfast?" he asked. "Or aren't we suppose to eat on duty?"

"Terribly sorry," said Young. "I almost forgot that you clean-living, non-smoking, non-drinking Canuck policemen have healthy appetites. Now what would you like?"

He took their orders, went over to another phone, placed the orders, and came back again. "While we're waiting, let me show you what we've got from the Gibbs collection in the British Museum about the way the Mongols dealt with the Assassins.

"And I've got something more. It's a special analysis of the activities of the Arab-based indiscriminate terrorist groups, the ITGs. A team of Scotland Yard Special Branch detectives worked it up in conjunction with orientalists from Oxford, Cambridge, and Leeds.

"They have made some suggestions, in very general terms of course, about how to handle the problem. These suggestions are based on the belief, in fact on the near certainty, that some of the present-day Palestinian terrorist attacks are a revival of the ancient cult of the Assassins.

"Gentlemen," said Young, "we are facing, the ghost of the Assassins. That's what it amounts to"

Paulisen sucked on his pipe and turned to Atherton. "So we're up against the ghost of the Assassins, eh?" said Atherton. "It sounds cute, poetic. Well, they're up against another ghost, only twenty-eight years dead. It takes a ghost to kill a ghost.

Each man fell into a thoughtful silence, interrupted by a knock on the door. Colins Young went to answer it. "Ah, breakfast. Trolley it right in, please."

They finished their brunch at twelve-thirty. Paulisen, still up from the Benzedrine, pushed the trolley away and turned to Young. "I'm ready for that history lesson now, Colin."

"Lay on, Macduff," said Atherton. "And damned be he . . ."

"Enough, enough," Paulisen said.

Colin Young stretched his legs and cleared his throat. "Well, here's what happened to the assassins," he said. "Fortunately, our chaps at the B.M. found an English version that someone seems to have translated. Here goes." He began to read.

The nine white yak tails of the imperial standard fluttered in the icy wind that swept the wintry Mongolian steppe.

As far as the eye could see, row upon row of horsemen, their lances flashing in the early morning sun, stood neatly spaced out in squadrons, regiments, and divisions that stretched out into the white horizon. These were the Tartars. The scourge of God. The most dreaded, most mobile army the world has ever seen. They faced south-west. And they stood still.

Only the war-loving, sturdy Mongolian ponies that stomped the snow betrayed that this was a real, live army—not a splendid oriental painting by some Persian master.

The Mongol troopers were in marching gear, not battle dress. They wore coats and breeches made of the hides of horses. Their headgear consisted of four layers of sheepskin, stitched together in a kind of cloak that also covered their neck and shoulders. Their footwear was from the hide of buffalo. Their main armament consisted of a lance, sword, mace, net and the terrible Mongol arrow—steel-tipped, launched from a short, very sturdy bow.

Mongol officers were dressed in the skins of wild animals—giant panda, tiger, leopard, boar. The skins of snakes were tightly wrapped around their legs from the ankle to the knee.

Hulagu Khan, grandson of Genghis Khan, was in command. He was very anxious to make himself conspicuous. He was about to launch a war of vengeance, probably the only popular war the Mongols ever fought in the two hundred years they terrified and dominated Asia and Europe. He was dressed in the white skins of polar bears and rode a white stallion.

Hulagu was fifty. Like his famous grandfather, he had red hair and a red beard, which was most unusual for pure-bred Mongols. Above his high cheekbones flashed coal-black slit eyes, capped by a thick, continuous line of red eyebrows.

This was October 19, 1253—the early morning of a short, wintry Mongolian day. Temperatures hovered around ten degrees below freezing.

Behind Hulagu's seven fighting divisions and his 2,000-strong bodyguard—a total of 72,000 men—were more than ten miles of caravans, horses, herds of cattle. This was Hulagu's supply train and his siege equipment.

The artillery consisted of one thousand mangonels, each with its Chinese team of bombardiers. They could hurl a 50-pound rock a distance of a mile, or pots of burning naphtha half that distance. Five thousand wagon loads of missiles and dismantled mangonels, drawn by ten times that number of cart horses and bullock teams, formed part of Hulagu's artillery train. Another five thousand wagons carried fodder and other supplies.

Each of the 72,000 fighting horsemen had two spare horses, attended by two personal servants. Under the saddle of each fighting horseman were 40 pounds of dried, salted meat.

Only Mongols had the privilege of fighting in Hulagu's army. And fighting was the only duty allowed for Mongols. This was a fighting race, a fighting nation par excellence. Its object was world conquest.

This vast army—perhaps half a million men and a million horses, cattle, buffalo, camels—was the smallest of three armies recently dispatched from Karakorum—Black Sands—the mobile capital of the Mongol empire, a city of a million giant felt tents.

Hulagu's army was part of the greatest campaign of conquest ever launched in the history of mankind. Hulagu's cousin, Batu, had already conquered Russia, Russia, Poland, and Hungary and had smashed the combined German principalities in the murderous battle of Liegnitz. The only reason Batu had not conquered the rest of Europe was because his uncle, the Mongol emperor Ogatai, had died in faraway Karakorum, and Batu had to return to Mongolia to help choose a successor. But he had left Mongol garrisons in Budapest. He had drawn the western borders of the Mongol empire roughly along the present-day border between East and West Germany, and then south to Hungary and northern Yugoslavia.

Hulagu's famous brother Kubla Khan, emerging from Peking, which his grandfather had captured nearly half a century earlier, had the toughest job and the biggest army. He had conquered the great Southern Chinese empire and sent his generals into present-day Vietnam, all the way to Saigon. They rode their Mongol ponies through the steaming jungles of Thailand and Malaysia all the way to the Straights of Malacca, and then built a fleet and subjugated the rulers of Sumatra and Java.

Hulagu was the last to launch his campaign. His orders, from his brother Mangu, who was the new emperor at Karakorum, were clear enough. "Ride to Baghdad and then West as far as your Mongol ponies will take you. But first make sure you destroy the Assassins."

And so, in the beginning of winter, Hulagu's horde moved forward in a campaign that would take his warriors to Damascus and the Mediterranean Sea—a distance of ten thousand miles on horseback!

Ahead of Hulagu lay a succession of four empires—each with a population of at least twenty-five million people. First of all, the Kwarizmian empire in Central Asia. This empire at the time extended from Siberia to the Indian Ocean and east as far as Pakistan. It had been subdued by Genghis Khan but was now in a state of revolt and anarchy.

Then there was the Persian empire, at that time consisting of the western part of present-day Iran. Then the empire of the Caliph of Baghdad. It incorporated present-day Iraq, the Arabian peninsula, Turkish Kurdistan, most of Syria, and Jordan.

Finally there was the Mameluke empire of Egypt, which controlled the area from southern Israel and the Sinai peninsula to Kenya and Algiers.

Wedged in between the Mameluke empire to the south and the Caliph's empire to the north and east were the Crusaders, who had set up a kingdom along much of the coast of Syria, Lebanon, and Israel.

By the time of Hulagu's onslaught, embassies had reached Karakorum

from the Pope and from various kings of Europe. Because of language dif-
ficulties. Mangu and his predecessor Kuyuk had thought that the
European emissaries were offering submission to the Mongols.

It was Mongol military policy to destroy all those who did not submit.
But once a prince, a city, a kingdom offered submission at the first request
(or preferably even before they were asked to do so), the Mongols
considered them part of their own empire. There was no reason, therefore, to destroy what belonged to them. Such people were friends and
allies as well as vassals. They must be treated accordingly, protected.
With this in mind, Hulagu was told that once he reached the
Mediterranean he would find friends and allies in the European
Crusaders fighting the Mamelukes and the Caliph.

During Genghis Khan's first foray into Central Asia several decades
earlier, the famous general Sabutay, later to conquer Budapest, had
surveyed the Assassin strongholds on the Erbruz Highlands. He had
found out that the Assassins had more than one hundred castles. The only
way an army could enter the mountain domain of the Sheik-el-Jebel was
by the solitary pass which led to Alamut—Eagle's Nest—the formidable
fortress and capital of the Assassins. Since this pass was always firmly
held, and Sabutay was riding light without artillery or other siege equipment, he bypassed the Assassins on his way to the Caucasus and Southern
Russia.

Years later, at the request of various Persian princes, the Old Man Of
The Mountain launched a campaign of terror against the Mongols. One
of Genghis Khan's stepsons was treacherously killed during a banquet.
Several Mongol generals were also stabbed to death. This had enraged
Genghis Khan. The great Mongol leader was by that time too old and sick
to begin a campaign against the Assassins. But he made his four sons
swear that they would avenge the murders and exterminate this nest of
killers in the Erbruz Highlands.

The Mongols never forgot. They waited for the right time. Then the
Caliph of Baghdad, enemy of the Old Man Of The Mountain, had sent
embassies to Karakorum. He described the horror unleashed by the Assassins. He urged the Mongols, in whose territory the Erbruz Highlands
lay, to do something about it. Mangu then ordered his brother to destroy
the Assassins on his way to Baghdad and the Mediterranean.

Mangu was anxious to publicize the fact that the Mongols would wipe
out the Assassins. First of all, this publicity would be good for military
morale. All the way from Budapest to Shanghai soldiers would know that
the Assassins, who had defied even the famous Sabutay, would finally
perish during Mangu's reign.

Second, it would improve the image of the Mongol administration
throughout the occupied territories. The Assassins had terrorized the entire Moslem World and much of Europe. The campaign against the Assassins would be very popular.

Third, it would strengthen the *yashak*, the law of Genghis Khan, among the hundreds of his descendants. The yashak was a code of ethics and military behavior, the Constitution of the Mongol empire. One of the rules of the yashak was that an order by the *Kakhan*—the emperor—must be obeyed, even if it took a hundred years.

Overriding all these reasons, of course, was revenge. But it was revenge combined with fear. If the Assassins were not destroyed, they might be able to get their hashishin killers even close to the Kakhan and the other princes.

The Mongols had studied the cult of the Assassins very carefully, over a long period of time. They had obtained the advice of Persian, Chinese, and Arab scholars, historians, army commanders. They had learned (through word of mouth, because the Mongol princes were illiterate) more about the origins and the way of operation of the Assassins than perhaps we know today, despite the various books on the subject.

The decision was therefore taken not only to destroy the Assassins and their castles but also their philosophy. The Mongols knew only too well that an idea can only be killed by another, better, idea. And they *had* a better idea. Peace. *Pax Tatarica*—Mongol peace. Universal peace within their subjugated dominions.

For all these reasons Mangu assigned to Hulagu's army a famous writer, historian, and philosopher of those days. His name was Ata Malik el Hudeini. Hudeini became the world's first, full-time war correspondent and propagandist, equipped with a captured Chinese press for his work, translators to put his writings into a variety of languages, and a team of secretaries and associated writers to help him compile the material he collected.

One of Hudeini's jobs was to write a history of the campaigns of Hulagu Khan, and particularly the part dealing with the destruction of the Assassins and their leader, the Sheik-el-Jebel. He had access to Hulagu at all times. And he was given comparative freedom to write the story as he saw it. He was even allowed to criticize the Mongols, if he felt they deserved criticism. And Hudeini did precisely that, though infrequently — because Hudeini was wise!

Young stopped reading and lit a cigarette. "What I'm going to tell you is not of course the full story of the destruction of the Assassins. That's available in a number of books, suitably embellished. I'll simply deal with the policy, the philosophy, the strategy which Hulagu used to wipe out the Assassins. And of course that's the only thing that we want right now.

"We're not likely to raise an army to go to Syria, Lebanon, Iraq, wherever the Assassins have their headquarters today, to kill off this sect."

Paulisen grinned, but said nothing.

"Sometimes I think I'd like to do just that," said Atherton.

"All right," said Young. He picked up his file and reopened it. He began to read again.

It took Hulagu two and a half years to travel the five thousand miles from northeastern Mongolia to central Persia, southwest of the Caspian Sea. Through skilful diplomacy and the ruthless use of military power he confirmed the submission of Central Asia, Afghanistan, and Persia. He razed some cities which had not submitted and exterminated the inhabitants to the last man.

This was standard Mongol strategy. It aimed to shock the population into quick submission. In other cases, Hulagu rebuilt previously destroyed cities, and rewarded their inhabitants for offering supplies to his army.

By May 1256, Hulagu's army, reinforced from other parts of the Mongol empire and by nearly one hundred thousand local levies, was encamped on the Persian flatlands in a semicircle around the 120-mile southern arc of the Erbruz mountain domain of the Assassins.

Hulagu had announced that he planned to subdue the Assassins, destroy their castles, and dissolve their terrorist network. But he had also announced that once they had submitted, their religious heresy would not be persecuted, and that he would declare a total amnesty for all crimes.

Even when a youthful Assassin was captured in Hulagu's tent and confessed that he planned to murder him on the orders of the Old Man Of The Mountain, the Mongol leader did not withdraw the amnesty offer.

The announcement that he would destroy the castles of the Assassins and stop terrorism was welcome news for the princes and the people of Persia and Central Asia. The Erbruz castles were crammed with treasure, collected over a period of nearly two centuries. So the prospect of seizing the castles stimulated the multitude of regular and irregular soldiers who obeyed Hulagu. Storming the castles meant plunder.

Through intensive diplomatic activity and the biggest, most sophisticated public-relations campaign ever, Hulagu suddenly became the champion of a population obsessed by fear of the Assassins and oppressed by the Old Man Of The Mountain.

The hereditary leaders of the people—the princes, religious potentates, generals, and other titled nobility—had been the main victims of extortion from the Erbruz. Once these men became convinced that Hulagu had the will and the power to stop this extortion, they propagated the views and the policies which Hulagu had come to enforce.

In short, before even considering an attack on the near-impregnable Erbruz, Hulagu first politically isolated the Old Man Of The Mountain.

The hereditary leader of the Assassins at that time was Rukn-ad-Din. A ruthless, cruel man, he had reportedly murdered his own father in order to ascend the throne of the Erbruz. It is impossible, at this historical distance, to confirm that Rukn-ad-Din had in fact killed his own father. The story comes to us from Hudeini.

So, in the summer of 1256, Rukn-ad-Din found himself completely cut off. To the east and south, Central Asia and Persia defied him and were in the hands of Hulagu. To the west was the empire of his archenemy, the Caliph of Baghdad. To the north, the Caspian Sea.

But even so, Rukn-ad-Din was safe. There was only one path into the Erbruz—a six-feet-wide trail blocked by Alamut at the far end. Alamut had defied 31 previous onslaughts. It had never been conquered. Inside the 10,000-square-mile Erbruz Highlands were no less than one hundred other castles. Even if the Mongols managed to storm the pass and take Alamut, which was unthinkable, they would wear themselves out in a long war of attrition trying to capture the castles, all held by fanatic hashishin who would rather die than surrender. Meanwhile, the Sheik-el-Jebel would have numerous chances to assassinate Mongol leaders, generals, even Hulagu himself.

Rukn-ad-Din's assessment of the military situation was sound. And it corresponded with the assessment of the Mongol divisional commanders. They reported to Hulagu that the pass could not be stormed, that it would be impossible to fight a successful campaign inside the Erbruz Highlands—even if the pass was stormed.

This information was a shock to Hulagu. The Mongols had never been stopped before. And his orders, his duty to his grandfather, were explicit. An attack from the sea was also considered. But the plan was dropped because it would take years to build a fleet to transport the Mongol army to the Caspian shores of the Erbruz.

Time was running out for Hulagu. His armies of men and horses had to be supplied. The Mongols had already denuded the countrysize of grazing pastures, beef cattle, flour, wine.

Hulagu had exacted a war levy from the Persians and the Kwariz-mians of 650 pounds of flour for each fighting Mongol soldier and 300 pints of wine. For his 72,000 Mongols, plus a division of 10,000 others who had reinforced him from other parts of the empire, this worked out to nearly a million bushels of wheat and 12,000 tons of wine—heavy taxation even for the fertile plains of Persia and Central Asia. In addition, of course, the vast number of auxiliaries had to be supplied and the army's horses provided for.

Hulagu held a war council, and it was agreed that the Assassins could not be destroyed by military means alone. The answer lay in a combination of military strength, intelligence work, diplomacy, propaganda.

Rukn-ad-Din, on the other hand, also decided to use diplomacy and negotiation to avert the Mongol onslaught. He offered to destroy some of the castles which were on the fringe of the Erbruz in exchange for a pledge by Hulagu that the Mongol army would strike camp and leave.

Hulagu encouraged him, but he also demanded that Rukn-ad-Din personally visit the Mongol camp and offer his submission. The Sheik-el-Jebel claimed he was sick and sent his brother instead. Time passed. The winter was about to set in. Hulagu knew he had to act quickly or fail. The Mongols and their advisers studied the situation. Exhaustively. They came up with only one answer. (This answer is very significant for us today.) There was only one way to stop the Assassins and their terrorist network. They must capture the Sheik-el-Jebel, Rukn-ad-Din, and then force him to order the surrender of the castles and the dissolution of the terrorist conspiracy. The fanatic hashishin would only obey an order from the Sheik-el-Jebel, the Old Man of The Mountain. Nobody else. terrorist conspiracy. The fanatic hashishin would only obey an order from the Sheik-el-Jebel, the Old Man of The Mountain. Nobody else.

The question was, how could they find and capture Rukn-ad-Din? The answer was intelligence work. Hulagu's spies penetrated into the Erbruz, some of them disguised as hashishin themselves. The news came back to Hulagu that Rukn-ad-Din planned to visit the formidable frontier fortress of Miamun-Diz, which stood on the top of a conical mountain on the very edge of the Erbruz.

One night in November 1256, a small Mongol detachment used rope ladders to scale a five hundred-foot sheer cliff left undefended by the Assassins because they had considered it safe.

The Mongols, one hundred all told, split into two parties. One party surprised and killed the Assassin sentries on two neighboring hills. The other party raced along the rugged mountainside to the point, 10 miles away, where stood the fortress of Maimun-Diz.

At dawn next day, fifty deadly Mongol archers, hidden among the rocks, on either side of the lone path which led to Maimun-Diz, blocked the exit from the fortress.

As soon as the situation was discovered, the drawbridge was lowered and out poured several hundred Assassin cavalrymen in full armor to dislodge the Mongols. It proved impossible. We must remember that the Mongol archers, as the Russians, Poles, Hungarians, and Germans had found out twenty five years earlier, could shoot through the plate armor of Western knights from a distance of one hundred yards. The Mongols were almost infallible marksmen. When dealing with knights in armor they oftened preferred to shoot the horses; the knights tumbled down helplessly and were massacred.

All day the Assassins tried to break out but failed. Rukn-ad-Din was trapped inside Maimun-Diz. More Mongols scaled the cliffs and overran sentry posts on either side of the bridgehead. Hulagu's Chinese engineers employed ten thousand men to cut and clear a winding, zigzag trail over which the Mongol cavalry now began to pass. The troopers dismounted and led their horses to the top. Wagonloads of equipment and supplies were hauled up on galleys. Soon the imperial standard with the nine white yak tails was planted on a hill across the deep ravine from Maimun-Diz.

The Mongols attacked the pass that led to Alamut from the rear. Then they brought up their mangonels and other siege equipment to Maimun-Diz. Day after day they pounded the fortress and attacked with infantry and scaling ladders. They were hurled back every time.

The answer still lay in negotiation, diplomacy, propaganda and public relations—not force!

Hulagu offered Rukn-ad-Din safe conduct for himself and all his followers, complete amnesty for everything the Assassins had done, freedom to practice their faith, even if other Moslems considered it heretic. All that Hulagu demanded was the surrender and destruction of the fortresses. "What is the reason for you to have castles," Hulagu asked, "if the mighty Mongol army protects you?"

The Mongols resumed the siege and continued to hammer the fortress with their mangonels. Rukn-ad-Din then visited Karakorum, to pay homage to Mangu, the Mongol emperor. While Rukn-ad-Din was in Karakorum, the news reached Mangu that the last Assassin fortress had been stormed, and that its commander had confessed that Rukn-ad-Din had urged him to resist. Mangu was enraged. He put Rukn-ad-Din to death. Then he sent messengers to Hulagu 5,000 miles away and ordered him to kill every captured Assassin because Rukn-ad-Din had broken his promise, thus canceling the safe-conduct promise. The order was duly carried out. That was the end of the Assassins in the Erbruz. But the Syrian branch of the sect continued to exist, until finally broken up by the Mamelukes of Egypt in a similar way, a few decades later.

However, the Syrian Assassins were never as thoroughly wiped out as their associates in the Erbruz. In the middle of the fifteenth century, Mohammet the Conqueror, Sultan of the Turks, was attacked by Assassins only weeks before he began his memorable siege of Constantinople. He survived.

The Syrian branch of the Assassins continued to operate, more or less openly, right up to the nineteenth century. Their headquarters was the fortress of Massiat in northeastern Syria. They also controlled more than a dozen other castles during the five hundred years Syria was under Turkish rule.

The Shi-as, together with other heretic groups, such as the Nossairis, the Motewellis, and the Druses, were condemned by the Moslem faith. The Turks called them *mumsoindiren*—extinguishers. But even at the very height of the Turkish empire, at the time of Suleiman the Magnificent, the Turks never tried to destroy the remnants of the hashishin.

Colin Young stopped reading. He put down his file of papers and lit a cigarette. "Well, gentlemen, this is how the Mongols handled the problem of indiscriminate terrorism from the Assassins.

"Now some conclusions. I haven't had much time to think them through, since we received this material only this morning. Tell me what you think.

"First, we must isolate the Assassins from all political support. Don't ask me how. Second, we must find and reach the top man—in other words, the Sheik-el-Jebel. We must try and negotiate from a position of strength and persuade him to call off his killers and dismantle the hashishin organization. That is by no means impossible.

"Third, we must reintroduce the death penalty for all acts of indiscriminate terrorism resulting in the death of people. Fourth, whenever hostages are taken, we have to negotiate with the terrorist—not just barge in with blazing machine guns. We have to remember that fedayeen, in true Assassin tradition, will die willingly after they have committed their assignment. They expect to go to paradise. They want to go to paradise. The sooner the better.

"The Israeli and Turkish attitude in this respect is wrong. Fruitless. The best way to deal with hashishin holding hostages is to find and bring to the scene one of their own leaders. If we don't know any of their leaders, Arafat will do. He's the top man in Al Fatah.

"For example, if Arafat had been brought to Khartoum when the U.S. and Belgian diplomats were held as hostages, the murders could have probably been averted. Arafat could have been flown over under a safe-conduct promise. In any case, he needs no such promise while traveling through Egypt and the Sudan. Then the negotiations for the release of the diplomats should have been carried out through Arafat.

"And of course we should be elastic and accommodating, as much as possible. When we deal with hashishin, we certainly do not deal with ordinary human beings. We should take into account their philosophy. It doesn't pay to use the hard line once the hashishin have taken hostages."

There was a knock on the door. Young got up, strolled over and opened it. A tall, slim, angular brunette in her thirties stepped in. She wore horn-rimmed glasses and a grim look on her pale, plain, paintless face. She gave Young a folder. "Here is the decoded message from Greece, sir," she said.

"Thank you, Miss Holme," said Young. She walked out and closed the door behind her.

Young read the message from Aris aloud:

The President of the government has agreed to cooperate with us. In a broadcast this P.M. he mentioned agreed code words intended to indicate Greece's approval of As Saiqa plan. Kokkinellis returned to Damascus and just reported that As Saiqa agent Shashikli provided him first installment of information relating to plot of Society of Seven. Remote-control trigger mechanism for three atomic bombs has been completed in secret laboratory situated in Latin-American country. Name of country was not mentioned. Full details of project to explode A-bombs in Paris, London, and New York will be provided when Greece orders a general mobilization against Turkey. Greek government not prepared to take this last step. This is the end of the line as far as Kokkinellis breakthrough is concerned. Over to us now. Returning to London hopefully tonight by way of Paris. Aris.

One of the phones on the desk began to hum and flash a blue light. Young went over and picked up the receiver. He listened for a while, said "yes, yes," a few times, returned and sat down.

"A call from crypto," Young said. "They say they've got something for us, but they don't think it's much. A messenger should be here in about ten minutes."

"Fine," said Paulisen. "Things are beginning to move. At last. Now, coming back to Aris' report, what do you make out of it?"

"Neither more nor less than Aris has told us," said Atherton. "As Saiqa is obviously aware of the Society of Seven plot. That in itself is quite significant. It shows a measure of collaboration between these two groups. Just about the only clue we've got is that the secret laboratory, where the A-bombs and their trigger mechanisms are being assembled, is somewhere in Latin America. I don't see why this information could not be true. By telling the Greeks that the laboratory is in Latin America, they haven't told them very much. Where in Latin America? So Shashikli hasn't really risked very much. In fact, practically nothing. Because of this, I'm inclined to believe that their laboratory *is* in fact in Latin America. And I'm also inclined to believe that the top man in the Society of Seven outfit is where the laboratory is."

"You mean the Sheik-el-Jebel?" asked Paulisen.

"No, no," said Atherton. "I mean the leader of the Society of Seven, the leader of this group of hashishin, or at least the leader of this particular operation of the Society of Seven."

"Yes," said Paulisen. "It seems reasonable to assume that the squad leader of this particular terrorist group is right there where the bombs are being equipped. That would be the obvious place for him to be."

There was a knock on the door. Young got up, was handed a sealed envelope, signed for it, and returned to his seat.

He opened the envelope and read for a few minutes. "They've drawn a blank," he said. "They're still trying, but so far they've seen nothing which may refer to our problem. They've broken three different codes so far, all dealing with instructions to terrorists inside Israel. There's also one significant observation: Whereas only three Falastin Al Thawra short-wave transmissions were beamed to North and Central America last week, this week we have nine.

Paulisen broke in, his voice eager, "Remember that guy—what's his name—Sidki? That's right, Sidki. The guy who committed suicide in an Athens jail?"

"Y-e-s," drawled Young.

"He had an airline ticket to Mexico," said Paulisen. "To Mexico City."

"Hey, hold it!" Atherton yelled. He looked Paulisen straight in the eye. "Are you thinking what I'm thinking?"

"Menzies!" Young and Paulisen said simultaneously.

"By Jove, he's right there!" said Young. "I better get down to the office and ask the Old Man to recall Carruthers, or at least revise his instructions. The Old Man will probably tell me to go to hell, he'll think I'm mad!"

Suddenly Paulisen sprang to his feet. He fiddled in his pocket, took out another Benzedrine tablet, and swallowed it with some cold coffee. "You think you've got problems? By the way, what's the latest on Carruthers?"

"Nothing," said Young. "Too early yet. We only got the message through to Carruthers and the embassy a few hours ago."

Paulisen looked at his watch. "I'm going down to the CIA office, and then I'm filing a report for Henry Kissinger.

"I think we're now justified in asking for a full hunt for the Society of Seven in Mexico. Christ, if they're there, they'll have to have a pretty big facility to produce atomic bombs. This isn't something you can build in your basement."

"But that's just the point," Atherton said. If those stolen birdcages are in London, Paris, and New York, they don't need to make them, you see."

"Right," Young said. "All they need to build is a detonating device."

"Well, they'll need scientists, technicians, security guards," said Atherton. "By the way, Rod, just a bit of advice. When the story comes out how some Mexican cops were conned into hunting for Menzies, how four of those cops got themselves creased while trying to collect the million-pesos reward, there'll be hell to play between the United States and Mexico."

"I think you better open up Fort Knox and hand over some hard currency to the families of the four dead Federales. And also make a donation to the Guadalajara Police Benevolent Society, or whatever it's called over there."

Paulisen nodded. "One problem is to sort things out with George Pappas. He runs our setup in Mexico. When I now turn and tell him to lay off Menzies, he's gonna blow his top."

Paulisen stuck his pipe in his mouth and puffed away. "Gentlemen, I think we all know what we have to do right now. But I suggest we postpone any other decision until we've had a chance to talk to Aris. If he's stepped off the plane in Paris to talk to the French, I don't think we'll see Aris until tomorrow morning. The guy needs a break. And he might find it in the Place Pigalle. And I wish to hell I was with him. By tomorrow we may also have some news from Carruthers.

"I don't know about you, but I've had it. I'm turning in the moment I get through with the CIA. Let's meet here at ten tomorrow morning."

"That's fine with me," said Atherton. "We've got a good man working out of the Ontario Government Tourist Office in Mexico City. He's code-named Cecil. Never met him. But I do know he operated with Stevenson out of New York in World War II. I'll see if I can get rhough to him some-how."

"Excellent," said Young. "I'll leave a message for Aris here, in case he comes over tonight. This shop is open 24 hours, of course. They have my phone number in case of emergency. And I know where I can find you two if anything terribly important crops up during the night.

"I'm putting a tail on all three of us. Routine security. So don't get alarmed if you notice anything. But I'm quite sure you won't." He grinned.

"Fine, that's a good idea," said Paulisen.

"Rod, you go first," said Young.

Paulisen stepped out of the room and Young went over to a phone and spoke briefly.

CHAPTER FOUR

A Matter of Trust

Menzies sipped a second cup of coffee and lit another cigarette. Quickly he reviewed the situation. Menzies could think of no hoodlum, no crime outfit, that could possibly be after him. Back in Vancouver, where he had been a police reporter for four years, he had stepped on the toes of the local Mafia brass a couple of times. But certainly not hard enough to invite a murder contract. In fact, he had had excellent relations with the local "Don" in Vancouver.

Menzies had a healthy respect for the Mafia. Because he happened to be a police reporter, the local Mafia had treated him well. They gave him a news break from time to time.

And their tips were always right. To be sure, the Don owed him a small favor. When the crime czar's eldest son was picked up on a drunken-driving charge by some rookie traffic cops who didn't know who he was, Menzies played the story straight. He reported it the way he would have re-ported a case involving any other citizen—a three-paragraph yarn, good only for an inside page of the first morning edition.

The Don had compared the way Menzies had handled the story with the big, sensational, front-page splash carried by the opposition morning paper. They had turned a drunken-driving arrest into an exposé, regurgitating back stuff, dropping inuendoes here and there, linking people all the way back to Lucky Luciano.

The Don felt obligated to Menzies. He was the sort of man who didn't like being obliged to anybody. So he repaid the courtesy by giving Menzies a credit card good for all seven Mafia nightclubs in Vancouver. Any time Menzies appeared at the door, he'd be ushered in without having to pay the cover charge. He'd be given the best table available, and the first couple of drinks were always on the house.

Could it have been a case of mistaken identity? That was out, too. The two cops at the roof-top restaurant had asked for him by name. What then? "Forget it, Johnnie boy," he told himself. "No good wasting any more time right now trying to solve that part. Who knows, with a bit of luck, the guerrilleros might come up with the answer. There are plenty of other matters that need your attention."

Menzies finished his coffee and snuffed out his cigarette. Then he got up and checked the whole house. He made sure that every door and window were locked or latched. He went to the first-floor bedroom, pulled the Luger from its holster, made sure the safety catch was off, put it on the dressing table, and covered it with a newspaper.

He took the cigarette lighter and hid it partially under the newspaper. The lighter was within inches of the pistol butt. Then he pulled the sheath with the throwing knives from his hip pocket, took the sheath off, and put it under the mattress. He strolled over to the living room, looked around, found a flowerpot with an artificial hibiscus planted in it, buried the blade of one of the knives in the sand and hid the handle of the knife near the stem of the plant. He hid another knife under the seat of an armchair, went back to the bedroom, took his jacket off, wrapped it around the third knife, and put the jacket on a chair. Then he stuck a cigarette in his mouth and reached for the half-hidden lighter. He practiced this move several times. The moment his right thumb touched the lighter, his index finger was on the trigger of the Luger. Menzies lit his cigarette, replaced the lighter, and then gave himself some more time to think.

He had to reach the British Embassy in Mexico City. They were the only ones who could really help. He was in big trouble. He had killed four cops. Even if he had ten witnesses to testify that he had killed them in self-defense, his chances, once the Federales got him, were nil. They just wouldn't believe him. They wouldn't believe witnesses. They wouldn't believe Jesus Christ himself. Menzies took that for granted. That's how it went if you killed four cops.

Menzies didn't underestimate the intelligence of the Mexican police. If they got him alive, they would find out, eventually, that the four cops he had killed were acting on their own, outside the law. But eventually was too late for Menzies. The cops would probably work him over on the way to the jail. And once they had done that, they wouldn't admit they had probably made a mistake.

If he were very, very lucky, he might get away with a couple of years in jail. Awaiting trial. And then, if he were again very lucky, he might get off. But he'd be a cripple, a physical and possibly a mental wreck. Angry, hate-filled friends, and other colleagues of the four dead cops, would give it to him. That's how it went. And if he beat the murder rap, even as a cripple, they'd get him on a conspiracy charge involving the guerrilleros. Menzies knew that one way or the other he was finished if he got caught. But that was a big "if."

The guerrilleros, if they really wanted to help, might just be able to smuggle him out of the country. But then, where could he go? To the States? Not a chance. An extradition treaty covers murder. To Britain? The same. Mexico subscribes to Interpol. He'd be hunted down, as a wanted murder suspect, in just about every country in the world. He'd have to change his name. Take up a new identity. Maybe a skin transplant on his hands to get rid of his fingerprints. Perhaps plastic surgery for his face.

This was too goddamn much!

Obviously then he had to get in touch with the British Embassy in Mexico City. Let them unravel the legalities, if they could be unraveled. Even if they finally did hand him over to the Mexican authorities, some of the heat would have cooled in the meantime. They'd probably hand him over directly to the Mexican attorney-general. They'd exact a pledge that he would not be tortured. They'd supervise the various legal procedures. Oh yes. That was by far the best course. Get in touch with the British Embassy. Tell them the whole story, his side of the story. After all, he was no crook. He could produce evidence that he was man of some standing. He could get one or two people right in the heart of the British Secret Service to vouch for him. Goddamit, he was an officer in the British intelligence reserves. Oh yes. The Embassy would try to help him, once they were satisfied he was innocent.

But he couldn't go to the embassy himself. Geralda was right. The police would have staked out the embassy by now. Maybe he could phone. But to whom? He didn't know anybody there. Hell, he hadn't even bothered to register with the consular section. He'd never get to the Ambassador on the phone, that was certain. Besides, if the Mexican police were convinced that he'd try to get Embassy help, they might wiretap all incoming calls. Unlikely they'd go to such lengths, in breach of diplomatic rules. Still, they might. Menzies knew he couldn't afford to take that chance.

He pondered the problem for over an hour. He chain-smoked, cursed, paced the living room. He had to get in touch with the Embassy, but he couldn't go there, and he couldn't phone. There was only one alternative. He had to find someone he could trust. This seemed to be the only way out. Next question: Whom could he trust in Mexico? Three names flashed in his mind. The first was Brian Donaldson, owner of the Red Snapper restaurant in Manzanillo and acting British Vice Consul there. Brian was a Scotsman, like himself, and a close friend. He was adventurous, quick-witted, and could recognize an emergency. Yes, Brian would do. But Brian was too far away—three hundred miles away. And the telephone connection to Manzanillo was a ghost. It might take hours, days, to reach him. Too bad. Menzies needed action right away.

The second name was that of Capitán Pedro Rodríguez Pérez de los Monteros. He was the officer commanding the Federales police detachment in Puerto Vallarta. Menzies grinned. It would be funny if a Federales captain would save him from a Federales manhunt. It seemed ironic to call on a Federales officer to help him escape from the rest of the Federales police! But it has happened before, he told himself.

Menzies had saved Pedro's life. It happened three months earlier. During a hunting trip. Pedro had fallen off his horse, and a wounded wild boar began to savage him. Menzies had leaped off his own horse and stuck the nine-inch blade of a hunting knife into the maddened animal's throat. Yes, Menzies was sure he could trust Pedro, even if it were Pedro's outfit that were now hunting him. The trouble was, the British Embassy wouldn't trust Pedro. Not in this case. The Embassy must know that the Federales were looking for him. And Pedro was a cop. The Embassy people would think that this was some kind of a plot to trap Menzies. They wouldn't cooperate.

If he could get to Puerto Vallarta and seek protection from Pedro, things might work out all right. Pedro was bound to help him all he could. But no. That wouldn't do. Pedro would be faced with a conflict of duties. His superiors in Mexico City wanted Menzies. They were convinced he had murdered four Federales policemen. Pedro would become an outlaw himself if he harbored a wanted killer—too much to ask from any man, even if you've saved his life.

The third name which flashed through Menzies mind was that of Morris Pizzen, in Mexico City. His real name was Chaim Beja, a Rumanian Jew who had settled in Natanya, Israel, some time before World War II. Menzies smiled at the thought of the short, chubby, bald-headed, timid-looking man he had first seen at the Café Vardan. It was in Tel Aviv's Nahlat Benjamin Street, way back in 1947. At a rough guess, Chaim must now be in his seventies, Menzies thought. Oh yes. He could trust Chaim. To the end of the world.

Menzies recalled that night in 1947 when he walked into the Café Vardan, together with two plain-clothes sergeants of the British Field Security Police. They had gone there to arrest Chaim for the explosion which had half-wrecked the British Army headquarters in Jerusalem's King David Hotel.

Chaim was a real pro. He was a member of the Jewish underground, in Palestine. The British had classified him as a terrorist. Most of the Jews called him a hero—a fighter for the liberation of Palestine. In effect, Chaim Beja was one of the founding members of the formidable and notorious Irgun Tsvai Leumi—a ruthless, hard-line, Jewish underground group. Chaim's boss at the time was Menahem Begin, most wanted outlaw in British Palestine and at present a successful leader of the Israeli Likud Party.

The harassed British intelligence groups in Palestine had been screaming for help to stop Jewish and Arab terrorism. And Uncle Tom, in Greece, had asked Menzies to go to Tel Aviv. "Take a holiday, go down to Tel Aviv and see what you can come up with," Uncle Tom had told Menzies. "And don't forget—bring me some Carmel wine when you get back."

Some holiday. After looking around for a couple of weeks he laid a trap for one of the terrorists. That was Chaim Beja. And he was only indirectly involved in the outrage. Chaim had been betrayed, quite accidentally, by a beautiful Jewish call girl. Her name was Vicki Schwarz, Menzies recalled. And she had the most lovely dark-brown hair he had ever seen. That was some broad! Any man would have fallen for her. Even a Greek Orthodox monk from Mount Athos, with ten celibacy vows to his credit. And Chaim was no monk.

Menzies had taken Chaim to the Field Security headquarters for questioning. And right there, under the most impossible circumstances, in the most unlikely atmosphere, began a friendship which Menzies knew, and Chaim knew, would last a lifetime. An Armenian interpreter, who spoke fluent Yiddish and was anxious to show his zeal, stuck the point of a knife at Chaim's throat. He hoped to frighten Chaim into a swift confession. Menzies hated brutality to prisoners, through he knew that he sometimes developed a sadistic strain himself under fire. At all other times, Menzies adhered to a nearly perfect code of behavior. He could think of nothing more degrading, to the inquisitor, then to torture a handcuffed, physically defenseless captive. Menzies leaped across the room and quickly disarmed the interpreter. He saw the thin trickle of blood descend from Chaim's neck and apologized—profusely.

Chaim was less upset by the incident than Menzies. He knew he wasn't going to talk, no matter what physical torture was applied.

Menzies had found out that Chaim's only son, Joseph, who was twelve, was dying of leukemia at a Tel Aviv hospital. He decided to take Chaim to see his son—possibly for the last time. He handed over his prisoner to the Field Security's interrogation section but next day he went back to see him—armed with a special permit from the British general who commanded the Tel Aviv garrison.

Chaim had been placed in solitary confinement—but twice a week, for two weeks. Menzies escorted him to the hospital to see his son and then brought him back. During these trips there grew an understanding between them. To Menzies it was touching to see this physically weak, but brave and formidable underground fighter dissolve into tears as he talked to the pale, skinny little boy who was about to die. To Chaim Beja, Menzies, his captor, had suddenly become a benefactor.

They struck a deal. Chaim confessed and gave details of the part he had played in the King David Hotel explosion. He implicated no one else. In exchange he was moved from solitary confinement at the interrogation center to a regular jail to await trial. Menzies went back to Uncle Tom with a dozen bottles of Carmel. A month later he returned to Tel Aviv to testify at Chaim's trial. Chaim got four years. But a few months later, when Britain withdrew her forces from Palestine, the new Jewish State was born; and Chaim was released.

In 1956, after the abortive Suez affair, Chaim visited London and went to see Menzies. In 1960 Menzies spent a two-week holiday as Chaim's guest in Jerusalem. From then on they corresponded regularly. Chaim, always connected with Jewish underground activity, went to Mexico in 1970. He changed his name to Morris Pizzen, obtained Mexican residence papers and lived there on a small pension and the rents from some real-estate investments. Menzies had gone to see him early in 1974. They had a lot to talk about. Menzies knew he could trust Chaim all the way.

As he paced around the room of the guerrilleros hideout, his mind a jumble of tortured and desperate thoughts, Menzies now decided to turn to Chaim for help. He looked up a number in his wallet, then strolled over to the phone.

Menzies spoke on the phone for less than five minutes. He used Arabic which Chaim understood, plus a sprinkling of Yiddish and English words. Chaim, instantly alerted, answered likewise. And he got the message.

Menzies replaced the receiver, decided to go to sleep in the first-floor bedroom, changed his mind, and walked down the corridor to the kitchen. He used half a dozen eggs to make himself a tomato omelette and washed the food down with a pint of fresh cold milk, which he sipped slowly, just as the nutrition books say one should.

Menzies glanced at his watch. It was ten o'clock. He looked out of the kitchen window and noticed a shed in the large garden behind the house. Tall eucalyptus trees and a row of cactus plants formed a fence around the garden, obscuring the view from the neighboring houses. Menzies unlocked the kitchen door, went out, closed the door behind him, walked over to the shed and got inside. There was no door in the shed. The place was crammed with garden tools, sacks of fertilizer, coils of old rope, and empty wooden boxes. He noticed that from the entrance of the shed he could see the gate in the front of the house. He moved three wooden boxes and placed them one after the other, used a fertilizer bag as a pillow, and stretched himself on the boxes. From the spot where his head was, he could see the gate.

Menzies went to sleep. He was awakened by the roar of thunder several hours later. The usual late-afternoon downpour followed. Big drops of water seeped through the leaky roof of the shed and began to drench him. He ignored the lukewarm rain and lay there, in a twilight sleep, his ears barely listening to the movement of traffic up and down the street less than fifty yards away. But when a car pulled up at the curb next to the gate, Menzies was instantly alerted. He sat and watched as three men and a woman—the men dressed in blue overalls—got out of a gray Volkswagen Combi painted with the Guadalajara public service insignia.

Menzies recognized the woman as Doña Tina—wearing the same shabby two-piece brown suit she had worn in the very early hours of the morning. But it was one of the men who drew Menzies' immediate attention. He was huge, so huge as to seem incredible. He was more like some upright pre-historic monster discovered intact in a Siberian cave, preserved in ice.

Menzies had never seen a man quite that big. Or had he? The giant seemed very familiar. In the lengthening shadows of the eucalyptus trees and the visual blurr caused by the pouring rain the awesome figure appeared to be eight, maybe nine feet tall! The breadth of his shoulders was twice that of the Miami Dolphins' Bill Stanfill. The giant moved with grace, the streamlined powerful grace of the professional athlete. His fingers hung stretched down from his hands like two bunches of overgrown Costa Rican bananas. But hell! Where had he seen this man before? Surely not in a nightmare!

Menzies switched his eyes to the other two men. Both were in their late thirties, about five-feet-eight, with sallow complexions. One was completely bald. He left the group and started walking toward the shed where Menzies was hiding. The other man, with black curly hair and a trim moustache, moved with the giant and Doña Tina towards the patio and the main entrance of the house.

Menzies tried to figure out why the baldheaded man was coming to the back of the house, to the shed. A danger signal flashed at the back of his mind. He flattened himself up against the inside wall of the shed just as the visitor entered. Then Menzies hit him with a short right to the jaw about two inches from the chin, his arm thrusting down with a slight twist. The bald man went down without as much as a grown-or even a whimper.

Menzies grabbed him by the armpits, lifted him up, and stretched him out on the wooden boxes which he had himself occupied a few minutes earlier. He took a piece of rope and tied his hands and feet, frisked him, found a *Beretta* pistol, checked it, and stuck the gun inside his shirt so that it was held in position by his belt. He found a handkerchief in the man's pocket, took it and stuffed it in his mouth. Then he leaped to the kitchen entrance of the house, got inside, unlatched the main entrance, and held the door wide open. Doña Tina led the way inside.

"Good afternoon Mr. Menzies," she said in English. "This is Don Carlos Heredia y Otero," she introduced the smaller of the two men. "Don Carlos is our Commissioner in Guadalajara."

"Mucho gusto," said Don Carlos, his eyes fixed on Menzies. They shook hands.

Doña Tina turned to the giant. "This is Leon," she said. "Leon is a compatriot of yours, Mr. Menzies. Well, perhaps not quite. You are from Britain, he is from Canada."

Leon growled something through heavily scarred lips, his blotchy face twisted, and he offered a ham-like hand which Menzies estimated was the size of his portable typewriter.

"Very glad to meet you gentlemen," said Menzies affably. "You've come right on time. I was just about to make myself some coffee. Would you care for some?"

"No thank you," said Don Carlos. His pale face was unsmiling, his intense eyes scrutinized Menzies. "Let us sit down. We have many things to discuss, and time is limited."

Leon picked up three armchairs and a sofa from various parts of the living room and placed them in a circle around a small table. Menzies swiftly chose the armchair where one of his knives was hidden and took another look at the giant. He noticed that Leon's right ear was missing. His nose reminded Menzies of a ripe Himalayan cucumber he had once seen during a visit to Tibet. Leon was completely bald, and there were numerous scars on his shiny scalp. At close quarters Menzies was able to assess Leon's size a bit more accurately. He reckoned Leon was about seven-feet-six-inches tall and close to four hundred pounds. *Where had he seen him before? And when?*

Don Carlos interrupted Menzies' thoughts. "Señor Menzies, we understand you have a gun and a knife and . . . you know how to use them," said

Don Carlos. He spoke in English, his voice was hoarse. The words were uttered slowly, casually. "Now, first of all, would you please give Leon these weapons."

Menzies looked hurt. He purposely hesitated before answering. "Of course, of course. If that's what you want. But I can't see why you want to disarm me, Señor, when I'm expecting you to help me, and when I'm going to help you."

"The gun and the knife, señor Menzies," Don Carlos repeated, his voice sounding bored. Menzies noticed that Don Carlos kept his right hand in the pocket of his jacket. He guessed there was a gun there.

"Very well, here's the gun," said Menzies, pointing at the bulge the Beretta made near his waist.

"Unbutton your shirt and keep your hands away from the gun," said Don Carlos.

Menzies obeyed. Don Carlos nodded to Leon. The next moment a huge, hairy hand scraped over Menzies' stomach, lifted the Beretta and gave it to Don Carlos. He emptied the gun, placed it on the table together with the loose cartridges.

"Now the knife," said Don Carlos.

"It's in my jacket, in the bedroom."

"Please go and get it."

Menzies got up and was followed to the bedroom by Leon. The floor creaked as the giant walked behind him. The monstrous frame blocked the dying gleams of daylight from a nearby window, casting an ugly shadow over Menzies.

Menzies told Leon where to find the knife. The banana fingers fumbled with the jacket, picked up the throwing knife and made it disappear into the huge palm. They both returned to the living room, where Doña Tina had switched the lights on. They sat down and Leon gave the knife to Don Carlos.

The Commissioner looked at the knife with curiosity. He seemed to weigh it in his left hand. He turned it around and around, noticed the hallmark and Arabic characters on the side of the blade, and finally put the knife in the breast pocket of his jacket. All this time his right hand never budged from the side pocket of his jacket." An unusual toy," he remarked.

"It has its uses," said Menzies.

"Now," said Don Carlos, "Will you please tell us who you are, exactly, what are you doing in Mexico, and what exactly happened last night."

"Oh, for heaven's sake!" said Menzies. "Surely, señor, you must know all this already. I'm a tourist, visiting Mexico for fun and taking the opportunity to do some writing."

"Which newspaper do you represent in Mexico?"

"I represent none. But I'm a special correspondent, a stringer, for the *London Daily Express,* the *New York Times,* the *National Enquirer,* and the *Sydney Daily Telegraph.*"

"This—special correspondent, stringer, what does it mean exactly?" Menzies told him.

"What happened last night?"

"Four Federales tried to kill me. To protect myself I had to kill them."

"Why did they try to kill you?"

"I don't know. I thought this is what you were going to find out."

Don Carlos paused, lit a cigarette, smoked silently for a while, seemed deep in thought. "Señor Menzies, you must speak truthfully. I do not have time to waste. And we cannot tolerate lies. You already know far too much about us. We want to know more about you. I do not wish to cause you undue concern, but in our organization a lie is the most serious offense. We have only one punishment for liars. I am sure you understand what I mean."

Menzies said nothing.

"Now you will answer me truthfully I hope, said Don Carlos. "What is your connection with the CIA?" He pronounced it *seeah.*

"None."

"This is impossible for me to believe." He snuffed out his cigarette, lit another.

"Why?"

"It is I who is doing the questioning." There was controlled anger in his voice.

"To hell with that," said Menzies. He got up, and instantly Leon did the same. "I don't have, I've never had any connection with the CIA."

"Sit down, Señor Menzies," said Don Carlos quietly. His voice sounded ominous.

Menzies sat down. "Give me one of your cigarettes, please," he said, irritably.

Don Carlos ignored the request. "Let me rephrase my question. Do you know, or have you ever known, anybody connected with *seeah?*"

"No."

"You're a liar, señor. I can see we are wasting our time with you." Don Carlos looked at Leon and the giant sat up stiffly, as if awaiting the command to attack. Steady, Menzies told himself. Steady. Doña Tina shifted in her seat and looked at Leon.

"I'm no liar. You're just out of your mind," said Menzies. His mind raced over possibilities, situations, distances, speed and power ratios, weapons. He came up with only one answer. He didn't have a chance—at that precise moment, in that particular position.

"Before we execute liars, our rules require that we provide one courtesy, one act of conclusive justice. You see, señor, we are not criminals, we are not gangsters, as some newspapers say. We are the democratic liberation movement of Mexico. We believe in justice. Perhaps rough justic, because of the situation we are in; but justice nonetheless. This courtesy and justice which we provide to people like yourself, is to prove to you that you are not speaking the truth. We like to provide this proof in public. Doña Tina over here and Leon are witnesses . . . that it has been proven that you have answered me with a lie."

"What the hell are you talking about?"

"Señor, here is the proof. I asked you whether you have any connection with *seeah*, whether you know anybody in *seeah*, and you denied it."

"That's right," said Menzies. His mind was wild with mental activity. If he could somehow get them to the bedroom, where his Luger was hidden, he might still have a chance. But how could he do that?

"In that case, it is proven that you are a liar, señor, because three months ago at Puerto Vallarta a senior *seeah* officer, a certain Col. Richard Paulisen, visited you and spent a week in the villa you were renting."

"What?" yelled Menzies. "Rod Paulisen? He's been a friend of mine since the days of the Second World War. He's got nothing to do with the CIA. Not as far as I know."

Don Carlos grinned. "You are very cunning, señor. We know that Colonel Paulisen is working for *seeah*. What were you discussing in Puerto Vallarta? I cannot believe, especially if you have known him for so long, that you do not know he works for *seeah*."

"Rod Paulisen is a publisher. I'm a writer. We discussed business. He's also a personal friend."

"What were you doing in the Second World War together with Colonel Paulisen?"

"We were in the same intelligence outfit. We hunted down Nazi killers, collaborators, spies."

"Oh I see. You hunted down Nazis," said Don Carlos. He paused, reflected for a while. "That was a very honorable undertaking at that time. . ."

"Now look here," Menzies interrupted him. "I asked you for a cigarette ten minutes ago. If you won't give me one I'll go over to the bedroom where I left my pack. This thing is getting so wild, it's gonna blow my nerves to pieces."

"My apologies, Señor Menzies," said Don Carlos. He offered him a cigarette, lit it for him, then continued, "But I do not think your nerves are in any . . . danger." He grinned, sarcastically. "Not after the episode last night at the Roma Hotel."

Don Carlos lapsed into silence and reflection. Menzies decided not to interrupt him. He knew he had scored a minor point with the explanation of the meeting with Paulisen. He also knew that Don Carlos was busy trying to make up his mind what to do with him. For Menzies, this was the moment of truth.

What bothered Menzies more than the gorilla-like creature next to him was Don Carlos' gun. Without that gun, Menzies felt he might just have a small chance against Leon, because he could grab his other knife under the seat of the armchair on which he was sitting and stick it into Leon's barrel-like guts in one fast movement. Suddenly he recognized who Leon was. Yes. That was him all right. And he had seen him at least twenty times. On TV ten years ago.

Leon was in fact Bear Killer Leo (The Rock) Kopechoff — a wrestler from Kamloops, British Columbia. He was one of the biggest, most successful wrestlers ever to come out of North America. He remembered reading a story the *Vancouver Sun* carried about Leo The Rock.

Leo was a Dukhobor—a member of a weird, isolationist, religious sect that had emigrated to Canada from Czarist Russia at the turn of the century. According to the wrestling promoters, Leo the Rock had discovered his fantastic strength and made his wrestling debut at the age of nineteen. At that time Leo was working for an upstate B.C. logging camp. He had accepted a $1000 offer to fight a captured grizzly bear in a ring-size cage. A muzzle was fitted onto the mouth of the 600-pound animal, so that it couldn't bite, and a padded suit was provided for Leo. The cage was set up on a flat clearing of the wooded mountainside, and the temperature was twenty degrees below freezing.

The memorable fight, for which the all-male audience of loggers paid $50 apiece, lasted four hours. There were no rounds and no referees. Half-way through the fight part of the bear's muzzle fell off. Leo's right ear was chewed off, a six-inch gash was torn in his thigh, and he was battered by the giant paws; but in the end it was the bear who quit. The grizzly was so badly injured that it had to be destroyed.

Since then, Leo had wrestled on live TV every Saturday night for years. He was disqualified from wrestling in Canada after killing Kerusheeto, the Giant Jap, a karate expert from the Ryukyu Islands. Leo had gone to the States, where he had done very well—until he was charged with manslaughter in Houston, Texas, after he hurled Osman, The Great Turk, out of the ring, smashing his head on the cement floor.

Leo had beaten the manslaughter charge, but he was banned from wrestling in the United States. After that episode Menzies, who always read the newspaper sports pages, had never heard of Bear Killer Leo (The Rock) Kopechoff again.

Don Carlos interrupted Menzies' reminiscences. "I am going to give you, señor, the benefit of the doubt," he said. "Even if it is a very, very, slight doubt. There are two reasons why I will give you the benefit of this doubt. First of all, you have most certainly killed four Federales. These people are our enemies. And so you are an outlaw like outselves.

"Second, Señor Menzies, we have found out, and this could well be a surprise for you, that the request for your . . . liquidation was made by *seeah,* through the FBI."

Menzies' eyes showed relief and surprise all at once. "Don Carlos, I've killed four cops in self-defense. That should be enough proof of my credentials. But what you say about the CIA and the FBI just doesn't make any sense at all. I—"

"Please, Señor Menzies, do not interrupt. The FBI asked our Federales to have you arrested for the murder of two Mexican farm workers at Indio, southern California. The murder was supposed to have happened last month. We do not know why this request was made, because we have found out that you have not left Mexico in the last four months. And the police knew that also. We have checked on your movements during this period."

"This is goddamn absurd," said Menzies. He got up, glared at Don Carlos with a mixture of anger and surprise. "Why should I want to kill two Mexican farm workers! I've been in Mexico all this time —"

"Please be calm, Señor Menzies," said Don Carlos quietly. "And please sit down."

Menzies sat down, reluctantly. "What the hell are you up to?" he said. "Is this some kind of a joke?"

"It is not a joke, Señor Menzies. I do not make jokes, and this is not the time for jokes. Let me continue, please.

"The Federales soon found out that you had not left Mexico for the last four months. But, of course, they tried to oblige the FBI. So they continued to search for you, though not intensively.

"Then *seeah* approached certain contacts they have in the Federales. *Seeah* offered one million pesos for your head, Señor Menzies. This should flatter you. It is a bigger price than I have on my head.

"Señor Menzies, you understand that this is an offer which is hard to resist, hard to refuse. But of course the offer is contrary to the laws, even of the present regime. The offer was also made known to certain police informers and underworld figures. We believe, we are convinced, that the four Federales you met last night had found out where you were and had quietly agreed, among themselves, to operate as a group, to kill you and collect the one million pesos. Señor Menzies, 250,000 pesos each is a lot of money in Mexico. This much money can tempt many, many people.

"Your position now is that several hundred people, including Federales and other police, are looking for you simply to collect the reward. In addition, of course, seeing that you have killed four Federales, every policeman in Mexico is looking for you officially. You are a hunted man, a killer. Interpol has been informed, in case you arrange to escape from the country.

"We do not know why *seeah* put a price on your head — an act which is contrary to the laws of Mexico. We understand this matter is now being investigated on the diplomatic level. Could you, perhaps, tell us why *seeah* is out to kill you?"

"I don't have a clue," said Menzies. "All this is news to me. It's just too fantastic for words. But what you've told me, makes everything fit. It explains what happened and the way it happened."

"Well, Señor Menzies, it appears that your salvation lies with us. Under certain circumstances, under certain conditions, we may be able to assist you. And you may be able to be of service to us.

"What do you know about the guerrilleros?"

"Nothing more than I've read in the newspapers," said Menzies.

"That is not very illuminating," said Don Carlos. "Almost all Mexican newspapers are controlled, are influenced, by the government. We know that. We do not trust most of our local newspapers. Their reports usually show their ignorance. To them, we are just bandidos, terroristas.

"Señor Menzies, the Federales are in possession of your personal files, of course. I mean the press clippings, correspondence files, etcetera, that you had with you at the Roma Hotel. We were able to obtain, through an associate, a photostatic copy of a biographical note published about you in a South African magazine." Don Carlos stuck his left hand into a breast pocket and pulled out a copy of a write-up about Menzies in *Wings Magazine* — the official publication of the South African Air Force. "Is all this information about you correct?"

"More or less."

"I see you are a linguist and have worked for various newspapers. It is just possible that you may be a useful person in our organization.

"But first we would need to see your identification papers. I suppose you do have a passport?"

Menzies nodded.

"And we would also need some proof that you are a person we can trust. If these two conditions are met to my satisfaction I am willing to recommend that you should become part of us—I mean part of our organization. But of course, this would be entirely up to you.

"I have authority to offer you assistance to leave Mexico—to go to the United States, Cuba, British Honduras, or Guatemala. We can help you reach any of these countries safely. But you could be extradited to Mexico from all of these countries—except, perhaps, Cuba.

"In exchange for this service, we would expect you to have certain articles published in the newspapers for which you are a special correspondent—particularly in the United States. We have no intention of censoring these articles. They will be based on your own observation, your own free judgement. We want you to help us stir the interest of public opinion in the United States about our movement.

"We expect you to write the truth about the guerrilleros in Mexico, about our purpose, the ideals we have. We know there is a great amount of good will in the United States towards people fighting oppression, injustice, social inequality. We are neighbors of the United States. We hope for North-American aid to reach us. I do not mean the aid which the United States government is providing, in hundreds of millions of dollars, to various countries—to the governments of various countries.

"I mean moral support, political activity in our favor in Washington, volunteers, private donations of money, equipment, weapons . . ."

Menzies listened, fascinated. What Don Carlos had said gripped his imagination. He could see the story angles. News. Features. Pictures. Interviews. Christ, what a break! He'd join the Mexican terrorist outfit. He'd bust wide open, from the inside, the story of a hundred assassinations and a thousand kidnappings. He'd have to be an outlaw himself. So what? He was one already. He had no alternative. Except . . . except diplomatic immunity. But did Chaim get to the ambassador? Was the Embassy going to act? In his favor?

Then another idea struck Menzies. Maybe the publicity he'd stir up around himself would provide the right atmosphere to give himself up when the time came. Where could he give himself up? The States, of course.

Jesus, if he handed himself over in the States after a spell with the guerrilleros, Menzies thought, and had enough money to hire a top lawyer, extradition proceedings would take months. Maybe years. During that time he could clear himself. After all, he *had* killed those cops in self-defense.

Like hell he had. He didn't have to kill the two cops in the *caballeros.* One was unconscious, the other was helpless. Well, that was true enough. But they had *tried* to kill him, to murder him. And there were no witnesses. A judge would have to believe him. For sure. No, that wouldn't do. He'd have to come clean in court. He'd tell it as it happened. He lost control of himself and he killed the two men because they had tried to murder him. Call it a human weakness—understandable in view of the circumstances. Manslaughter? Justifiable homicide? Well, he couldn't figure out all the legalities—not right now. Maybe a couple of years' suspended sentence.

But where? Not in the States. The crime, if it was a crime, had been committed in Mexico. Is there a manslaughter or a lesser homicide charge extraditable between the States and Mexico? Doubtful. Hell, he'd get off scot-free, in the States, if he had a good lawyer, and the exact truth came out.

Menzies heaved a sigh of relief. He looked at Don Carlos. "All right," he said. "I'll go along with your suggestion. As long as I've got an absolutely free hand to report what I see, and as long as nothing I write is censored."

"Of course, Señor Menzies, of course. We here in Mexico are associated, we are affiliated with similar groups in other countries. Newspapers often use the term 'terrorists' to describe us. This is unfair and untrue. We are fighting for a political cause. Others, in other countries, are also fighting for their political causes. We have the greatest sympathy for the Irish Republican Army in your own country, Señor Menzies. Their activities are in a more advanced stage than ours. But they also are fighting for a just cause. And the same applies to the people your newspapers often describe as Palestinian terrorists. They are freedom fighters, like ourselves."

Don Carlos paused, seemed to be weighing his words. "We have provided a special facility for our Arab friends. Since you speak Arabic, you have lived in Egypt, and you have a degree from a Cairo university, I think you will find our Arab friends most interesting. I take it that you are not a Jew and that you can prove it."

A new, fantastic series of ideas flashed through Menzies' mind. A new angle. What an angle! "I'm not a Jew," he said, the words almost bursting through his lips. "But I don't know how you want me to prove it. Unless you hire a genealogy-tracking agency in London . . . and I don't know how far back they'd get."

Don Carlos smiled. "There are ways, Señor Menzies, there are ways." He lit another cigarette, then continued, "I'm sure our Arab friends could provide you with very interesting material for your articles. But before we go into this, I must first see your passport. Also I must have some proof that you can be trusted."

"I can show you my passport," said Menzies. "It's in my jacket in the bedroom. But as for proof being trustworthy—I don't know what you'd consider proof. I'd have thought you got all the proof you need." He paused and snuffed out his cigarette. Suddenly a new idea struck him. It was so exciting that it showed all over his face. "Just a moment. I think I've got all the proof you need," he said. "If what I'm going to show you doesn't convince you that you can trust me, then nothing will." He stood up. "Come along with me. I'll show you the passport at the same time."

The sofa squeaked as Leo shifted and slowly rose to his feet. Doña Tina picked up the Beretta and the bullets and stuck them in her handbag. She got up when she saw Don Carlos following Menzies and Leo to the bed-room. Menzies noticed that Don Carlos' right hand was still in his pocket. Menzies went over to the chair where he had left his jacket. He pulled his passport out with his left hand and offered it to Don Carlos, slightly touching the guerrillero leader's right arm as he did so. It was a very old trick, based on knowledge of human nature and natural reflex action. Unconsciously Don Carlos released his grip on the invisible gun in his pocket and took the passport. He began looking at it, page by page. Menzies thought Don Carlos was a bit naive—in this particular kind of work, anyhow. Passports nowadays were only good for the cursory, standard, immigration inspection. They could be forged in ten different ways. And unless someone was trained to spot flaws, he had no chance of finding out which passport was genuine and which wasn't.

Menzies pretended he had just noticed the pack of cigarettes he had left on the bed. "Oh, there's my cigarettes," he said. He looked at Don Carlos. "I've been smoking yours all night." He went over, picked up the pack, stuck a cigarette in his lips, and touched his trouser pockets. "I'm sure I've got a lighter somewhere," he said.

"You should," said Doña Tina. "Geralda gave it back to you."

"There it is," said Menzies, pointing at the half-hidden lighter on the dressing table. He noticed that Leo kept his eyes on him.

Menzies' right hand slipped forward and the next instant the Luger was pointing straight at Don Carlos' face. "Make one move and I'll blow your heads off," he said.

Don Carlos went pale. His jaws sagged. He dropped the passport. Leo froze. Doña Tina moved her handbag upward and Menzies said "Hold it, lady, or you're dead."

Don Carlos moved his right hand towards his pocket. Menzies turned to him and said, "Stop it, señor. I seldom miss."

Don Carlos recovered from his surprise. "You're a fool," he hissed. "We're the only ones who can help you."

"I believe you," said Menzies. "You asked for proof. That you can trust me." He grinned. "This is the proof. I could kill all three of you. Right now. But I won't." Slowly he lowered the Luger and stuck it in his pocket.

Leo growled and took a step forward, but Don Carlos raised his hand and stopped him. It was his turn to smile. "Señor Menzies, I understand you perfectly. And I am satisfied. I am—what do you say—amazed." He offered his right hand. Menzies shook it. Leo relaxed. They walked back to the living room and sat down.

"I want to make one thing clear," said Menzies. "I accept your offer. And I'm going to write about what I see, about what you show me. But I'll do this on my own terms. Not as your prisoner. But I don't want to be smuggled out of Mexico. Not right now. Not until I've seen and written about you as fairly as I can."

"Sí, señor," said Don Carlos. "I hope to make some arrangements for you tonight. You'll be leaving this place before dawn tomorrow." There was respect in his voice.

"I'm very interested in your Arab friends," said Menzies. "Their work is very much in the news right now. I don't think I'll have any trouble getting some suitable articles published about them. That's for sure!"

"I will do my best to satisfy your request, señor. We have provided them with a very elaborate facility. In the State of Michoacán. We don't even know exactly what they are doing. But they employ some of our people, including two of the top nuclear scientists in Mexico. We had to persuade them to go there. The newspapers, of course, called it abduction.

"But the commandos are paying them very well. They pay us very well, too." Don Carlos smiled. "They are most generous. They can afford to be, you know. I'm sure you will find them cooperative. And very generous, too. They absolutely insist on paying for services. If you explain to the people of the United States how much this particular group of Palestinian commandos has been misunderstood, I know they will compensate you to your absolute satisfaction. They are members of a group called Society of Seven."

Menzies was about to make a suitable reply to the suggested bribe but changed his mind. "Thank you, Don Carlos. I understand exactly what you mean."

Don Carlos rose. Leo and Doña Tina followed him.

"Hasta luego, Señor Menzies," he said. Menzies go up, smiled, and shook hands.

"By the way," said Menzies. "The Beretta, the gun you took from me, belongs to your friend, the one who came along with you. He's in the shed, in the garden behind the house. I'm sure he's all right, but you better release him. He's all tied up."

Don Carlos looked at Menzies steadily. "That was not very friendly. Why did you do that? We have come here to help you. To find out if we could help you."

"Neither was it very friendly of you to surround me, to block the back exit of the house. You play it straight with me, Don Carlos, and I'll never do anything harmful to the guerrilleros. Never. Your quarrel with the government isn't mine. I'll report exactly what I see. But I'll never be your enemy. You can bet on that."

"That is a fair answer, señor," said Don Carlos. "I understand you now.

You are a real *hombre*—a hombre to my liking. You know this Mexican expression?"

"Thank you. I do."

"Take this back, Señor Menzies," said Don Carlos, handing him the knife. "I hope the *Madre de Dios* guides your hand, when you use the knife, the gun, or the pen." There was emotion in his voice. He turned to Leo and said something, and Leo walked away toward the kitchen door and the shed.

"Thank you, Don Carlos," said Menzies. Then he turned to Doña Tina. "How's Geralda?" he asked.

"She will get her car back," said Doña Tina. "She stayed with the Federales for three hours this morning. They allowed her to leave. I think they are satisfied with her explanations. She has taken a holiday from her work. She will not be singing at the Roma Hotel tonight."

"The Señorita Porras-Castro will be your guide, Señor Menzies," said Don Carlos. "Seeing that your relationship is so excellent, I am certain that you will find this news very pleasant." He smiled.

"My dear Don Carlos, nothing escapes you."

"Many things escape me, Señor Menzies. Many things do. This reminds me of something. Did you use the telephone?"

Menzies answered without hesitation. "Yes, I did. I'm afraid I broke your rules there. But I didn't know you then. I just did what I thought was best for myself at the time."

Don Carlos' face turned serious. "To whom did you speak on the telephone?"

"To a friend of mine in Mexico City."

"That was not very wise, Señor Menzies. What did you discuss?"

"I asked him to go to the British Embassy and give a message to the Ambassador. I felt the Embassy people were the only ones who could really help me."

"How long ago was that?"

Menzies looked at his watch. "About eight hours ago."

"Did you give this address?"

"I told him what the house looked like and approximately where it is. I don't know the exact address myself."

"That was stupid, dangerous," yelled Doña Tina.

"Doña Tina is right, Señor Menzies, but you could not have known how right she is at that time. You see, if *seeah* has put a price of one million pesos on your head, knowing you to be a British journalist of some standing, do you think they could have done that without some consultation with the British? We know that *seeah* and British intelligence in Mexico are cooperating. It is easy for the British to find out that is was *seeah* that asked the Federales to hunt you. Did you tell your friend in Mexico City that you were cooperating with us?"

"No, I didn't. There was no need to."

"Señor Menzies, you may have compromised yourself, and possibly us. We cannot know for sure. And it is too late now to make other arrangements. But at least I admire you for being truthful." He turned to Doña Tina, spoke to her in rapid Spanish, then looked at Menzies. "We must go now. Hasta luego, Señor Menzies. Our people will be here an hour before dawn. They will come in a school bus. Just three people altogether, including the Señorita Porras-Castro. You should be waiting for them at the gate, at five o'clock. Do you understand?"

"Yes," said Menzies.

Don Carlos turned and walked out of the house, with Doña Tina at his heels.

Menzies looked at his watch. It was 8:00 P.M. He heard the Volkswagen Combi pull away from the curb, checked the locks in the back and front doors, and switched off all the lights. Then he stood by the kitchen door for a few minutes to let his eyes get adjusted to the darkness, broken only by a gleam of moonlight coming from a window.

Menzies found a chair and sat down. He sighed with relief. He was glad the guerrilleros had gone. He was not the only one relieved to see the guerrilleros leave. Out in the thick shadows of the eucalyptus trees a tall, willowy figure moved. It was Archibald Carruthers, agent of the British Secret Service, a trained killer like Menzies.

And his mission was murder.

CHAPTER FIVE

Nothing Personal...

ARCHIBALD Carruthers got the call from the Embassy at 2:00 P.M. He asked his secretary to reschedule two afternoon dental appointments. Then he left the surgery, flagged a cab, and reached the Embassy ten minutes later. He was ushered into the office of Sir Kenneth Sinclair, the Ambassador, the moment he arrived.

Twenty minutes later, from the Embassy, he phoned the Aero Club and reserved a two-seater Cessna. He got a taxi to his home, picked his Walther PPK automatic from a drawer, and fastened it with two rubber bands to the inside of his left calf. From another drawer he got a two-inch hypodermic syringe and two tiny ampoules. One contained cyanide, the other morphine. Then he hopped into his 3.5 litre Jaguar and roared out of the garage.

Carruthers was an experienced flier. He had served as a **Spitfire** pilot in the now-famous No. 11 Group, Royal Air Force, during the Battle of Britain. In 1943 he had been transferred to intelligence and posted to an undercover job in Guatemala City. But in the intervening years he had never lost interest in flying. He had a valid commercial pilot's license and often flew hired planes to Acapulco, where he usually spent his brief vacations.

During the war days in Central America, Carruthers was nothing more —or less—than an executioner. Central America in those days was a thriving center of espionage. Nazi and Japanese agents had made arrangements with local authorities to resupply U-boats operating in the Caribbean and the Pacific. This meant that enemy submarines could prolong their stay astride vital Allied shipping lanes and cause havoc.

Carruthers had done no investigating himself at that time. His superiors pointed out certain people to him, and Carruthers arranged their elimination. He spoke fluent Spanish. He had his contacts. He seldom carried out murder contracts himself. He hired other people to do the job. The people he hired were often members of the local underworld—big-time hoodlums operating in the drug traffic, disgruntled former cops out to make a fast buck, free-lance killers who all but advertised their trade in the papers. Carruthers paid them well. But he sometimes had to arrange for the murder of his own hired killers in order to break the chain of evidence that could lead to himself.

When the war ended, Carruthers became second-in-command of the Central American branch of the British Secret Service operating out of Guatemala City. His work became more streamlined, more polished. Murder was all but wiped out from his assignment list. In the early 1950s, the British government, harassed by money problems, slashed the budget of the Secret Service, and Carruthers found himself out of a job. He had been studying dentistry before he was called up to serve in the RAF. So he went back to London, got his degree, struck a deal with the Old Firm, returned to Central America, and set himself up in Mexico City. He was no longer on staff. He was on a retainer for the Old Firm. But his operation was just about as efficient as ever before. Carruthers was once quoted: "The British can do with a hundred thousand dollars what would cost the Americans a million." And there were many people who thought he was right, at least as far as Mexico was concerned. This was because the key men in the British network in Mexico operated without pay. They did their job mostly for patriotic reasons. And they were paid expenses only. Plus a few personal favors now and then. There was only one other group that could do an intelligence job as cheaply and as effectively as the British could in Mexico. That was the Israelis. And the head of the Israeli outfit, also operating on an unpaid, expenses-only basis, was Chaim Beja, alias Morris Pizzen.

As the small plane soared to the 8,000-foot level and began to dodge the mountain peaks around Mexico City, Carruthers reviewed his assignment. It was clear enough. He had to find Menzies and ask him to return to London. If Menzies agreed, he'd have to smuggle him out of Mexico somehow. If not, Menzies would have to be eliminated.

All Carruthers knew about Menzies was that he was a former agent who had got himself into trouble in Mexico and had to be brought back to London. In response to a message from London a few days earlier, Carruthers had gone down to Manzanillo, to Menzies' seaside bungalow. His trip had proved a waste of time. This had angered Carruthers. A two-day absence from his surgery cost him two hundred dollars. The Old Firm didn't compensate him for earnings lost. Just straight expenses. Carruthers blamed Menzies. Stupid bastards like Menzies got themselves into trouble in a foreign country and then expected someone to get them out of it. Carruthers knew about the Roma Hotel shootings and that Menzies was involved. He had also been in touch with George Pappas, chief CIA agent in Mexico City. Pappas, a burly man in his forties with bushy black eyebrows and a pale, sallow complexion, had found it necessary to tell Carruthers that in response to a request from a newly-created Anglo-American intelligence outfit in London, he had posted a one-million-peso reward for Menzies.

Carruthers was also annoyed with his London boss, whom he didn't know. London had told Carruthers to go out and get Menzies, one way or another, as soon as Menzies contacted the embassy. But Carruthers had to do the job on his own, without CIA knowledge and facilities. Why on earth did London want him to find out if Menzies was willing to be smuggled out of Mexico? Why not a simple elimination? On the spot. Carruthers hoped that Menzies would refuse to leave Mexico. Then he could finish the job right there and fly back to Mexico City in time for his first surgery appointment the next day. If Menzies agreed to be smuggled out of the country, it would mean at least another couple of days' work for Carruthers. It would take time to organize this. Didn't London know that? Lost surgery time cost Carruthers a lot of money.

Carruthers waited a few minutes after the guerrilleros had left and then slipped across the shadows to the front of the house. He had no idea who they were, but he was pretty sure Menzies was now alone.

Quickly Carruthers strolled to the main entrance of the house and at that moment noticed that the lights inside were switched off. Carruthers cursed. He didn't like this. It could mean that Menzies had noticed a prowler around the house and was taking precautions.

After a moment's hesitation, Carruthers noisily climbed the few steps to the patio and banged on the door.

Menzies instantly snuffed out his cigarette. He tiptoed across the corridor and the living room to the entrance and switched on the patio light. Menzies touched the curtain of a window and peeped outside. He saw a tall, lanky man, in his middle fifties. About six-feet-two-inches, 180 or 190 pounds, blond hair graying at the temples, blue eyes, distinguished appearance, immaculate light-blue suit, RAF tie. Menzies figured this was the Embassy contact he had been expecting. Old Chaim had managed to get through.

Menzies used his left hand to unlock the door and swing it open. His right hand hung limply by his side, within easy reach of the Luger in his right trouser pocket.

Carruthers looked at him, casually. "Menzies?" he asked.

"Yes."

"Carruthers, Embassy."

"Come in."

Menzies killed the patio light, locked the door behind Carruthers, and switched on the living-room light.

They sat down. Carruthers crossed his legs, the left calf on the right knee, his hands over the bulge in the calf hiding the invisible Walther. Menzies stretched his legs out, his left hand on the cushion of the arm chair, his right hand on his right thigh.

"Sir Kenneth sent me. Some old friends want you in London. I'm here to help you get there."

"Thanks." Menzies grinned. He thought Carruthers looked awkward in that particular position. The way he sat didn't seem to suit him. Menzies lit a cigarette, using only his left hand. "A couple of hours ago, I'd have given my right arm for such an offer. But let me tell you what's happened since. It's fantastic and—"

"I'm afraid I haven't got much time," Carruthers interrupted him. His face cracked in a sardonic smile. "Neither have you."

"Listen, Carruthers. Right now I'm in the hands of the guerrilleros." He looked for any sign of interest, but was disappointed. "Do you understand what I'm saying?"

"Hardly, old chap. And I'm not really concerned. My job's to ask you to go over to London. And I think I can arrange it. You've been enough bother as it is."

"Now just a moment," Menzies interrupted. "What I'm going to tell you will make London's hair stand up. At least it should. There's a secret Arab terrorist setup called Society of Seven. They've kidnapped two of Mexico's top physicists. They have an elaborate facility some place in Michoacán. I'm going in there as the guest of the guerrilleros. There's a fantastic story there for me."

Carruthers had no idea what a stir even the mention of the words "Society of Seven" would have caused in the right circles in Washington, London, Ottawa, Paris. Carruthers looked bored.

"What makes you think that anybody in London would be interested in this Society of Seven, as you call it?"

"Just a hunch," said Menzies. "I must presume that the Old Firm is interested in international terrorism." There was sarcasm in the tone of his voice.

Carruthers didn't budge an eyelid. He was a highly trained operative. He knew Menzies was no longer connected with the Old Firm. He was going to tell him nothing. Menzies was obviously bluffing, Carruthers thought. For reasons which didn't really matter.

"Look, Menzies." His voice was crisp, sharp. "I don't know what you're talking about. And I'm not interested. But I'm getting bored. Are you coming along with me, yes or no?"

Menzies was mad. Too late he noted the implied threat in Carruthers' words. "Goddamnit no!" he yelled, and even before he had finished speaking, he saw the Walther in Carruthers' fist. It was pointing straight at his stomach.

"Hey hold it! What is this?" said Menzies.

"Put your hands on your head and stand up," said Carruthers.

Menzies obeyed. "Hm! So that's how it goes, eh? A million pesos is too hard to resist, even for you!"

Carruthers quickly stepped behind Menzies. "It is tempting, old boy, very tempting. But I'm afraid you're wrong, this time. Now do as I tell you, or I'll put a bullet in your spine."

"Sure. . . sure. . ." said Menzies, his voice trailing away.

Menzies knew he was up against a real pro. Even by the way Carruthers held the gun. He didn't hold it forward, ahead of his body, the way gunmen often hold their weapons on TV. Carruthers held the Walther close to his body on his right side, the barrel of the gun no more than an inch or two ahead of the most forward part of his suit, which in this case was the lower button of his loose-hanging jacket. This meant that it was almost impossible to kick the gun away from Carruthers' hand. In fact, it would be near-suicidal to attempt it. The way Carruthers held the gun, plus the swift way he had drawn it from a leg holster, plus his use of the expression "some old friends in London want you" convinced Menzies that Carruthers was no Embassy employee. He belonged to the Old Firm, the British Secret Service. For nobody except a Secret Service agent was likely to be told that Menzies had, in fact, at one time worked for the Secret Service.

Suspecting that Carruthers was about to hit him on the back of the head with the butt of his gun, Menzies gradually eased his hands, which were on his head, to protect the base of his skull. But Carruthers had other plans.

Carruthers hated messy jobs. The sound of a gun shot in a quiet suburban street at night travels some distance. Carruthers didn't know who else might be near the house. And there was a lot more evidence left behind in a killing involving a gun than in a tiny cyanide pinprick in the small of the back.

Carruthers transferred the gun to his left hand and with his right hand frisked Menzies. He found the Luger and threw it away. "Now stand still and you won't get hurt," he told his intended victim. Safe in the knowledge that Menzies couldn't see behind his back, Carruthers put the Walther in his pocket, took out the syringe and snapped the top off the cyanide ampoule.

Menzies noticed that Carruthers' voice had come from a position very close behind him. This was very welcome news. He was now half-convinced that Carruthers planned to kill him. Why was there any need to frisk him, to disarm him. Once Carruthers had pulled a gun on him, Menzies, with his backlog of Secret Service training and experience, was sure it could lead to only one thing. Death. But whose?

As Carruthers finished drawing the liquid into the syringe, Menzies slashed down and backward with his right elbow knocking the syringe and the cyanide ampoule out of Carruthers' hands. Carruthers reached for the Walther and Menzies caught his wrist and forced it upward.

Suddenly Carruthers jerked his head down and swung it up into the base of Menzies' jaw. The blow jarred Menzies' brains and sent a jab of pain to his nose and eyes. His vision was blurred and his head seemed to spin all over the room, all over Guadalajara, but he kept his grip on Carruthers' gun hand. Carruthers rammed his left fist into Menzies' liver, and the force of the blow turned his knees into jelly.

They stood there, almost face to face, in the middle of the room, panting, sweating, the best part of a century of fighting experience between them. Both had underestimated each other. And both knew that in that situation Menzies was doomed. His chances were next to nil. Both of Menzies' hands were busy keeping Carruthers' gun hand out of the way, while Carruthers could use his left fist to do the damage.

Carruthers hurled another low punch and Menzies tightened his stomach muscles to receive it. And another left hook by Carruthers ripped into Menzies' lower stomach, only a fraction of an inch above the vulnerable groin. Menzies saw yet another swing coming and jerked his head down, taking the blow on his forehead instead of on his nose.

Menzies was dazed. He felt his hands on Carruthers' wrist loosening. And then Carruthers jerked up the stiffened thumb of his left fist and rammed it like a mini-dagger into Menzies' right kidney. Menzies was in agony. He couldn't take this kind of punishment for another minute. He made an effort to push Carruthers back, and as Carruthers pushed forward to resist it, Menzies jerked Carruthers forward, towards him, and at the same time let his knees sag from under him.

Carruthers fell over Menzies and they rolled on the floor, knocking over chairs, flowerpots, vases, and tables as they went along—a mass of tangled legs and swinging feet and knees, fighting for some advantage. Menzies won brief relief from the vicious left hook, and he didn't let go of the right wrist he held with both hands.

Menzies knew that if he could manage to stay in the fight a bit longer and keep away from Carruthers' murderous left fist, his greater strength and better condition were bound to change the odds in his favor, sooner or later.

For an instant they lay on the floor exhausted, side by side, and Menzies tried to pull Carruthers' gun hand to his teeth, but Carruthers knew this trick and quickly interposed his head, the blond, freckled forehead smashing into Menzies' chin.

Blood poured from Menzies' face and mouth, the taste of it spurred him into renewed action. He shot his legs upward, twisting his shoulders at the same time, and brought his knees down together towards Carruthers' face. Carruthers jerked his head out of the way, and at the same time smashed another left hook into Menzies' ribs. Menzies happened to look sideways and noticed the syringe on the floor. "You bastard," he hissed through bruised, bleeding lips.

Carruthers jerked his gun hand, but Menzies held on to it, then lifted it up and smashed it on the floor. The bang caused Carruthers' trigger finger to tighten, and a succession of shots like a machine gun roared through the living room, the bullets chipping plaster off the walls and ceiling.

Carruthers released his grip on the now-empty Walther and rammed his knee into Menzies' stomach. Menzies gasped and let go of Carruthers' right hand to clutch his belly. Carruthers sprang up, picked up the Walther and hurled it at Menzies' head. The barrel of the gun grazed Menzies' neck as he lay on the floor, but he rose to his feet—just in time to catch a vicious straight right to the heart.

Menzies swayed backward, dazed, groggy, his eyelids heavy, his hands hanging limply along his side, his shirt splattered with blood, blue welts rising all over his battered face.

Carruthers, unhurt, lifted his fists in the standard boxing stance. He knew Menzies was mauled, but he also knew that Menzies was more powerful then he. He certainly wasn't going to grapple with him. Carruthers had great confidence in his fists. He had a punching bag in his basement and practiced regularly. Many years ago he had won the amateur heavyweight championship of Yorkshire. He decided to play it safe, to hammer Menzies into a pulp from a safe distance, to knock him out, and then finish him off.

Carruthers' left fist flashed forward, and Menzies barely saw it in time to duck under the punch. But Menzies never saw where the right fist came from until it smashed up against his nose. It rocked Menzies and for a moment blinded him. He sneezed some blood and launched a wild combination of counterpunches which slashed the air harmlessly yards away from Carruthers.

Carruthers began to circle his target for another attack, and Menzies wiped some blood from his nose and mouth.

Another straight left from Carruthers smacked against Menzies' chin, but the follow-up right uppercut just missed. Menzies saw Carruthers coming in again and swung his left foot in a karate kick that would have torn Carruthers' guts out, had it connected.

"Hold it, Carruthers," Menzies growled through swollen lips. "What the hell do you want from me? Who really sent you here?"

"None of your business," said Carruthers. His left fist flew forward again and jarred Menzies when it crashed into his forehead. "Nothing personal, you understand," said Carruthers. "Nothing personal at all." He waded into Menzies again with a flurry of body punches, most of which Menzies took on his arms.

Menzies swung a wild right which grazed Carruthers' chin, and Carruthers swiftly stepped out of range. They were both out of breath and put seven feet of floor space between them as they gasped for air.

But the brief interval was soon over. Carruthers resumed his fighting stance. Then he went in for the kill.

Quickly Menzies leaped back. Suddenly his hands flew up. His left hand thrust forward, the open palm turned up. The bent, rigid fingers were separated and looked like claws. His right hand, kept close to the right side of his face, was held in the same way, but the palm and talon fingers faced down. Menzies growled. His left foot stepped forward and his neck sunk between his shoulders in the standard Kung-Fu menacing position.

Carruthers back-stepped smartly. He took a close look at the bleeding, messy spectacle of Menzies' face. He watched Menzies' eyes. He knew the Kung-Fu growl was a psychological weapon. But it could also mean that Menzies was scared. Carruthers bent his head slightly forward and those trained, powerful fists swung into action. A left hook thudded into Menzies' ribs, but the follow-up straight right to the jaw was deflected by an arm and only grazed the chin. Menzies flung himself sideways and back, his Kung-Fu position unchanged.

Carruthers, his eyes fixed on the eyes of Menzies, moved in again, and at that very moment Menzies leaped, and his legs shot forward in a Kung-Fu killer scissors blow. The left foot missed Carruthers' face by an inch but the right foot, traveling in the opposite direction, thumped onto Carruthers' left shoulder. The force of the blow sent Carruthers rolling to the other side of the room.

Carruthers sprang to his feet, shaken. And for the first time that night fear gripped him. He saw the Luger lying under an armchair and slowly edged in that direction. Menzies blocked his path.

Carruthers now rushed at Menzies, his fists hammering away from all directions. Menzies parried one blow to his head, absorbed another in his taut stomach muscles. Then his right, claw-like hand descended onto Carruthers' face. Three red weals, which soon became bloody, mutilated Carruthers' face, and his head jerked backward. Carruthers swung sideways and put an armchair between himself and Menzies. His blood began to drip on the floor, and Menzies grinned at the sight of it. "This is where we settle an old argument, Carruthers," he said. "Boxing versus Kung Fu."

Carruthers grabbed a heavy porcelain ashtray and flung it at Menzies. Menzies side-stepped in time. Carruthers reached for a flowerpot, but before he could lift it, Menzies had again leaped in the air, this time sideways. He turned around in midair and struck back with his foot in a classical Kung-Fu mule kick. The blow caught Carruthers on the mouth, and he fell on the floor stunned, spitting mouthfuls of shattered teeth.

Menzies landed on the armchair and rolled over. As he did so his right hand slid under the cushion and grabbed his knife. He stepped over to the spot where Carruthers had fallen. He saw him struggle to get up. He let him get up. Carruthers saw the left-handed karate chop coming and lifted his arms to block it, but then Menzies' knee thudded into Carruthers' ribs. Carruthers began to cough. He seemed to be choking. He stumbled away from Menzies, tried to steady himself against the wall and slowly sagged to the floor.

His right hand held behind his back, Menzies went over to Carruthers. Using the wall as a support for his back, Carruthers began to rise. He took a look at his assailant. Menzies looked wild. Even the black eye, the bruises, and the blood didn't conceal the strange, crazy grimace which twisted his face. Carruthers raised his hands above his head to protect himself from another karate blow, but then Menzies shoved the blade into his stomach. "Sorry about this," said Menzies. "Nothing personal, you understand. Nothing personal at all." He pulled the blood-smeared blade out and chucked the knife away. "Just business."

Carruthers gasped, and his eyes bulged halfway out of their sockets when he felt the cool, seven-inch blade enter his body. But then his eyes began to close; he sagged and went pale.

Menzies looked alarmed. He bent over him, began to slap him across the face. "Carruthers!" he yelled. "Now get hold of yourself, old man. You're not dead. You should know that. You're still alive, Carruthers. You've got a long life head of you—at least an hour." There was a sadistic look in Menzies' eyes. "Now Carruthers," he yelled and shook him. "What's a few inches of Damascus steel between old comrades, eh?"

Carruthers' eyes reopened. He mumbled something through shattered lips. He said quietly, clearly. "Get on with it and finish the job." Then he gasped, spat some blood out. Carruthers, the killer, was in tears. "Or — if you're going to let me live—look into my jacket. There's a morphine ampoule there," he groaned. He went into shivers. "There's a . . . syringe . . . on the floor . . . Stick it anywhere . . . Then . . . phone for an ambu. . . lance."

"That's my boy," said Menzies. "Now that's much better." Suddenly remorse gripped him. Could it be that Carruthers had only tried to drug him with morphine, not to kill him? He found the ampoule in the jacket. It had "morphine" written all over it. He strolled over and picked up the syringe and also the broken other ampoule with "cyanide" written on it. Menzies grinned. He went back to Carruthers. "Which of the two do you want me to use?" he asked.

"For God's sake, Menzies . . . rinse . . . that syringe with warm water . . . . Refill it with morphine and inject me. Anywhere will do." His voice was pleading.

"Sure, sure," said Menzies. "But first I want to hear who sent you here and why you tried to kill me."

"I . . . I had . . . no . . . option," Carruthers gasped. He groaned, began to cough, spat a mixture of broken teeth and blood. "London . . . asked me to smuggle you out of the country . . ." he coughed again. "And if you resisted . . . if you . . . even . . . hesitated . . . I was to kill you. Nothing. . . personal. . . at all. For. . . God's sake, hurry up. The . . . morphine," he began to cough again, "I . . . just can't stand . . . the pain.. . ."

"All right, Carruthers," said Menzies. "I'll be back in a moment." He strolled over to the kitchen, rinsed the syringe again and again, filled it with the morphine, and went back. "Carruthers, I got the morphine right here," he said. "But first of all I want you to tell me, "Why, why? Goddamnit, why?" he yelled and shook him.

"Really . . . don't know," said Carruthers. He looked very pale now. The blood on his face had ceased to flow. "Sorry . . . old chap . . . I just don't. . . know."

"Who sent you the message from London?"

Carruthers' cloudy eyes focused briefly on Menzies. "You . . . should know . . . better," he whispered, began to cough again. "Just . . . routine message . . . code of course . . . presume . . . came from the Old Man . . . he's the only one who . . . okays this sort of thing . . . now days. . . ."

"Think Carruthers, think," yelled Menzies. "Why do they want me in London?"

". . . the morphine . . . please . . . Menzies . . . for God's sake . . . the morphine. . . ."

"Here's the morphine," said Menzies, sticking the needle into the side of Carruthers' neck. He pushed the liquid in, then withdrew the syringe and threw it away. "Why did they want me to go to London, why?"

"Heard . . . through the grapevine . . . some new . . . Anglo-American . . . unit . . . just been formed . . . don't really know . . . anything about them . . . plenty of pull in the . . . right places . . . top priority and that sort . . . of thing . . . maybe it's them who . . . want you for some . . . reason that can't . . . wait. . . ." Suddenly Carruthers' head flopped onto one side.

Menzies looked at him for a long while. Then he stood up. Suddenly he felt very sick. His mind was a jumble of thoughts. His face and his head ached. He strolled over to the other end of the room, picked up the Luger, checked it, stuck it in his pocket. Then he went to the bathroom, put his head and neck under the cold tap, washed his face gently with soap, and regarded himself in the mirror. His face reminded Menzies of the bare, red, blotchy, swollen, and scarred arse of an old Colobus monkey which had just given birth to twins in the San Diego zoo. He looked at his watch. It was past ten o'clock. The fight with Carruthers had lasted a long time.

He went back to Carruthers, lifted his eyelids, noticed the dilated pupils. He felt for a pulse; there wasn't any. Carruthers looked very dead. Or was he just mercifully asleep, unconscious, drugged? One thing Menzies didn't want was a live Carruthers spilling his guts out, giving his side of the story. Menzies picked the knife up from the floor, noticing the grease and blood marks right up to the hilt. He went back to Carruthers, lifted his shirt up, saw the small cut about three inches above the navel. Could anybody live for long with such a wound in his stomach? Who knows? Only a doctor could answer that question. After an examination.

Menzies was tired of the gory spectacle of himself, of Carruthers. But he felt he had to do it. He just had to make sure. And he was trained to do what was necessary, regardless of his feelings. He shoved the blade into Carruthers' throat and twisted it. No blood came out. Carruthers didn't move.

Menzies frisked the corpse. He found nothing of interest; he pulled some professional cards from Carruthers' pocket. Archibald Thaxted Carruthers, Oral Surgeon and Endodontist. Maybe a root-canal expert, eh? One less endodontist for the Secret Service.

Menzies got up and switched off the lights. He sat in an armchair, lit a cigarette and began to consider the situation. Who wanted him in London, and why? What was this new Anglo-American outfit Carruthers had mentioned? What compelled the Old Man to issue an order for his liquidation if he didn't agree to be smuggled to London?

Liquidation. What a euphemism for plain, cold-blooded murder. But the war days were over. Liquidation orders weren't issued lightly. There were civil-rights groups, investigative reporters, parliaments, opposition parties. Goddamit, there were also peace-time democratic ethics. Nobody went around murdering people for nothing. The national security bogey was being scrutinized in the United States as never before. In good old England there was the House of Commons, mother of parliaments, cradle of democracy. And the Old Firm was the most fair, most considerate, most humane outfit of its kind in the world.

Menzies recalled one other time when an intelligence agent on his side of the war had tried to murder him. Stacey, in Salonika, in 1947. Hm! Yes, Stacey. It was a long, long story. But presumably Stacey had been rooted out after the Philby defection.

What then? Here's what then, he reasoned with himself. First of all, it had to be something very, very big. Something on which the lives of other people might depend. A national emergency. The kind of emergency that would overrule the law, justice, principles of democracy. It had to be something like that for a murder order to be issued against anybody, but especially against him.

Second, it obviously involved both the United States and the British secret outfits. The CIA had placed a million pesos on his head, Don Carlos had told him. Anglo-American. What the hell could it be? Don Carlos was concerned, especially about Paulisen. Paulisen! Paulisen had asked him if he'd participate in a new E Force emergency job. What for? Paulisen never told him. Carruthers had gone all the way to Manzanillo to find him. He couldn't find him. Then the death warrant in Mexico.

That was the answer. It had to be. They needed him in London for something to do with the revived E Force. And it was so damned important and urgent that they had to kill him if they couldn't get him there. Reasonable enough. Yes, reasonable enough indeed! He was one of the very few people who knew about E Force. He just couldn't be left out. He either had to be in or dead.

Menzies stood up. He threw his cigarette butt on the floor. He stepped on it, and lit another. He had to get in touch with Paulisen. But where? In London, of course. Where the hell in London? How about Colin Young? He was with the *Daily Telegraph*. At least he had been there five years ago. A cable to Young. In some kind of crypto-language.

Goddamit, Carruthers. If you had talked straight, if you had just sat down and discussed the whole matter, you'd be alive now! Dammit, dammit!

Menzies heard footsteps on the wooden patio and quickly snuffed out the cigarette and froze. His right hand slipped into his pocket and pulled out the Luger.

There was a soft knock on the front door. Menzies slipped his shoes off and crawled along the floor. He flattened himself against the wall, slowly rose, reached for the patio light and switched it on.

"Señor Menzies, please switch off that light," he heard Geralda say.

Menzies breathed with relief. He did what Geralda had asked. But he kept the Luger in his right fist as he unlocked the door with his left. Silhouetted in the soft moonlight Geralda quickly stepped inside.

"Baby, I'm so glad it's you," said Menzies. He closed the door behind her, put the Luger in his pocket and reached for her hand. She didn't draw it away. A halo of gardenia perfume surrounded him, wiping out the stench of sweat and death.

"I'm pleased to see you too, Juan," she said.

She stood there in the dark, close to him, so that he could almost feel her breathe. A wave of suppressed emotion overflowed insided him. He was trembling. His fingers drifted to her elbows, to the inside of her arms.

His touch had an electrifying effect on her. She felt a shiver of excitement down her spine. When she spoke, there was an audible tremble in her voice. "Juan, I have come to tell you about tomorrow; about the trip to Michoacán . . . to the Sierra Madre Occidental."

His caressing finger tips had moved up almost to her armpits, they were moving toward her bulging breasts, towards the upright nipples. Suddenly he pulled her up against him, his bruised lips touching the side of her neck, his tongue caressing the tiny earlobes.

Her whole body shook as she raised her arms up, up, and then over his neck and clung to him, fitting every curve of her body into his.

Menzies felt the dampness of tears descending down her face. "Baby, you're crying," he said. "What's the matter?"

She didn't answer, and his right hand moved down to her legs and lifted her up. He carried her to the bedroom and when he couldn't unfasten her bra, impatiently he slashed the cord with his teeth.

His clothes chucked all over the floor, Menzies caressed her naked body until Geralda was in convulsions. Then he climbed between her legs, lifted her feet over his shoulders and loved her violently like this twice in succession.

They lay side by side for a while, relaxed, and Menzies lit a cigarette. His thoughts began to drift to his problem of getting out of Mexico, but she interrupted them.

"Tell me, Juan, why did you ask me to sing 'El Manicero,' that old Cuban song?"

Menzies reflected before answering. "It's been my favorite tune ever since I was a kid, that's all. I didn't even know it was called 'El Manicero.'"

"Do you know what El Manicero means?"

"Yeah. The peanut seller."

"I didn't mean just that. Do you know the real meaning of the words of this song?"

"No. I don't know any of the words," said Menzies.

"They have a very special meaning, Juan; a very special meaning. It's a revolutionary song. That's why when you asked me to sing it for you, for a while I thought you might be one of us."

"Honey, I'm sorry to disappoint you; I just like the tune, that's all."

"Juan, the words of 'El Manicero' speak about the oppression of the poor people by the rich; they speak about the hungry children, their desperate mothers in Cuba, who had nothing to give their children for dinner except a handful of peanut shells."

Menzies remained silent. Geralda's words seemed to throw light on yet another aspect of his present situation.

"You know, Juan, this sort of thing is also happening today in Mexico. It's happening all over Latin America. Rich people, absentee landlords, own thousands of acres of land. They let it stay untilled, desolate, unproductive. And while this happens, hundreds of thousands of farm workers remain unemployed. That's why here in Mexico also, desperate mothers have nothing to give their children for dinner, except perhaps a handful of peanuts, or a stale tortilla. This is what we, the guerrilleros, are fighting against."

Menzies reflected some more about what Geralda was saying. Last thing he wanted to do at present was to get mixed up in a political discussion. He had never been to Cuba, but he had seen enought of Mexico to know that the country, over the past twenty years, had made good progress toward providing more economic, social, and political freedom. And providing political freedom wasn't something Castro's Cuba could boast about. He decided to change the subject to something which seemed to him at the moment a little more urgent. He began to caress Geralda again, and when he felt she was responding, he turned her face down, lifted her hips so that they were supported by her knees, climbed behind her and loved her again, this time with a long, relaxed passion.

Geralda seemed to roll her hips in rhumba style, in rhythm with his strokes, and she reached such a delirium of sexual thrill that she began to mutter incoherent, meaningless words, calling his name at times, mumbling half-spoken English and Spanish sentences, while Menzies loved her endlessly, for what appeared to both of them at least an hour.

The noon sun blazed down on the 8,000-foot slopes of the Sierra Madre Occidental. A rolling, uneven, carpet of forest hugged the mountain sides, the high-rise flatlands, the cone-shaped volcanic hills. Swift mountain streams split the Sierra and joined together to form rivers which wandered through tropical valleys to the shores of the Pacific. A tarred road twisted and turned, disappearing behind hills and re-emerging to continue its snaky trail.

Menzies focused his field glasses on the gray, dusty Indian town of Uruapan, perched on rolling hills near the junction of three mountain streams. His face ached. His right, bloodshot eye was half-buried in an egg-size swelling over the cheek bone. His lips hurt, his head hurt, his whole body hurt. He stared for a while at the high spirals of the fortress-like abbey of Nuestra Señora Magdalena de los Ríos ten miles away. Then he lowered his glasses and let his naked eyes roam over the clearing in the forest. The army of General Juan Antonio Vargas Heredia, commander-in-chief of the guerrilleros in the State of Michoacán, lay sprawled all around him. It consisted of perhaps one hundred men and twenty women, a mixture of Indians and *mestizos* of every shade.

Bandoliers crossed the chests of the guerrilleros. Huge sombreros shaded their heads. Hand grenades clung to their belts. Half-moon-shaped water canteens of white goat skin hung from long straps on their shoulders. Rifles, Tommy guns, and sten guns lay handy beside them.

Several hundred horses, donkeys, and mules were tied to nearby trees, attracting swarms of flies. The animals grazed on the short green grass under the giant trees. The smell of sizzling meat filled the clear mountain air. On a huge spit a 400-pound steer was slowly being barbecued over a flameless, dampened pine-cone fire.

The aroma made Menzies hungry. He also felt exhausted. He had just spent three hours climbing mountains to reach the command post. And this had come after a five-hour nightmare of a ride from Guadalajara, a trip that he could only describe as fantastic. He had spent the first hour crammed in the false ceiling of a school bus. It was worse when they let him out—four hours of a most breathtaking, hair-raising, head-spinning driving he had ever seen.

Lopez, the driver, had pushed the 30-seat fifteen-year-old heap into eighty-mile-an-hour sprints. He had taken hair-pin curves 7000 feet high above Morelia and Patzcuaro on two wheels. He had missed 2000-foot unprotected drops by inches. The anguished tires screamed and skidded and groaned when he braked. It had been just too much! Even for *his* nerves. Especially after the sleepless night, the three-hour love tangle with Geralda, the death duel with Carruthers.

While climbing the mountain alongside Geralda, Menzies had kept his mind busy. He had to reach Young. The sooner the better. He knew Young was still connected with the Old Firm.

Following the line of thought projected during his talk with Don Carlos, Menzies told *el general* that he had to send a cable to London to make arrangements for the publication of some articles on the guerrilleros. Heredia had agreed. The organization in Uruapán would send the cable for him. All he had to do was scribble the message. Menzies got a piece of paper and thought. Then he wrote:

TO: COLIN YOUNG DAILY TELEGRAPH FLEET STREET LONDON HAVE OBTAINED MATERIAL FOR SERIES OF SEVEN STORIES RE MEXICO'S EXPANDING TOURIST ATTRACTIONS STOP REGRET THAXTED DEPARTED STOP REMAIN AVAILABLE BUT REQUEST URGENT REMITTAL PESOS EQUIVALENT ONE THOUSAND POUNDS THROUGH BANCO NACIONAL DE MEXICO URUAPAN STOP REGARDS TO ROD REPLY GENERAL DELIVERY URUAPAN

Menzies read the message several times. THAXTED was the middle name of Carruthers. Menzies guessed that Young would get the message. If Carruthers was dead, he had died trying to kill Menzies, Young would reason. And this could also mean that Carruthers had told Menzies everything he knew before he died, including the bad news that the CIA had placed a million pesos on Menzies' head at the request of London. The mention of ROD would alert Young that Menzies now knew that E Force was being recalled to duty. The words SERIES OF SEVEN would puzzle Young, unless, of course, he had heard about the Society of Seven Arab terrorist group, in which case he would be most interested. MEXICO'S EXPANDING TOURIST ATTRACTIONS could be taken as necessary padding to the wording of the cable, but he hoped Young would read it as an indication of increased international terrorist activity in Mexico. It didn't matter which way Young interpreted these words. REMAIN

AVAILABLE was plain enough—and it would be understood that he, Menzies, was willing to cooperate in any revival of E Force. URGENT REMITTAL PESOS could be understood as a reference to the pesos reward for the bounty hunters. ONE THOUSAND POUNDS THROUGH BANCO NACIONAL DE MEXICO could be taken either as necessary padding to the crypto-message or as a request for money. Either way it didn't matter. But Menzies knew that in view of all the circumstances, the Old Firm would make sure he wasn't left without money. They'd wire cash . . . about two thousand four hundred dollars. Menzies grinned. Let them pay. They can afford it. They've caused enough trouble already. GENERAL DELIVERY URUAPAN gave Young a contact address.

Menzies handed the message to Heredia. He was a short, swarthy, bearded man in his late thirties. He spoke no English, so Geralda interpreted the message for him. "What do you need the money for, señor?" Heredia asked, grinning.

"It is for you, General Heredia, and for your men," Menzies promptly replied. "I may be your guest for a long time and I would like you to accept a small gift as a token of appreciation for the hospitality."

Heredia burst out laughing. "Señor Menzies," he said, "We do not need money." He turned and looked at the rough, unshaven guerrilleros lounging on the grass, leaning up against trees, cleaning rifles. "Do you really think, señor, that caballeros such as ourselves do not already have unlimited credit in Uruapán?"

Some of the guerrilleros overheard him and also burst out laughing. "Señor Menzies, this beautiful town, with its hotels, banks, churches, shops, is ours. It belongs to us. Any time we want it. Keep the money for yourself, señor. It is not money that we need from you." He paused, seemed to change his mind, perhaps fearing that he might have offended Menzies. "But your offer, señor, is very welcome, and we appreciate it. Now if you like to order some good Scotch whiskey from Morelia—not more than a case or two—my men and I will be honored to drink to your health." His mouth broke into a wide, friendly grin. He offered his hand to Menzies. Menzies shook it cordially.

"But señor, you have not signed the telegram," Heredia added. "Sign it Teresa Smith. That's the name of Doña Teresa, a gringo lady from California who is an English language teacher at Uruapán. She works with us. She is one of us."

Menzies did so and handed the message back to Heredia. The general looked at it once more, nodded to Geralda, turned and called out to a short teenage boy. "Hey! *Pablito!* Take this paper to Doña Teresa and ask her to send the telegram."

Heredia glanced up at the sun, then turned to Menzies. "I think your tele-gram will go out today. But now we have important business. We must eat, eh?" He slapped Menzies on the shoulder and grinned.

Miss Audrey Philbury-Jones, secretary of the literary and features editor of the *Daily Telegraph,* was a punctual, painstaking, imaginative young woman. She arrived at the office exactly at a quarter to nine every morning five days a week. Her first job was to sort out the mail for Colin Young's attention.

This Friday morning she opened the telegram delivered an hour earlier. She read it again and again. She knew of nobody by the name of Smith with an outstanding assignment from Mexico. As for the request for one thousand pounds, it was preposterous! The *Daily Telegraph* did not pay that kind of money, even for a series of seven articles. Obviously there had to be some mistake. The cable might be from some crazy American free-lance who had opened the *Author's and Writer's Year Book,* found the *Daily Telegraph,* and sent the cable. She hoped to convince the most authoritative, best-informed newspaper in the world, with a circulation of well over a million a day, to make space for a series of seven — seven, mind you—articles on Mexico's tourist trade!

Miss Philbury-Jones thought this impertinent. She crumpled the tele-gram in her tiny fist and threw it into the wastebasket. Then she remembered it was addressed personally to Colin Young. She knew there was no mention of Colin Young in the one-paragraph section devoted to the *Daily Telegraph* in the *A & W Year Book.* She picked up the telegram and smoothed it out.

Miss Philbury-Jones did not expect to see Young that day. He had told her he would be busy attending an emergency meeting of the executive committee of the National Union of Journalists, and he must not be disturbed under any circumstances. She pondered the matter for a while. After all it *was* a telegram. And it *was* addressed to Colin Young. She looked at her watch. Perhaps she could reach him at home. She dialed an unlisted phone number.

When Young answered, she read him the telegram, noticing with sur-prize that his voice betrayed excitement. He made her read it twice over.

"Would you like me to answer it?" she asked. "It's obviously from some crackpot freelance writer, sir."

"I'm inclined to think you are absolutely right. Audrey," Young said evenly. "It most certainly is. But please don't bother to answer it. I'll handle it myself."

"Do you know this Smith, sir? She's not in our file of stringers."

"Y-e-s, Audrey. I'm quite sure I do know her. Thank you so much." He abruptly put the phone down to avoid further explanations.

Young took his time finishing his scrambled eggs on toast. Then he kissed his wife, went down to the garage, and hopped into his Jaguar.

The VC-10 jetliner of BOAC's Flight 121 roared out of London's Heathrow airport precisely at 1:15 P.M. Among the 79 passengers on board for the non-stop trip to Mexico City were Aris, Atherton, and Young. They had arrived at the airport separately and were traveling separately — but all in the tourist section of the plane.

Paulisen was already on his way to New York by Pan-Am. He had arranged to switch planes in New York for Washington, where Secretary of State Henry Kissinger awaited his report. Then Paulisen, too, would fly to Mexico City.

E Force would reassemble at noon the following day. At Mexico City's luxurious Fiesta Palace Hotel, situated on Paseo de la Reforma.

CHAPTER SIX

Unholy Retribution

Chief Inspector Andreas Spanos (retired), formerly of the Special Security Section (Idiki Asfalia) of the Athens City Police, stepped onto the tenth-floor balcony of his luxurious penthouse apartment which over-looked Patision Street. The last glimmer of daylight was fading away from the top of the Akropolis and the spires of the church on Mount Lykavitos. Spanos, in his early sixties—a pale, gray-haired man going bald—had his hands firmly clamped on the lower part of his back, on his kidneys. He had been suffering from recurring kidney trouble for twenty years—the result of an old, half-cured dose of gonorrhea. This disability had caused his five-foot-nine-inch frame to bend into the most improbably S-shaped posture.

Spanos lived alone. How he could afford to live in luxury on his pension was a mystery to all but himself. Knowing that his circumstances might arouse suspicion, Spanos had encouraged the rumor of successful invest-ments, which were being handled for him by the Banque de Geneve, Switzerland.

Every three months a check for twenty-seven thousand Swiss francs—about nine thousand dollars—was deposited in his account with the Na-tional Bank of Greece in Athens. The money enabled Spanos to spend a week out of every month at the luxurious Kylini spa in the Peloponnese, to run a late-model, chauffeur-driven Mercedes-Benz, to gamble moderately at chemin-de-fer at the Loutraki resort south of Athens, or to take occasional trips to the sun-drenched Isle of Rhodes.

Spanos had it made financially. He also had the satisfaction of knowing —or at least believing—that he was working for a good cause. He was an agent of British Intelligence—at least he thought he was. And British Intelligence was fighting the same enemy that he had been fighting in Idiki Asfalia. This enemy was international communism. The threat, the danger to be averted, was a communist takeover in Greece. Spanos' conscience was clear. He was in the pay of a foreign power, but it was an allied foreign power whose objectives in Greece were to safeguard the country against a communist takeover. This was his own personal belief—his own credo, his own Bible, and his political purpose.

During World War II, Spanos, then only a sergeant, had also served the Abwehr—the war-time Nazi secret service—at the request of Herr Otto Blumentritt, Abwehr's chief in Greece. The Greek government of General Isolakoglou, which collaborated with the Nazi forces occupying Greece, had arranged for Spanos to be "detached" from Idiki Asfalia for full-time service with the Abwehr. Spanos had been enrolled in the Abwehr's dreaded Abteilung III (counterespionage and security) and operated out of a three-story building on Kifissia Avenue. The Abwehr had also been fighting a communist takeover in Greece. Spanos was ready to serve the devil if need be, if the devil were anticommunist.

Spanos did not fear that his connection with British Intelligence might expose him to prosecution; such being the situation in Greece in early 1974, that his link with an allied intelligence outfit gave him prestige among certain police circles in Athens. Of course, he never admitted that he was a foreign agent. And he made sure no evidence linked him to foreign intelligence. Just the lingering suggestion that he might be linked with British intelligence was helpful to him. And he knew it surrounded him with a halo of mysterious power, which flattered his ego and placed him one step above other retired Idiki Asfalia old hands.

Spanos had been recruited, ostensibly for British Intelligence, back in 1948 by a man of seemingly impeccable credentials, a man named Stacey. Stacey served in the Balkan Counter Intelligence Service; he even wore an officer's uniform with the initials B.C.I.S. stitched into his epaulettes. The first two words on the name of this unit were irrelevant, Spanos had felt at the time. The words that counted were Intelligence Service. That was it. The real thing. The all-powerful, world-renowned Intelligence Service mentioned in countless books.

When the Second World War had ended, Spanos had every reason to fear British Intelligence. After all, he had helped the Abwehr hunt down scores of British spies infiltrating Greece from the Middle East. So when Stacey had approached Spanos with the friendly suggestion that he work for British Intelligence, Spanos was not only delighted; he felt he had been saved by a miracle of the celebrated Holy Mary of Tinos.

When Stacey left Greece, he gave Spanos a contact in Athens, a code system, and an alternative contact in Paris. Stacey had made all necessary financial arrangements. And he had warned Spanos not ever to attempt to contact any other British Intelligence agent in Greece whom he might accidentally discover. Stacey had explained that British Intelligence worked in tiny, self-sufficient cells with no direct contact between them. For Spanos to disclose to another British agent his own affiliation would mean that he had broken a cardinal rule, that he was unreliable. Unreliable agents could be dealt with in only one way, Spanos understood.

Oh, yes. Spanos understood the situation perfectly well. He banked his check every three months and secretly acknowledged that he was being grossly overpaid. He liked the people he worked for. They had displayed British sportsmanship. He had been an implacable enemy of the British during World War II; but once the war was over, they were ready to forget everything, shake hands, and be friends.

What he also liked about the British was that he did not have to do very much for his money. If only that idiot Churchill had been on the side of Hitler in World War II and had helped Hitler fight Stalin, he, Spanos, would rather have worked for the British than for the Germans. The British never gave him any questionnaires; he never knew what they really wanted to know. They trusted him so implicity that they left everything to his own judgment. His main job, almost his only duty, was to keep his eyes and ears open, to keep in close touch with his former colleagues in Idiki Asfalia, and pass on the news. All the news. Sometimes they would also ask him to elaborate. Generally, he told them about hunted-down anarchists and other political dissidents, plus occasional profiles of senior Greek police officers.

Spanos found his work exceedingly simple. As an oldtimer in Idiki Asfalia he knew some of the present senior officers, who trusted him. Some of the rookie cops he helped train in the late forties and early fifties were now heads of departments—inspectors, chief inspectors, superintendents. It wasn't hard to get information from them — especially when he got them to his penthouse apartment for an all-night poker game, filled them with the best retsina wine, and made sure they all left next day a few thousand drachmas richer.

Yes. It was easy. Dead easy. And it all revolved around good public relations. That was all. And for this work, the Banque de Genève sent him nine thousand dollars every three months. How lucky can one get! If it hadn't been for that bitch he was shacked up with for a while down in the Piraeus in 1952, that Katarina, who had given him that first, incurable dose of clap! Hm! What a bit of bad luck! An antibiotic-resistant strain of gonorrhea which no doctor could completely cure.

Spanos had even flow to Paris to see if he could get curative treatment there. No luck. A celebrated French professor of medicine who had treated him gave up after seven weeks. The elderly, bearded doctor had patted him in the back and said: *"Mon vieux,* you have been infected with gonorrhea only seven times in your life so far. And you have been remarkably successful in curing the infection the last six times. Alas! The first infection persists. You can control this, but you cannot cure it. You cannot have children of course. But who wants children at your age, eh?

"What you have, we call in France *la goutte matinale.* It is often a sign of genius. Even Robespierre, Maréchal Soult, and Jean-Jacques Rousseau had it. But look what they were able to achieve, eh?"

Spanos had no idea what these three Frenchmen had achieved. Maybe they, too, had been British Intelligence agents. You can never tell whom you can trust these days. Spanos felt reasonably proud that he had been eminently successful in curing the last six doses of gonorrhea. He left Paris reassured. He hadn't completely cured the first dose, of course. But them, you can't win them all!

As he now surveyed the darkening Athenian skyline, Spanos reviewed the sensitive information he had received during the past three days. Spanos was a methodical man. He sifted all details and made careful assessments before putting everything on paper and coding it.

A Palestinian Arab by the name of Sidki had committed suicide in a most unusual way while in solitary confinement in an Idiki Asfalia cell. Only a few hours before he died, Sidki had disclosed under interrogation (hm! They called that stupid modern stuff interrogation) that an Arab organization calling itself the Society of Seven—SS—(he liked the parallel with the Nazi outfit which carried the same initials) planned to smuggle three 100-kiloton atomic bombs into London, New York, and Paris and detonate them.

That sonofabitch Aris, who headed the Greek Secret Service, was in charge of the Sidki investigation. He had screwed the whole thing up. He had let Sidki commit suicide. Why if he, Andreas Spanos, had been in charge of the investigation, he'd have made Sidki talk, all right. Half an hour of *falaga* — beating on the soles of the feet with an iron bar — plus the *enesis*—injection of lemon juice into the spinal cord—would have done the trick in no time.

But there you have it. Aris had bungled the whole thing with his psychological interrogation. He blew it. That bastard Aris. If only Spanos had managed to catch him during World War II, when Aris traveled back and forth into German-occupied Greece from the Middle East, Greece would now be a happier place.

So Aris had bungled the interrogation and had allowed Sidki to die before compromising his associates and giving more specific details of the plot.

The Society of Seven. Bullshit! This wasn't an Arab terrorist group at all. It was a commie setup, operated by the KGB from the Kremlin. It had to be. The three cities it planned to destroy were the leading capitals of NATO.

It was clearly obvious, yet Aris couldn't see it. He didn't want to see it. Because Aris was a commie himself. He had always been one. He used to come into Greece during World War II to help the Greek communist guerrillas fighting the anticommunist Germans. If Aris wasn't a commie, how come the Abwehr and the Gestapo hunted him? Spanos reasoned, Hitler didn't want to fight the British and the Americans. He was only fighting the Russian communists. They were the enemy.

If that stupid sonofabitch Churchill had only realized this, Russia wouldn't be in the heart of Europe today, and there would be no need for NATO. All Hitler wanted was to fight the communists and be friends with Britain and America. Yet, that Churchill! He was the greatest criminal; he had caused more damage to Europe and the rest of the world than anybody else. Churchill had ruined Greece. All this stuff about democracy and horseshit was just a cover up for communism. What Greece needed was a good national socialist government, with a strong man like Himmler to control the police and wipe out all the communist and crypto-communist scum. And of course the Jews.

He, Andreas Spanos, was one of a brave band of Greek Nazis who had dominated certain sectors of the Greek security forces since the end of World War II. Spanos recognized that his Nazi band was dying, but he was proud of them nonetheless. People like Stacey and his organization had appreciated the services that Greeks could still provide in the anti-communist cause. For it was part of the job of BCIS immediately after the end of World War II to clean up former Abwehr, Gestapo, and Reischs-sicherheitshauptamt (RSHA) agents in Greece. The fact that they had not done so was proof of British political genius, Spanos felt.

As soon as Aris had received the bad news that Sidki was dead he had flown to London. Then he had returned to Greece. But within a few days Aris had again made arrangements to fly to London, this time by way of Paris. In fact, (Spanos looked at his watch) if his information was right, Aris was due to fly from Tatoi Airport in just over an hour. There was no time to lose, therefore. Britist Intelligence must be alerted to pick up Aris' trail in London and find out what he was doing there.

Spanos had managed to obtain a word-for-word transcript of the Sidki interrogation. He incorporated this in his report, put it all in code, then took the elevator to the ground floor, walked across Patision Street to a public phone, dialed a number, and made arrangements for his report to be picked up straightaway.

The phone jangled in Room 21 of the Hotel Studio, in the Rue des Vieux Colombiers, on the fringe of Paris' Latin Quarter.

The sole occupant of the room, registered as Monsieur Alphonse Herman Boudieny, reputedly a traveling lingerie salesman from Lyons, picked up the phone. He said *mais oui, oui, naturellement, d'accord* a few times in a gruff, foreign accent. Then he replaced the receiver.

Monsieur Boudieny, a stocky, swarthy man in his early thirties, went over to the bidet in the bathroom and pissed in it. Then he spat into the adjacent toilet bowl and began cursing softly in a strange language. *"Maitkata puitkata na glava na gulema,"* he hissed. What the hell did they think he was? An electronic machine? He had to put a tail on a man coming out of an international flight due at Orly in seven minutes, then meet the *directeur* at the Café Danton in the Carrefour de l'Odéon half a dozen blocks away. Monsieru Boudieny walked back to the phone and dialed a number, spoke briefly in the same strange language, a Bulgarian-Macedonian dialect, then adjusted his black tie, put on his jacket and dark overcoat, and walked out into the street.

The directeur—his name was Georgi Efraimovitch Bogdanoff—was a tall, gray-haired man in his seventies who looked and felt at least fifteen years younger. Besides being the boss of a special intelligence unit of the Warsaw Pact powers in France, code-named *Zena,* he was also cultural attaché of the Bulgarian Embassy in Paris. Bogdanoff was a Macedonian Bulgarian. He had been only a little boy, back in 1913, when the advancing Greek army entered the spacious stone house in the town of Poroia where the Bogdanoff family had lived for countless generations.

Greek soldiers had ravaged and plundered their house and ravished his two teenage sisters. They would have shot his father, had not a Greek officer arrived just in time to stop his men at the point of his pistol. The tall, burly, mustachioed officer was from the nearby Greek town of Sidirokastron and had known the Bogdanoff family for years. Protected by the Greek officer, the Bogdanoffs were allowed to pile the remainder of their belongings onto two bullock-drawn carts and make their way through the perilous, 5,000-foot, freezing passes of Mount Rupel to the Rumelia province of southern Bulgaria.

Bogdanoff never forgot the looting and the destructive frenzy of the victory-flushed Greek soldiery. He never forgot the please, the screams, and later the anguished sobbing of his sisters, who had been dragged to an upstairs bedroom and raped by nearly a dozen vengeful, bearded, filthy men. He never forgot the rape of his sisters even though he was supposed to forget it, because the girls could not get married decently unless they were virgins. Bogdanoff never forgot how his mother had to sell family heirlooms to pay a doctor to sew up the torn virginal hymens of the girls a week after the outrage, thus ostensibly restoring their virginity and their self-respect. Even during the wedding ceremonies, a few years later when the girls were respectably married off, Bogdanoff could not forget the nightmare of Poroia. He knew, of course, that in the war-torn Balkans of the 1912-1913 wars such things had happened regularly and that no side was without blame, not even the Bulgarians.

But Bogdanoff still hated the Greeks—more so than he hated the Turks who had controlled Poroia before the Greeks had arrived. And Spanos' reports, intended for British Intelligence, for more than twenty years had been reaching Bogdanoff's Warsaw Pact *apparat*—Bogdanoff's communist spy cell—instead. For that was precisely Stacey's arrangement.

Bogdanoff was well aware that at seventy-six he was past retirement age. He knew that while he still held the post of directeur of Zena he could still do something to avenge the insult of 1913.

Bogdanoff was not really a communist. How could he be? His family for generations had been part of the Bulgarian-Macedonian aristocracy. Rich land-owners, they could afford to send their male children to study medicine, architecture, and literature at the Sorbonne.

Bogdanoff did not actually dislike the Russians. He just considered them uncouth but still friendly peasants. Russia was a nation of drunks lacking in personal refinement. Bodganoff tolerated his Soviet KGB bosses because Bulgaria was, and had to be, a member of the Warsaw Pact. And the Warsaw Pact protected Bulgaria against its implacable enemies—the Greeks and the Turks.

When Bogdanoff got Spanos' reports, his mind began to work at a feverish pace. He decided to act on his own, to stray a bit from routine which required Zena Apparat to pass on the information to the Joint Intelligence Commissariat and await instructions.

So the Greeks had discovered an Arab terrorist plot to blow up London,

Paris, and New York, eh? The Greeks would then claim credit for this discovery. Greece's position and prestige would be enhanced. This was something which Bogdanoff could not allow to happen. He would screw up everything. He would hit the Greeks where it hurt them most—in their credibility. He, Georgi Bogdanoff, would now avenge the insult to his family in 1913. He could do this quite easily. It required only one phone call. And the call would go to Alamut—the *nom de guerre* of a young Palestinian he had met at a Libyan Embassy cocktail party only a few weeks earlier.

The young Arab with the black intense eyes and the taut, light-brown leathery skin had told Bogdanoff: "My name is too long and difficult for you to remember it; but I would very much like you to know me and remember me. So please just call me Alamut. Here is my phone number." Bogdanoff had stuck the piece of paper with Alamut's phone number in his pocket. A week later, when he had found out who Alamut was, he quickly memorized the telephone number and burnt the piece of paper.

Bogdanoff had inquired at KGB headquarters. He was told that Alamut was an Arab terrorist leader, and that he must have nothing to do with him. The KGB was careful not to identify itself with Arab terrorism, which in any case was not directed against communist countries. On the other hand the KGB recognized that indiscriminate terrorism directed against the West from any quarter was valuable. If for no other reason indiscriminate terrorism absorbed much of the energy, the personnel and the finances of NATO security—an effort that left fewer resources to combat espionage activities of the KGB.

Incredible though it seemed, the KGB had reached a gentleman's agreement with Western intelligence agencies, Bogdanoff knew. There was to be no indiscrimnate terrorism initiated by either side against the other. This agreement had been quietly established long before the recent *détente*. But nonagression did not imply an obligation to assist the West in suppressing indiscriminate terrorism.

Because of all these considerations, Bogdanoff was in some doubt whether he would be displeasing his KGB bosses by contacting Alamut. In any case, this particular consideration did not bother him too much—not at this stage of his life and service to the KGB. He hated the Greeks and now saw his chance to undermine Greek intelligence. What's more, with a little bit of luck he might be able to infuse a suspicion in the minds of Allied intelligence that Aris had betrayed them.

So after meeting and briefing Boudieny, whose real name was Semeon Aliksandr Fedoroff, Bogdanoff walked down the steps into the *Métro*. He used the telephone in the public urinals to dial Alamut's number; and when a young woman answered he said: "This is Bogdanoff; I have bought tickets for the midnight show at the Moulin Rouge for yourself and

Alamut and will meet you there at eleven forty-five precisely." Bodganoff then climbed up the steps of the Métro station, gave himself a double Pernod at a nearby bistro, and walked briskly along Boulevard St. Germain to stimulate his appetite.

Seven young men arrived separately between 2:30 and 3:30 A.M. at the 13th floor of Appartements El Mirador in Montparnasse and were admitted to the luxurious Suite 133. It consisted of a huge reception hall, a dining room, three bedrooms—each with a bathroom *en suite,* a library, kitchen, servants' quarters, wine cellar, and utility room. A forty-foot long balcony extended from the reception hall, from which one could pick out all the famous Paris landmarks—Notre Dame, La Madeleine, the Bastille, the Arc de Triomphe at the far end of the Champs Elysées, the Palais de Justice, the Pantheon, and of course the Eiffel Tower.

Suite 133 had been rented three months earlier by a man who identified himself on the phone as an official of the Libyan Embassy at the rate of twelve thousand francs (about $2,400) a month, unfurnished. Six months' rent had been paid in advance, as the agents for Appartements El Mirador required. A further 270,000 francs (about fifty-four thousand dollars) had been spent only for the local French component of the furnishings. These consisted mostly of modern electrical kitchen equipment and lighting fixtures, curtains, drapes, appliances, a wall safe, and some exquisite reproductions of famous French paintings.

But the bulk of the furnishings had arrived in a truck from Marseilles, where they had been disgorged from the hold of a Liberian-registered freighter which had sailed from Tripoli with general cargo a week earlier.

Among the imported furnishings were thick Persian carpets; sheepskins; various wall decorations including six pairs of early eighteenth-century muzzle-loading pistols; an assortment of enormous goose-feather pillows with colorfully embroidered covers portraying warlike scenes; Moslem praying rugs of various sizes; low divans with upholstery embroidered in geometric figures; scores of hand-woven blankets, eiderdowns, bedspreads; enormous silver-lined cooking pots, food-serving platters, teapots, and other kitchen utensils; about half a ton of books and Arab encyclopedias; and a circular, 10-foot-high Senusi Arab sheik's tent, complete with colorful interior decorations and a heavy, low, mahogany eating table.

The tent, about 20 feet in diameter, had been pitched right in the center of the reception hall of suite 133, so that its top just about touched the ceiling at the very point where the giant Louis XIV-style chandelier had once been.

The moment a visitor entered the tent, he was almost completely transferred to the typically Bedouin surroundings of Senusi Arab aristocracy. There was only one flaw to this illusion. It was the lighting. The seven oil lamps around the interior of the tent did not exude the smell of burning kerosene. They looked like oil lamps, but they operated on standard French electric current, through colorful, shaded 75-watt bulbs.

At 5:00 A.M., five hours after Bogdanoff had met Alamut at the Moulin Rouge, breakfast was served in the tent of ~uite 133. It consisted of a huge bowl containing large chunks of fatty, half-cooked boiled lamb, swimming in thick, oily gravy. Another huge bowl contained boiled rice spiced with cinnamon and nutmeg.

The seven young men in the tent sat in a circle on cushions around the low magogany table. They ate with their fingers from the same bowl. From time to time they dipped their hands into containers of water beside them; the water had been spiced with clover and lemon juice.

Nothing in the appearance of the seven men would identify them as Arabs, let alone as members of a fanatic sect whose chief function was extortion and terrorism. They wore business suits in muted tones of gray and brown. Their ample dark hair was well-trimmed. Their sideburns were modest, their faces clean-shaven. Their eyes were a variety of hues, from coal-black to light brown. They ranged in age from twenty to thirty-five.

Alamut, broad-shouldered and about five-foot-ten, wore a tiny silver pin on the left lapel of his herring-bone tweed jacket. If one had the opportunity to examine the head of this pin with a magnifying glass, one would notice engraved upon it the characteristic outline of the seven-handed Ryukyu dragon. To cognoscenti, the design of the pin signified that the wearer was a black-belt karate expert who had graduated with first-class honors from the *Bushido-kai Karate-do Sheetu-Ryo Ryukyu* College of Martial Arts in Japan.

Alamut sat on a higher pillow, overlooking the other six at the far end of the tent, facing the narrow slit which was the entrance.

When they had finished eating and had dipped their hands in the bowls of water for the last time, Alamut pulled a cord. Two veiled women appeared at the entrance of the tent. They were dressed in black velvet, which completely covered their bodies including their hair and feet. Their faces were covered by a *yasmak* of transparent black tulle cotton which did not unduly obstruct their vision.

One of the women cleared the table, while the other brought seven tiny cups of thick, pitch-black, honey-sweet, over-cooked tea that had been boiling for over an hour. The first woman returned with a pint-size clay container inside of which glowed seven small pieces of charcoal. Alamut reached under the mahogany table and picked up a long-stem, silver-bowl pipe. In it he put a black, round substance about the size of a match head and thrust the bowl of the pipe in the charcoal brazier. When the smell of hashish began to permeate the tent, Alamut lifted the pipe to his lips and then passed it around for inhalation by the others.

When the pipe was returned to him he placed it in a thick leather pouch and zipped it closed. One of the women reappeared at the entrance of the tent and removed the clay container. Alamut's black eyes intensely surveyed the men around him. Then he lifted the cup of tea to his lips, and the others instantly did the same. Alamut took a few sips. Then, very slowly and gently, he put the cup down. He began to speak in a hoarse, monotonous voice:

"My beloved fedayeen brethren. The illustrious Sheik-el-Jebel, the only true missionary of Allah on earth, has interceded for us. And Allah has been merciful."

Alamut paused for several minutes. The funereal silence was oppressive. They sat motionless, not even allowing their eyes to wander or blink.

Alamut spoke again, his voice a tone deeper:

"May the glory and the brilliance of the Sheik-el-Jebel eclipse the midday sun of our own Moslem heretics and of the foreign infidels who obey them."

"*Ah! Aiua! Inshallah!*" murmured the other six in unison. Their eyes were glazed. Tiny drops of perspiration had gathered on their foreheads.

"My beloved brethren," Alamut continued, "Our courier Sidki fell into the hands of our enemies. He is now among the chosen of Allah, enjoying perpetual happiness in paradise.

"The Greek police found the message Sidki was carrying. They were able to decode it. They know about Operation Mushroom in London, Paris, and New York. We must expect that they have alerted the French, British, and American dogs."

There were sounds of "Ah!" and muffled curses by the other six.

"We must expect our enemies are taking precautions," Alamut continued. "But Allah will deliver the infidel dogs into our hands.

"Ah! Inshallah! Hassan-i-Sabbah and his legitimate successors, the only true missionaries of Allah on earth, be praised and worshipped throughout eternity," murmured the six in unison.

Alamut continued, his voice gradually rising to a high pitch: "As the viper kills its mate after copulation, as the hyena eats the bodies of its dead offsprings, so do the infidel dogs eat the intestines of each other"

"Ah! Aiua! It is true, oh Alamut," whispered the audience.

"Last night, my beloved fedayeen brethren," Alamut continued, "a Bulgarian agent of the Russians gave me the full transcript of Sidki's interrogation. He gave me the details of the action planned by our enemies."

His voice rising to a crescendo, the finger of his right hand waving,

Alamut yelled: "They think, they hope they can stop us! But they are too late!"

He let his eyes roam around the tent until they rested on the two-foot-high central mahogany table.

"Under this table, my brethren, is the atomic bomb for Paris. It is in an iron box which fits under this table. But it will blow this degenerate infidel city to the devil. So that the whole world will know, and the stars will know, and paradise and hell will know, that the Yehudi infidels who took our sacred land in Palestine, who pollute our drinking water with their excrement, who eat the livers of our newborn sons, will never and must never rest in peace!"

"Aiua, aiua, so be it!" said the six hashishin.

"The other two bombs are already in Paris and New York," Alamut continued. "So how can they stop us?"

"Ah! It is true, oh Alamut. They cannot stop us."

"The blessings of the Sheik-el-Jebel are upon us. That is why, my beloved brethren, the plans of the enemy, and the information he has, have been delivered into our hands."

"Ah! Aiua! It is true, oh Alamut."

"Now we are waiting for the triggers from Mexico. They are ready. They should arrive in a week. Three of us are going to Mexico to get them."

"Our enemies have taken precautions. But as the sky has many stars, so do their cities have many suitable points for our bombs."

"Praise be to Hassan-i-Sabbah, heart of our spirit and father of our thoughts. We will carry out the will of Allah, as transmitted by his only true missionary on earth, the illustrious Sheik-el-Jebel."

"Ah! Inshallah! This is the will of God. It will be done," said the other six hashishin. They chanted in perfect unison.

Alamut once again relapsed into a tense silence. Then, turning to the short, thick-set man on his immediate left, he said in a crisp, businesslike voice: "You, Hassan. You will go to New York immediately and leave the American bomb atop the World Trade Center. I know where to find you. I will bring you the trigger within a week."

The sharply changed tone of Alamut's voice, and the mention of his name, had an electrifying effect on Hassan. The glaze vanished from his eyes. "Yes, Alamut," he said eagerly.

"You must go now, Hassan," Alamut said.

Hassan sprang to his feet. He bowed slightly in the direction of Alamut. "Salaam aleikum—peace be with you," he said. With the open palm of his right hand he touched, in quick succession, his stomach, chest and forehead, in the traditional Arab salute. Then he briskly walked out of the tent.

Alamut turned to the man sitting next to Hassan's empty seat. "Abdul," he said. "You will go to London. Hide your bomb in the rotunda of St. Paul's Cathedral. I will bring the trigger to you as soon as I finish my work in New York."

"Yes, Alamut," said Abdul, a tall thin man. He got up, saluted as Hassan had done, and quickly left.

"You, Mahmoud, and you, Zoltan," said Alamut addressing the next two men around the table. "You will stay here in Paris and make new arrangements. Be very careful. For us, the French are more dangerous than either the British or the Americans. The French know more about us. I repeat: Take no chances."

"Yes, Alamut," said Mahmoud and Zoltan simultaneously. They stood up, but with a wave of his hand Alamut stopped them from leaving.

"You will stay in this apartment," Alamut continued. "We have comfortable divans in the bedrooms. Go, now, and get some rest."

Mahmoud and Zoltan bowed, saluted, and left the tent.

Alamut turned to the remaining two hashishin. "You, Omar, and you, Mohammet, are coming with me to Mexico."

"Yes, Alamut," they both said, recovering from the spell.

Alamut was silent for several minutes, his mind immersed in thought, his eyes fixed on the table before him. Then he continued, emphasizing each word: "But before we go to Mexico, we are going to see our first enemy. Aris. He is here. In Paris.

"He is staying at the Hotel Terminus St. Lazare. This infidel Greek dog must not die, not yet. He questioned Sidki. What he knows is all that the enemy knows.

"We will follow Aris and discover his other associates. Then we can dispatch them all to hell together.

"We now have a big advantage. And we must use it. We know who Aris is. But he doesn't know who we are.

"We are able to recognize him. But he cannot recognize the humble servants of the Sheik-el-Jebel."

For the first time that night Alamut's leathery face broke into a grin. His lips parted to show the tips of perfect, strong teeth. Then he continued his monologue: "Aris, I think, is the name for the god of war in Greek mythology, in Greek history. By the grace of Allah we will ensure that he returns to history, to past history; that he and his like become a myth in the burning bowels of hell!" Alamut allowed a further long pause before he spoke again.

"I have asked Al Fatah's international office in Zurich for a profile on Aris, and full details about his background.

"Al Fatah's Zurich office does not know they are helping us. And we don't want them to know. Because they could betray us. They are not believers in Hassan-i-Sabbah. This we must never forget. Though we have our fedayeen among them. Like the eminent Sheik Abu Daoud, may his flocks of goats multiply and his camels never cross the desert without water, and may his sons have the paramount honor of serving the Sheik-el-Jebel as their father does."

"It is true, Alamut," said Omar and Mahommet. "May the blessings of Allah rest with Abu Daoud, as the sweet, nourishing dew of dawn rests upon the young grass of the Sinai."

"It is time for us to go now, my brethren," said Alamut, rising to his feet. Omar and Mahommet followed him.

One of the first acts of the newly-elected French President, Monsieur Valéry Giscard d'Estaing, was to reorganize France's police, internal security, and foreign intelligence services. In the last two categories, France had been served, in early 1974, by no less than seven independent or semi-independent outfits. There had been a certain amount of overlapping responsibilities and resulting professional jealousies. There had also been extravagance, top-heavy administration, waste of manpower, petty politicking. The net result had been a measure of confusion, heart-breaking red tape, contradictory and often illiberal activities which did no credit to France's democratic constitution.

When Monsieur d'Estaing took over, France's internal security and foreign intelligence required an overhaul. And also the advice of what could be described in U.S. business circles as a good firm of efficiency and management consultants.

The new president did precisely that. In a series of drastic administrative measures, certain security and intelligence outfits were guillotined. Other were amalgamated. New ones were created. Staff dismissed, reshuffled, engaged. Budget allocations were reviewed and adjusted.

One of the new units to emerge from these revolutionary changes was the *Service de Renseignements Spéciaux,* (SRS). It was a secret outfit, whose existence and purpose were known only to Monsieur d'Estaing and a handful of his cabinet ministers, outside of the SRS boss himself and his senior officers.

Head of SRS was Commissaire Henri Montjoie, scion of a noble French family from Artois, whose ancestors had somehow escaped the blade of the guillotine at the time of *le terreur,* during the French Revolution.

Commissaire Montjoie had been chief of *Sûreté Générale* of a town in

Alsace before being elevated to his new post He had won distinction there
—though not much publicity—as a result of a series of spectacular
French-German border police activities, which involved the seizure, over a
period of years, of nearly a ton of heroin, opium, cocaine, and other hard
drugs, nearly all of which had been earmarked for the flourishing United
States market.

Commissaire Montjoie had drawn the attention of Monsieur d'Estaing
when the latter was campaigning for election in Alsace. After a suitable
background investigation, Montjoie resigned from the Sûreté
Générale, ostensibly to go into private business—to head a large private
detective agency in Paris which had offered him double the salary he was
getting with the Sûreté.

The Service de Renseignements Spéciaux operated out of a massive
three-story converted villa in the Avenue des Chasseurs in Paris. It pur-
ported to be a private detective agency which specialized in global industrial espionage.

The choice of this particular cover for the operations of what was one of
France's most sensitive intelligence outfits was Montjoie's. He had decided
to use this cover despite the initial reservations of d'Estaing himself. Using
a private detective agency cover for a government intelligence and security
outfit was so oldfashioned, so well-worn, so obvious, that it was no cover at
all—Monsieur d'Estaing had been advised by his cabinet colleagues in the
know.

However, it was precisely here that Montjoie's genius shone. What self-
respecting foreign-intelligence chief would ever think that the French were
so stupid, so clumsy, and so backward as to choose a private detective
agency cover for a secret French security agency? "Non, non, *Monsieur le
Président,*" Montjoie had argued. "The very fact that such an obvious
cover is used is a guarantee that it is an excellent cover."

The finesse, the Gallic humor, the subtlety of Montjoie's exquisite thinking and deception were not wasted on Monsieur d'Estaing, himself a man
of the most refined thought and humor. And Montjoie's suggestion was accepted.

The function of SRS, and Montjoie's terms of reference, had been
defined in one brief, clear, Napoleonic sentence: Prevent the operation of
indiscriminate terrorist groups within France. And Commissaire Montjoie
—a short, bald-headed, be-spectacled man in his early forties—launched
himself upon this task with the élan, the vigor, and the enthusiasm of
Maréchal Ney.

In addition to his own carefully selected full-time staff, Montjoie enjoyed the services of more than three thousand informers, half of whom

were in Paris itself. These informers had been inherited by Montjoie from several disbanded government security agencies. Montjoie could also call upon the assistance of the full international intelligence services of France's formidable Service de Documentation Extérieure et du Contre-Espionage (SDECE), the post-war French secret service which originally had been the Second Bureau Intelligence of the French General Staff, but now was a mammoth political as well as military intelligence and counter-intelligence agency operating independently of the French General Staff.

One of these SRS informers was the *concierge*—the janitor—of Appartements El Mirador in Montparnasse. His contact name with SRS was simply Michel. He was a Frenchman—but born, educated, and raised in Tripoli, Libya. And it was not at all by accident that Michel had managed to obtain this position at Appartements El Mirador.

This luxurious block of 72 apartments in the most fashionable and expensive part of Montparnasse housed no fewer than six foreign diplomats and agents. One of them was the military attaché of the Polish Embassy. Another was the First Secretary of the Brazilian Embassy. The third had recently been rented for the Ambassador of Chile. The fourth, also recently, had been rented by the Libyan Embassy. The fifth belonged to Hank Margolis, UPI deputy Bureau Chief in France, who, SRS had reason to suspect, doubled as a senior CIA agent whose activities were independent from the accredited CIA office in Paris.

Yet another El Mirador apartment had been rented and used, SRS had found out, by Sheik Ibn el Fahmi, acting Minister of National Resources (that meant exclusively oil) of the Arabian Gulf Kingdom of Kuwait. He had once been overheard at a cocktail party claiming he had screwed every chorus girl in the 1973 line-up of the now defunct Trianon nightclub of the Place Pigalle. Defunct, no doubt, Commissaire Montjoie had enviously surmised, because the chorus girls had been so lavishly rewarded that they had decided to take a year off and spend some time screwing young, penniless Spaniards on the Costa Brava.

So it was with excellent reason that SRS had arranged for Michel to obtain the position of concierge at Appartements El Mirador.

Michel spoke Arabic without a flaw, of course, but with the distinctive, harsh-sounding, Libyan accent. Michel could not only recognize the Arab-background intonation of Arabs speaking in fluent French; but he also recognized some of the various Arab accents, which betrayed geographical origin, when they spoke Arabic.

Just as an American can sometimes recognize that an overseas visitor who speaks to him in fluent English has a Russian, Greek, German, or French linguistic background, Michel could recognize a foreigner speaking to him in fluent French as having a Russian, German, Chinese, or

Arabic linguistic background. Having lived in an Arab country for so long, Michel could instantly recognize Arabs speaking to him in fluent French. Moreover, Michel could recognize the particular geographic origin of anybody speaking to him in Arabic—the same as an American can recognize a United States Southern accent, a Canadian English accent, a British English accent, or an Australian English accent.

Michel had overheard, on several occasions, visitors to the Libyan suite of El Mirador speaking Arabic. Nothing he had heard could possibly give grounds for suspicion; but their Arabic accents *had* aroused Michels curiosity.

Though the occupants and visitors to Suite 133 were ostensibly Libyan Arabs, they spoke with the kind of accent that he usually associated with Lebanese, Palestinians, perhaps Syrians.

Michel's curiosity was further aroused when he noticed the unusual activity in the Libyan Embassy suite in the early hours of Friday morning. Michel was paid by SRS on the basis of results and valid information provided, not on a retainer arrangement. So he wasted no time to try and make some money. He dialed the number of his SRS contact and reported what he had noticed He tried to embellish what he had noticed, of course, in order to arouse SRS interest. And to convince his SRS contact that he, Michel, considered his news important, he made sure he phoned the moment Alamut and his two companions had left the building. He also told his contact that he had not wasted a single minute to pass on this vital information.

At SRS headquarters Michel's news was examined, sifted, typed on a proper information sheet with the comments of two department heads at the bottom, and did not finally reach Commissaire Montjoie until just before lunch.

Montjoie then arranged for a routine check. He sent two "electricity inspectors" in blue coveralls to visit the hashishin apartment, under a suitable excuse, early the same afternoon. They found the door double-locked and Michel's passkey useless. Moreover, one of the women in the apartment yelled at the inspectors through the locked door that there was absolutly nothing wrong either with the lights or with the appliances, and that her instructions were not to receive any visitors that day.

The inspectors left, as they had been told to do under such circumstances, and reported to Montjoie. His suspicions were aroused, and he decided to place the whole building under discreet but constant surveillance.

Aris' report to President d'Estaing the previous evening had been the subject of an emergency meeting of the French cabinet. It took place just about the time the two inspectors had returned to report to Montjoie. And several hours later, while Commissaire Montjoie was having an early dinner at *La Vache Rouge,* an inconspicuous little restaurant half a dozen blocks from his office, an SRS messenger, disguised as a taxi driver, came over and told him to get back to the office straightaway to receive an urgent communication from President d'Estaing.

Monjoie read Aris' report and the President's comments; then he read Michel's report again, and the report of the two agents. Nothing really connected the two—even though Sidki, a Palestinian Arab, had been traveling on a Lybian passport and posed as a Lybian Arab, just as the seven apparently Palestinians at El Mirador posed as Lybians. But one of Montjoie's hobbies was numerology—the study of the occult significance of numbers. For example, why is 13 often considered an unlucky number, whereas 9 and 27 so often proved to be lucky numbers for him at roulette? Things like that bothered and fascinated Montjoie. So, when he connected the Society of Seven disclosed by Sidki with the seven Arab visitors to suite 133 reported by Michel he metaphorically put two and two together and came up with a strong, persistent hunch.

Montjoie went to interview Michel at El Mirador. There he obtained the welcome and exciting news that though apartment 133 had been rented by the Libyan Embassy, all Embassy personnel lived elsewhere. He also found out that six months' rent had been paid in advance in cash. Montjoie thought this most unusual.

Early Saturday morning, Montjoie, at the head of his SRS agents, forced the door of apartment 133. They found nobody there. They searched the place thoroughly but very discreetly. They found the Bedouin tent nearly folded under a sofa. The chandelier in the hall was in its right place. They also found the heavy mahogany table and noticed the empty compartment underneath it. Montjoie thought this compartment adequate to smuggle into France at least seventy kilos of opium. They took fingerprints and checked for traces of heroin. They found none. Then they tidied up, leaving the place as they had found it. They even fixed the broken latch on the front door and used fine paint brushes to retouch the chipped woodwork. Then they returned to the Avenue des Chasseurs, where part of the basement had been turned into a police scientific laboratory.

Montjoie was now more than ever convinced that the apartment had been used by some kind of criminals. What kind of criminals he had no way of knowing for sure. The two hashishin who had been in the apartment when the phony inspectors arrived had become suspicious. They had not forgotten Alamut's warning. They removed the 180-pound container with the 100-kiloton atomic device by way of a fire escape during the two-hour interval between the time the two inspectors left and the time the block of apartments was placed under SRS surveillance.

The SRS raid had proven fruitless. But Montjoie's hunch remained very much alive. He got through to the Sûreté and the SDECE and launched his SRS into an intensive hunt for the seven Arabs. One of the first steps the Sûreté took was to check the passenger lists of all outgoing international flights and compare them with descriptions provided by Michel.

Flight BA121 from London arrived in Mexico City a few minutes after 9:00 P.M. Friday. Less than an hour later, Aris, Atherton, and Young had booked in at the Fiesta Palace Hotel. Young and Atherton were in suites 913 and 966 respectively—both on the ninth floor. Aris was in suite 627—three floors below.

Throughout the long trip from London, the subsequent airport formalities, the airline bus ride to the hotel, they had given no sign of recognition. As far as anybody was able to tell, these three passengers of BA121 did not know each other.

The reservations for them at the luxurious Fiesta Palace had been made by BOAC's Mexico City office. Malcolm Sanderson, assistant press officer of the British Embassy in Mexico City, had been at the airport to greet Young. Sanderson, a short, dark-haired man in his middle twenties with the youthful face of a teenager, had stepped up to Young after the customs inspection and introduced himself.

"Mr. Young?" he asked.

"Yes," said Young.

"Sanderson, from the Embassy Press Office. We have a cable for you from the *Daily Telegraph.*" He gave Young an envelope.

"Thank you so much," said Young. He opened the envelope and read the message:

CASSIDY NO LONGER AVAILABLE TO ASSIST YOU BUT RE- QUIRE YOUR URGENT ATTENTION THREE PIECE FOLLOW UP RE LONDON MEXICO MANGO FRUIT EXPORT PACT ALERT ARIS WALTER

Young did not pause to consider the real meaning of the cable. He was standing in the middle of the airport's arrivals lounge and was conscious of the probability that the eyes of many people might be fixed on him at that moment. Ostentatiously he crumpled the cablegram in his fist and stuck it in his pocket. "Dammit," he told Sanderson. "They got me working over- time again. Confound the editors. Aren't I supposed to get any sleep?"

Sanderson grinned but remained silent.

Young continued, "I'm really most grateful to you for taking all this trouble. Would you care for a drink?"

Sanderson looked at him closely and seemed to hesitate.

"Well, not really; I mean I'd love to, but I'm supposed to play squash with a friend and—"

"That's quite all right," Young quickly interrupted him. "Thank you so much." They shook hands and Sanderson left.

Young decoded during the bus trip to the Fiesta Palace. CASSIDY NO LONGER AVAILABLE TO ASSIST YOU was plain enough. It confirmed Menzies' cable that Carruthers was dead or at least out of action. Since Carruthers headed the Secret Service in Mexico and was the only one in direct contact with London, this part of the message also meant he could not expect any immediate help from the British organization in Mexico.

REQUIRE YOUR URGENT ATTENTION meant precisely what it said, Young concluded. The rest of the message puzzled Young, but only for a few minutes. Obviously any fruit trade between the two countries would involve export of fruit from Mexico to Britain, not the other way about. Menzies had used, in his cable, the form SERIES OF SEVEN ARTICLES to refer to the Society of Seven. So the reference to THREE PIECE FOLLOW UP RE LONDON MEXICO could well mean that a three-member team (of the enemy) had followed the three E Force agents from London to Mexico. ALERT ARIS (why only Aris?) also was in plain language. WALTER stood for the "W" Section of the Secret Service—the section through which Young communicated with the Old Man.

Young got up and stepped over to the bus driver. He asked how long it would be before the bus arrived at the Fiesta Palace. Young didn't quite catch what the driver told him in broken English, but on his way back to his seat he dropped the cablegram into Aris' lap.

Aris quickly covered the piece of paper with his hands. When he was convinced that none of the nine other passengers was observing him, he picked up a Mexico City publicity folder from the empty seat next to him and put the cablegram inside it. Then he casually lifted the publicity folder and opened it. In the dim light he read the cable.

In the spacious foyer of the Fiesta Palace was George Pappas, Chief CIA agent in Mexico, together with two of his assistants—Sammy Aielo, grandson of the infamous Mafia Don Vincenso Aielo who was murdered in a Detroit gang war in the 1940s, and Johnny Bruskowitz, a Harvard graduate in political science.

Pappas was lounging in a huge leather chair, smoking and pretending to read the newspaper. Aielo and Bruskowitz were standing nearby, talking animatedly in Spanish, but casually scrutinizing the passengers who had just arrived on the Flight BA121 bus.

Pappas and his assistants had received accurate descriptions of the three

E Force men and recognized them instantly. They also had descriptions, via the British M.I.5 of three other passengers on Flight BA121. None of the people who got out of the airline bus fitted the descriptions of these three other passengers.

Pappas and his team already knew the rooms the three E-Force men would occupy, because the night desk clerk, Enrique Gonzalez Cartin, had been on the CIA payroll for years.

Pappas, whose parents had emigrated to the United States from the town of Pyrgos in the Peloponnese noted Aris with particular interest. He would have loved to go up to him, talk to him in Greek, and ask him some questions about the old country. But he knew that this course might turn out to be disastrous for both of them. Pappas had learned, only three hours earlier, that Aris had been compromised. How, by whom, he didn't know. But the CIA office in London had notified him that the Special Branch agent tailing Aris in London had noticed that there were two, possibly three, other men also tailing Aris. The Special Branch detective had at first thought that the other men following Aris might also be from Special Branch, or from M.I.5, as a sort of double insurance that Aris was effectively shadowed. However, when the detective reported his observations to his superiors, it had been ascertained that there had been no other tail on Aris, either from Special Branch or M.I.5. Unfortunately, by the time this information had been received and processed by Special Branch headquarters, BA121 was already on its way to Mexico City.

A howling storm over the Caribbean had rendered radio communications difficult. And this factor, coupled with the obvious need for absolute security, had dissuaded the Old Man from alerting Young while the plane was in flight.

Alamut, Mohammet, and Omar, traveling on forged French passports, had picked up Aris at the Terminus St. Lazare Hotel early that morning and followed him to London. It took Alamut only a few minutes and a couple of telephone calls to make some alternative arrangements for the London end of Operation Mushroom, and the three of them followed Aris to the Strand Palace Hotel and then to Heathrow airport in time for the flight to Mexico City.

At no time had the three hashishin seen Aris in the company of either Young or Atherton, because the E Force meeting had been held in tight security in the fifth-floor suite at the Strand Palace. So they had no idea that two of Aris' associates were also on Flight BA121.

When Alamut saw that Aris was heading for Mexico City, his worst suspicions were confirmed. Aris, who had broken the Society of Seven code during the interrogation of Sidki, had obviously also found out that the triggers for the three atomic bombs were being made in Mexico, Alamut had concluded.

After some anxious moments at BOAC reservations, the three hashishin boarded the flight to Mexico City. At first, Alamut had thought of killing Aris on the plane—a task which he considered easy.

The then Alamut decided that this would be pointless and premature. Aris was bound to have already communicated with the British and other intelligence agencies. In any case, the mysterious death of a passenger during an international flight was bound to cause delays in "processing" the new arrivals in Mexico City. Immigration, police, and customs clearance would be delayed. And Alamut could not afford delay. He had to alert his organization in Mexico that the game was up, that the scheme had been betrayed, before the Mexican authorities and a host of international security agencies descended upon them.

The hashishin had no reservations at the Fiesta Palace. However, a $100 bill in the eager hands of the chief bell hop worked miracles.

Another $100 bill caused two extra beds to float into the honeymoon suite as if on a magic carpet. The hotel registration documents were brought up to their suite for them to sign. Three more $100 bills were sent down to pay for the suite for three days, with a $30 tip for the desk clerk.

Señor Enriques Gonzales Cartin, through whom the documentation had passed, had no idea that the three had just come from Flight BA121. As far as he knew, they were visiting businessmen whose previous address in Mexico had been the exclusive Hotel Acapulco Malibu, on Acapulco's Avenida Miguel Alemán. Neither had Pappas or his two colleagues had any reason to notice the three young men who swiftly moved through the foyer without luggage nearly half-an-hour before the expected arrival of the airline bus.

The three hashishin had entered the hotel foyer from the side entrance on the Paseo de la Reforma, by way of the hotel's ground-floor cocktail lounge, and not from the sumptuous main entrance on the driveway. In this busy, luxurious hub of international travel, hundreds of people criss-crossed the acre-size foyer at every hour of the night.

When the last bell hop and desk clerk had muttered words of gratitutde in French for the regal *pourboires* and had bowed out of the honeymoom suite, Alamut picked up the phone and dialed a number. He first spoke certain code phrases in French. Then he switched to Arabic.

"I bring you greetings from the one and only Sheik, I, Alamut, his eternal servant and humble messenger.

"Through the intercession of the Sheik-el-Jebel—may happiness and glory be with him forever—Allah has graciously brought us safely to Mexico City on the wings of justice and holy retribution. I now seek your help and your news.

"We are about to have dinner, my brother, but the three of us have no utensils with which to cook, nor knives with which to cut the meat which Allah has provided, nor salt to spice our food.

"We are in suite 773 of the Fiesta Palace Hotel and hope that the wings of the fastest eagle inspired by the eternal spirit of Hassan-i-Sabbah can bring you here immediately.

"And we anxiously await your news, which like honey will pour from your lips to refresh our hearts and minds."

Half an hour later, while the three E men were still completing the hotel registration forms, two men strolled through the foyer of the Fiesta Palace Hotel carrying briefcases and wearing large, clumsy looking raincoats. They took the elevator to the seventh floor and were admitted to suite 773.

The visitors supplied the three hashishin with two Berettas and one Browning pistol, the latter with a silencer. They also brought three British made Mills No. 36 pin-operated, fragmentation grenades; one World War II-vintage German-made, 32-bullet Schmeisser submachine gun (which had to be reassembled); and nearly twenty pounds of ammunition of various kinds. That was not all. From one of the briefcases the visitors produced three scimitar-shaped, narrow-blade, ten-inch daggers, whose beautifully ornamented solid silver handles were engraved with various Oriental designs and an inscription in Persian. Translated into English, the inscription read: *From the Rekindled Beacon of Alamut Comes Holy Retribution.*

After a brief exchange of appreciation and humble assurances of eternal faithful service, the two visitors gave Alamut the news. First and most important, the triggers were ready for delivery. Alamut could pick them up the next day at Massiat—the secret workshop in the State of Michoacán. The scientists would explain the working of the triggers, how they could be fitted onto the atomic bombs, and how they could be controlled and operated electronically by means of a radio signal from a distance of up to 50 miles. It was all quite simple, Alamut was assured.

Second, a coded signal had arrived through the Paris Libyan Embassy from Al Fatah's international headquarters in Zurich. Alamut handed the message to Mohammet, who was the code expert.

While they waited for Mohammet to complete his task, the visitors gave Alamut the third item.

A British journalist by the name of John Menzies had killed four

Federales policemen in Guadalajara. He was granted political asylum by the Mexican Liberation Army on condition that he assist the guerrilleros with a world-wide publicity campaign. Its purpose would be to focus attention on the indignities and the oppression experienced by the people of Mexico at the hands of the government of President Echeverria.

Menzies was also hunted by the CIA and British Intelligence for reasons unknown, Alamut was told. The CIA had even posted a one-million-pesos reward for his death. Menzies had also killed a British agent sent to Guadalajara from Mexico City to assassinate him. This Menzies was obviously a desperate, proficient killer. He spoke Arabic fluently, as well as several other languages, and he might also serve to publicize the just cause of the Palestinian Liberation Organization.

The reliability and the credentials of this man Menzies, Alamut was told, had been proved beyond any doubt whatsoever. He had definitely killed the four Federales policemen and the British secret agent. Even at this moment every policeman in Mexico and the entire apparatus of the CIA were hunting him.

Alamut's informer was full of praise for Menzies. With suitable teaching in the eternal religion and philosophy of Hassan-i-Sabbah, Menzies could become an excellent fedayeen. He could become deadly to the enemies of the true faith and the Sheik-el-Jebel, because nobody would suspect an *inglis* of being a fedayeen. So, with this in mind, Menzies had been given permission to visit Massiat, so that his reactions could be observed as part of the preliminary training.

"I want to meet this man while I am in Mexico," Alamut said. "It will not be the first time than an infidel has been converted to our cause with everlasting advantage and to the glory of the Sheik-el-Jebel. Our Japanese recruits at the Lydda airport operation performed with outstanding devotion.

"Yes, I would like to interview this man Menzies. Good reliable men who are ready to serve Allah faithfully through the medium of the illustrious Sheik-el-Jebel will always find a place in the eternal happiness palace of paradise—"

Mohammet interrupted him. "Here is the decoded message, Alamut. It's about the infidel dog Aris, and this man John Menzies is mentioned."

Alamut's eyes suddenly darkened as he grabbed the seven sheets of closely written Arabic. Silently he began to read:

Aristides Dimitrakopoulos (Aris), head of the Greek secret service since 1957. Born September 21, 1919, at Karpenisi, mainland of Greece. Educated Third Public (Junior) School of Karpenisi and Karpenisi Gymnasium. Enrolled Athens Polytechnic College, September 1937, and simultaneously took French-language night studies with Athens branch of Alliance Française Institute. Greek-Italian war interrupted studies, volunteered, second lieutenant, III Battalion, First Evzone Regiment . . .

Alamut skipped the details of Aris' military service and his description since, having tailed him for the last twenty-four hours, he knew already what he looked like. Then he continued reading:

. . . escaped from Greece to the Middle East December, 1941, by way of Turkey. No information available re activities from December, 1941, to January, 1945, during which period he apparently served with Allied (possibly British) intelligence. 1945 to 1948—close business associate in marble-export company with Thomas Buchanan, British Vice-Consul in Athens, believed to have been British Secret Service chief for Greece. Arrested but quickly released by Salonika General Security police when he impersonated lawyer in order to visit British journalist John Menzies, held in solitary confinement in Salonika. Menzies believed to have been wartime secret agent, probably associate of Aris. Held in custody, unspecified charges, at the request of British Intelligence. Details unknown.

1949—Aris Joined Hellenic Fertilizer Company, believed to have been cover for Greek secret service . . .

Suddenly Alamut threw the decoded report on the floor and banged his fist on a bedside table. He began to curse, softly and rapidly.

Finally Alamut composed himself and politely told the two visitors: "Thank you my brethren. But Menzies happens to be our most dangerous enemy.

"That he is to visit Massiat is not your fault of course. As you said, his credentials were perfect."

"But Alamut, Menzies definitely killed four Federales and a British intelligence agent," said Abbas, one of the two visitors.

Alamut interrupted him with a wave of his hand. "Yes, you've told me all this. It was all part of a satanic cover plan for Menzies. The only kind of cover plan that could have fooled us, my brethren. And it did.

"That is why Aris is here. He was alerted by Menzies. This explains everything." Alamut paused, and the other four respectfully kept their silence.

Abruptly Alamut got up and began to pace the room. After a while he stopped and turned to Abbas. "How can we reach Solis in Massiat?"

"It is impossible, Alamut," Abbas replied. "There is no phone. And we purposely did not install a radio link for fear of detection."

"No way at all we can reach Solis at this moment?" Alamut persisted.

"None, Alamut," said Abbas. "From six in the morning to six at night we can phone a number in Uruapan and send a messenger to Massiat. It usually takes serveral hours. But at night, there is no way."

"In that case," said Alamut, "I want a driver and a car to be ready to leave for Uruapan within an hour." He looked at his watch. "By midnight at the latest. Can you arrange that, my brother?"

"Yes, of course, Alamut," Abbas replied. "You will also need a guide. They will not let you through to Massiat unless they know you. I will arrange a guide for you."

"Thank you, my brother," said Alamut. "Can you estimate the length of the journey?"

"Perhaps seven hours, if the driver is really good. And then three or four hours on foot."

"Would it be quicker for us to charter a plane early tomorrow morning and fly to Uruapan?"

"No, Alamut," said Abbas. "There is no landing strip in Uruapan. The nearest one is at Morelia, three hours away."

"We will go by car," said Alamut. "My brother, I beseech you to phone our contact in Uruapan at six in the morning and give a message from me to Solis."

"Yes, Alamut, it will be done," said Abbas.

"The message is: Kill Menzies now."

"Yes, Alamut," said Abbas. He bowed and mumbled "Peace be with you." Then the two visitors to suite 773 left, discreetly closing the door behind them.

Alamut turned to Omar. "My brother, Aris must not meet Menzies. He is here in this hotel. Do not fail, Omar. May the blessings of Hassan-i-Sabbah be with you for eternity."

Aris had just tipped the bell hop and closed the door of suite 627 when the phone rang. He looked at his watch. It was 10:30 p.m. He picked up the receiver and listened.

"Gia sou Aris," a husky voice said in Greek.

"My name is Pappas," the caller continued. "I have an urgent message for you from Rod. I'm waiting for you right now at the El Caracol bar on the second floor. Make it quick."

"Very well," said Aris, also in Greek. Then he put the receiver down and lit a cigarette.

Aris had heard Paulisen refer to Pappas as the CIA chief in Mexico. The mention of Rod during the recent phone call and the use of the Greek language were evidence that the caller was, in fact, Pappas.

Aris had read and understood the crypto-wording of the cable Young had dropped in his lap during the bus trip from the airport. This cable, plus the urgency of Pappas' call, convinced Aris that either the whole E Force, or only himself, had been compromised.

Aris unlocked his briefcase. From it he took out a thick-stemmed, seven-inch-long, leather-covered French-made Longchamps pipe, which he had never smoked in his life. He unscrewed the bowl and checked the magazine containing four .22-caliber bullets. Then he lifted the stem of the pipe, which was the barrel of the pistol, to the light. He was satisfied that there was nothing in the barrel to obstruct the passage of bullets. He emptied the magazine, checked the press-button trigger mechanism on the bowl of the pipe, refilled the magazine, and screwed the two pieces of the pistol back together. Aris then stuck the pipe into the outside breast pocket of his jacket, left his room and took the elevator to the second floor.

The El Caracol bar and night club was nearly deserted so early in the evening. The contrast between the brilliant lighting of the hotel second-floor lounge and the dim, shadowy environment of El Caracol was so striking that Aris at first felt he'd need a torch to find his way around. As his eyes adjusted, he noticed the bar. He stepped over and climbed onto a stool at the far end, next to the wall, from where he could see the entrance.

A three-piece combo, calling itself Los Brazilleros, struck up the opening strains of La Cucaracha. Aris had to yell at the tuxedoed barman for a double White Horse whiskey on the rocks. When the drink arrived, Aris casually took the pipe from his pocket and let the barrel rest on the bar, his grip on the pipe bowl.

Pappas, who had been sitting alone at a nearby table, got up and slid onto the next bar stool. They talked rapidly in Greek, whenever the barman was out of earshot. Pappas gave Aris the bad news that he had been followed from the moment he arrived in London, probably all the way from Paris, possibly even from Athens. Aris told Pappas about the cable Young had received. Prodded by Pappas, Aris tried to revive in his memory the faces and appearance of the flight passengers.

By eleven o'clock several patrons began to enter El Caracol. One of them was Omar. He sat at a table only fifteen feet away from Aris and Pappas. The waiter brought him a dry martini, which Omar left untouched. From his wallet Omar took a piece of paper and scribbled on it in French: *From the rekindled beacon of Alamut comes holy retribution.* He signed it with the number "7" and let the piece of paper drop on the floor.

Omar pulled the pin off the Mills grenade, got up and walked over to Aris. "Monsieur, you have dropped your wallet," Omar said in French. He offered the live grenade to Aris.

Aris reacted instantly. But he was still too late.

Omar dropped the grenade at Aris' feet and plunged sideways, even as the .22 bullet from the Longchamps pipe hit him in the shoulder. The roar and the blast of the fragmentation grenade in the confined space of El Caracol had the effect of a Richter-Scale No. 9 earthquake on a Central American shanty town sitting over the epicenter.

Aris' legs were shattered. Shrapnel riddled the left side of his body. But Pappas got it worse. He had bent down to see what Omar had dropped, and the blast tore off his head and sent it spinning like a football along the well-polished floor of El Caracol. By some incredible reaction of the dying nervous system, the headless corpse of the CIA agent took several unsteady steps away from the bar. It then sagged onto the floor, drenched by spurts of blood from the severed jugular veins, the legs and arms in convulsions.

The angry whizz of the fragments which ricocheted again and again off the concrete walls and ceiling of El Caracol soon mingled with the hysterical screams of women and the groans and curses of men.

Omar got it, too. Half his guts were spilled onto the floor, like a big mass of thick, tomato-tinted spaghetti. He lay on the floor, his eyes glazed, muttering incoherent prayers. But then, incredibly, he managed to get up. The fearsome ogre of the hashishin, dragging long strings of intestines over shattered glass and pools of blood, moved toward the exit, where Sammy Aielo suddenly appeared. He had to put four bullets from a Colt .38 into Omar, all neatly grouped around the sternum, before the hashishi finally went down.

The two barmen, the three members of Los Brazilleros and six other patrons were also injured in the explosion. The rows of bottles behind the bar, the chandeliers and crockery of the Fiesta Palace Hotel were in a shambles.

Soon the Federales, the Mexico City Police, the Mexican Political Police, the undercover agents of the National Anti-Terrorist Squad began to arrive. And so did the ambulances, from three separate stations.

Superintendent Jim Atherton of the Royal Canadian Mounted Police heard the muffled explosion in his ninth-floor suite. Atherton had just had a shower and a shave and was talking to Young, who had arrived to give him the news contained in the cable. They had been unsuccessfully trying to raise Aris on the phone for the past 20 minutes and had decided to go down to his room, when the tremor of the explosion reached Atherton's suite.

Atherton and Young went down to El Caracol and saw what had happened. Atherton showed his RCMP badge and mingled with the Mexican cops. He looked around, noticed the piece of paper blown by the blast of the explosion up against a curtain. He picked it up, read the message and showed it to Young.

Atherton threatened his way into the ambulance where the shattered bodies of Aris and two of Los Brazilleros were being taken to San José de Dios Hospital.

Young slowly strolled across the polished, imported-marble floor toward a row of public telephones. Before picking up the phone he noticed that his blood-stained shoes were leaving imprints all over the place. He used a newspaper to wipe off the soles of his shoes.

Young dialed the night number of the British Embassy and persuaded the woman who answered to give him the private number of the First Secretary. He reached him and convinced him to send a coded cable to Walter.

Young then went to the front desk and drafted a wire to "Smith," in Uruapan. He shuffled the words around for a while; finally he was satisfied that Menzies would get the message. He handed the wire to the desk clerk, together with a 100-pesos tip, and asked him to send it quickly.

Young strolled to the other end of the foyer. As he waited for the elevator to the restaurant, Sammy Aielo and Johnny Bruskowitz came over. They introduced themselves, exchanged a few words, then walked away.

Young got to the restaurant, ordered a steak *tartare* and a bottle of St. Emilion. He thought the price of French wine in Mexico was more than fantastic. It was absurd, ridiculous. Five hundred and thirty pesos, about $40, for a bottle of French wine you could buy in Paris for four dollars!

"My God! You need the income of an oil sheik to live over here, at least to live in the Fiesta Palace," he told the *Maître d',* who was fussing around, preparing the raw steak next to his table.

Young wondered whether the Old Man, way back in London, who sometimes personally scrutinized outrageous expense accounts, would approve a bill for $40 for a bottle of St. Emilion. "Goddammit, he better approve it; he bloody well better approve it," Young told himself. Then, with a wave of the hand he told the wine steward to dispense with the ritual of letting him taste the wine before filling his glass. Young knew he needed a long drink. And fast.

John Menzies was awakened by the wriggling of Geralda's bottom up against his crotch. He looked at the luminous dial of his black-faced Eternamatic calendar wrist watch and noticed that it was Friday, 3:30 a.m. Above him, amid the tall pine trees, he could see thousands of stars. Nature's thick mattress of pine needles beneath him was comfortable. The clean, 7,000-foot-level mountain air filled his lungs. He felt good. He also felt philosophical. "That's the way to live," he told himself. "I guess this kind of outdoor living suits me. It's part of my personality. Camping on a mountain side, sailing in an open boat, sunbasking and swimming along some tropical beach—that's all that counts. Well, not quite *all;* but near enough, anyway."

Menzies was in one of his rare, self-analytical moods. Now, what was it in his personality, if anything, that might have contributed to the load of trouble he was in? Hell, nothing! Just bad luck and circumstances, he reassured himself. Could he have avoided the mess and the murder at Guadalajara?

Menzies didn't get time to answer that last question. Because Geralda wriggled herself up against him even closer, and his prick swiftly reacted to the warm softness of her eager buttocks. Sensing it, Geralda took his hand and put it inside her blouse, squeezed it up against the fullness of her heaving breasts.

That did it. Every philosophical thought evaporated from his mind in order to allow his undivided attention to more earthly matters. He began to caress the back of her neck with his lips, fondled the upright nipples in his hands, and adjusted her body so that he could love her with sudden, violent, overwhelming passion. Geralda reached her climax only just ahead of him. And then they lay on their backs, their nostrils and open mouths sucking the sweet mountain air.

Some time later, Menzies noticed shadows moving among the pine trees. He heard footsteps and knew that the camp was awake.

Geralda adjusted her clothing and discreetly slipped from underneath the double blanket and began to walk away. She changed her mind, returned, bent over him, and kissed him long and hard. "Oh, I love you. My God, I love you as no woman has ever loved a man," she whispered between kisses, her voice choking with emotion.

The sincere, overwhelming intensity of her words almost frightened Menzies. He stroked the back of her head and her hair, feeling much more composed than Geralda. To relieve the tension he said, "Baby, you got the kind of hip movement that would make the Tahitian *tamuré* dancers turn green with envy.

"I'm nuts about you. I'm so crazy about you that to please you, I'd even volunteer to spend half an hour with Leo the Bear Killer in a Saskatchewan ring—even if Leo had just had a molar extracted without an anesthetic, and the referee was King Kong."

She smiled but didn't seem to appreciate him humor. "You're not taking me seriously," she said and pulled herself away. "Keep away from Leo. He doesn't like you very much." She pressed her lips to his once again, then stood up. She lingered there for a while, looking at him. The shadows of the early twilight played on her pale beautiful face framed by the luxurious masses of her golden hair. Then Geralda turned and walked away.

And Menzies had no idea that this was the last time he'd ever see her again—alive.

CHAPTER SEVEN

El Salvador

When Colonel Rod Paulisen arrived in Washington, he reported to Secretary of State Henry Kissinger. An emergency meeting of the National Security Council was then called for the same evening, Friday. Paulisen attended the NSC meeting at 9:00 P.M. in the White House. The Council considered the threat to New York.

After discussions which lasted nearly an hour, FBI director Clarence Kelley was entrusted with ultimate responsibility for all precautionary arrangements in New York and was provided with extraordinary powers. These included blanket permission to use wire-tapping methods at his discretion for a period of three weeks. It also included authority to form a special New York defense team with suitable personnel drawn from any law enforcement agency he wished.

The Council realized the danger of a stampede if the story got out that New York was being threatened. It also realized the danger of a massive witch hunt. For this reason the NSC decided to keep silence on the matter. The NSC secretarial staff was excluded from the meeting, and all tape recorders in the Oval Room were switched off.

After Paulisen had repeated his report to Kissinger, this time in the presence of the NSC, he was closely questioned. Then he was asked to leave the meeting, so that even he would have no knowledge of the counter-measures planned by the Council.

The minutes of the meeting and the written instructions of Kelley were typed out by members of the NSC themselves. As an added precaution and at the suggestion of Kissenger, a code name was adopted for the peril posed by the hashishin. The use of this code name would facilitate communications in the administrative machinery now being geared to deal with the problem. At the same time, it would improve security. The code name selected was KOBOLD, which Kissinger explained stands for an evil spirit in Teutonic mythology.

Kelley's New York special defense operation was then named Anti-Terrorist Tactical Agency for the Control of Kobold (ATTACK). Kelley told the Council that the man he hand in mind to head ATTACK was Capt. James O'Flynn, 59, Deputy Chief of Homicide, New York City Police.

Before leaving to organize ATTACK, Kelley told the Council that in 1974 there had been nearly three thousand bombings of various kinds throughout the United States. He said that many of these bombings were caused by terrorist organizations, and that with the emergence of newer and more sophisticated bombing methods, it could be expected that the death and injury toll, already heavy, would increase unless more stringent methods were adopted.

When the meeting was over, Kissinger strode to the phone. There he began a long series of telephone conversations. He alerted key congressmen of a national emergency but didn't tell them very much.

After some hesitation and reflection, Kissinger also called Soviet Ambassador Anatoly Dobrynin. He told him that the emergency precautions the United States was taking were not aimed against the Soviet Union but against a terrorist threat to place an atomic bomb in a U.S. city.

Kissinger told Dobrynin that the United States had evidence that the head of the As Saiqa, Colonel Mohsen, had been repeatedly seen in the company of Major General Alexei Fournikoff, believed to head the Middle East apparat of the KGB. Kissinger said that he, Kissinger, trusted that any pertinent information that might come to the knowledge of the Soviet government would not be withheld from the United States in this national emergency. He said the situation could easily be misunderstood. It could deteriorate into an international crisis of grave proportions particularly if it were later established that the Soviet Union had prior knowledge of this outrage.

Having thus warned Dobrynin, Kissinger casually mentioned as a sort of parting joke that the city threatened with an atomic bomb explosion could well be Washington, where Dobrynin happened to be.

Another person who was busy on the phone early Saturday morning was Paulisen. Aielo got through to him with the bad news that Pappas was dead and Aris critically wounded. There was no way Paulisen could get to Mexico City before noon next day. But he did manage to speak with Young on the phone.

In Mexico City the Federales and the CIA had checked all visitors registered at the Fiesta Palace as of midnight Friday. The night desk clerk, Señor Cartin, proved invaluable in this respect. But the rich Frenchmen who had briefly occupied the honeymoon suite on the seventh floor had vanished; except, of course, for Omar, who was dead in the city mortuary.

Several bell hops remembered the French visitors very well: how could they ever forget them after the generous, regal tips! They identified Omar as one of them. They also gave excellent descriptions of Mohammet and Alamut.

At 4:00 A.M. Saturday morning, Federales headquarters in Mexico City ordered a top-priority, full-scale hunt for the two missing hashishin. Particular attention was to be paid to all international and local airports.

Simultaneously (but very reluctantly) the Mexican police called off the "kill-on-sight" order against Menzies and substituted for it "arrest and detain." That was as far as they were prepared to go, even at the request of President Echeverria.

It was just past midnight when Kissinger spoke to Dobrynin on the phone. Less than an hour later, Dobrynin had reported to Moscow the recorded text of his conversation with Kissinger, with some pertinent comments of his own.

Pres. Leonid Brezhnev was pouring himself his first cup of tea of the day from a giant silver samovar when the decoded message from Dobrynin reached him. He was so infuriated by Kissinger's preposterous suggestion that the KGB might be in league with Arab terrorists that he took a fast gulp of boiling-hot, lemon-flavored tea. It burned his tongue and the lining of his throat.

President Brezhnev coughed, cursed, and dictated a sharp denial of Kissinger's allegation. Then he picked up the phone and got through to KGB headquarters in the Kremlin.

A very frank KGB report reached Brezhnev a few hours later. Yes, General Fournikoff had met Colonel Mohsen in Damascus a number of times. But Mohsen also happened to be a senior official of the ruling Ba'ath Party. That was the reason why Fournikoff cultivated Mohsen. Mohsen had never mentioned any international terrorist plot to Fournikoff. Fournikoff had never heard, from any source, the alleged plot to bomb

Washington. However, the head of Zena Apparat in Paris, Comrade Georgi Bogdanoff, a Bulgarian, had reported to the head of the Warsaw Pact Joint Intelligence Commissariat that one of Bogdanoff's agents, a Greek by the name of Spanos, had given certain information about the matter. It had not been reported to Brezhnev immediately because it was not thought to be absolutely urgent. Measures were being taken to ensure that the Soviet Union would not be embarrassed. The measures included the liquidation of all possible evidence that the KGB had any knowledge whatsoever, in any shape or form, from any source.

Brezhnev considered the KGB report carefully. He concluded, quite justifiably, that the West already knew what the Soviet Union knew about the plan to bomb London, Paris, and New York. After all, the KGB had gleaned the information from the West! From the Greek police! What puzzled Brezhnev a little was that Kissinger had suggested to Dobrynin that the threatened American city might be Washington, not New York. He asked the KGB to investigate this particular point further but decided there was no need to tell Kissinger anything more, because the United States already had all the information that the Soviet Union was able to obtain.

The doorbell rang at the penthouse apartment of Andreas Spanos just as he began shaving—a chore to which he now subjected himself irregularly, but always prior to his usual Sunday-morning drive to the Loutraki resort.

"Who is it?" yelled Spanos approaching the front door.

"It's me, Mitsos, Mr. Chief Inspector," answered a familiar voice from behind the door.

Recognizing the voice of his driver, Spanos opened the door and said: "But it's too early; I told you to come at . . ."

Spanos never finished his sentence. A snub-nosed automatic with a silencer began to spit. Three slugs hit Spanos in the chest. As he began to fall, Mitsos swiftly pushed him inside and closed the door behind them.

Mitsos waited a few minutes until he was sure Spanos was dead. Then, before rigor mortis set in, he placed the pistol in Spanos' left hand, because Mitsos knew Spanos was left-handed. Mitsos then looked around the apartment. He found Spanos' wrist watch on a bedside table, changed the time to an hour earlier, strapped the watch onto Spanos' right wrist and smashed it onto the floor.

Mitsos was about to leave when he noticed that Spanos was only half-shaven. This was a bit tricky, he thought. Do people commit suicide when they're only half-shaven? Who knows? Only the coroner would have to decide. Better play it safe and clean up properly. He got the Gillette safety razor from the bathroom, shaved the rest of Spanos' dead face, and cleaned up in the bathroom. Then he left, went down to the parking lot, and sat in the Mercedes-Benz.

An hour earlier, Mitsos had been at a nearby coffee shop having breakfast, in the presence of at least fifteen people. Mitsos figured that if the matter did reach the point where he needed an alibi, he had one.

In Paris, three hours later, Georgi Bogdanoff was strolling along the Seine when a black Peugeot came by. Federoff urgently waved to Bogdanoff to get in. Bogdanoff, trusted KGB agent for a quarter of a century, had no idea that this black Peugeot was going to be his funeral bier. Not even when Fedoroff affably put his arm around his shoulders, and he felt the sharp jab of a needle in his side.

Bogdanoff was dead in fifteen seconds. He was driven to Fontainebleau forest, dragged out of the Peugeot when there was no other traffic along the road, and placed in a sitting position with his back up against a tree.

The name of the poison injected into Bogdanoff was Cardioemphragma No. 13—a fairly recent discovery of a Hungarian veterinary laboratory. The poison had been found useful in dispatching cattle suffering from hoof-and-mouth disease prior to burning the remains to avoid contamination.

Cardioemphragma No. 13 caused an occlusion of the aorta, which in turn caused cardiac arrest. The victim of such poisoning displayed all the superficial symptoms of death through what is commonly called heart attack. And of course, that was exactly what Bogdanoff had died of. Heart attack. Only in this case, it was artificially induced.

The Mexican sun had dipped behind the pine-clad western foothills of the Sierra Madre Occidental and plunged into the calm, emerald-green Pacific Ocean when John Menzies, Manuel, six other guerrilleros, and eighteen heavily laden mules began the long climb to Massiat.

In the fading daylight, framed against the skyline, Menzies saw the massive, conical-shaped, ten thousand-foot mountain commonly known in those parts as El Salvador—The Savior—because on its very peak stood a seven-foot-high chapel, with a large cross on top, dedicated nearly three centuries earlier to San Bartolomeo El Salvador.

The guerrilleros, no longer concerned about the hot tropical sun, had tilted their huge sombreros back. Their rough, unshaven faces glistened with sweat as they plodded up the winding mountain trail. From time to time they prodded the mules with short, sharp sticks and exchanged crude jokes.

Quickly the night grew cooler. Menzies was glad he wore his jacket, which also served to hide the Luger, cradled in the French leather holster at his side. His three knives lay embedded in the three-piece sheath stuck in his right-hand hip pocket.

Manuel went over to Menzies. *"Olá, compadre,"* he said. "How do you like this night walk?"

"It's fine with me," said Menzies, carefully avoiding big chunks of manure.

"You know, you have been very lucky," said Manuel.

Menzies was a long time in answering. "Why so?" he asked.

"Juancito, the way you handled those four Federales delights my father in his grave. But you also needed luck, plenty of luck, *amigo."*

"You are right, Manuel. Nothing works when luck is against you."

"You know about Massiat, this place we're going to visit?"

"Very little."

"It's a workshop for our Arab friends."

"What do they use it for?"

"I don't know. None of us know." Manuel paused, then continued. "They are friends. They pay well. Sometimes they bring us guns. New guns. Like this Armalite rifle." He patted the weapon he was carrying.

"How long have they been in Massiat?"

"It will be three years on the fifteenth of next month. I remember this well. Because we started work on Massiat exactly a month after Geralda's eighteenth birthday."

"They've been here a long time, Manuel, eh?"

"Yes. But now their job is finished."

"Finished?"

"Yes." Manuel looked at the last three heavily-laden beasts of the mule train. "You know what they're carrying?"

"No."

"Gelignite."

"What for?"

Manuel smiled. "The Arabs will be leaving tomorrow."

"You mean Massiat is going up?"

"Yes. That is why I said you are lucky. You will see Massiat before we blow it up."

"You're gonna blow up this mountain? Blow up El Savador?"

"Madre de Dios, of course not." Manuel crossed himself. "El Salvador will stay where he is. Massiat is only a big cave in the side of El Salvador." He paused. "You know the prophecy of El Salvador, gringo?"

"No."

Manuel looked at the moon, then at the craggy skyline formed by the peak of El Salvador. "We are about halfway," he said. "It is time to give the mules some rest." He turned and yelled at the leading muleteer. "Olá! Antonio! We stop for half an hour here. And come over, all of you. I'm going to tell this gringo the prophecy of El Salvador."

The guerrilleros tied the mules to nearby trees, then gathered around Manuel. They stretched out on the damp grass and the mattress of pine needles, supporting themselves on their elbows, or resting on their sides. One of the men got up and fetched a bag from one of the mules. It contained *tortillas,* raw onions, chiles, salt, several over-ripe tomatoes and a pot of boiled beans in a thick, black sauce.

The guerrilleros filled the tortillas with swift, deft movements and began to eat. From time to time they passed around a half-gallon jug of home-brewed Michoacán tequila. It tasted and burnt like pure alcohol and caused Menzies to shudder.

"Many, many years ago," began Manuel, "before the time of my grand-father's grandfather, a very beautiful Indian maiden lived near Uruapan. She belonged to the Chapaqa Indian nation.

"She was called Aruntechek. In the Chapaqa language this meant Flower of the Goddess.

"Aruntechek was willowy and tall. She had blue eyes and golden hair. Because the Chapaqa were one of those tribes we call White Indians."

"White Indians?" Menzies asked.

"Yes. White Indians," Manuel repeated. "Few White Indians are left today. Some of them still live in the mountains of Oaxaca.

"Aruntechek's skin was so white that, compared to it, the skin of Don José Miranda of Castille seemed black!

"Don José owned all the land around Uruapan, as far as the eye could see. His herds of cattle and horses grew fat on the rich grass of these mountains.

"Don José had three sons. Antonio, Enriques, and Bartolomeo. All three of them fell in love with Aruntechek. But only the youngest son, Bartolomeo, drew favor with the White Indian maiden.

"Bartolomeo asked his father's permission to marry Aruntechek. But old Don José became very angry. How could the son of a Spanish aristo-crat marry an Indian? Such things were unheard of. Besides, Aruntechek was a pagan Indian, from a tribe which had refused Christianity.

"Aruntechek's people were stubborn. They rejected the new religion which came to Mexico from Spain. They even defied the threats of the bishops from Guadalajara.

"The Chapaqa still believed in the religion of the Aztecs. They even practiced human sacrifice, once every three years. The mountain we now call El Salvador, which is an old volcano, was then called Arazu.

"On the day of the sacrifice, the Chapaqa, thousands of them, treked from many directions to the top of Arazu. There, on the very peak, was and still is a big white stone. Late in the day, at the moment the edge of the sun touched the waters of the ocean, the most beautiful maiden of the Chapaqa nation was sacrificed. She was killed. With a long stone knife. Stabbed in the heart by the red-robed Chapaqa priests.

"The sacrifice was a tribute to the sun, the god of all life. The sun would not climb into the sky again if it did not receive the soul and the body of the most beautiful Chapaqa maiden once every three years.

"The maidens to be sacrificed were called brides of the sun. This was a great honor. A pride to their families. And before they died, they were raped, in full view of the Chapaqa nation, by the priests who later killed them.

"Aruntechek was chosen, because of her beauty, to become bride of the sun. She was very proud of this honor. But she was also sad. Because she knew her death would cause distress to Bartolomeo. And she loved him dearly.

"Don José knew about the human sacrifice of the Chapaqa. He had the power to stop it. His caballeros, the Spanish knights of his private army, were many. They wore chain mail. They wore steel helmets. They carried steel-tipped lances, swords, and fire daggers. And they rode strong, fearless horses.

"But Don José didn't want to stop the sacrifice of Aruntechek. Six months before the sacrifice, he had sent Bartolomeo to Spain to get over his love for Aruntechek. Don José thought that with Aruntechek's death, his son would recover from the magic spell which this Indian woman had cast upon him.

"Bartolomeo's brothers—Antonio and Enriques—had been rejected by Aruntechek. They had no desire to save her from death.

"When Bartolomeo arrived in Spain, he was forced against his will to join the military academy at Seville. Through he was brave, a born fighter, he hated military discipline. He thought the Spanish ideas about war were useless in Mexico. Bartolomeo's love for Aruntechek never faded. The charms of the many well-bred Spanish ladies he met did not compare with the grace, the honesty, the innocent manner, and the exotic beauty of Aruntechek. He knew she loved him with the purity of an untouched mountain flower. And he wanted to make that flower his own. Forever.

"Bartolomeo deserted the military academy. He went down to Cadiz and boarded a galleon for Villa Rica de la Vera Cruz—the city we now call Veracruz, on the Caribbean coast.

"Two months later the ship dropped anchor in this busy Spanish port.

Bartolomeo bought a horse and rode to the Chapaqa Indian camp. It was near the spot where we are now sitting.

"Bartolomeo carefully avoided his father's caballeros. He knew that if his father found out he had deserted the military academy, he would have him sent back to Spain in chains to serve a term of punishment in the dungeons of the Castillo Montalban, south of Madrid, where captured criminals were kept.

"Bartolomeo found out that Aruntechek would be sacrificed in a few days. He was allowed to see her, but not to speak to her or touch her. Bartolomeo wanted to save her and thought of many desperate plans. But in his heart he knew they could not succeed. He would get himself killed without saving Aruntechek.

"Bartolomeo left the camp of the Chapaqa. He disguised himself as an Indian and went to see Father Aloysius, at the small church of San Bartolomeo de las Piñas Blancas. Don José, his father, had built this church and donated it to the Diocese of Guadalajara at the time of Bartolomeo's birth, twenty years earlier.

"Bartolomeo pleaded with Father Aloysius to help him. He asked him to intercede with San Bartolomeo, his own patron saint, to save Aruntechek. Father Aloysius took pity on him. But he also realized that it would take more than prayers. It would take a miracle to save the young Indian maiden.

"But God has various ways to assist those who seek and deserve his help. In this case, the help came in the shape of an idea. If Aruntechek deserted the pagan beliefs and became a Christian, she would be considered polluted according to the faith of the Chapaqa, Father Aloysius told Bartolomeo. And no polluted virgin, who believed in a different god, could be offered as a bride to the sun—the god of all life. That would be sacrilege.

"So when Aruntechek and other Indians came to Uruapán, a day or two later, to exchange hides and woven mats for copper pots and machetes, Bartolomeo approached her.

"He asked her, he pleaded with her, he begged her to go with him to the Church of San Bartolomeo de las Piñas Blancas where Father Aloysius was waiting for them. They embraced and cried together. She told him she loved him, but she refused to change her faith. She had been picked to become bride of the sun. It was the greatest of all honors to her family. She would do nothing to alter her fate.

"Bartomomeo was strong-willed. He was impetuous. And his strength came from the greatest power that a human being came muster. Love.

"He grabbed Aruntechek, lifted her in his arms. Her legs kicked and she screamed, but he carried her off to the church. Father Aloysius baptized her into the Christian faith and called her Geralda. But she had been baptized against her will."

"Geralda?" asked Menzies. "The same name as your sister?"

"Yes," said Manuel. Have you ever heard, in all your travels, any other woman called Geralda?"

"Come to think of it, no," said Menzies. "Unusual name."

"It was the first name that came to Father Aloysius' mind. Because at the time he was reading some ancient scripts, about San Geraldo of Andalusia. And my sister is called Geralda because she was born on the day of the Fiesta of El Salvador. Tomorrow is her birthday.

"What happened then?" asked Menzies.

"As soon as Bartolomeo let her go, she rushed out of the church, to the Chapaqa crowd gathering outside. They had been afraid to enter the church because they thought they would be polluted by the Christian faith."

"And then?"

Manuel smiled and lit a cigarette. "I see you are interested in the prophecy of San Bartolomeo el Salvador," he said. "Well, Geralda did not tell the other Indians that she had been baptized. She did not wish to be disqualified from becoming bridde to the sun.

"The Indians went on with their preparations. Father Aloysius climbed onto his mule and rode all the way to the camp of the Chapaqa. He told them that Aruntechek was now Geralda. He told them she had been baptized, that she was a Christian. But they did not believe him. And Geralda denied it.

"Then Father Aloysius told the Indians that if a Christian baptized in his church of San Bartolomeo de las Piñas Blancas was sacrificed on top of Arazu, the Christian saint would never forgive them. He told them that the volcano would explode. The mountain would tremble. Thousands of rocks would fall from the sky. A black, fiery snake of molten lava would creep down the mountainside.

"The Chapaqa laughed. They told him to take his religion away. Father Aloysius was very distressed. He went back to Uruapan and saw Don José. He begged and exhorted him to send his caballeros to stop the human sacrifice of the pagan Indians.

"But Don José remained firm in his decision. He said he would not meddle with the Indian religion. He said he employed many Indian *peones* in his cattle ranches, orchards, and vegetable gardens. All these men would leave his service if he interfered with their religion. They would become his enemies. The times had changed since the days of the *conquistadores*. The problem of human sacrifice and Christianizing the Indians was up to the Church, not his private army.

"Father Aloysius went back to his priory. Bartolomeo was waiting for him. Father Aloysius broke the bad news to the young man. They prayed and prayed together.

"Father Aloysius, who knew he was acting in a very good cause, pronounced a curse. If ever a woman was slaughtered on Arazu, the wrath of San Bartolomeo and God should fall upon the killers; the mountain would tremble, and the pagan faith should be destroyed.

"The day of the sacrifice came. As the sun began its downward journey into the western horizon, young Bartolomeo, dressed in the panoply of his father's caballeros, mounted an angry black charger. He rode out, and up the mountain trails, toward the top of Arazu. He was on his way to fight a lone crusade against the heathen Chapaqa. He hoped to die if he could not save Geralda.

"Up and up the black horse galloped along the winding trails, its mouth filled with white froth. Its hide glistened with sweat like black velvet.

"But Bartolomeo was too late. As the edge of the sun touched the reflected red surface of the ocean, the stone dagger plunged into the heart of Geralda. Her blood painted the white sacrificial stone crimson red.

"And then the earth trembled. The mountain roared, and its side exploded. Millions of rocks flew into the air and rained down on the Chapaqa. The black horse neighed with anger. It reared on its hind legs and its coal-black eyes flashed.

"Thousands of screaming, terrified Chapaqa Indians came running down the mountain side. Their faces were twisted with horror. Bartolomeo waylaid the red-robed sacrificial priests. He killed them all. His dagger, his lance, his sword were covered with the blood of the men who had butchered Geralda.

"Next day all the Indians from the various Chapaqa camps gathered around the church of San Bartolomeo de las Piñas Blancas. They begged to be forgiven, to be accepted in the Christain faith. They knew nothing about Christianity. But they had been convinced of the power of Father Aloysiuss' magic.

"Father Aloysius told them that the fierce knight on the black horse was San Bartolomeo himself, taking vengeance on the priests who had murdered Geralda.

"And so this horrible custom of human sacrifice came to an end. In time, the Indians became genuine and devout Christians. Under the guidance of Father Aloysius, they built the chapel to San Bartolomeo on the very spot, around the same sacrificial white stone, where hundreds of people had been murdered from the beginning of time, all in the name of Chapaqa faith.

"And they called San Bartolomeo, who saved the lives as well as the souls of the Indians from this cruel custom, El Salvador.

"That, amigo, is the prophecy of El Salvador."

"And what happened to young Bartolomeo?" Menzies asked.

"Well, Don José was killed when his hacienda collapsed in the earthquake. But Bartolomeo didn't go home. He had no home. His heart heavy with unspoken grief for Geralda, he just rode away, down the same mountain trails, into the tropical valleys of our neighboring State of Colima and up again the other branch of the Sierra Madre Occidental. He was never heard of again."

Menzies lit a cigarette. "This is some story," he said. "A very interesting legend."

"It isn't just a story, amigo. And it isn't a legend. This is true. It's what happened. Ask anybody in Uruapán, anybody right here."

The other guerrilleros nodded sullenly.

"That was the prophecy of El Salvador," Manuel continued. "If ever a woman is slaughtered on Arazu, the wrath of God and San Bartolomeo will fall upon the killers. Their pagan faith will be wiped out from these parts, and the mountain will tremble, roar, and explode.

"And these prophetic words are written inside the chapel of El Salvador.

"Come to think of it, by the Indian calendar, tomorrow should be the fiesta of El Salvador. But by tradition it can only be held on a Wednesday. So next Wednesday, amigo, thousands of people from Uruapán and the nearby villages will climb to the op of El Salvador. The fiesta is held once every three years, on the same day that the Chapaqa held their human sacrifice."

Manuel got up and dusted the pine needles off his clothes. "Vamos muchachos, vámonos," he told his guerrilleros.

The mule train resumed the climb to Massiat.

It was shortly after 11:00 P.M., just about the time the fragmentation grenade was exploding at El Caracol, that the mule train with Manuel and Menzies in the lead reached the end of the trail. It had suddenly stopped at the edge of a precipice, on the lip of a deep ravine through which raged and roared the white-foamed waters of the Rîo Bravo.

The mules neighed and backed away. Manuel put his arm on Menzies' shoulder as if to warn him that only a black chasm lay ahead.

The moonlight, coming at an angle, did not disperse the black shadows of the ravine. Menzies held on to the branch of a tree and looked down. When his eyes adjusted, he saw the moving white foam of the mountain stream. He reckoned the ravine was at least one hundred fifty feet deep at that point. It was also very narrow. Perhaps no more than fifty feet across.

The guerrilleros began to unpack the mules. Manuel flicked a signal with his torch, and then Menzies saw furtive shadows moving on the other side of the ravine. The edge of a string, tied onto a small rock, was tossed across the Rio Bravo. One of Manuel's men picked it up and began to pull. Soon a one-inch thick nylon rope was brought over. Six guerrilleros grabbed the rope and began to pull some more. Bit by bit a bridge of woven nylon rope and two-inch thick aluminum piping appeared on Menzies' side of the Rio Bravo. Ropes were fastened onto thick tree trunks and the heavily-laden guerrilleros began to cross the suspension bridge to the other side of the ravine.

Manuel and Menzies were the last to cross. They were greeted with handshakes and pats on the back by Santos, Geralda's youngest brother, who commanded the guerrilleros on the other side.

All the supplies were brought over, including twelve black tin boxes containing twenty-five pounds of gelignite each. Then Manuel and his men recrossed the bridge.

"Hasta luego, gringo," yelled Manuel from the other side.

"Hasta la vista, Manuel," said Menzies. Then he followed Santos and his men to the tunnel-shaped, pitch-black entrance of a cave.

Santos' men had torches fitted into their belts, like miners about to descend a shaft. They walked along the level tunnel for several hundred feet. The atmosphere grew hot, damp, and oppressive. Finally Santos pulled a switch. Instantly the tunnel was lit up by scores of electric lights.

Santos noticed Menzies' surprise and said: "Yes, amigo. We do have electric lights. Civilization has reached Massiat.

"Where we are now standing, is the crater of the volcano Arazu. But do not fear. It is dead. Well, at least asleep. Last time it exploded was three hundred years ago.

"Believe me, it was big problem bringing the diesel engines and the generators to produce electricity up here. Each one of the three diesel engines weighs nearly two hundred fifty pounds.

"But the longest job was building up our oil stocks. In the last three years we had to bring over to Massiat more than two hundred tons of oil, all in four-gallon drums, five or six drums on each mule. You know how long that takes? If you only use fifteen or twenty mules for one, possibly two, trips every night?"

"I have no idea," Menzies confessed. "At least not without working it out on paper."

"It took a long, long time, amigo. But in the last month we didn't have to bring up any oil. Because the job of Massiat is finished. We've been using the stocks we piled up.

"Yes, amigo. You have come up just in time to see Massiat. By tomorrow night, there will be no Massiat left. That's why we brought up all this gelignite. We're going to blow the place up. The mountain will cave in and cover up everything."

"That seems a pity," Menzies said. "After all this work, all this effort, there will be nothing left."

"Yes, amigo. It is a pity. It took a long time to build Massiat. We brought up thousands of bags of cement and other material. We had 120 guerrilleros working up here, forty in each of three shifts, day and night, for nearly ten months. And now everything will be blown up. But that's how our Arab friends want it. And that's how it's going to be. They had a job to do. They've paid us well. We have no complaints."

They reached a stone bench, which Menzies figured was about a quarter of a mile inside the tunnel.

"Let's sit down," said Santos. "Solis doesn't expect you until midnight. He's a very busy man. He's a civil engineer, you know. And he is very precise with his time table."

They sat down on the bench. They were alone, because Santos' men had stayed near the entrance of the tunnel.

"When Massiat goes up in the air, there will be no more pay for you," said Menzies. "Your men will be unemployed. At least as far as Massiat is concerned. Do your men like this idea?"

Santos laughed. "Not so, my friend. We will ge paid for another three years. All in one lump sum. A bonus." He paused, then continued. "Now let me see. What do they call this kind of bonus in trade union language?"

"Severance pay," said Menzies.

"Ah, yes. Severance pay. That's it. Severance pay. We all get three years' severance pay the moment Massiat ends. And we expect more work for the Society of Seven. Who knows? Some other time, maybe some other place.

"Believe me, Don Juan, they are a good company to work for. Yes, a very good employer." He grinned.

"You know, Santos, what amazes me is how you were able to bring up all this machinery, all these supplies. How did you manage to move so many mules up and down the mountain for so many years without being discovered? By the police? The Federales? The ordinary people?"

Santos' grin grew wider. "I see you do not understand the situation, Juancito. Let me explain. The Society of Seven has bought protection from us. They have bought from us supplies, services.

"We, also, have bought protection. With Arab money. From certain people in well-placed positions. And this is also *mutual* protection. Becuase these well-placed people have also bought protection from us! We can capture anybody we wish in the State of Michoacán. We can execute anybody we wish. We can take the town of Uruapán, anytime we wish. All we have to do is set up a few roadblocks, and it will be days before anybody outside can get through to Uruapán. Better still, we can just blow up half a dozen bridges. Then Uruapán is isolated. We have many friends and sympathizers in the town.

"But we do not abuse our power. We do not abduct or kill. Not during the last three years, anyhow. We *buy* what we need for ourselves and the Society of Seven at Massiat. We do not steal. Uruapán is a peaceful town. Plenty of dollars pour into Uruapán because of the workshop at Massiat. This is very good for the tourist business. Other tourists come and go. Nobody interferes with them. We pay a few hundred thousand pesos here and there just to keep our friends happy. We don't bother anybody. And we don't make ourselves obvious.

"All this diesel oil and food supplies and other things going to Massiat could be going to any of a dozen Indian villages in this area. Only two of them are linked by road to Uruapán. And this road is not open year-round. Trucking supplies to these villages is very expensive. So the supplies have to go by mule. That's the explanation of the mule trains, if anybody notices them. And our supplies move up at night. The villagers who may travel through these trails are our friends. Practically every family around here has a son, a brother, a husband, a father who is a guerrillero. So nobody wants to betray us. No that this would do them any good!

"But on Wednesday it will be different. Thousands of people will start trekking to the top of the mountain, many of them from areas outside Michoacán. And on Wednesday, Massiat will no longer be there. It will go up at dusk tomorrow, as the sun dips into the sea. So those pilgrims who will be brave enough to climb the mountain to the chapel of El Salvador will see nothing of Massiat. Just a landslide on the side of the mountain. There have been earthquakes here before. Have you heard the prophecy of El Salvador?"

"Yes, I have," said Menzies. "Your brother Manuel told me about it. It's very interesting."

"Well, you know about that. Everybody will think a woman was killed on El Salvador. God knows by whom, or how. And the mountain has trembled and exploded, as the prophecy said it would if such a thing happens."

"And what will your next job be?" asked Menzies. "I mean, what are you guerrilleros up here going to do when there is no more Massiat?"

"Amigo, I have no idea. It will be up to the Mexican Revolutionary Army headquarters to give us another job."

"Whatever the Society of Seven is doing up here must be very important. They have gone to all this trouble, to all this expense," said Menzies.

"Oh, yes," said Santos. "It is very important. But I have no idea what they're doing. We are not allowed to speak to the two Mexican scientists we brought here. For this, you must ask Solis. He is the leader of the Society of Seven up here. Tomorrow we also expect Alamut. He is *el comandante*. The man who controls everything about the Society of Seven. He is the chairman of the board and its chief shareholder.

"Solis will tell you about him. Solis is very interested in meeting you. He knows about the way you fought the Federales in Guadalajara. He is full of admiration for you. And he also knows about that dentist. Our people in Guadalajara buried that dentist in the back yard of the house the same night you left. Nobody will ever find him.

"To protect you from your own countrymen, we are telling the newspapers in Guadalajara that the dentist has been taken by the guerrilleros. We are asking a $500,000 ransom for his release. *Inglaterra* still has plenty of money. They will pay to get back their chief agent in Mexico."

Menzies forced himself to laugh. "But my friend, how can you demand ransom for a man who is already dead? It is not fair. I thought the Mexican Revolutionary Army never broke its word!"

"Ah! But we will not break our word. All we have promised is that we will deliver this man to his surgery in Mexico City for $500,000. We didn't say whether he would be alive or dead when we deliver him, eh?"

Menzies patted him in the back. "Muchacho," he said, dragging the word in the usual Mexican style to denote admiration. "You think of everything, everything!"

"Yes, yet," said Santos. Nobody can ever say the guerrilleros have broken their promise!" He paused, reflected a bit, and the possible sarcasm of Menzies' remarks did not escape him. "But of course, let me remind you Don Juan. It was not we who killed this man—how do you call him—Curachas?"

"Car-ru-thers," said Menzies, pronouncing very slowly each syllable.

"*Sí, sí*, Cucarachas," said Santos. He burst out in laughter. "I like your gringo language, amigo. Cucarachas is a good name for that dentist . . . .

"But as I was telling you, it was you who killed the cucaracha dentist. And you did a pretty good job on him, too.

"When we abduct people who are our enemies and then offer to return them to their homes for the payment of ransom, we do not kill them. It is against our principles. We are not murderers. We do not kill people who are in our custody, unarmed. Never. This is a matter of honor with us. We are honorable fighters, not assassins. We kill national traitors, sadists who capture and torture our men. But we kill them with honor. We do not capture them first, take them away, and then kill them. We prefer to shoot them down in the street or in their office. There is a big difference. That's why we admire you, Juancito. You killed the four Federales and

Cucaracha because they tried to kill you. You didn't capture them, tie them up, and then torture them to death. That is why we call you a real hombre."

Menzies felt he could not argue against Santos' philosophy on the issue of honorable killing. "Thank you, Santos," he said. "I like what you say and I agree with you. And that is the reason why I feel honored that I am here to serve the guerrilleros. And I know I owe you my life."

Santos looked at him very carefully. Then, with a flourish, he offered him his hand. Menzies shook it, warmly and sincerely.

"I am glad Geralda brought you to us," said Santos. "She recognized you for what you are. And that is why she loves you."

"Where *is* Geralda?" Menzies asked.

"In Morelia, together with Leon. They will meet Alamut and his friends there. Then they'll escort them to the crossways near Uruapan. Then Manuel will lead all of them to Massiat. They should be here tomorrow afternoon.

"Did you say Alamut? The name sounds strangely familiar."

"Yes, Alamut. Do you know him?"

"No, no," said Menzies. "It's just that I've read something about this name. I think in history . . . medieval Persian history . . . oh yes, I remember now. Alamut, it means Eagle's Nest in ancient Persian . . . it was a fortress, a big castle in Persia, the headquarters of . . ." Menzies stopped midway through the sentence. The wrinkles around his eyes became a shade deeper. His mind eagerly began to sort out, bits and pieces of information he had picked during the few days he had spent with the guerrilleros.

Santos interrupted his thoughts. "If it's history, Solis will know about it. He is a professor of history as well as a civil engineer. He'll enjoy talking to you, because you speak Arabic and like the history of those countries."

"I want to meet him, too," said Menzies. He paused, and his voice changed as he asked: "What happens to me when Massiat is finished? I mean, do I stay with you, in the Uruapan district?"

"Juan, I don't really know. We want you with us. But the Society of Seven also wants you. You are popular, Juancito! I think they have some plans for you. They may take you out of Mexico. You'll be lucky if they do, because they pay very well. They look after their people. And they are part of a big international organization. They could smuggle you out of Mexico without any problem at all."

"Oh, I see," said Menzies. The idea of joining the Society of Seven, in whatever project they had in mind, did not appeal to him. All he knew was that they were some sort of Arab secret society, financed no doubt with oil funds. Projecting his thoughts further, Menzies figured that an Arab international secret society, financed with oil money, was likely to be linked to any of a number of movements for the liberation of Palestine. He thought it was bad enough to be linked with the Mexican guerrilleros. Joining up with an Arab secret society, which could turn out to be a terrorist outfit, was just too much. Even for him in his present predicament. He reckoned he had had more than his share of trouble in the last week alone!

Picking his words carefully, Menzies said: "Santos, I'm grateful and honored by the interest of the Society of Seven. But I happen to be in love with your sister, Geralda. And I want to stay with her."

"Juan, Juan," Santos interrupted him. "The world all around us is in trouble. It's in flames.

"What choice do people like me and you have? We are just pawns, ants. We are insignificant, amigo! And in your position, if I were in your position, I would take every opportunity to get out of Mexico. There are traitors even among ourselves. There's a million pesos on your head!

"I'm saying this amigo, because I love you. All of us guerrilleros like you. We would like you to stay with us. But you will be able to help our cause better from outside Mexico. We must consider that, too.

"Anyhow, whether you will stay with us or go with the Society of Seven is still unsettled. So relax, amigo. Solis will meet you in a few minutes and talk to you.

"We will be busy all night preparing this place for the explosion tomorrow. Whatever the scientists and Solis have been preparing here is now finished. And it must be very light. Because they will not even need a single mule to carry it. It's just three small cases, each about the size of that typewriter we brought for you from Uruapán yesterday. Everything else is going up."

"What happens to the two Mexican scientists working over here? Are they leaving Mexico with Alamut?"

Santos' face grew serious. "Solis told me they had an accident. They were electrocuted. We buried them this morning down in the ravine."

"Accident?" asked Menzies.

"Yes, amigo. That's what I was told, anyhow. But I am not happy about this. We have lost a million pesos in ransom money. We took them from their homes and told their wives we would bring them back. Now we cannot keep our promise. They are dead. But it was not our fault. I saw their bodies myself. No bullet holes, no knife wounds. Just some burns on their fingers. They were electrocuted. I believe Solis."

"And the nine other assistants? What about them?"

"They are fine. They are Arabs, all of them from the universities of Cairo and Baghdad. They will be leaving with Solis and Alamut tomorrow. And so will the two Arab guards who came with Solis." Santos looked at his watch. "Well, amigo, it is time. Let us go to meet Solis."

CHAPTER EIGHT

For Geralda

S antos pulled a lever behind them, and a section of the tunnel wall began to move. It opened and they entered an acre-size, oval-shaped area where the hum of air conditioners and the draft of cool air was a welcome change from the oppressing heat and humidity inside the tunnel.

On the far side of this cavern, brightly lit by scores of fluorescent tubes, were three thirty-foot tables. Masses of electronic equipment lay on them. A four-foot-square panel of switches and colorful indicator lights was built into the rock above them. The cement floor of the cavern showed a number of cracks. Over them hovered tiny clouds where the damp heat of the rock was constantly eliminated by the cool dry air of the air conditioners. On one side of the cavern there was a huge, L-shaped desk, several filing cabinets, and half a dozen sheepskin-covered armchairs. The air conditioners operated through three circular, two-foot ventilation shafts in the ceiling. An intricate system of tubing carried the cool, dry air to two dozen points in the cavern.

A door opened behind the workshop tables, and a tall; slim, bearded figure appeared, dressed in white overalls and a red fez. He was followed by two shorter men, similarly dressed, who carried Tommy guns.

The tall man went over to Menzies with extended arms. He embraced him, kissed him on both cheeks in the traditional fashion, then took his hand and led him to an armchair near the desk. "Welcome, Menzies," said Solis, in a deep, throaty voice. "Peace be with you, my son, and may the glory of Allah put steel and fire in your right arm to punish those who have sought to kill you. So say I, your eternal fried, Eredin Kara Aslan. But please, call me Solis."

"And with you, may peace rest forever," Menzies replied in Arabic. "Divine providence has bestowed upon you a splendid name, Kara Aslan—black lion."

"Ah! I see! You are not only an Arab scholar, but you also understand the Turkish language," Solis said graciously.

"Not so, my beloved host," Menzies said.

"I am delighted, my son, that providence has brought to me such an erudite visitor. Living here for the last three years deprived me of much good conversation."

Menzies nodded. "You are Turkish, *effendi?"*

"I am not a Turk, though my name is of Turkish origin. I am a Kurd, from Sivas, in Anatolia. And for ten years before coming here I was dean of the faculty of history and political sciences of the University of Basra in Iraq. But this background has been of no use to me over here. Only by engineering knowledge has been of help to me. I am an associate member of the Institute of Civil Engineering of Britain."

"I am honored to meet you, Solis," said Menzies, with a trace of respect in his voice, as etiquette required.

Solis sat down behind his desk. His two bodyguards, whom Solis introduced as Palestinian liberation workers, moved a few paces away but remained standing.

"I have heard of your recent auspicious deeds, my son, performed in the name of justice and holy retribution. And I understand the kind of man you are. So I will dispense with protocol and hope you will excuse my manners, which require me to let you rest after your long trip to Massiat.

"But I must ask you certain questions, my son, which I know you will answer with the clarity of a pure mountain stream descending from Mount Ararat. May the sound of your words be refreshing and musical to my ears."

Menzies realized that his life might well depend on the answers he gave. So he mentally braced himself. He also recognized that Solis was anxious to come to the point of Menzies' visit. "I am ready, Solis," he said.

"What do you consider happiness, my son, when you view the question from the uncertainties of your present position?" Solis' voice was sweet, soothing.

Menzies didn't take long to answer. "Happiness is peace," he said. He had stolen a well-worn cliché from the vocabulary of some pot-headed intellectual hippies he had once interviewed while covering a marijuana-smuggling story for a Vancouver daily newspaper. He knew that nobody, certainly nobody in the Arab world, could fault that answer. Nonetheless he quickly decided to qualify it. "I mean peace of soul and mind as well as peace of body," he added.

"I'm glad you've put peace of soul and mind ahead of peace of body," said Solis. "Most people think that peace is indivisible, but it is not. For what good is peace of soul if it can be terminated with the body?

"Nobody knows exactly when he is going to die—not even those condemned to death; even when the executioner approaches there still lingers the hope of a last-minute reprieve. Not even the incurably ill know when they are going to die, though they see their most beloved relatives begin to fight over the possessions which they hope to inherit."

"That is quite true," said Menzies. "Peace of soul, eternal peace, is the one peace worth pursuing."

"And how can such peace be achieved, my son?" asked Solis.

Menzies thought fast. He sensed a loaded question. He had already begun to guess, from the word "Alamut," that the Society of Seven might be linked with the infamous *hashishin.* "Peace achieved in the pursuit of a noble and just cause is eternal peace," he said, groping for oracular obfuscation.

"Your answer is correct but not complete," said Solis. "Peace in the pursuit of a noble and just cause can only be eternal if eternity of soul and thought is guaranteed by God. And the only true God is He who can prove to the satisfaction of your mind and soul that He is the true "God."

"Yes," said Menzies.

"To what religion do you belong, my son?"

"I was baptized a Scottish Presbyterian. But I know very little about religion."

"Are you circumcised, my beloved son?"

"No."

"Very well. That is all I have to ask you for the moment. I know you must be very tired. Please excuse me for keeping you up so late with these questions.

"I am about to light a pipe, and I hope you will do me the honor to join me in this traditional token of peace, hospitality, and friendship."

"My pleasure," said Menzies.

Solis took out a long, silver-stemmed pipe with a half-pint silver bowl. He placed the bowl of the pipe on an electric heater and dropped a tiny ball of a black, oily substance into it. Menzies sniffed the smell of burning hashish. Solis inhaled a couple of times and passed the pipe to Menzies, who knew he had to go through with the ritual. He took a puff, tried not to inhale, blew the smoke out of his nostrils, and began to cough. He was choking. He coughed and coughed, and went all red in the face and around the neck, so that Solis had to get up and pat him on the back.

"Breathe deeply, my son," Solis said. "And do not be afraid. You will soon recover. You have not inhaled, but you have tried. You have much to learn."

Menzies recovered. "I'm sorry," he said. "I thought I was going to choke."

"I understand, I understand," said Solis. "It is difficult at first. In time you will see that this pipe brings peace of mind, which in turn contributes to peace of soul. And that is the most exquisite state which a human being can achieve—eternity with the only true God."

"Yes, Solis," said Menzies.

"Now, my son. You have answered my questions. I am ready to answer yours." He returned to his seat behind the desk. Even that single puff of hashish had clouded his mind. A nebulous cobweb had spread over his brain; he fought to keep himself balanced and alert. He now knew why people who smoked marijuana and hashish were called potheads. Though perhaps it did produce a temporary serenity, hashish destroyed coordination. It was the serenity which comes from the death of all logical thought, not the serenity which results from a philosophical acceptance of life. Hashish numbed the mind.

Menzies chose his words very carefully. "I am here to publicize the cause of the guerrilleros," he said. "And I will be glad to help you in any way I can. My first question is, in what way? I would also like to know what *is* Massiat? What are you doing here on this mountain?"

Menzies didn't really expect full answers to these direct questions. But neither did he expect Solis to lie. Lies are dreadful traps in any kind of questioning, because once they are discovered the credibility of the speaker is gone forever. When this happens, the suspect (in this case himself) is constantly on his guard. Then the business of getting at the truth becomes infinitely more difficult.

Menzies also knew that the very bluntness of his questions would help convince Solis that he, Menzies, was on the level, that he did not fear Solis, and that he had nothing to hide. Long experience in interrogation had taught Menzies that sometimes you learn more about a person from the questions he asks than from the answers he gives. Menzies did not want to appear too discreet, too cautious, and therefore a man whose intentions could be suspect.

Solis took his time to answer. "Massiat will be destroyed tomorrow," he said. "This you have probably heard from Manuel and Santos. Our job here has ended." He paused before continuing.

"But because I am speaking to *you,* I do not think I am any longer bound by the strict secrecy which has been essential for our work in Massiat."

It was Solis now who picked his words carefully. "My son, we have completed here certain instruments which are valuable to us in our world-wide campaign against oppression. To fight oppression, you must have weapons, as well as dedicated men motivated by justice and inspired by the pursuit of eternal happiness.

"The instruments we have built here will be used in conjunction with certain defensive weapons. Two Mexican scientists have helped us produce these instruments. This morning, I regret to say, they met with an accident and are now dead. But their work, which to some small extent I was able to supervise, lives on.

"Because our cause is misunderstood in so many parts of the world, we did not have the facilities to build these instruments elsewhere. So we went to the expense, and the labor, to build Massiat and equip it suitably in order to produce these instruments in peace, away from possible interference.

"We are a religious group, my son. We believe in God, who ordains our acts. Our religion originates from what you Christians would call the eleventh century. As an Arab-history scholar, no doubt you have heard about us. We have inherited the original, pure, honorable Ismailite faith. Our Moslem enemies have called it the Shi-a heresy. But it is they who are heretics. We believe that the true missionaries of Allah on earth are not those installed in power right now. We believe that usurpers have betrayed the true faith. They have distorted the true meaning of the Koran, and by doing this they have brought the wrath of God upon our Moslem World.

"The Aga Khan is an impostor. Besides being of doubtful ancestry himself, the fact is that his ancestors deviated from the true Ismaili faith and usurped the title with the help of Egyptian lances. The line of the Aga Khan survived the centuries only with the help of Mongol arrows and the armored cavalry of the Mamelukes of Egypt.

"But we are the disciples of Hassan-i-Sabbah, the only true missionary of the Ismaili faith. We are the faithful followers of the Sheik-el-Jebel, whom you, in your Western histories, call the Old Man Of The Mountain.

"At one time, in our part of the world, they called us *hashishin*—users of hashish. This was true, in a sense; but then, everybody in our world used hashish, which has universally-accepted healing properties. What we object to is that the world hashishin implied that we were the only users of hashish, that the use of hashish is something bad, criminal, and outrageous.

"Then your Crusaders came. In their utter ignorance, they corrupted this simple Arabic word and turned us into 'Assassins.'

"Now, I know, my son, that you have studied history from our own Arab sources. Therefore you may be more prejudiced against the religion of Hassan-i-Sabbah than other Westerners.

"But the truth is that we are neither heretics nor assassins.

"We are simply defenders of our faith. And we have always been defenders of our faith. Do you know what the purpose of our faith has always been? Let me tell you. It has always been, it still is, to shake despotism to its foundations; to strike fear into the hearts of the oligarchs, to dispossess the oppressors of the people.

"In many ways, we are revolutionaries. We collect money from the rich and protect the poor. And we make no distinction among the oppressors, though naturally we must first strike at those oppressors who profess the same faith as ourselves, the Moslem oppressors.

"You have heard of the Arab League, of course?"

"Yes, I have," said Menzies.

"They are our worst enemies. We have marked them all for execution when the call comes from the Sheik-el-Jebel. Arab League members know this. But it is too late for them to do anything about it. They hope to appease us with various donations and gifts. We accept these gifts. But only when they repent and acknowledge the true faith of Hassan-i-Sabbah, only when they express regret for persecuting our religion—the only true Moslem religion, only when they display humility, will they save themselves from destruction. Their gifts just buy time. And not very much time.

"Our faith, my son, is based on principles. It is not restricted by narrow, religious boundaries. There are many cases in history, acknowledged even in the history of our most implacable Moslem enemies, in which we supported infidel Christians oppressed by Moslem conquerors. We help all peoples oppressed by dictators.

"During my many months here I have been translating into modern Arabic one of the few genuine histories of our religion. This history escaped the destructive frenzy of the Mongol soldiery when they captured Alamut. And to be sure, they captured it by treason; because the Mongols obtained the services of a man who was the spitting image, the absolute double of Rukn-ad-Din, the Sheik-el-Jebel at the time. The Mongols brought this impersonator before the gate of Alamut and he called upon the garrison commander to surrender to the Mongols. The commander believed he was speaking to the real Sheik-el-Jebel and obeyed. He opened the gates. That is how Alamut fell to the Mongols. They would have never taken it otherwise.

"When I finish the translation of this real history, of our faith, I will have it published, so all the world can see how we helped defend the poor against the rich, how we struck fear in the hearts of the emirs, the sheiks, the *atabegs,* and even the sultans—who had surrounded themselves with harems, gold, jewelry, and mercenaries while the people starved and begged.

"These rich, powerful men used and continue to use, our own Moslem faith to bind and blind the Arabs, to drug them with false promises and turn them into willing tools of their own destructions. The Christian religion has been used by your dukes, counts, earls, kings, dictators, financiers, communist commissars, industrialists, bankers, governments, to subdue and enchain your own spirit of freedom, justice, and equality."

Solis stopped talking, and Menzies remained silent. When Solis resumed speaking, his voice quickly rose to a high pitch of excitement.

"My son, as long as there is oppression and injustice, true men and true religions will rise, inspired by the teachings of Hassan-i-Sabbah—which are universal—to strike down the oppressors. That is why we have risen, at the command of Hassan-i-Sabbah, after so many centuries, to defend the people of the world—all the world—against exploitation, oppression, and indignity.

"And our first target must be this hideous Yehudi State of Israel. This cancerous growth thrives in the very heart of our Moslem region. This nation of criminals uses military power to frighten and oppress the people of Palestine.

"The Egyptians, the Jordanians, the Lebanese, and even the Syrians are led by traitors. These traitors are ready to accept almost any solution which the United States and the Soviet Union—both oppressive powers—are likely to impose. But not we. Not the true Ismailites, inspired by the voice of Hassan-i-Sabbah."

Solis lapsed into a long silence, and Menzies felt no urge to interrupt it. When Solis spoke again, his voice had reverted to its soothing earlier tone. "I must apologize to you, my son. I have been carried away by what I was saying. You must be very tired." Solis looked at his watch. It was past two.

"Let me show you to your room," said Solis. "We shall talk again tomorrow."

He led the way to a ten-foot-square, cell-like room. Through a ventilation shaft in one corner blew cool mountain air. The only furniture was a bed and a small bookcase containing the seven-volume *History of the Prophet,* in Persian, by His Eminence The Emir Shafrulillah Mahmoud el Mansour, May His Brilliance Light The Sky of Ignorance Forever. The date of this massive work—after Menzies figured out the difference between the Moslem and Christian calendars—was September 1372. About the time of Tamerlane, thought Menzies.

With a polite bow and the words "Peace be with you," Solis left the room. Menzies looked around and saw another door. It led to a private bathroom with spartan but adequate facilities. There was another ventilation shaft in the bathroom. Menzies returned to the bedroom, noticed that Solis had left the exit door open, closed it, switched off the lights, and lay on the bed fully clothed.

He was soon immersed in thought. The long talk with Solis had left him mentally and psychologically shaken.

Physicial threats he understood. What he feared was a powerful, incontrovertible ideology. His mind groped years back to everything he had read about the Assassins. Arab books, particularly Moslem religious books, condemned this criminal heresy much more than Western history books did, and with good reason. For itwas the Moslems who had suffered most from the extortion and murder unleashed upon the world from the Erbruz.

And now, by a strange twist of misfortune, he was in a modern Assassin stronghold. What's more he was a potential ally. They were grooming him for service among the suicidal hashishin.

From what he had read about the Assassins, their brainwashing system was superior to anything devised so far. Through drugs they had been able to penetrate the minds and the psyches of prospective recruits and to distort their values. In due course, the hashishin indoctrination system was able to subdue and totally eclipse even the most elementary human instinct—that of self-preservation. Hashishin were ready to die. In fact, they sought death in carrying out the will of the Old Man Of The Mountain.

And he, Menzies, a fugitive from law, a wanted killer, had already been subjected to the first mild brainwashing, to the first "lesson" in the system of the Assassins. And he had felt the effects—a slight haze over his mind which for a while dimmed his sense of values, his sense of balance, and his perspective.

Menzies was gripped by a strange fear, one against which his Luger and his three knives, provided little reassurance. Of one thing he was glad. His thoughts were still his own. They were completely private. No one could see them, nobody could read them, nobody could sense them. Not yet. . . .

Menzies lit a cigarette and quickly reviewed the events of the last few days. The ugly affair at the Roma Hotel, Carruthers, Geralda, the guerrilleros, his cable to Young and Young's reply, the prophecy of El Salvador, the talk with Solis.

He didn't like his situation at all. He was worse off now than the night he faced the four Federales in Guadalajara. He had never figured, not even in his wildest nightmares, that his link with the guerrilleros would lead to the hashishin. God! No wonder Young in London pricked up his ears the moment he mentioned the series of seven. No wonder the Secret Service, the CIA, and God knows who else were anxious to know more about the Society of Seven.

Menzies had no way of telling whether his former E Force colleagues, who had been brought together obviously for some very good reason, had realized that the Society of Seven were hashishin—Assassins. And he had no way of telling whether Rod and the others knew what the Assassins were doing at Massiat.

What the hell were those "instruments" Solis had mentioned? Judging by what little he had seen, they appeared to be some kind of electronic devices, built by two of Mexico's best electronics engineers, who were now dead. Menzies didn't doubt for a minute that the two engineers had been murdered by Solis when they had done their job. For security reasons, obviously.

And what *were* these electronic devices, these . . . instruments? They were to be used in conjunction with some "defensive" weapon. What kind of weapon? Must be some weapon big enough, destructive enough, to justify all this trouble, all this expense. Atomic bombs! Could be other weapons, too. Gas, for example. Or even germs. Maybe laser beams. Who knows what else? But the most likely mass weapon would be atomic bombs. Yes, atomic bombs. An atomic bomb is much more spectacular and sensational than either gas or germs. Judging by history, the hashishin preferred sensational, spectacular killings.

Menzies snuffed out his cigarette and lit another. What had all this got to do with him, anyhow? So the Society of Seven was planning to explode atomic bombs somewhere, maybe kill a million people. What could he do about it? Nothing. What was he supposed to do about it? Get himself killed in some fool-hardy effort to stop them? To hell with that! He was already in plenty of trouble right now. His first responsbility must be to stay alive, to save his own life, to try and get out of this mess. He was already an outlaw, wanted for murder in Mexico, and probably in most countries of the world.

And what about his former E Force colleagues? Aris, Atherton, Young, and Rod. Forget them, Johnny boy, Menzies told himself. Goddammit, Rod had instructed the CIA to kill him. The CIA had even put one million pesos on his head. He probably would have done the same thing in Rod's position. He, Menzies, knew too much about E Force. And since they couldn't find him to persuade him to work with them, they had to eliminate him. That's all very fine—for Rod. His life wasn't at stake.

Coming back to E Force and the old, wartime comradeship, he rejected it. Dammit, the war was over—a long, long time ago. Screw the E Force. If the others had been chosen by their governments to hunt down the Society of Seven, that was their business. They figured things out from the safety of London or Washington. They had at their disposal the resources of the CIA, the Royal Canadian Mounted Police, the whole gamut of the British security services. His only resources were his instinct to survive, his Luger and his knives.

As for his colleagues in British intelligence, they could go to hell. Dammit, Carruthers was one of them and had tried to murder him. Sure, sure! He could guess why. And from the point of view of the Old Man in London, the attempt was probably justified—at that time. But why the hell should he, John Menzies, be mixed up in all this? He was just having a good time in Manzanillo, minding his own business, swimming. He had done no one any harm. He hadn't even been indiscreet about his wartime activities thirty years ago, even though he knew that the twenty-year period of secrecy had long since expired.

Then and there Menzies decided he's hadve nothing more to do with E Force, with the Society of Seven, the guerrilleros, even with Geralda. It was better that way. He had tipped off E Force about the Society of Seven. They could take that as his final contribution, a parting gift to an association he had once belonged to.

As for Geralda, it was best that he left her. This poor Mexican girl was stuck on him. He could see that. He knew she'd follow him anywhere. She had taken a few risks with her own outfit by introducing him to the guerrilleros. But that's how it went. He couldn't take her along with him. There were too many uncertainties ahead.

Menzies' thoughts again drifted to E Force. The trouble was that nobody was ever expected to resign from it. Well, he was going to resign. He would disappear, change his name. He'd vanish to some place where nobody could find him. Not Interpol, not E Force, not the CIA, not the Secret Service, not the RCMP. Not anybody.

Menzies never doubted his ability to get out of Massiat. Right now the Society of Seven considered him a potential recruit. They did not suspect that he was planning to leave. He'd surprise them. His main problem wasn't getting out of Massiat; it was getting out of Mexico and evading his pursuers afterward.

Now, where could he go, so nobody would find him? It didn't take him long to settle on a hideout. It would be the tiny, one-square-mile island of

Manono, in western Samoa, in the South Pacific. It was a delightful little island, with wonderful sandy beaches all around it, with terrific swimming and fishing inside the coral reef.

On Manono live five hundred care-free, beautiful, lovable, honest Polynesians. Their chief, Aaa-tofau Faalimanau, was a good friend of his. He was bound, by Polynesian tradition, to offer him hospitality. And Menzies didn't intend becoming a bum on the island. He'd teach the children English, bring over a short-wave radio and a tape recorder, so they could listen to American jazz, which they loved.

What a delightful way of life these Polynesian islanders had, Menzies ruminated. They owned everyting communally. The lacked nothing really necessary in life. They went to church every Sunday and listened to the good word of the Bible. They swam, fished, raised chickens and pigs. They didn't have to cultivate anything; everything they need grows naturally year-round. They have breadfuit and eggplant and butter fruit and mangoes; papayas, coconuts, pineapples, bananas; avocados and half a dozen other tropical fruits and vegetables.

Nothing that conceivably can harm a human being lives on the island. No snakes, poisonous spiders, scorpions, mosquitoes, or stinging bugs of any kind. No sharks within the reef, no poisonous stonefish, absolutely nothing that can do any harm. He could walk naked in the jungle that covers the center of the island and sleep at night in the bush, without fear of harm. People don't really need clothes, anyhow, because temperatures range from 78 to 88 degrees, day and night, year-round. People don't really need houses, because when it rained, regularly every afternoon, everyone rushes out to have a shower. Yes, he'd get out of this mess and go to Manono, Menzies decided.

Having made this decision, Menzies somehow felt happier. Now he had an objective, a philosophy, a goal, a cause to fight for, a haven, and a paradise of his own—a better paradise than that which motivated the hashishin.

Once again Menzies' thoughts reverted to the CIA, to E Force, to the British Secret Service. Come to think of it, there was a good chance that Young had called off the search. They should have realized that at least for the moment, he was a valuable asset, an investment in the right place—among the Society of Seven in Massiat.

The more he thought about this angle, the more he realized that this line of thinking was justified. After all, he had already provided a valuable service. Menzies could make an educated guess about what the other E Force men were thinking. They would guess that he was close to the Society of Seven, closer than they had managed to get. He had already provided a valuable service by tipping them off. They would figure that he was the key to Massiat. So they'd want him to stay alive and in excellent health. _____

His problem was now the Mexican police. Four Federales had been killed; someone would have to explain their death; and the only one who could do so was Menzies. So they would keep looking for him.

What made it easier to resign from E Force was that he wasn't on anybody's payroll. He had asked for one thousand pounds, and they had sent it to him. This thought was a little disturbing. Maybe they thought this money obligated him to serve.

Well, they could keep their money. He wouldn't go to the bank to pick it up. Since the money was addressed to "Smith," the guerrilleros would pick it up on his behalf. That was just too bad. He'd have to cable Young, first chance he had, and tell him that he had changed his mind, that he wasn't going to take it, And Young would believe him; he should know him well enough to believe him.

Menzies looked at his watch. It was 4:00 A.M. His thoughts once more drifted to Geralda. What a lovely girl! How lucky he was that she had fallen in love with him! The only woman he had met, in six months, that really appealed to him. And now, what a bit of bad luck! He'd have to leave her. After all the promises they had exchanged! Geralda, who had helped him get over his broken marriage, who had risked her life for him, would never know, never, that he just had to leave without her. For her own sake! Sadness and despair filled him as his mind lingered on Geralda.

Menzies looked at his watch again. It was four-fifteen. No point looking back, only ahead, and at the blue Pacific horizon, where that enchanting, lonely little island beckoned him. Menzies felt the need to encourage himself. "Come on, John Menzies," he whispered to himself. "One more battle, one last fight; and if you win, maybe with luck you'll find a new and happier life." He swung his legs off the bed and stood in the dark. His eyes were adjusted to the darkness, broken only by the faintest gleam of reflected moonlight creeping through the ventilation shaft. He moved around the room, examined the walls, examined the shaft. Too small for his 200-pound frame to wriggle through. He went to the bathroom, examined the walls there, returned to the bedroom, took another look at the door. It was still unlocked. But he knew this could be a trap.

Menzies switched the lights on and began to cough loudly. He picked up one of the volumes of *The History of the Prophet* and pretended to read. He hoped he could draw attention, then somebody might knock at the door and ask him if he wanted anything. He was disappointed. But a little while later he heard people talking in the oval-shaped cavern, so he opened the door. He noticed that one of the large tables had been cleared, and that the two guards he had met earlier that night were busy serving breakfast to nine other men sitting around the table.

Menzies went out and joined them. They were the Arab technicians assisting in the Massiat project. They exchanged customary greetings and polite remarks as Menzies pulled up a chair and sat down. Breakfast consisted of a large bowl of hot milk into which large pieces of bread had been dipped and softened. He ate, then asked the two guards, who still carried Tommy guns slung over their shoulders, to take him to Solis.

The huge door opened, and Menzies stepped out of the cavern. Followed by the two guards, he walked along the tunnel to the spot near the entrance where Solis was standing. Solis and Santos were busy laying wires and setting fuses. Around them hovered the guerrilleros, digging holes in the rock, carrying cases of gelignite, untangling coils of cord.

Solis went over to Menzies. "And what, my beloved son, has brought you up so early?" he asked.

"I got used to getting up early when I was at the guerrilleros camp," said Menzies. "I know this is going to be a glorious day for you, Solis. And since I hope to be associated with you, this will be a glorious day for me, too. So I want to see and enjoy all of it."

Solis looked at him steadily. "All right, my son. Ahmed and Hamdi will show you whatever you wish to see." He nodded at the two guards. "I will be with you as soon as I can."

Followed by Ahmed and Hamdi, Menzies went to the mouth of the tunnel. The first gleam of daylight was just rising over the peak of El Salvador. The roar of the waters of Rio Bravo was audible again, but the suspension bridge had been withdrawn.

Menzies stepped over to the edge of the ravine and then turned and looked back. He could see no one outside the tunnel. But he noticed a long piece of leftover cord. He knew there was no time to waste. He had to act while the shadows of night still lingered. Casually he drew a packet of Mexican Fiesta cigarettes from his pocket and lit one. Making it look like an afterthought, he offered cigarettes to the two guards beside him.

With his left hand Menzies flicked his cigarette lighter but held the flame low, forcing Ahmed to bend his head down to light his cigarette. Then Menzies' right hand, the palm open and stiff, came down like an axe on Ahmed's neck. And his left fist, with the cigarette lighter now in it, at the same time swung in a heavy uppercut that crashed halfway between Hamdi's chin and the base of his jawbone.

The action was so sudden and swift, the blows so surgically accurate, that the two hashishin hit the ground without as much as a groan.

Menzies quickly relieved them of the Tommyguns. He slung one over his shoulder, threw the other into the Rio Bravo. Then he grabbed the cord, tied one end of it to the protruding root of a tree near the precipice and began to climb down to the Rio Bravo.

It took him less than fifteen minutes to make his way about five hundred feet downsteam, wade across the shallow waters, climb the hundred feet on the other side of the slope, and hit the muletrain track. His heart pounded, and his temples throbbed. He breathed huge draughts of clear mountain air to restore the oxygen to his blood.

Menzies guessed that at Massiat they were already looking for him. But he reckoned it would take some time before they got the suspension bridge across to the other side. They might not even bother to chase him at all. There was little that Menzies could do against them. He could not report the existence of Massiat to the Mexican police, because he was wanted by the police.

He started down the mountain trail and from time to time stopped to listen for pursuers. He heard nothing. He also stopped to gaze at the imposing silhouette of El Salvador, now clearly visible in the emerging daylight.

He was free. He was on his own. He liked it that way. Because he could rely on himself. But Menzies wasn't happy. Far from it. How could he be happy when yet another dream, another illusion, was quickly vanishing—this time among the mountains of Michoacán. It was the dream of Geralda and the illusion of an end to the wanderings which had taken him all over the world.

The sun rose behind the mountains. Soon the night dew began to evaporate, creating a haze along the mountain sides. Menzies stopped and once again turned his eyes to the little chapel with the huge cross on top of El Salvador, now perhaps four or five miles away. It seemed to sparkle in the early morning sunlight and turn from white to yellow, to gold, and crimson red. He stood there for a while, watching the top of El Salvador, remembering the prophecy which Manuel the previous night had told him. Then he turned and continued down the mountain.

The winding trail, often hidden amidst the pine forest, twisted and turned and crossed half a dozen clear, cool, fast-moving streams. Menzies reached the spot where Manuel's muleteers had stopped for dinner, the spot where the Chapaqa Indians once had their camp. He felt tired after his sleepless night. So he got off the trail, climbed a few hundred feet to the top of a nearby hill, and lay down on the mattress of pine needles to give himself some rest. He was soon asleep.

He dreamed he was at the Roma Hotel in Guadalajara, and Geralda was singing his favorite tune, the old Cuban song, "El Manicero." The lyrics of the song did not mean very much to Menzies. His knowledge of Spanish was limited, his understanding of the Spanish-American culture modest, and he had never been to Cuba. So it was mostly the music, the exquisite rhythm, the tune, which stirred and fascinated him. Plus, of course, the dim memory of the movie he had seen many many years ago. In his dreams, Menzies now relived the story of the movie.

He was a U.S. Marine in Cuba who had fallen in love with a beautiful Cuban girl. But then he broke some military regulations and was banned from Cuba. He was posted to Guam, and it took him seven years to get his release from the Marine Corps. But the memory of that Cuban girl never faded; he returned to Cuba to find her. She had disappeared. Then, in a remote village where he had been searching for her, he heard a little boy humming "El Manicero." This was a very old Cuban song which very few people knew at the time, and his Cuban girl friend had often sung it when he had served in her country with the Marines. Menzies—the U.S. Marine in his dream—asked the little boy where he had learned that tune. The boy told him that his mother had taught it to him, and that she was now dead. Menzies—the Marine—took another look at the little boy, asked him his age, and realized it was his son.

Menzies himself was only a little boy when he had seen that movie, but for some reason the story and the tune had stuck in his mind throughout the years. It became his favorite Latin-American tune, and he had danced to its exotic rhythm in night clubs from Beirut to Algiers, and from Athens to Barcelona, Lisbon, London, Brussels, New York, and Rio.

Menzies woke up from his dream, and to his surprise the strains of "El Manicero" were still in the air. He looked around. There, faraway on the top of another hill, he noticed a young shepherd singing. . .

> *Maaaniiii . . . .! Maaaniiii . . . .!*
> *Caserita no te vayas a dormir,*
> *Sin comerte un cucurucho de mani.*
>
> *Cuando la calle sola está,*
> *Casera de mi corazón.*
>
> *El manicero entona su pregón,*
> *Y mi negra sale a su balcón,*
> *En busca de su mani.*
>
> *Maaaniiii . . .! Maaaniiii . . .!*
> *El manicero se vááááá . . .!*

Menzies looked at his watch. It was 2:00 P.M., and the sun had already dipped in the sky. He got up. His plan was simple. And he knew it was also feasible. He'd strike the track again and make his way to the tarred road east of Uruapan. He'd then hijack a passing car and drive right through the night to Acapulco, using a variety of mountain roads and avoiding the main intersections. He reckoned if he got a suitable car at dusk, he should be able to make Acapulco by midday. Sunday. He'd dump the car at a spot before Acapulco, then get lost there.

He'd take time to write a report to Young, telling him all he knew about the Society of Seven, as a sort of final gesture to E Force. This gesture would also discharge his obligation to society—the obligation that compelled him to report the outrageous crime planned by the hashishin. Then he'd phone his Jewish friend in Mexico City, Chaim Beja, and ask help in getting out of Mexico. And he knew Chaim would help him, because Chaim understood Menzies personality. For Menzies wouldn't be asking Chaim for charity. In exchange for Chaim's help, Menzies would tell him all he had learned about the Society of Seven. This information, Menzies knew, would help to alert Chaim's Zionist organization. But Chaim's strongest motivation in helping him, Menzies felt sure, would be friendship, trust, and respect.

Confident that his escape plan would succeed, Menzies quickly began to descend towards the brown line which trailed down from Massiat.

The strains of "El Manicero" were still in his ears as he bounded over rocks and fallen logs. Less than a hundred yards from the trail, his eyes caught movement. He abruptly stopped.

First appeared a huge sombrero and then under it the stocky little figure of Pablito, the guerrillero messenger boy, strolling up the hill on his way to Massiat.

Menzies yelled: "Hey! Pablito! Where are you going, muchacho, in such a hurry?"

Pablito stopped. "Don Juan, it's you!" he yelled back. His pale face lit up into a wide grin. "Don Juan, I have a message for you, come over."

Menzies leaped onto the trail and gave Pablito a few friendly slaps on the face. Pablito's eyes were bulging with admiration for Menzies. The story of Menzies in Guadalajara, exaggerated and embellished, had gone around the guerrilleros campfires until in Pablito's boyish mind Menzies had become the greatest hero of all time. Menzies had fought and killed, single-handed, four dreaded Federales. For Pablito, Menzies personified everything that was good, honorable, brave and fearless.

"Here, Don Juan," said Pablito. "This message came for you today. But what are you doing over here? I thought you were at Massiat."

Menzies took the telegram form, unfolded it, and read:

DAILY TELEGRAPH EDITOR UTOM WARNS THAT OWING
SERIOUS LACK OF SPACE YOU MUST ELIMINATE REPEAT
ELIMINATE ALL SUPERFLUOUS COPY RE SERIES OF SEVEN
ARTICLES ON MEXICO STOP SUGGEST YOU USE SAME STYLE
AS IN ABAB THREE ARTICLES YOU HANDLED FOR UTOM IN
THE PAST STOP SUBEDITOR STIDES WHO CHECKED YOUR
COPY BEFORE NO LONGER AVAILABLE OWING SERIOUS ILL-
NESS STOP INTERNATIONAL SYNDICATION THROUGH ROD
ASSURED BUT COULD COME LATE STOP IMPERATIVE YOU
ACT QUICKLY AND SAVE YOURSELF EXTRA REWRITE WORK
BY KEEPING ORIGINAL COPY TIGHT GOOD LUCK YOUNG

Menzies read the telegram, date-marked Mexico City, 23:37 hours, Friday, over and over again. And the smile which played on his face when he
greeted Pablito slowly vanished.

He understood the message perfectly well. UTOM was Uncle Tom, Tom
Buchanan, who headed E Force during World War II but was now dead.
The word ELIMINATE was plain enough, as was the SERIES OF
SEVEN. The words AS IN ABAB THREE ARTICLES puzzled him, but
only for a few seconds. It stood for Abwehr's Abteilung III—the Nazi wartime security and counterespionage section against which E Force had often fought. STIDES no doubt was Aristides, Aris for short. Hell! So they
got Aris, eh?

Deciphering the rest of the wording presented no problem to Menzies.
Rod was coming, with overwhelming forces no doubt, but he might arrive
too late! Too late for what? Too late to stop the destruction of Massiat by
three hundred pounds of gelignite? No, it couldn't be that. Too late to stop
the three "instruments" for the atomic bombs from being delivered to Alamut, and through him God knows where. IMPERATIVE YOU ACT
QUICKLY was in plain language, and so was SAVE YOURSELF. The
rest of the message was just padding.

Menzies sat on a rock and buried his head in his hands. He felt sick at this
twist of events. There he was, groping with a desperate plan to get out of it
all, to be on his way to Manono Island; and now—now Young had placed
the whole damned responsibility on his shoulders. Eliminate the Society of
Seven, said Young. Imperative you act quickly, he said. How the hell could
he eliminate the Society of Seven? Dammit, he didn't even want to eliminate the Society of Seven even if he could. This whole bloody business had
nothing to do with him any more. In fact, it never had anything to do with
him. If E Force, his old buddies, hadn't got the Federales after him, there
would have been no need for him to kill those four cops at the Roma Hotel.
The same for Carruthers. It was they, E Force, who had started all his trou-

bles. Let the sons of bitches finish their job with the Society of Seven by
themselves. He was through. He had resigned. For good. Forever.

Why the hell should he be mixed up in all this? Right now! His brief
career with E Force had consisted of just about only one thing. Murder. He
had been a killer. Not a hired killer, of the Mafia type. More like a hashishin, a killer for a cause. The only difference was that he didn't need hashish to put him into the right frame of mind for murder. He had done it because there happened to be a war on. He believed in the cause for which his
country was fighting. And he had been selected to become a special kind of
killer. Goddammit, that's what soldiers are supposed to do—kill the
enemy. Even Montgomery said that. But he, Menzies, was no longer a soldier. He had been honorably discharged. And on top of it, he had just resigned!

Menzies' mind swiftly moved back three decades to a place in Libya
called Wadi Zem-Zem, about half way between Benghazi and Tripoli. This
was some time before he joined Intelligence and eventually E Force. He
was only a private then, in the Fifth Black Watch Battalion, 153rd Brigade;
51st Highland Division.

The word had spread around the desert camps of the Eighth Army that
Montgomery was going to attack Rommel the next day. Late in the afternoon, when the scorching desert heat had abated, a stream of staff cars had
roared into the Black Watch bivouac area. Out stepped Monty, followed
by the brass.

The troops gathered, informally stretched out on the sand, and Monty
gave them one of his pep talks. He told them that the only job soldiers were
called to do in the army—Monty's army—was kill the enemy.

Menzies, a volunteer and only eighteen at the time, did his job well the
next day at Wadi Zem-Zem. In fact, he did it so well that he was recom-
mended for a commission from the field. He was the first, and youngest,
soldier to be picked for this honor since the 51st Highland Division had arrived in the Middle East.

Menzies first taste of action had been at El Alamein. But after Wadi
Zem-Zem he had developed such a military enthusiasm that he volunteered
for just about every reckless operation available.

Soon the Eighth Army was racing toward Tripoli. One company of his
regiment was chosen to ride on the tanks of an armored brigade and lead
the way into this biggest city of Mussolini's North African empire.

Menzies, riding on the hood of the leading tank, entered Tripoli in the
small hours one morning. Using a tourist map and a torch, he had led the
armored brigade through the deserted city streets, feeling bitterly disappointed that there were no German or Italian troops to shoot at with his

Tommygun. When they reached the sumptuous villa which had been head-quarters for the Italian commander-in-chief in Lybia, Menzies was first off the tank. He raced up the steps to the second floor in pitch darkness and kicked opn the door of the general's office. There was nobody there. The Italians had left, even before the Germans, a few hours earlier. But Menzies found the Italian general's ceremonial sword, with a note to Montgomery, in which he officially surrendered Tripoli. Menzies took the sword and the note, and the next day they were handed over to Montgomery. It had been from this background that he had been eventually picked for Uncle Tom's E Force.

These memories raced through Menzies' mind as he held his head in his hands, torn by conflicting instincts and loyalties, wondering what he should do, what was right for him to do, what his common sense and his maturing wisdom told him he must do.

Menzies got up. He tore Young's telegram to shreds. "I'm leaving," he told Pablito. "I'm going away from here."

"Don Juan, where are you going?" asked Pablito, concern in his voice. "Stay with us, Don Juan."

Menzies shook his head as if clearing it of fumes. Then he noticed another telegram in Pablito's hand.

"Is that one also for me, Pablito?"

"No, señor. It is for the Arab *jefe.*"

"You may give it to me," Menzies said.

"Sí, señor."

Menzies took the other envelope and opened it. There was a message for Solis, all right. It had been scribbled out in Roman characters, but the language was Arabic, and it was signed "Alamut." Translated, the message said: "Kill Menzies now."

Menzies grinned. "So that's how it goes," he whispered to himself. His mind shook off its lethargy. What appeared probable was that Alamut found out about his connection with E Force. This could mean that the Society of Seven had busted wide open the tight security of E Force. That's why Alamut got Aris. E Force and his old buddies were all but beaten. Alamut had got the upper hand in this international contest where those who were vanquished almost invariably died. No wonder Young was screaming for help. And that explained that desperate request, ELIMINATE ALL, which Young must know would be near-suicidal for Menzies.

He read this second message again and again, while Pablito stood beside him in respectful silence.

A deep-rooted, long-dormant instinct urged Menzies to accept Alamut's challenge. Who was this sonofabitch who thought it was going to be so easy to kill Menzies? If he let that challenge unanswered, perhaps something would nag him, deep inside, even if he got as far as Manono Island. He, Menzies, who really had little to live for in any case, had been scared. By a drug-crazed terrorist called Alamut!

But no. To hell with Alamut. Slowly Menzies returned the second message to Pablito. "I'm leaving," he repeated.

"Don Juan, Don Juan," said Pablito, his face a picture of concern and worry. "Geralda is also going to Massiat. She loves you, Don Juan. I know it, I know it. She left for Massiat this morning. Together with Manuel, Alamut, another Arab, and big Leo. They bought many horses. They are going along the other trail, on the other side of the river, the one that joins this trail further up. Don't tell Manuel, Don Juan, but I fell asleep on the way up here. Geralda and the others may have passed already. She's waiting for you at Massiat, Don Juan. Come with me, Don Juan."

But Menzies had made up his mind. His heart choked with conflicting emotions, he raised his hand to Pablito. *"Adiós, muchacho,"* he said. Then he turned and continued down the trail, followed only by the fading voice of the shepherd, still singing "El Manicero".

"Look, Don Juan!" Pablito yelled, pointing at the forest on the other side of the Rio Bravo. "You see those black birds flying around? That's where the other trail is. Go there and wait for them. They'll give you a ride to Massiat on their horses. Wait for them there, Don Juan!"

Menzies wasn't listening. His eyes were on the big black birds, circling a spot on the mountain. He had seen those huge black birds before, riding in the air with dead wings. They were vultures, Mexican vultures commonly known in Michoacán as *zonchos.*

Menzies continued down the mountain. The next turn of the trail brought him closer to Rio Bravo. Once again his eyes drifted to the zonchos. They seemed to be coming down less than two hundred yards away. Instinct, curiosity, a lurking desire to see Geralda for the last time and say adiós, and a subconscious defiance of Alamut drew him toward the other trail.

He climbed down the slope to the Bravo. Holding the Tommygun above his head, he waded into the cool river waist-deep and crossed to the other side. The vultures had desceneded to tree-top level. Frightened by his appearance, they perched in the top branches of the tallest trees.

He reached the other trail and noticed the hoof marks of many horses on the damp ground. Then he saw a blur of contrasting bright yellow under the dark-green trees. He stepped over and saw Geralda. She was dead, lying on her back. Her long, golden hair lay dishevelled around her head. Her bright-yellow skirt was lifted above her thighs. She was naked underneath, her pale legs bruised blue and purple. Her hands tied with a cord. Her white blouse was stained red where the big knife had plunged into her chest, into her heart. She had been raped and stabbed to death. Or possibly the other way around.

Menzies noticed the handle of the knife. It had strange oriental designs on it. It was made of pure silver. He grabbed it and pulled hard to get it out of her body, where rigor mortis had already set in.

He wiped the blood-smeared scimitar on the grass and read the Persian inscription. It said: FROM THE REKINDLED BEACON OF ALAMUT COMES HOLY RETRIBUTION. Menzies also noticed a small gray stamp imprinted on the blade, near the hilt. It was identical to the stamp of his knives, made by the same celebrated Syrian swordsmith, Salah el Faisal & Company. They claimed to use the secret formula by which Saladdin's terrible sword had been fashioned.

Menzies threw the scimitar away. He saw a piece of paper lying near Geralda's neck and picked it up. Someone had scribbled on it in French: "For the treason of this woman, who brought the mad dog Menzies to Massiat, the Sheik-el-Jebel has pronounced the only sentence." It was signed "ALAMUT."

Menzies stuck the piece of paper in his pocket. He sat beside the corpse and lit a cigarette. A tear swelled in his eye. "El Manicero" rang in his ears, growing stronger and stronger. He heard Geralda singing it.

Menzies snuffed out his cigarette and got up. He took another look at the horror in Gerald's face, imprinted there at the moment of her death. He took the silver band from his right wrist and looked at it. On top was his name, engraved in a plaque of gold. Beneath were the Latin words *nemo me impune lacessit.* He let the silver wrist band fall on Gerald's bloody breast. Then he turned and started up the trail towards Massiat.

Menzies passed the corpse of Manuel, recrossed the Rio Bravo a mile upstream, then hit the muletrain path to El Slavador. He noticed the lengthening shadows of the trees as the sun edged closer to the ocean. He hastened his step. Up and up the mountain trail he walked, glad that after the month-long training at Manzanillo he was in top condition.

Then the earth suddenly shook beneath him. The mountain roared as an explosion hammered his eardrums. But not even this muffled the strains of "El Manicero."

Menzies heard voices ahead of him, and the thunder of hooves. He got off the trail, crouched behind a rock, and unlimbered the Tommygun.

In the fading daylight he saw more then a dozen riders coming down the hill, followed by Santos' guerrilleros on foot. They were slowly following the trail, the riders two abreast, bunched together, talking, laughing. One of the riders he recognized as Solis, two others were his bodyguards, the fourth he recognized as Santos, some others were Massiat's Arab technicians, the men he had shared breakfast with that morning.

Menzies leaped into the middle of the trail, blocking their path. "Who's Alamut," he asked.

A man on a big black horse stirred and reached for his pistol and Menzies pressed the trigger of the Tommygun.

It blazed and coughed and shook, sending a spray of .45 bullets in the direction of the riders. Menzies leaped sideways and rolled on the ground, firing short bursts all the way to the cover of the rock, where bullets began to whiz all around him.

He peeped over and saw that the column of riders was in a shambles. Horses reared and neighed, trampling fallen men into pulp, Solis among them. But Alamut, the man on the black horse, was unhurt and rallying his supporters.

The blaze and the rat-a-tat of a machinegun crackled through the shadows and sent chips of rock flying in front of Menzies' nose. He recklessly rose behind the rock, aimed the Tommygun at Alamut and at the mingling remaining riders and pressed the trigger, but the magazine was empty. As he threw the now useless gun at Alamut, something hit him under the right shoulder with such force that it tossed him sideways.

He knew he'd been hit by a bullet but had no idea how bad the wound was. So he stuck his fingers in his mouth and checked the saliva for blood. There was none. But a narrow stream of blood began to seep out from two holes near his armpit where the bullet had entered and left.

Menzies noticed some movement behind the trees about thirty yards to his left. The Luger blazed, and a groan told him that the flat-nosed bullet had found its mark. Again and again the Luger thundered, and two men who had tried to rush him dropped within yards of the spot where Menzies crouched.

"Mohammet! Go behind him!" Alamut yelled in Arabic.

Menzies saw some movement in the grass and switched the Luger to his left hand.

Mohammet rose above the grass and threw something at Menzies. Simultaneously Menzies' free right hand reached for his hip pocket and the blade of a knife flashed through the moonlight before thumping into Mohammet's chest. The object Mohammet had thrown rolled near Menzies' legs. He reached for it and his sense of touch instantly told him what it was, so he threw it at the mass of horses and men. The Mills grenade exploded in midair, tearing flesh beneath it and stampeding horses.

Menzies saw more shadows crawling around him and knew his position was hopeless. His right arm was already feeling stiff. He had two more bullets in his Luger and two more knives. A thought flashed through his mind. "Santos!" he yelled. "Alamut has killed your sister and your brother Manuel. Santos! Can you hear me? It's true!"

A burst of machinegun fire answered him. Chipped pieces of rock exploded into his face and riddled it with scores of deep scratches which soon began to ooze blood.

"Hold your fire, Santos!" Menzies yelled again, quickly changing his position behind the rock. "Alamut has murdered your sister. Geralda is dead. He raped and killed her."

"Don't believe him!" Alamut screamed. But the guerrillero guns suddenly fell silent.

"Let me kill this infidel dog," shouted Alamut and stuck his spurs into the black horse. It moved forward, its mouth full of white froth, and cleared the rock in one giant leap, its hooves hissing through the air as they passed overhead.

Alamut and Menzies fired almost blindly into the respective moving shadows and both missed. The big horse turned around and again they both fired at moving dark targets and missed.

Alamust threw his empty pistol at Menzies and drew a long scimitar. "In the name of Hassani-i-Sabbah you will now die," he said. Menzies, whose gun was also empty, got up and drew a second knife from his hip pocket, but he was unable to throw it, because the black horse had reared again, masking Alamut.

Alamut leaped off his horse and rushed at Menzies. Two Damascus blades clashed, sending sparks into the night. Again and again Alamut thrust at his elusive target, and every time the scimitar met the knife of Menzies.

Santos and his *guerrilleros,* their eyes shining in the moonlight and bulging with excitement, gathered around to watch this mortal duel on the slopes of El Salvador.

The two men thrust and parried and circled each other; twisted and turned and leaped like jungle cats fighting over the carcass of a fresh kill. Their shadows played on the mountainside, on the trail, on the dead and dying horses and men, on the shocked eyes of the guerrilleros, like ghosts of devils performing a dance of death.

Menzies felt the growing numbness in his right arm and knew he couldn't stay in the fight much longer. Sensing this weakness, Alamut lunged at Menzies, but the burning blades clashed again and the two men stood almost face to face, their eyes blazing with hatred, testing each other's strength at the edge of their knives.

A karate kick on the legs from Alamut sent Menzies rolling on the ground. His dart knife fell from his weakened right hand. He got up, shaken but unhurt, and Alamut rushed in for the kill. Menzies suddenly stepped aside and kicked the scimitar from Alamut's hand.

Alamut didn't even bother to look where his knife had fallen. He took up a classical karate stance, his left hand rigidly straight in a vertical position at face height, his right hand held above his head like an axe. Menzies took up his Kung-Fu position and they rushed at each other. A flurry of blows and counter-blows, parried and driven home, rained from almost every quarter on both of them.

The giant Leo Kopechoff, the killer-wrestler from Kamloops, roared from the circle of spectators: "Kill him, Alamut; kill this bastard."

All the guerrilleros had now taken sides, either in favor of Alamut or Menzies, and they were obviously thrilled by the spectacle on the slopes of El Salvador.

Little Pablito was among those who supported Menzies. "Fight him, Don Juan; get him, get him!" he shrieked. "He killed Geralda, I believe you. I know it. Leo was there, too."

Again Alamut rushed at Menzies, his hands and feet hissing through the air as they aimed a succession of blows. A kick from Alamut struck home in Menzies' stomach and sent a shudder through his body. Menzies' right hand was almost useless now, and he backed away, coughing, tasting his own blood, knowing he had suffered a serious injury.

Menzies saw Alamut move in again and let himself roll backward. Alamut rushed over to him. Standing almost above him, he lifted his foot to smash Menzies' head. But then Menzies suddenly twisted his body, and supporting himself on his head, shoulders, and left hand, kicked upward and into Alamut's neck.

Alamut's neck jerked and cracked as he was lifted off his feet by the violence of the blow. A loud sigh rose to his lips, and he tumbled backward and lay still in the gentle mattress of pine needles which covered most of the arena.

Slowly Menzies rose to his feet. His right arm hung limply by his side. Jabs of pain tore his body as he took the few steps to the spot where Alamut lay. Menzies looked at him and knew that Alamut wasn't dead—not yet, anyhow. The broken neck had paralyzed him, but the Assassin leader was still conscious.

Menzies reached for his pocket and took the piece of paper which Alamut had left on Geralda's body. He stood over Alamut, showed him the paper. Then he took his cigarette lighter, opened the bottom, poured the fluid on the paper and let it drop on Alamut's face. "For Geralda. . . ." he said, and lit it.

A foot-high flame flared around Alamut's face. The burning eyes and brows stirred. His hair caught fire, and the flames spread to the pine needles. The reflection of the light from the burning paper twisted and contorted the face of the dying hashishin.

And Menzies saw in the flame the fleeting image of Geralda's death mask. But then this image disappeared, and all he could see through the flames was the grimace of pain which was the face of Alamut. Menzies brought his foot down on the burning face with such force that the heel of his boot caused Alamut's mouth and jaw to cave in, trapping his boot so that he had to shake his leg hard to extricate it.

Alamut's fall had been so sudden and unexpected, and the hideous sight of his burning face so fearsome, that the spectators had been stunned into silence.

Leo was the first to recover. "I'll kill this cruel bastard," he said, and his monstrous, inhuman frame moved out of the circle.

He seemed as tall as the pine trees, his 370-pound frame towering over everybody. The giant hands rose. He stepped in the direction of Menzies and growled. But then Menzies' left hand reached for his hip pocket and the last knife whisked through the air and thudded into the big target of Leo's chest.

Leo's hands went for the hilt of the knife, which was the only part of it left out of his body. Then the hands sagged, and a stream of blood poured out of his mouth.

A gasp of surprise and awe rose from the lips of the guerrilleros. Their stunned eyes bulged as they watched the giant tumble to the ground. The lifeless corpose of the wrestler rolled over and over again down the hill until it came to rest in a grotesque position against a tree trunk.

Menzies stepped forward, and the circle of speechless spectators opened to let him pass. His right arm hung limp; blood oozed from the wound under the shoulder; his face was scarred and covered with blood. He walked over to the spot where the big black horse grazed and watched the death all around him. Menzies grabbed the three cases strapped on the horse's saddle and smashed them on the rocks. Then he took the reins in his left hand, steadied his left foot on the stirrup, and mounted.

Menzies' head sagged on his chest, and the horse turned and took the downhill trail.

The *guerrilleros* stirred. They seemed to have recovered from a spell.

"Hey, gringo!" yelled Santos. "Don't go! Stay with us, Don Juan! We love you gringoooo. . .!"

But the black horse was already trotting away.

Little Pablito ran after it. "Don Juan, come back, Don Juan!" he screamed. "Come back Juan! You're bleeding, Juan! You need a doctor! We love you Juan!"

Streams of tears were pouring down Pablito's face, and he ran so fast that he caught up with the black horse. "Juan, come back! Come back! You're wounded, Juan! The Federales are waiting for you, Juan! And you don't even have a gun!

"Here's your gun, Juan," said Pablito waving the Luger.

Menzies heard the desperation in Pablito's voice and pulled up. He saw the tears in the pleading eyes and the heavy Luger in the small hand. "Keep it for me, Pablito," he said. "If I need it again, I'll come back to get it."

Then the black horse stamped its legs impatiently and neighed. Menzies loosened the rein and quickly vanished down the winding mountain trail.

Pablito wiped the tears off his face. He stuck the Luger in his shirt and knelt on the grass. He crossed himself and whispered: "El Salvador!"

Epilogue

In the spacious card room of London's exclusive Athenaeum Club, four men sat down to a bridge table just as Big Ben boomed 7 P.M.

With Paulisen, Atherton, and Young was a man officially known only as *Doubledeegeeses,* which stood for the initials of his position, Deputy Director General of Secret Services. His real name was a national secret, and public disclosure of it, by the few in the know, could render them liable to prosecution under at least two different clauses of Britain's Official Secrets Act.

However, calling a senior officer in Her Majesty's Service "Doubledeegeeses" was awkward, besides being jaw-breaking. The word could be mispronounced in so many different ways. For example, it was mildly blasphemous to call this potentate of British Intelligence "Double-O-the-Jesus"—though that was precisely what some members of his staff thought he was. And it was absurd to have his name mispronounced "Double-the-Geysers." It was also embarrassing when he was called "Double-Kisses."

So the DDGSS, a man of considerable sense of humor despite the more somber aspects of his work, had discreetly let it be known that he had no objections if his staff called him "Doubleday," just like the name of the well-known American publisher. And his intimate circle of friends and close associates had even abbreviated this appellation. They called him "DD."

The four men settled down, ordered drinks and drew for partner and the deal.

Young dealt and looked at his cards. He held the ace, king and queen of spades; queen, ten, nine of heart; queen, ten, nine, three of diamonds; ace, five, three of clubs. He bid one no trump.

DD, appropriately perhaps, said "double." Paulisen, playing in partnership with Young, passed and Atherton said, "two spades."
Atherton raised it to four hearts.

Young doubled, DD passed, and then Paulisen stunned everybody by biding seven diamonds—a grand slam! Atherton and Young passed, DD doubled, and Young put his cards on the table. Atherton led the seven of hearts, and Young got up to take a look at his partner's hand. Paulisen held the four and three of spades, no hearts; the ace, jack, eight, six, four, and two of diamonds; queen, seven, four, two of clubs.

Young thought the bidding of this hand would have caused Charles Goren to pass out!

At that moment a steward came into the card room carrying a blackboard on which was written "paging Mr. Doubleday."

DD apologized and got up. The other three sipped their drinks and talked about London's frightful weather.

DD came back, and after noticing that there was nobody within earshot he said: "By the way, has anybody heard anything about Jim? You know who I mean—the chap who vanished from Mexico a few months ago."

The other three looked at DD in silence, pondering the question.

Atherton, always alert, was the first to speak. "You mean the former police reporter in Vancouver?"

DD hesitated only for an instant. "Why yes; yes," he said.

Atherton looked at Young.

"Not a word," said Young, "other than that last report about Massiat, the Society of Seven, and that he refused to accept that one thousand pounds we sent him."

"Any idea at all where he might be?" DD persisted.

"None at all," said Young. "Last thing I know he was convalescing in a private clinic in Acapulco. Our new man in Mexico tried to reach him, as you know, but he had already left."

"I see," said DD. "No doubt he'll turn up somewhere, when he's least expected." He lit a cigarette. "Trouble is, we want him now."

"Why, any problem?" asked Paulisen.

"Well, not really," said DD. "Just happens he's the only one on fil who knows anything about voodoo."

"Voodoo?" asked Ahterton, allowing an extra wrinkle around his eyes.

"Yes. Does sound strange, doesn't it?" said DD. He puffed at his cigarette, thinking. "Confound this damned business. This Mad Saint, or whatever else he's called, mentioned in the papers in the last couple of weeks—you know who I mean. That witch doctor in Haiti. Our man in Miami is dead, just like three of your men (DD looked at Paulisen) in Casablanca, Panama, and Costa Rica."

"I don't get it," said Atherton. "What has this got to do with voodoo, and what has voodoo got to do with us—I mean *you?*"

Paulisen took out his pipe, filled it and lit it. "DD, I'm afraid I've also lost you," he said.

"I don't blame you at all," DD quickly replied, a slight trace of irritation in his voice. "Would you three come to my office at 9:00 A.M. tomorrow? I'd like you to see some reports."

"And what's Jay-em got to do with it?" asked Young.

DD took a few more puffs at his cigarette. "Have you seen the series of articles he wrote some time ago for the Johannesburg *Golden City Post?* About African witchcraft in the Caribbean? Haiti and Jamaica particularly? And a new voodoo cult in Florida and London?"

Young pondered a while. "Well, no—just a minute—yes, I *did* read something the Sunday *Times* carried. Something about a new, virulent strain of the bubonic plague; transmitted by human carriers who have been immunized to the disease by voodoo . . . by the Mad Saint of Haiti. Is that it?"

Paulisen said, "The *Chronicle* had something about it in San Francisco just before I left. But it seems to me what you need here is an exorcist, not Jay-em or anybody else!"

DD's face broke into a sardonic smile. "My dear Rod, you won't think so when you get back to your office at the Embassy. There's a message there waiting for you from K."

Paulisen took a couple of puffs at his pipe before answering. "I follow you," he said.

"What's more," DD continued, "We have good reason to believe that our old friends are mixed up in this business. And Jay-em, besides breaking the story initially—confound him—also speaks their language. He could pass as one of them himself. You see now why he's our first choice?"

DD got up. "I'm terribly sorry, but I have to leave," he said. "In any case, I'm sure you two gentlemen would like to adjourn the game." He smiled and looked at Young and Paulisen. "You would never have made seven diamonds. . . ."

"Wait a minute," said Atherton. "What makes you think Jay-em would want to get mixed up in a thing like this?"

"I didn't say he'd *want* to," said DD, still smiling.

"I think I can understand Jay-em," said Paulisen. "He's disillusioned. Probably wants to be left alone."

"Would you blame him—after what happened in Mexico?" said Young.

DD's face grew serious. "Yes, yes, I know all this. He's probably basking on some lonely beach, swimming, fishing, fornicating. The point is, he's the right man for the job. Let's find him first, and answer his objections afterward. And there's also another matter. We've just been informed by the *Bundesnachrichtendienst* in Bonn, the West German secret service, that the Baades-Meinhoff terrorist group have been . . . shall we say retained for ten million dollars, by our old and somewhat implacable friends, to kidnap Prince Philip during the forthcoming royal tour of Central America. I have a feeling that Menzies would be useful in this problem, too." DD looked at his watch. "I really must go," he said. "See you tomorrow".

"What I'm worried about is the bill. One hundred and thirteen thousand dollars! I just can't justify it in my budget. Goddammit, I haven't got that kind of money! I got to get K to fix it. And he won't find it easy, either. The Democrats are looking for another Watergate in just about everything we do."

Young grinned. "Money is your side of the problem," he said. "Come, come, Rod. If Uncle Sam can't pay, no one can. Why not put it on your American Express card?"

"Oh, shudup, Colin," Paulisen said. "Don't be so smug. Your problem's going to be finding John Menzies—Jay-em, Jim, whatever you want to call him.

"And I wish you guys would stop being so security-conscious. Half the time you're talking in riddles and confusing yourselves more than anybody else!"

Young took a fast gulp of Scotch. "I'm not going to argue with you there, not completely, anyhow," he said. He looked at the cards on the table. "I'm wondering whether you would have made seven diamonds."

"You bet I would," Paulisen said. "I've played bridge with DD before!"

"Where do we start with Menzies?" asked Atherton, pronouncing the word "Mingis," the Scottish way.

"Search me," said Paulisen. "Obviously he'd have gotten out of Mexico by now. Let's try in Central America first. There are only ten thousand beaches there."

"Uh-uh," said Atherton, shaking his head. "Menzies doesn't know the Federales have called off the hunt. But he does know there's a foolproof extradition agreement between Mexico and the Central American republics.

"My guess is he's gotten right out of the area, Maybe to some island in the Pacific." Atherton got up, picked up a copy of *The Times World At-las* from a shelf, and brought it back to the table.

Young tapped the huge volume with his fingers. "Excellent. Let's start looking for Menzies," he said, sarcastically.

Paulisen ordered another round of drinks. "You star looking," he told Young. "Remember, my job is to pay the bill!"

Atherton pulled his chair away from the table and stretched his long legs. "Relaaax. . ." he said. "We'll find Menzies. Just leave it all to the Royal Canadian Mountain Police!"